ISAAC ASIMOV

PRESENTS

THE GREAT SF STORIES

#20

(1958)

EDITED BY ISAAC ASIMOV AND MARTIN H. GREENBERG

D1547870

DAW BOOKS, INC.
DONALD A. WOLLHEIM, PUBLISHER

1633 Broadway, New York, NY 10019

DAW Book Collectors No. 808.

First Printing, February 1990

1 2 3 4 5 6 7 8 9

PRINTED IN THE U.S.A.

ACKNOWLEDGMENTS

CONTENTS

Introduction   **9**

THE LAST OF THE DELIVERERS   **13**
  Poul Anderson

THE FEELING OF POWER   **29**
  Isaac Asimov

POOR LITTLE WARRIOR!   **41**
  Brian W. Aldiss

THE IRON CHANCELLOR   **49**
  Robert Silverberg

THE PRIZE OF PERIL   **77**
  Robert Sheckley

OR ALL THE SEAS WITH OYSTERS   **99**
  Avram Davidson

TWO DOOMS   **111**
  C. M. Kornbluth

THE BIG FRONT YARD   **167**
  Clifford D. Simak

THE BURNING OF THE BRAIN   **229**
  Cordwainer Smith

THE YELLOW PILL   **243**
  Rog Phillips

UNHUMAN SACRIFICE   **259**
  Katherine MacLean

THE IMMORTALS   **297**
  James E. Gunn

INTRODUCTION

On the film front, the good news was the release of Alfred Hitchcocks' *Vertigo* and Orson Welles' *Touch of Evil*. Other important movies of the year included *South Pacific, Gigi, The Young Lions, Auntie Mame, Cat On A Hot Tin Roof* with Elizabeth Taylor and Paul Newman, and Delbert Mann's *Separate Tables*. *Gigi* copped the Academy Award for Best Picture because there's just no justice in the world.

The year in sports saw the Yankees win the World Series over Milwaukee, Tim Tam win the Kentucky Derby, Althea Gibson win the U.S. Open, Jim Brown break the rushing record in the NFL, Ernie Banks lead the majors in homers with 47, Richie Ashburn lead in batting with .350, and Arnold Palmer win a lot of money on the PGA Tour. But the highlight of the year had to be Baltimore's overtime win over the Giants in the NFL's championship game, which some believe was the greatest pro football game up to that time. The winning touchdown was scored by Alan "the horse" Ameche, the nephew of actor Don Ameche.

On the book front, such works as *Ice Palace* by Edna Ferber, *Doctor Zhivago* by Boris Pasternack, *Only In America* by Harry Golden, *Lolita* by Vladimir Nabokov, and *Anatomy Of A Murder* by Robert Traver flew off the shelves, but the "best" books of the year had to be *Dear Abby* by Abigail Van Buren and *The Sundial* by the great Shirley Jackson. The first Pizza Hut opened.

The best play of 1958 was *Sunrise At Campobello* with Ralph Bellamy as FDR. Artistic highlights included the opening of the Four Seasons restaurant in New York and Van Cliburn's great victory in the International Tchaikovsky Piano Competition. NASA was organized in 1958 to get man into deep space, James Van Allen had cosmic radiation belts named after him, and Decca brought out the first "stereo" records.

Death took Pope Pius XII, Mike Todd, Ronald Colman, Tyrone Power, Christian Dior, W.C. Handy, and Robert Donat. Mel Brooks was Mel Brooks.

1958 was a significant year for man's attempts to leave this planet—the United States finally got Explorer, our first artificial satellite, launched from Cape Canaveral and into Earth orbit; later in the year, Pioneer would be successfully fired. But on a grimmer note, the first ballistic missile units were declared operational by the United States Air Force.

The Middle East was the Middle East—serious riots in Beirut eventually led to the landing of American marines, who waded ashore amidst sunbathers, a quite different fate than that which would await American marines in the 1980s. Egypt, Syria, and Yemen combined to form the United Arab Republic, but this broke apart three years later. The mainland Chinese were lobbing shells against the islands of Matsu and Quemoy; the U.S. response would become an issue in the Presidential election of 1960. The eventual loser of that election, Vice President Nixon, was attacked by an angry crowd on a visit to Caracas. In a desperate attempt to avoid an army coup, Charles de Gaulle agreed to take leadership in France, but only if the rules of government were changed; this gave rise to the Fifth Republic. Castro continued his struggle against Batista in Cuba.

Closer to home, Alaska became a State of the Union while Martin H. Greenberg graduated from Miami Beach High

School. The scandal of the year involved the resignation of President Eisenhower's Chief-of-Staff Sherman Adams, who admitted accepting an expensive coat from somebody who wanted something in return.

Popular culture stayed popular, as such songs as "Tom Dooley," "Bird Dog," "Twilight Time" by the wonderful Platters, "Pink Shoe Laces," "Fever," and Johnny Cash's unforgettable "Ballad of a Teenage Queen" all were big hits. *Flower Drum Song* was the top Broadway musical, while new hit television shows included Steve McQueen's *Wanted: Dead or Alive*, *The Donna Reed Show*, which was as pure as the driven snow, the great *Peter Gunn*, and the not so great *77 Sunset Strip*. Elvis got drafted.

In the real world it was a terrible year in spite of excellent stories and novels, for 1958 saw the death at 35 of Cyril M. Kornbluth and at 43 of Henry Kuttner, both major figures in the *genre*.

The paperback explosion continued, with new publishers introducing lines of science fiction books. Important works included *Immortality Delivered* by Robert Sheckley; *The Space Willies* by Eric Frank Russell; *The Cosmic Rape* by Theodore Sturgeon; *Of Men and Monsters* by William Tenn; *The Edge of Time* by Donald A. Wollheim; *The Path of Unreason* by George O. Smith; *Undersea City* by Frederik Pohl and Jack Williamson; the outstanding *The Lincoln Hunters* by Wilson Tucker; *A Touch of Strange* (collection) by Theodore Sturgeon; the landmark *The Languages of Pao* by Jack Vance; and *Invaders from Earth* by Robert Silverberg.

The magazine scene was not nearly as healthy as five publications bit the dust—*Science Fiction Quarterly*, *Science Fiction Adventures*, *Imagination Science Fiction*, *Space Travel*, and *Infinity Science Fiction*. The latter was a particularly fine magazine and was much missed by fans and writers. In addition, two of the most promising new ventures in the field lasted only one issue each—Frederik Pohl's *Star Science Fiction* and James Blish's *Vanguard Science Fiction*. The innovative *Venture Science Fiction* was combined with *The*

Introduction

Magazine of Fantasy and Science Fiction, making things even worse. Important editorial developments of the year included Isaac Asimov joining *Venture* and then *F&SF* as Contributing Science Editor, a role that continues to this day, Robert Mills replacing Anthony Boucher (who became Book Editor) as Editor of *F&SF*, and Damon Knight becoming Editor of *IF*.

In the real world, more important people made their maiden voyages into reality: in February—John Rackham with "Drog"; in July—Thomas Burnett Swann with "Winged Victory; in September—Rosel George Brown with "From an Unseen Censor" and Richard McKenna with "Casey Agonistes"; and in November—Colin Kapp with "Life Plan."

Fantastic films (in terms of category, not always quality) of 1958 included *The Brain From Planet Arous, Escapement, Strange World of Planet X*, the lusty *She Demons*, the campy and unforgettable *Attack of the Fifty Foot Woman, War of the Satellites*, the underrated *Fiend Without A Face, The Space Children*, the kind-of-neat *The Colossus of New York, It! Terror From Beyond Space*, Zsa Zsa Gabor as the *The Queen of Outer Space, War of the Colossal Beast, Attack of the Puppet People*, Steve McQueen in *The Blob*, the soapy *I Married a Monster From Outer Space, The Trollenberg Terror, The Spider Terror* (it was a big year for terror) *From the Year 5,000, The Brain Eaters, From the Earth to the Moon, The Lost Missile*, and *Night of the Blood Beast*.

The Family gathered in Los Angeles for the 16th World Science Fiction Convention—the Solacon. Hugo Awards went the *The Big Time* by Fritz Leiber, "Or All the Seas With Oysters" by Avram Davidson, *The Magazine of Fantasy and Science Fiction*, to Frank Kelly Freas for Best Artist, to *The Incredible Shrinking Man* as Outstanding Movie, and to Walt Willis as Outstanding "Actifan."

Let us travel back to that honored but tragic year of 1958 and enjoy the best stories that the real world bequeathed to us.

THE LAST OF THE DELIVERERS

BY POUL ANDERSON (1926–)

THE MAGAZINE OF FANTASY AND SCIENCE FICTION
FEBRUARY

We have discussed the career of Poul Anderson several times in this series. Suffice it to say for now that he is still going strong, still producing wonderful science fiction, and increasingly, wonderful fantasy.

"The Last of the Deliverers" shows us a future political system that is decentralized, one where formal ideology is no longer necessary, but where human beings still cling to the old beliefs. Poul captures the fanaticism and the ultimate loneliness of such people with the skill and emotion that he brings to all of his work. (MHG)

In Katherine MacLean's "Unhuman Sacrifice" later in this volume, there is involved a missionary in the religious sense.

Not all missionaries, however, are busy retailing religious truths, or what they consider to be religious truths.

Unfortunately, we all of us have beliefs that are not amenable to rational investigation. For instance, I have a fixed idea that the world would be a sweeter, cleaner place if the New York Mets baseball team were to win the division title, then the pennant, and then the World Series, in any given year. No amount of evidence to the effect that in that given year the Mets might not deserve these victories would sway me. No rational demonstration that it doesn't really matter which baseball team wins in a particular year, and that a situation in which every team wins now and then is actually better for baseball as a whole, will argue me out of my view.

Such irrationalisms, insofar as they involve baseball, or some other comparatively trivial affair (forgive me, O mighty spirit of Babe Ruth), doesn't really do harm. It may even do good in working off some of my naturally combative and pugnacious attitudes into harmless side-issues.

But there are political and economic beliefs that have almost the force of religion, and that can give rise to dangerous conflicts despite anything that reason can do. Poul Anderson's satire shows this. (Of course, Poul is a libertarian, and some day I may punch him in the nose for that—except that I am very fond of him.) (IA)

Till I was nine years old, we had a crazy man living in our town. He was almost a hundred himself, I suppose, and none of his kin were left. But in those days every town still had a few people who did not belong to any family.

Uncle Jim was harmless, even useful. He wanted to work, and did a bit of cobbling. His shop was in his house, always neat, and when you stood there among the good smells of leather and oil, you could see his living room beyond. He did not have many books, but shelf after shelf was loaded with tall bright sheaves cased in plastic—cracked and yellowed by age like their owner. He called them his magazines, and if we children behaved nicely he sometimes let us look at the pictures in them. After he was dead I had a chance to read the texts. They didn't make sense. Nobody would worry about the things the people in those stories and articles made such a fuss over. He also had a big antique television set, though why he kept it when there was nothing to receive but announcements and the town had a perfectly good set, I don't know. Well, he was crazy.

Every morning he took a walk down Main Street. The trees along it were mostly elms, tall, overshadowing in summer except where gold sunflecks got through. Uncle Jim always dressed his long stiff body in ancient clothes, no matter how hot the day, and Ohio can get plenty hot; so no doubt the shadiness was the reason for his route. He wore frayed white shirts with scratchy, choky collars and a strip of cloth knotted around his neck, long trousers, a clumsy kind of jacket, and narrow shoes that pinched his feet. The outfit was ugly, though painfully clean. We children, being young and therefore cruel, thought at first that because we never saw him unclothed he must be hiding some awful deformity, and teased him about it. My aunt's brother John made us stop, and Uncle Jim never held our bad ways against us. In fact, he used to give us candy he had made himself, till the dentist complained. Then we had solemn talks with our parents and learned that sugar rots the teeth.

Finally we decided that Uncle Jim—we called him that, without saying on which side he was anyone's uncle, because he wasn't really—wore those things as a sort of background for his button that said "WIN WITH WILLARD." He told me once, when I asked, that Willard had been the last Republican President of the United States and a very great man who tried to avert disaster but was too late because the people were already far gone in sloth and decadence. That was a big lading for a nine-year-old head and I still don't really understand it, except that the towns did not govern themselves then and the country was divided between the two big groups who were not even clans but who more or less took turns furnishing a President; and the President was not an umpire between towns and states, but ran everything.

Uncle Jim used to creak down Main Street past Townhall and the sunpower plant, then turn at the fountain and go by my father's great-uncle Conrad's house to the edge of town where the fields and Trees rolled to the rim of the world. At the airport he would turn and come back by Joseph Arakelian's, where he always looked in at the hand looms and sneered and talked about automatic machinery; though what he had against the looms I don't know, because Joseph's weavery was famous. He also made harsh remarks about our ratty little airport and the town's half-dozen flitters. That wasn't fair; we had a good airport, surfaced with concrete ripped out of the old highway, and plenty of flitters for our longer trips. You'd never get more than six groups going anywhere at any one time in a town this size.

But I wanted to tell about the Communist.

This was in spring. The snow had melted and the ground begun to dry and our farmers were out planting. The rest of our town bustled with preparations for the Fete, cooking and baking, oh, such a smell as filled the air, women trading recipes from porch to porch, artisans hammering and sawing and welding, the washlines afire with Sunday-best clothes taken out of winter chests, lovers hand in hand whispering of the festivals to come. Red and Bob and Stinky and I were playing marbles by the airport. It used to be mumbletypeg, but some of the kids flipped their knives into Trees and the Elders made a rule that no kid could carry a knife unless a grown-up was along.

So it was a fair sweet morning, the sky a dizzy-high arch of blue, sunlight bouncing off puffy white clouds and down to the earth, and the first pale whisper of green had been breathed across the hills. Dust leaped where our marbles hit, a small wind blew up from the south and slid across my skin and rumpled my hair, the world and the season and we were young.

We were about to quit, fetch our guns and take into the woods after rabbit, when a shadow fell across us and we saw Uncle Jim and my mother's cousin Andy. Uncle Jim wore a long coat above his other clothes, and still shivered as he leaned on his cane, and the shrunken hands were blue from cold. Andy wore a kilt, for the pockets, and sandals. He was our town engineer, a stocky man of forty. In the prehistoric past before I was born he had been on an expedition to Mars, and this made him a hero for us kids. We never understood why he was not a swaggering corsair. He owned three thousand books at least, more than twice the average in our town.

He spent a lot of time with Uncle Jim, too, and I didn't know why. Now I see that he was trying to learn about the past from him, not the dead past mummified in the history books but the people who had once been alive.

The old man looked down at us and said: "You boys aren't wearing a stitch. You'll catch your death of cold." He had a high, thin voice, but steady. In the many years alone, he must have learned how to be firm with himself.

"Oh, nonsense," said Andy. "I'll bet it's sixty in the sun."

"We was going after rabbits," I said importantly. "I'll bring mine to your place and your wife can make us a stew." Like all children, I spent as much time with kinfolk as I did with my ortho-parents, but I favored Andy's home. His wife was a wonderful cook, his oldest son was better than most on the guitar, and his daughter's chess was just about my speed, neither too good nor too bad.

I'd won most of the marbles this game, so now I gave them back. "When I was a boy," said Uncle Jim, "we played for keeps."

"What happened after the best shooter had won all the marbles in town?" said Stinky. "It's hard work making a good marble, Uncle Jim. I can't hardly replace what I lose anyway."

"You could have bought more," he told him. "There were stores where you could buy anything."

"But who made those marbles?"

"There were factories—"

Imagine that! Big grown men spending their time making colored glass balls!

We were almost ready to leave when the Communist showed up. We saw him as he rounded the clump of Trees at the north quarter-section, which was pasture that year. He was on the Middleton road, and dust scuffed up from his bare feet.

A stranger in town is always big news. We kids started running to meet him till Andy recalled us with a sharp word and reminded us that he was entitled to proper courtesy. Then we waited, our eyes bugging out, till he reached us.

But this was a woebegone stranger. He was tall, like Uncle Jim, but his cape hung in rags about a narrow chest where you could count the ribs, and under a bald dome of a head was a dirty white beard down to his waist. He walked heavily, leaning on a staff, heavy as Time, and even then I sensed the loneliness like a weight on his thin shoulders.

Andy stepped forward and bowed. "Greetings and welcome, Freeborn," he said. "I am Andrew Jackson Welles, town engineer, and on behalf of the Folks I bid you stay and rest and refresh yourself." He didn't just rattle the words off as he would for someone he knew, but declaimed them with great care.

Uncle Jim smiled then, a smile like thawing after a nine year's winter, for this man was as old as himself and born in the same forgotten world. He trod forth and held out his hand. "Hello, sir," he said. "My name is Robbins. Pleased to meet you." They didn't have very good manners in his day.

"Thank you, Comrade Welles, Comrade Robbins," said the stranger. His smile was lost somewhere in that tangled mold of whiskers. "I'm Harry Miller."

"*Comrade?*" Uncle Jim spoke it slowly, like a word out of a nightmare. His hand crept back again. "What do you mean?"

The wanderer straightened and looked at us in a way that frightened me. "I meant what I said," he answered. "I don't make any bones about it. Harry Miller, of the Communist Party of the United States of America!"

Uncle Jim sucked in a long breath. "But—" he stammered, "but I thought . . . at the very least, I thought all you rats were dead."

"Now hold on," said Andy. "Your pardon, Freeborn Miller. Our friend isn't, uh, isn't quite himself. Don't take it personally, I beg you."

There was a grimness in Miller's chuckle. "Oh, I don't mind. I've been called worse than that."

"And deserved it!" I had never seen Uncle Jim angry before. His face got red and he stamped his cane in the dust. "Andy, this, this man is a traitor. D'you hear? He's a foreign agent!"

"You mean you come clear from Russia?" murmured Andy, and we boys clustered near, our ears stiff in the breeze, because a foreigner was a seldom sight.

"No," said Miller. "No, I'm from Pittsburgh. never been to Russia. Wouldn't want to go. Too awful—they *had* socialism once."

"Didn't know anybody was left in Pittsburgh," said Andy. "I was there last year with a salvage crew, after steel and copper, and we never saw anything but birds."

"A few. A few. My wife and I. But she died, and I couldn't stay in that rotten empty shell of a city, so I went out on the road."

"And you can go back on the road," snarled Uncle Jim.

"Now, please be quiet," said Andy. "Come on into town, Freeborn Miller—Comrade Miller, if you prefer. May I invite you to stay with me?"

Uncle Jim grabbed Andy's arm. He shook like a dead leaf in fall, under the heartless fall winds. "You can't!" he shrieked. "Don't you see, he'll poison your minds, he'll subvert you, we'll end up slaves to him and his gang of bandits!"

"It seems you've been doing a little mind-poisoning of your own, Mister Robbins," said Miller.

Uncle Jim stood for a moment, head bent to the ground, and the quick tears of an old man glimmered in his eyes. Then he lifted his face and pride rang in the words: "I am a Republican."

"I thought so." The Communist glanced around and nodded to himself. "Typical bourgeois pseudo-culture. Look at those men, each out on his own little tractor in his own field, hugging his own little selfishness to him."

Andy scratched his head. "What are you talking about, Freeborn?" he asked. "Those are town machines. Who wants to be bothered keeping his own tractor and plow and harvester?"

"Oh . . . you mean—" I glimpsed a light of wonder in the Communist's eyes. He half-stretched out his hands. They were aged hands; I could see bones just under the dried-out skin. "You mean you do work the land collectively?"

"Why, no. What on earth would be the point of that?" replied Andy. "A man's entitled to what he raises himself, isn't he?"

"So the land, which should be the property of all the people, is parcelled among those kulaks!" flared Miller.

"How in hell's name can land by anybody's property? It's . . . it's land. You can't put forty acres in your pocket and walk off with them." Andy took a long breath. "You must have been pretty well cut off from things in Pittsburgh. Ate the ancient canned stuff, didn't you? I thought so. It's easy enough to explain. Look, that section yonder is being planted in corn by my mother's cousin Glenn. It's his corn, that he swaps for whatever else he needs. But next year, to conserve the soil, it'll be put in alfalfa, and my sister's son Willy takes care of it. As for garden truck and fruit, most of us raise our own, just to get outdoors each day."

The light faded in our visitor. "That doesn't make sense," said Miller, and I could hear how tired he was. It must have been a long hike from Pittsburgh, living off handouts from gypsies and the Lone Farmers.

"I quite agree," said Uncle Jim with a stiff kind of smile. "In my father's day—" He closed his mouth. I knew his father had died in Korea, in some war when he himself was a baby, and Uncle Jim had been left to keep the memory and the sad barren pride of it. I remembered my history, which Freeborn Levinsohn taught in our town because he knew it best, and a shiver crept in my skin. A *Communist!* Why, they had killed and tortured Americans . . . only this was a faded rag of a man, who couldn't kill a puppy. It was very odd.

We started towards Townhall. People saw us and began to

crowd around, staring and whispering as much as decorum allowed. I strutted with Red and Bob and Stinky, right next to the stranger, the real live Communist, under the eyes of the other kids.

We passed Joseph's weavery. His family and apprentices came out to join the gogglers. Miller spat in the street. "I imagine those people are hired," he said.

"You don't expect them to work for nothing, do you?" asked Andy.

"They should work for the common good."

"But they do. Every time somebody needs a garment or a blanket, Joseph gets his boys together and they make one. You can buy better stuff from him than most women can make at home."

"I knew it. The bourgeois exploiter—"

"I only wish that were the case," said Uncle Jim, tightlipped.

"You would," snapped Miller.

"But it isn't. People don't have any drive these days. No spirit of competition. No desire to improve their living standard. No . . . they buy what they need, and wear it while it lasts—and it's made to last damn near forever." Uncle Jim waved his cane in the air. "I tell you, Andy, the country's gone to hell. The economy is stagnant. Business has become a bunch of miserable little shops and people making for themselves what they used to buy!"

"I think we're pretty well fed and clothed and housed," said Andy.

"But where's your . . . your drive? Where's the get-up-and-go, the hustling, that made America great? Look—your wife wears the same model of gown her mother wore. You use a flitter that was built in your father's time. Don't you want anything better?"

"Our machinery works well enough." Andy spoke in a bored voice. This was an old argument to him, while the Communist was new. I saw Miller's tattered cape swirl into Si Johansen's carpenter shop and followed.

Si was making a chest of drawers for George Hulme, who was getting married this spring. He put down his tools and answered politely.

"Yes . . . yes, Freeborn . . . sure, I work here . . . Organize? What for? Social-like, you mean? But my apprentices got too damn much social life as is. Every third day a holiday, damn near. . . . No, they *aren't* oppressed. Hell, they're my own kin! . . . But there aren't any people who haven't got good furniture. Not unless they're lousy carpenters and too uppity to get help—"

"But the people all over the world!" cried Miller. "Don't you have any heart, man? What about the Mexican peons?"

Si Johansen shrugged. "What about them? If they want to run things different down there, it's their own business." He put away his electric sander and hollered to his apprentices that they could have the rest of the day off. They'd have taken it anyway, of course, but Si was a wee bit bossy.

Andy got Miller out in the street again. At Townhall the Mayor came in from the fields and received him. Since good weather was predicted for the whole week, we decided there was no hurry about the planting and we'd spend the afternoon welcoming our guest.

"Bunch of bums!" snorted Uncle Jim. "Your ancestors stuck by a job till it was finished."

"This'll get finished in time," said the Mayor, as if he were talking to a baby. "What's the rush, Jim?"

"Rush? To get on with it—finish it and go on to something else. Better things for better living!"

"For the benefit of your exploiters," cackled Miller. He stood on the Townhall steps like a starved and angry rooster.

"What exploiters?" The Mayor was as puzzled as me.

"The . . . the big businessmen, the—"

"There aren't any more businessmen," said Uncle Jim. A little more life seemed to trickle out of him as he admitted it. "Our shopkeepers? . . . No. They only want to make a living. They've never heard of making a profit. They're too lazy to expand."

"Then why haven't you got socialism?" Miller glared around as if looking for some hidden enemy. "It's every family for itself. Where's your solidarity?"

"We get along pretty well with each other, Freeborn," said the Mayor. "We got courts to settle any arguments."

"But don't you want to go on, to advance, to—"

"We get enough," declared the Mayor, patting his belly. "I couldn't eat any more than I do."

"But you could wear more!" said Uncle Jim. He jittered on the steps, the poor crazy man, dancing before our eyes like the puppets in a traveling show. "You could have your own car, a new model every year with beautiful chrome plate all over it, and new machines to lighten your labor, and—"

"And to buy those shoddy things, meant only to wear out, you would have to slave your lives away for capitalists," said Miller. "The people must produce for the people."

Andy traded a glance with the Mayor. "Look, Freeborn," he said gently, "you don't seem to get the point. We don't *want* such gadgets. It isn't worthwhile scheming and working to get more than we have, not while there are girls to love in springtime and deer to hunt in fall. And when we do work, we'd rather work for ourselves, not for somebody else, whether you call the somebody else a capitalist or the people. Now let's go sit down and take it easy before lunch."

Wedged between the legs of the Folks, I heard Si Johansen mutter to Joseph Arakelian: "I don't get it. What would we do with that machinery? If I had some damn machine to make furniture for me, what'd I do with my hands?"

Joseph lifted his shoulders. "Beats me, Si. Personally, I'd go nuts watching two people wear the same identical pattern."

"It might be kind of nice at that," said Red to me, "having a car like they show in Uncle Jim's ma-gazines."

"Where'd you go in it?" asked Bob.

"Gee, I dunno. To Canada, maybe. But shucks, I can go to Canada any time I can talk my dad into checking out a flitter."

"Sure," said Bob. "And if you're going less than a hundred miles, you got a horse, haven't you? Who wants an old car?''

I wriggled through the crowd toward the Plaza, where the women were setting up outdoor tables and bringing food for a banquet. The crowd was so thick around our guest where he sat that I couldn't get near, but Stinky and I skun up into the Plaza Tree, a huge gray oak, and crawled along a branch till we hung just above his head. It was a bare and liver-spotted head, wobbling on a thread of neck, but he darted it around and spoke shrill.

Andy and the Mayor sat near him, puffing their pipes, and Uncle Jim was there too. The Folks had let him in so they could watch the fireworks. That was thoughtless, but how could we know? Uncle Jim had always been peaceful, and we'd never had two crazy men in town.

''. . . forces of reaction,'' Comrade Miller was saying. ''I'm not sure precisely which forces engineered the dissolution of the Soviet Union. News was already getting hard to come by, not many telecasts anymore and—well, I must admit I doubt either the capitalists or the Chinese were behind the tragedy. Both those systems were pretty far gone by then.''

''Whatever did happen in Russia?'' wondered Ed Mulligan. He was the town psychocounsellor, who'd trained at Menninger, clear out in Kansas. ''Actual events, I mean. I never would have thought the Communists would allow freedom, not from what I've read of them.''

''What you call freedom,'' Miller said scornfully. ''I suspect, myself, revisionism took hold. Once that had led to corruption, the whole poor country was ripe for a counterrevolutionary takeover.''

''Now that isn't true,'' said Uncle Jim. ''I followed the news too, remember. The Communists in Russia got corrupt and easygoing of their own accord. Tyrants always do. They didn't foresee what changes the new technology would make, and blithely introduced it. Soon their Iron Curtain rusted away. Nobody *listened* to them anymore.''

"Pretty correct, Jim," said Andy. He saw my face among the twigs, and winked at me. "Some violence did occur, the breakup was more complicated than you think, but that's essentially what happened. Trouble is, you can't seem to realize it happened in the U.S.A. also."

Miller shook his withered head. "Marx proved that technological advances mean inevitable progress towards socialism," he said. "Oh, the cause has been set back, but the day is coming."

"Why, maybe you're right up to a point," said Andy. "But you see, science and society went beyond that point. Maybe I can give you a simple explanation."

"If you wish," said Miller, grumpy-like.

"Well, I've studied the period. Technology made it possible for a few people and acres to feed the whole country, till millions of acres were lying idle; you could buy them for peanuts. Meanwhile the cities were overtaxed, underrepresented, and choked by their own traffic. Along came the cheap sunpower unit and the high-capacity accumulator. Those let a man supply most of his own wants, not work his heart out for someone else to pay the inflated prices demanded by an economy where every single business was subsidized or protected at the taxpayer's expense. Also, by living in the new way, a man cut down his money income to the point where he had to pay almost no taxes—he actually lived better on a shorter work week.

"More and more, people tended to drift out and settle in small country communities. They consumed less, which brought on a great depression, and that drove still more people out to fend for themselves. By the time big business and organized labor realized what was happening and tried to get laws passed against what they called un-American practices, it was too late; nobody was interested. Everything happened so gradually, you see. But it happened, and I think for the better."

"Ridiculous!" said Miller. "Capitalism went bankrupt, as Marx foresaw two hundred years ago, but its vicious influence was still so powerful that instead of advancing to collectivism you went back to being peasants.''

"Please," said the Mayor. I could see he was annoyed, and thought that maybe peasants were somebody not Freeborn. "Uh, maybe we can pass the time with a little singing."

Though he had no voice to speak of, courtesy demanded that Miller be asked to perform first. He rose and quavered out something about a guy named Joe Hill. It had a nice tune, but even a nine-year-old like me knew it was lousy poetics. A childish a-b-c-b scheme of masculine rhymes and not a double metaphor anywhere. Besides, who cares what happened to some little tramp when we have hunting songs and epics about interplanetary explorers to make? I was glad when Andy took over and gave us some music with muscle in it.

Lunch was called. I slipped down from the Tree and found a seat nearby. Comrade Miller and Uncle Jim glowered at each other across the table, but nothing much was said till after the meal, a couple of hours later. People had kind of lost interest in the stranger as they learned he'd spent his time huddled in a dead city, and wandered off for the dancing and games. Andy hung around, not wanting to but because he was Miller's host.

The Communist sighed and got up. "You've been nice to me," he said.

"I thought we were a bunch of capitalists," sneered Uncle Jim.

"It's man I'm interested in, wherever he is and whatever conditions he has to live under," said Miller.

Uncle Jim lifted his voice with his cane: "Man! You claim to care for man, you who killed and enslaved him?"

"Oh, come off it, Jim," said Andy. "That was a long time ago. Who cares at this late date?"

"I do!" Uncle Jim started crying, but he looked at Miller and walked toward him, stiff-legged, fingers crooked. "They killed my father. Men died by the tens of thousands—for an ideal. And you don't care! The whole damn country has lost its guts!"

THE LAST OF THE DELIVERERS

I stood under the Tree, one hand on the rough comfort of its bark. I was a little afraid, because I did not understand. Surely Andy, who had been sent by the United Townships Research Foundation the long black way to Mars, just to gather knowledge, was no coward. Surely my father, a gentle man and full of laughter, did not lack guts. What was it we were supposed to want?

"Why, you bootlicking belly-crawling lackey," yelled Miller, "it was you who gutted them! It was you who murdered working men, and roped their sons into your dummy unions, and . . . and . . . what about the Mexican peons?"

Andy tried to come between them. Miller's staff clattered on his head. Andy stepped back, wiping blood off, looking helpless, as the old crazy men howled at each other. He couldn't use force; he might hurt them.

Perhaps, in that moment, he realized. "It's all right, Freeborns," he said quickly. "It's all right. We'll listen to you. Look, you can have a nice debate tonight, right in Townhall, and everybody will come and—"

He was too late. Uncle Jim and Comrade Miller were already fighting, thin arms locked and dim eyes full of tears because they had no strength left to destroy what they hated. But I think, now, that the hate arose from a baffled love. They both loved us in a queer, maimed fashion, and we did not care, we did not care.

Andy got some men together and separated the two and they were led off to different houses for a nap. When Dr. Simmons looked in on Uncle Jim a few hours later, he was gone. The doctor hurried off to find the Communist, and he was gone, too.

I only learned that afterward, since I went off to play tag and pom-pom-pullaway with the other kids down where the river flowed cool and dark. It was in the same river, next morning, that Constable Thompson found the Communist and the Republican. Nobody knew what had happened. They met under the Trees, alone, at dusk, when bonfires were being lit and the Elders making merry around them and lovers stealing

27

off into the woods. That's all we can be sure of. We gave them a decent funeral.

It was the talk of the town for a week, and in fact the whole Ohio region heard about it; but after a while the talk died and the old crazy men lay forgotten. That was the year the Brotherhood came to power in the north, and men wondered what this could mean. The next spring they learned, and there was an alliance made and war went across the hills. For the Brotherhood gang, just as it had threatened, cut Trees down wholesale and planted none. Such evil cannot go unpunished.

THE FEELING OF POWER

BY ISAAC ASIMOV (1920–   )

THE MAGAZINE OF FANTASY AND SCIENCE FICTION
FEBRUARY

Aha, one of my own. This story is one of the most frequently anthologized of any of my stories and I think I see why.

It's one of those cases where some aspects of the future are clearly seen. Not that I set out to do any predictions, you understand. I was just writing a satire.

To begin with, I described a society in which pocket computers were common and did so in 1958, when computers were still huge, lumbering beasts, just beginning to be transistorized. (However, just to show you how little I listen to myself, when pocket computers came in about fifteen years later, I was caught completely unprepared. I had just published a book on how to use a slide-rule, which instantly became equivalent to writing one on how to use Roman numerals.)

Secondly, I described (ha, ha, ha) a society in which computing had come to be so common that people had forgotten how to do arithmetic without one. (That's not so funny, you know. Can you start a fire without a match? People once knew how to do that.)

And, actually, people now worry about schoolchildren never learning how to work out simple problems without a computer. Listen, I catch myself depending on it. These days, if I must subtract 387 from 7,933, I don't put my pen to paper. I say "where the devil is the calculator?" and I go and get it, and push buttons.

Anyway, in reading my satire, keep an eye out for grim echoes here and there. (IA)

Jehan Shuman was used to dealing with the men in authority on long-embattled Earth. He was only a civilian but he originated programming patterns that resulted in self-directing war computers of the highest sort. Generals consequently listened to him. Heads of Congressional committees, too.

There was one of each in the special lounge of New Pentagon. General Weider was space-burnt and had a small mouth puckered almost into a cipher. Congressman Brant was smooth-cheeked and clear-eyed. He smoked Denebian tobacco with the air of one whose patriotism was so notorious he could be allowed such liberties.

Shuman, tall, distinguished, and Programmer First Class, faced them fearlessly.

He said, "This, gentlemen, is Ladislas Aub."

"The one with the unusual gift that you discovered quite by accident," said Congressman Brant, placidly. "Ah." He inspected the little man with the egg-bald head with amiable curiosity.

The little man, in return, twisted the fingers of his hands anxiously. He had never been near such great men before. He was only an aging low-grade Technician who had long ago failed all tests designed to smoke out the gifted ones among mankind and had settled into the rut of unskilled labor. There was just this hobby of his that the great Programmer had found out about and was now making such a frightening fuss over.

General Weider said, "I find this atmosphere of mystery childish."

"You won't in a moment," said Shuman. "This is not something we can leak to the first comer. —Aub!" There was something imperative about his manner of biting off that one-syllable name, but then he was a great Programmer speaking to a mere Technician. "Aub! How much is nine times seven?"

Aub hesitated a moment, his pale eyes glimmered with a feeble anxiety. "Sixty-three," he said.

Congressman Brant lifted his eyebrows. "Is that right?"

"Check it for yourself, Congressman."

The Congressman took out his pocket computer, nudged the milled edges twice, looked at its face as it lay there in the palm of his hand, and put it back. He said, "Is this the gift you brought us here to demonstrate? An illusionist?"

"More than that, sir. Aub has memorized a few operations and with them he computes on paper."

"A paper computer?" said the General. He looked pained.

"No, sir," said Shuman, patiently. "Not a paper computer. Simply a sheet of paper. General, would you be so kind as to suggest a number?"

"Seventeen," said the General.

"And you, Congressman?"

"Twenty-three."

"Good! Aub, multiply those numbers and please show the gentlemen your manner of doing it."

"Yes, Programmer," said Aub, ducking his head. He fished a small pad out of one shirt pocket and an artist's hairline stylus out of the other. His forehead corrugated as he made painstaking marks on the paper.

General Weider interrupted him sharply. "Let's see that."

Aub passed him the paper, and Weider said, "Well, it *looks* like the figure seventeen."

Congressman Brant nodded and said, "So it does, but I suppose anyone can copy figures off a computer. I think I could make a passable seventeen myself, even without practice."

"If you will let Aub continue, gentlemen," said Shuman without heat.

Aub continued, his hand trembling a little. Finally, he said in a low voice, "The answer is three hundred and ninety-one."

Congressman Brant took out his computer a second time and flicked it. "By Godfrey, so it is. How did he guess?"

"No guess, Congressman," said Shuman. "He computed that result. He did it on this sheet of paper."

"Humbug," said the General, impatiently. "A computer is one thing and marks on paper are another."

"Explain, Aub," said Shuman.

"Yes, Programmer. —Well, gentlemen, I write down seventeen and just underneath it, I write twenty-three. Next, I say to myself; seven times three—"

The Congressman interrupted smoothly, "Now, Aub, the problem is seventeen times twenty-three."

"Yes, I know," said the little Technician earnestly, "but I *start* by saying seven times three because that's the way it works. Now seven times three is twenty-one."

"And how do you know that?" asked the Congressman.

"I just remember it. It's always twenty-one on the computer. I've checked it any number of times."

"That doesn't mean it always will be, though, does it?" said the Congressman.

"Maybe not," stammered Aub. "I'm not a mathematician. But I always get the right answers, you see."

"Go on."

"Seven times three is twenty-one, so I write down twenty-one. Then one times three is three, so I write down a three under the two of twenty-one."

"Why under the two?" asked Congressman Brant at once.

"Because—" Aug looked helplessly at his superior for support. "It's difficult to explain."

Shuman said, "If you will accept his work for the moment, we can leave the details for the mathematicians."

Brant subsided.

Aub said, "Three plus two makes five, you see, so the twenty-one becomes a fifty-one. Now you let that go for a while and start fresh. You multiply seven and two, that's fourteen, and one and two, that's two. Put them down like this and it adds up to thirty-four. Now if you put the thirty-four under the fifty-one this way and add them, you get three hundred and ninety-one and that's the answer."

There was an instant's silence and then General Weider said, "I don't believe it. He goes through this rigmarole and makes up numbers and multiplies and adds them this way and that, but I don't believe it. It's too complicated to be anything but hornswoggling."

"Oh, no, sir," said Aub in a sweat. "It only *seems* complicated because you're not used to it. Actually, the rules are quite simple and will work for any numbers."

"Any numbers, eh?" said the General. "Come then." He took out his own computer (a severely styled GI model) and struck it at random. "Make a five, seven, three, eight on the paper. That's five thousand seven hundred and thirty-eight."

"Yes, sir," said Aub, taking a new sheet of paper.

"Now"—more punching of his computer—"seven two three nine. Seven thousand two hundred and thirty-nine."

"Yes, sir."

"And now multiply those two."

"It will take some time," quavered Aub.

"Take the time," said the General.

"Go ahead, Aub," said Shuman, crisply.

Aub set to work, bending low. He took another sheet of paper and another. The general took out his watch finally and stared at it. "Are you through with your magic-making, Technician?"

"I'm almost done, sir. Here it is, sir. Forty-one million, five hundred and thirty-seven thousand, three hundred and eighty-two." He showed the scrawled figures of the result.

General Weider smiled bitterly. He pushed the multiplication contact on his computer and let the numbers whirl to a halt. And then he stared and said in a surprised squeak. "Great Galaxy, the fella's right."

The President of the Terrestrial Federation had grown haggard in office and, in private, he allowed a look of settled melancholy to appear on his sensitive features. The Denebian war, after its early start of vast movement and great popularity, had trickled down into a sordid matter of maneuver and counter-maneuver, with discontent rising steadily on Earth. Possibly it was rising on Deneb, too.

And now Congressman Brant, head of the important Committee on Military Appropriations, was cheerfully and smoothly spending his half-hour appointment spouting nonsense.

"Computing without a computer," said the President, impatiently, "is a contradiction in terms."

"Computing," said the Congressman, "is only a system for handling data. A machine might do it, or the human brain might. Let me give you an example." And, using the new skills he had learned, he worked out sums and products until the President, despite himself, grew interested.

"Does this always work?"

"Every time, Mr. President. It is foolproof."

"Is it hard to learn?"

"It took me a week to get the real hang of it. I think you could do better."

"Well," said the president, considering, "it's an interesting parlor game, but what is the use of it?"

"What is the use of a new-born baby, Mr. President? At the moment, there is no use, but don't you see that this points the way toward liberation from the machine? Consider, Mr. President," the Congressman rose and his deep voice automatically took on some of the cadences he used in public debate, "that the Denebian war is a war of computer against computer. Their computers forge an impenetrable shield of countermissiles against our missiles, and ours forge one against theirs. If we advance the efficiency of our computers, so do they theirs, and for five years a precarious and profitless balance has existed.

"Now we have in our hands a method for going beyond the computer, leapfrogging it, passing through it. We will combine the mechanics of computation with human thought; we will have the equivalent of intelligent computers; billions of them. I can't predict what the consequences will be in detail but they will be incalculable. And if Deneb beats us to the punch, they may be catastrophic.''

The President said, troubled, ''What would you have me do?''

''Put the power of the administration behind the establishment of a secret project on human computation. Call it Project Number, if you like. I can vouch for my committee but I will need the administration behind me.''

''But how far can human computation go?''

''There is no limit. According to Programmer Shuman who first introduced me to this discovery—''

''I've heard of Shuman, of course.''

''Yes. Well, Dr. Shuman tells me that in theory there is nothing the computer can do that the human mind cannot do. The computer merely takes a finite amount of data and performs a finite number of operations upon them. The human mind can duplicate the process.''

The President considered that. He said, ''If Shuman says this, I am inclined to believe him—in theory. But, in practice, how can anyone know how a computer works?''

Brant laughed genially. ''Well, Mr. President, I asked the same question. It seems that at one time, computers were designed directly by human beings. Those were simple computers, of course; this being before the time of the rational use of computers to design more advanced computers had been established.''

''Yes, yes. Go on.''

''Technician Aub apparently had, as his hobby, the reconstruction of some of these ancient devices, and in so doing he studied the details of their workings and found he could imitate them. The multiplication I just performed for you is an imitation of the workings of a computer.''

''Amazing!''

The Congressman coughed gently. ''If I may make another point, Mr. President—the further we can develop this thing, the more we can divert our federal effort from computer production and computer maintenance. As the human brain takes over, more of our energy can be directed into peacetime pursuits and the impingement of war on the ordinary man will be less. This will be most advantageous for the party in power, of course.''

''Ah,'' said the President, ''I see your point. Well, sit down, Congressman, sit down. I want some time to think about this. But meanwhile, show me that multiplication trick again. Let's see if I can't catch the point of it.''

Programmer Shuman did not try to hurry matters. Loesser was conservative, very conservative, and liked to deal with computers as his father and grandfather had. Still, he controlled the West European computer combine and if he could be persuaded to join Project Number in full enthusiasm, a great deal would have been accomplished.

But Loesser was holding back. He said, ''I'm not sure I like the idea of relaxing our hold on computers. The human mind is a capricious thing. The computer will give the same answer to the same problem each time. What guarantee have we that the human mind will do the same?''

''The human mind, Computer Loesser, only manipulates facts. It doesn't matter whether the human mind or a machine does it. They are just tools.''

''Yes, yes. I've gone over your ingenious demonstration that the mind can duplicate the computer but it seems to me a little in the air. I'll grant the theory, but what reason have we for thinking that theory can be converted to practice?''

''I think we have reason, sir. After all, computers have not always existed. The cavemen with their triremes, stone axes, and railroads had no computers.''

''And possibly they did not compute.''

''You know better than that. Even the building of a railroad or a ziggurat called for some computing, and that must have been without computers, as we know them.''

''Do you suggest they computed in the fashion you demonstrate?''

''Probably not. After all, this method—we call it 'graphitics,' by the way, from the old European word *grapho*, meaning 'to write'—is developed from the computers themselves so it cannot have antedated them. Still, the cavemen must have had *some* method, eh?''

"Lost arts! If you're going to talk about lost arts—''

"No, no. I'm not a lost-art enthusiast, though I don't say there may not be some. After all, man was eating grain before hydroponics and if the primitives ate grain, they must have grown them in soil. What else could they have done?''

"I don't know, but I'll believe in soil-growing when I see someone grow grain in soil. And I'll believe in making fire by rubbing two pieces of flint together when I see that, too.''

Shuman grew placating. "Well, let's stick to graphics. It's just part of the process of etherealization. Transportation by means of bulky contrivances is giving way to direct mass transference. Communications devices become less massive and more efficient constantly. For that matter, compare your pocket computer with the massive jobs of a thousand years ago. Why not, then, the last step of doing away with computers altogether? Come, sir, Project Number is a going concern; progress is already headlong. But we want your help. If patriotism doesn't move you, consider the intellectual adventure involved.''

Loesser said, skeptically, "What progress? What can you do beyond multiplication? Can you integrate a transcendental function?''

"In time, sir. In time. In the last month I have learned to handle division. I can determine, and correctly, integral quotients, and decimal quotients.''

"Decimal quotients? To how many places?''

Programmer Shuman tried to keep his tone casual. "Any number!''

Loesser's lower jaw dropped. "Without a computer?''

"Set me a problem?''

"Divide twenty-seven by thirteen. Take it to six places.''

Five minutes later, Shuman said, "Two point oh seven six nine two three.''

Loesser checked it. "Well, now, that's amazing. Multiplication didn't impress me too much because it involved integers, after all, and I thought trick manipulation might do it. But decimals—"

"And that is not all. There is a new development that is, so far, top secret and which, strictly speaking, I ought not to mention. Still—we may have made a breakthrough on the square-root front."

"Square roots?"

"It involves some tricky points and we haven't licked the bugs yet, but Technician Aub, the man who invented the science and who has an amazing intuition in connection with it, maintains he has the problem almost solved. And he is only a technician. A man like yourself, a trained and talented mathematician, ought to have no difficulty."

"Square roots," muttered Loesser, attracted.

"Cube roots, too. Are you with us?"

Loesser's hand thrust out suddenly. "Count me in."

General Weider stumped his way back and forth at the head of the room and addressed his listeners after the fashion of a savage teacher facing a group of recalcitrant students. It made no difference to the General that they were the civilian scientists heading Project Number. The General was the overall head, and he so considered himself at every waking moment.

He said, "Now square roots are all fine. I can't do them myself and I don't understand the methods, but they're fine. Still, the project will not be side-tracked into what some of you call the fundamentals. You can play with graphitics any way you want to after the war is over, but right now we have specific and very practical problems to solve."

In a far corner, Technician Aub listened with painful attention. He was no longer a Technician, of course, having been relieved of his duties and assigned to the project, with a fine-sounding title and good pay. But, of course, the social distinction remained and the highly placed scientific leaders could never bring themselves to admit him to their ranks on a footing of equality. Nor did he, himself, wish it. He was as uncomfortable with\them as they with him.

The General was saying, "Our goal is a simple one, gentlemen; the replacement of the computer. A ship that can navigate space without a computer on board can be constructed in one-fifth the time and at one-tenth the expense of a computer-laden ship. We could build fleets five times, ten times as great as Deneb could if we could but eliminate the computer.

"And I see something even beyond this. It may be fantastic now; a mere dream; but in the future I see the manned missile!"

There was an instant murmur from the audience.

The General drove on. "At the present time, our chief bottleneck is the fact that missiles are limited in intelligence. The computer controlling them can only be so large, so they can meet the changing nature of antimissile defenses only in an unsatisfactory way. Few missiles, if any, accomplish their goal, and missile warfare is coming to a dead end; for the enemy, fortunately, as well as for ourselves.

"On the other hand, a missile with a man or two within, controlling flight by graphitics, would be lighter, more mobile, more intelligent. It would give us a lead that might well mean the margin of victory. Besides which, gentlemen, the exigencies of war compel us to remember one thing. A man is much more dispensable than a computer. Manned missiles could be launched in numbers and under circumstances that no good General would care to undertake as far as computer-directed missiles are concerned—"

He said much more but Technician Aub did not wait.

Technician Aub, in the privacy of his quarters, labored long over the note he was leaving behind. It read finally as follows:

"When I began the study of what is now called graphitics, it was no more than a hobby. I saw no more in it than an interesting amusement, an exercise of mind.

"When Project Number began, I thought that others were

wiser than I; that graphitics might be put to practical use as a benefit to mankind: to aid in the production of really practical mass-transference devices perhaps. But now I see it is to be used only for death.

"I cannot face the responsibility involved in having invented graphites."

He then deliberately turned the focus of a protein depolarizer on himself and fell instantly and painlessly dead.

They stood over the grave of the little Technician while tribute was paid to the greatness of his discovery.

Programmer Shuman bowed his head along with the rest of them, but remained unmoved. The Technician had done his share and was no longer needed, after all. He might have started graphitics, but now that it had started, it would carry on by itself overwhelmingly, triumphantly, until manned missiles were possible, along with who knew what else.

Nine times seven, thought Shuman with deep satisfaction, is sixty-three and I don't need a computer to tell me so. The computer is in my own head.

And it was amazing the feeling of power that gave him.

POOR LITTLE WARRIOR

BY BRIAN W. ALDISS (1925–   )

THE MAGAZINE OF FANTASY AND SCIENCE FICTION
APRIL

Brian Aldiss is a distinguished British writer (not all his work is science fiction) who emerged in the late 1950s as one of the most important voices in sf. 1958 saw the publication of his first novel, Non-Stop *(*Starship *in the United States). He served as the Literary Editor for the* Oxford Mail *from 1958 to 1969, was the Co-Founder and Chairman of the John W. Campbell Award, and served as President of World SF in the mid-1980s. His many honors include a Hugo Award in 1962, a Nebula Award in 1965, a Pilgrim Award for his work in science fiction criticism in 1978, and the Campbell Award in 1983.*

His major novels are almost too numerous to mention, but one must note at least Greybeard *(1964),* Report on Probability A *(1969),* Barefoot in the Head *(1970),* Frankenstein Unbound *(1973), and especially his ''Helliconia Trilogy,''* Helliconia Spring *(1982),* Helliconia Summer *(1983), and* Helliconia Winter *(1985).*

''Poor Little Warrior'' ranks with Carol Emshwiller's ''The Hunting Machine'' as the most powerful hunting story in science fiction. (MHG)

It's always interesting (and difficult, which makes it more interesting) to handle things that are very different in scale—

41

to get across what it feels like to deal with things much larger than yourself, or much smaller.

Convincing stories about the large dinosaurs require a certain expertise in description and the two best science fiction stories I know of in this respect are Ray Bradbury's "The Sound of Thunder" and Brian Aldiss's "Poor Little Warrior!"

Incidentally, I generally don't like artificialities of style. For instance, it is quite fashionable now to write stories in the "historical present." This is supposed to give you a greater feeling of immediacy. You say, "I go there" instead of "I went there": and you feel as though you are really going at the moment of reading. For myself, I find that irritating in the extreme, because I don't want to be going there myself.

I also purse my lips at any attempt to tell a story in the second person, saying "You went there" instead of "I went there" or "He went there." Again this is supposed to drag the reader, more effectively, into the story. For myself, I usually find that an invasion of my privacy.

However, I suppose that, well done, any bit of experimentation becomes acceptable. "Poor Little Warrior!", except for the first sentence, is told in the second person and I don't mind at all. (IA)

Claude Ford knew exactly how it was to hunt a brontosaurus. You crawled heedlessly through the grass beneath the willows, through the little primitive flowers with petals as green and brown as a football field, through the beauty-lotion mud. You peered out at the creature sprawling among the reeds, its body as graceful as a sock full of sand. There it lay, letting the gravity cuddle it nappy-damp to the marsh, running its big rabbit-hole nostrils a foot above the grass in a sweeping semi-circle, in a snoring search for more sausagey reeds. It was beautiful: here horror had reached its limits, come full circle, and finally disappeared up its own sphincter movement. Its eyes gleamed with the liveliness of a week-dead corpse's big toe, and its compost breath and the fur in its crude aural cavities were particularly to be recommended to anyone who might otherwise have felt inclined to speak lovingly of the work of Mother Nature.

But as you, little mammal with opposed digit and .65 self-loading, semi-automatic, duel-barrelled, digitally-computed, telescopically sighted, ruthless, high-powered rifle gripped in your otherwise-defenceless paws, as you slide along under the bygone willows, what primarily attracts you is the thunder lizard's hide. It gives off a smell as deeply resonant as the bass note of a piano. It makes the elephant's epidermis look like a sheet of crinkled lavatory paper. It is grey as the Viking seas, daft-deep as cathedral foundations. What contact possible to bone could allay the fever of that flesh? Over it scamper—you can see them from here!—the little brown lice that live in those grey walls and canyons, gay as ghosts, cruel as crabs. If one of them jumped on you, it would very likely break your back. And when one of those parasites stops to cock its leg against one of the bronto's vertebrae, you can see it carries in its turn its own crop of easy-livers, each as big as a lobster, for you're near now, oh, so near that you can hear the monster's primitive heart-organ knocking, as the ventricle keeps miraculous time with the auricle.

Time for listening to the oracle is past: you're beyond the stage for omens, you're now headed in for the kill, yours or his; superstition has had its little day for today; from now on only this windy nerve of yours, this shaky conglomeration of muscle entangled untraceably beneath the sweat-shiny carapace of skin, this bloody little urge to slay the dragon, is going to answer all your orisons.

You could shoot now. Just wait till that tiny steam-shovel head pauses once again to gulp down a quarry load of bullrushes, and with one inexpressibly vulgar bang you can show the whole indifferent Jurassic world that it's standing looking down the business end of evolution's sex-shooter. You know why you pause, even as you pretend not to know why you pause; that old worm conscience, long as a baseball pitch, long-lived tortoise, is at work; through every sense it slides, more monstrous than the serpent. Through the passions: saying here is a sitting duck, O Englishman! Through the intelligence: whispering that boredom, the kite-hawk who never feeds, will settle again when the task is done. Through the nerves: sneering that when the adrenalin currents cease to flow the vomiting begins. Through the maestro behind the retina: plausibly forcing the beauty of the view upon you.

Spare us that poor old slipper-slopper of a word, beauty; holy mom, is this a travelogue, nor are we out of it? "Perched now on this titanic creature's back, we see a round dozen—and folks let me stress that round—of gaudily plumaged birds, exhibiting between them all the colour you might expect to find on lovely, fabled Copacabana Beach. They're so round because they feed from the droppings that fall from the rich man's table. Watch this lovely shot now! See the bronto's tail lift. . . . Oh, lovely, yep, a couple of hayricksful at least emerging from his nether end. That sure was a beauty, folks, delivered straight from consumer to consumer. The birds are fighting over it now. Hey, you, there's enough to go round, and anyhow, you're round enough already. . . . And nothing to do now but hop back up onto the old rump steak and wait for the next round. And now as the sun stinks in the Jurassic West, we say 'Fare well on that diet'. . . ."

No, you're procrastinating, and that's a life work. Shoot the beast and put it out of your agony. Taking your courage in your hands, you raise it to shoulder level and squint down its sights. There is a terrible report; you are half stunned. Shakily, you look about you. The monster still munches, relieved to have broken enough wind to unbecalm the Ancient Mariner.

Angered—or is it some subtler emotion?—you now burst from the bushes and confront it, and this exposed condition is typical of the straits into which your consideration for yourself and others continually pitches you. Consideration? Or again something subtler? Why should you be confused just because you come from a confused civilization? But that's a point to deal with later, if there is a later, as these two hog-wallow eyes pupilling you all over from spitting distance tend to dispute. Let it not be by jaws alone, O monster, but also by huge hooves and, if convenient to yourself, by mountainous rollings upon me! Let death be a saga, sagacious, Beowulfate.

Quarter of a mile distant is the sound of a dozen hippos springing boisterously in gymslips from the ancestral mud, and next second a walloping great tail as long as Sunday and as thick as Saturday night comes slicing over your head. You duck as duck you must, but the beast missed you anyway because it so happens that its co-ordination is no better than yours would be if you had to wave the Woolworth Building at a tarsier. This done, it seems to feel it has done its duty by itself. It forgets you. You just wish you could forget yourself as easily; that was, after all, the reason you had to come the long way here. Get Away From It All, said the time travel brochure, which meant for you getting away from Claude Ford, a husband as futile as his name with a terrible wife called Maude. Maude and Claude Ford. Who could not adjust to themselves, to each other, or to the world they were born in. It was the best reason in the as-it-is-at-present-constituted world for coming back here to shoot giant saurians—if you were fool enough to think that one hundred and fifty million years either way made an ounce of difference to the muddle of thoughts in a man's cerebral vortex.

You try and halt your silly, slobbering thoughts, but they have never really stopped since the coca-collaborating days of your growing up; God, if adolescence did not exist it would be unnecessary to invent it! Slightly, it steadies you to look again on the enormous bulk of this tyrant vegetarian into whose presence you charged with such a mixed death-life wish, charged with all the emotion the human orga(ni)sm is capable of. This time the bogey-man is real, Claude, just as you wanted it to be, and this time you really have to face up to it before it turns and faces you again. And so again you lift Ole Equalizer, waiting till you can spot the vulnerable spot.

The bright birds sway, the lice scamper like dogs, the

marsh groans, as bronto rolls over and sends his little cranium
snaking down under the bile-bright water in a forage for
roughage. You watch this; you have never been so jittery
before in all your jittered life, and you are counting on this
catharsis to wring the last drop of acid fear out of your system
for ever. O.K., you keep saying to yourself insanely over and
over, your million-dollar, twenty-second-century education
going for nothing, O.K., O.K. And as you say it for the
umpteenth time, the crazy head comes back out of the water
like a renegade express and gazes in your direction.

Grazes in your direction. For as the champing jaw with its
big blunt molars like concrete posts works up and down, you
see the swamp water course out over rimless lips, lipless
rims, splashing your feet and sousing the ground. Reed and
root, stalk and stem, leaf and loam, all are intermittently
visible in that masticating maw and, struggling, straggling, or
tossed among them, minnows, tiny crustaceans, frogs—all
destined in that awful, jaw-full movement to turn into bowel
movement. And as the glump-glump-glumping takes place,
above it the slime-resistant eyes again survey you.

These beasts live up to three hundred years, says the time
travel brochure, and this beast has obviously tried to live up
to that, for its gaze is centuries old, full of decades upon
decades of wallowing in its heavyweight thoughtlessness until
it has grown wise on twitterpated-ness. For you it is like looking into a disturbing misty pool; it gives you a psychic shock,
you fire off both barrels at your own reflection. Bang-bang,
the dum-dums, big as paw-paws, go.

Those century-old lights, dim and sacred, go out with no
indecision. These cloisters are closed till Judgment Day. Your
reflection is torn and bloodied from them for ever. Over their
ravaged panes nictitating membranes slide slowly upwards,
like dirty sheets covering a cadaver. The jaw continues to
munch slowly, as slowly the head sinks down. Slowly, a
squeeze of cold reptile blood toothpastes down the wrinkled
flank of one cheek. Everything is slow, a creepy Secondary
Era slowness like the drip of water, and you know that if you

had been in charge of creation you would have found some medium less heart-breaking than Time to stage it all in.

Never mind! Quaff down your beakers, lords, Claude Ford has slain a harmless creature. Long live Claude the Clawed!

You watch breathless as the head touches the ground, the long laugh of neck touches the ground, the jaws close for good. You watch and wait for something else to happen, but nothing ever does. Nothing ever would. You could stand here watching for a hundred and fifty million years, Lord Claude, and nothing would ever happen here again. Gradually your bronto's mighty carcass, picked loving clean by predators, would sink into the slime, carried by its own weight deeper; then the waters would rise, and old Conqueror Sea would come in with the leisurely air of a card-sharp dealing the boys a bad hand. Silt and sediment would filter down over the mighty grave, a slow rain with centuries to rain in. Old bronto's bed might be raised up and then down again perhaps half a dozen times, gently enough not to disturb him, although by now the sedimentary rocks would be forming thick around him. Finally, when he was wrapped in a tomb finer than any Indian rajah ever boasted, the powers of the Earth would raise him high on their shoulders until, sleeping still, bronto would lie in a brow of the Rockies high above the waters of the Pacific. But little any of that would count with you, Claude the Sword; once the midget maggot of life is dead in the creature's skull, the rest is no concern of yours.

You have no emotion now. You are just faintly put out. You expected dramatic thrashing of the ground, or bellowing; on the other hand, you are glad the thing did not appear to suffer. You are like all cruel men, sentimental; you are like all sentimental men, squeamish. You tuck the gun under your arm and walk round the land side of the dinosaur to view your victory.

You prowl past the ungainly hooves, round the septic white of the cliff of belly, beyond the glistening and how-thought-provoking cavern of the cloaca, finally posing beneath the switch-back sweep of tail-to-rump. Now your disappointment is as crisp and obvious as a visiting card: the giant is not half as big as you thought it was. It is not one half as large, for example, as the image of you and Maude is in your mind. Poor little warrior, science will never invent anything to assist the titanic death you want in the contra-terrene caverns of your fee-fo-fi-fumblingly fearful id!

Nothing is left to you now but to slink back to your time-mobile with a belly full of anti-climax. See, the bright dung-consuming birds have already cottoned on to the true state of affairs; one by one, they gather up their hunched wings and fly disconsolately off across the swamp to other hosts. They know when a good thing turns back, and do not wait for the vultures to drive them off; all hope abandon, ye who entrail here. You also turn away.

You turn, but you pause. Nothing is left but to go back, no, but A.D. 2181 is not just the home date; it is Maude. It is Claude. It is the whole awful, hopeless, endless business of trying to adjust to an over-complex environment, of trying to turn yourself into a cog. Your escape from it into the grand Simplicities of the Jurassic, to quote the brochure again, was only a partial escape, now over.

So you pause and, as you pause, something lands socko on your back, pitching you face forward into tasty mud. You struggle and scream as lobster claws tear at your neck and throat. You try to pick up the rifle but cannot, so in agony you roll over, and next second the crab-thing is greedying it on your chest. You wrench at its shell, but it giggles and pecks your fingers off. You forgot when you killed the bronto that its parasites would leave it, and that to a little shrimp like you they would be a deal more dangerous than their host.

You do your best, kicking for at least three minutes. By the end of that time there is a whole pack of the creatures on you. Already they are picking your carcass loving clean. You're going to like it up there on top of the Rockies; you won't feel a thing.

THE IRON CHANCELLOR

BY ROBERT SILVERBERG (1935–   )

GALAXY SCIENCE FICTION
MAY

1958 was the last major year for Robert Silverberg in the science fiction field for almost a decade. That year he published five sf novels—Invaders From Earth, Invincible Barriers (as David Osborne), Stepsons of Terra, Starhaven (as Ivar Jorgenson), and Aliens From Space (as Osborne). Although a fair number of sf novels appeared from 1959 to 1966, they were either for kids or were rewritten versions of stories and books published earlier. He turned his attention to nonfiction, producing numerous works that include a number that are still in print today. His "return" to science fiction in 1967 was heralded by the publication of the wonderful Thorns and "Hawksbill Station." The "new" Silverberg quickly established himself as one of the finest writers in the history of the genre.

Isaac, George R.R. Martin, and I reprinted "The Iron Chancellor" in The Science Fiction Weight Loss Book (Crown, 1983), one of my personal, if ill-conceived from a marketplace point of view, favorite anthologies. That book sank without a trace, so it is a pleasure to present the story to you again. (MHG)

I read robot stories with a proprietary air. After all, I am supposed to be the father of the modern robot story. This means that I tend to be captious and hard to please.

This one, however, I approve of. Just as a velvet glove is most effective if there is an iron fist inside, so a humorous story is most effective if there is a grim echo to the laughter.

Now I'm not a person who makes a big deal out of looking for symbolism in a story, but the notion of being taken care of in spite of yourself seems to echo something that predates robots.

Come, we've all been children, haven't we? We've all had wonderful, caring, loving mothers, haven't we? And we all remember her sweet way of saying, "Put on your rubbers before you go out or you'll catch cold." Or "Eat those vegetables, they're good for you. And you can't have another piece of cake. You'll rot your teeth." Or, "How do you manage to get your clothes so dirty?"

And those among you who are masculine have the great fortune to hear delightful comments of that sort even in adult life, for we develop new mothers called "wives" who make precisely similar remarks about rubbers, vegetables, and clothes.

Now I don't recall that Bob Silverberg (unlike me) has ever been fat, or has ever needed to diet, but that's just a detail. I'm sure that he has had occasion to grind his teeth over being inconveniently loved, and this story may be an exorcism thereof. (IA)

The Carmichaels were a pretty plump family, to begin with. Not one of the four of them couldn't stand to shed quite a few pounds. And there happened to be a superspecial on roboservitors at one of the Miracle Mile roboshops—40% off on the 2061 model, with adjustable caloric-intake monitors.

Sam Carmichael liked the idea of having his food prepared and served by a robot who would keep one beady solenoid eye on the collective family waistline. He squinted speculatively at the glossy display model, absentmindedly slipped his thumbs beneath his elastobelt to knead his paunch, and said, "How much?"

The salesman flashed a brilliant and probably synthetic grin. "Only 2995, sir. That includes free service contract for the first five years. Only two hundred credits down and up to forty months to pay."

Carmichael frowned, thinking of his bank balance. Then he thought of his wife's figure, and of his daughter's endless yammering about her need to diet. Besides, Jemima, their old robocook, was shabby and gear-stripped, and made a miserable showing when other company executives visited them for dinner.

"I'll take it," he said.

"Care to trade in your old robocook, sir? Liberal trade-in allowances—"

"I have a '43 Madison." Carmichael wondered if he should mention its bad arm libration and serious fuel-feed overflow, but decided that would be carrying candidness too far.

"Well—ah—I guess we could allow you fifty credits on a '43, sir. Seventy-five, maybe, if the recipe bank is still in good condition."

"Excellent condition." That part was honest—the family had never let even one recipe wear out. "You could send a man down to look her over."

"Oh, no need to do that, sir. We'll take your word. Seventy-five, then? And delivery of the new model by this evening?"

"Done," Carmichael said. He was glad to get the pathetic old '43 out of the house at any cost.

He signed the purchase order cheerfully, pocketed the facsim and handed over ten crisp twenty-credit vouchers. He could almost feel the roll of fat melting from him now, as he eyed the magnificent '61 roboservitor that would shortly be his.

The time was only 1810 hours when he left the shop, got into his car and punched out the coordinates for home. The whole transaction had taken less than ten minutes. Carmichael, a second-level executive at Normandy Trust, prided himself both on his good business sense and his ability to come quickly to a firm decision.

Fifteen minutes later, his car deposited him at the front entrance to their totally detached self-powered suburban home in the fashionable Westley subdivision. The car obediently took itself around back to the garage, while Carmichael stood in the scanner field until the door opened. Clyde, the robutler, came scuttling hastily up, took his hat and cloak, and handed him a Martini.

Carmichael beamed appreciatively. "Well done, thou good and faithful servant!"

He took a healthy sip and headed toward the living room to greet his wife, son and daughter. Pleasant gin-induced warmth filtered through him. The robutler was ancient and due for replacement as soon as the budget could stand the charge, but Carmichael realized he would miss the clanking old heap.

"You're late, dear," Ethel Carmichael said as he appeared. "Dinner's been ready for ten minutes. Jemima's so annoyed her cathodes are clicking."

"Jemima's cathodes fail to interest me," Carmichael said evenly. "Good evening, dear. Myra. Joey. I'm late because I stopped off at Marhew's on my way home."

His son blinked. "The robot place, Dad?"

"Precisely. I bought a '61 roboservitor to replace old Jemima and her spluttering cathodes. The new model has," Carmichael added, eyeing his son's adolescent bulkiness and the rather-more-than ample figures of his wife and daughter, "some very special attachments."

They dined well that night, on Jemima's favorite Tuesday dinner menu—shrimp cocktail, fumet of gumbo chervil, breast of chicken with creamed potatoes and asparagus, delicious plum tarts for dessert, and coffee. Carmichael felt pleasantly bloated when he had finished, and gestured to Clyde for a snifter of his favorite after-dinner digestive aid, VSOP Cognac. He leaned back, warm, replete, able easily to ignore the blustery November winds outside.

A pleasing electroluminescence suffused the dining room with pink—this year, the experts thought pink improved digestion—and the heating filaments embedded in the wall glowed cozily as they delivered the BTUs. This was the hour for relaxation in the Carmichael household.

"Dad," Joey began hesitantly, "about that canoe trip next weekend—"

Carmichael folded his hands across his stomach and nodded. "You can go, I suppose. Only be careful. If I find out you didn't use the equilibriator this time—"

The door chime sounded. Carmichael lifted an eyebrow and swivelled in his chair.

"Who is it, Clyde?"

"He gives his name as Robinson, sir. Of Robinson Robotics, he said. He has a bulky package to deliver."

"It must be that new robocook, Father!" Myra Carmichael exclaimed.

"I guess it is. Show him in, Clyde."

Robinson turned out to be a red-faced, efficient-looking little man in greasy green overalls and a plaid pullover-coat, who looked disapprovingly at the robutler and strode into the Carmichael living room.

He was followed by a lumbering object about seven feet high, mounted on a pair of rolltreads and swathed completely in quilted rags.

"Got him all wrapped up against the cold, Mr. Carmichael. Lot of delicate circuitry in that job. You ought to be proud of him."

"Clyde, help Mr. Robinson unpack the new robocook," Carmichael said.

"That's okay—I can manage it. And it's *not* a robocook, by the way. It's called a roboservitor now. Fancy price, fancy name."

Carmichael heard his wife mutter, "Sam, how much—"

He scowled at her. "Very reasonable, Ethel. Don't worry so much."

He stepped back to admire the roboservitor as it emerged from the quilted swaddling. It was big, all right, with a massive barrel of a chest—robotic controls are always housed in the chest, not in the relatively tiny head—and a gleaming mirror-keen finish that accented its sleekness and newness. Carmichael felt the satisfying glow of pride in ownership. Somehow it seemed to him that he had done something noble and lordly in buying this magnificent robot.

Robinson finished the unpacking job and, standing on tiptoes, opened the robot's chest panel. He unclipped a thick instruction manual and handed it to Carmichael, who stared at the tome uneasily.

"Don't fret about that, Mr. Carmichael. This robot's no trouble to handle. The book's just part of the trimming. Come here a minute."

Carmichael peered into the robot's innards. Pointing, Robinson said, "Here's the recipe bank—biggest, and best ever designed. Of course it's possible to tape in any of your favorite family recipes, if they're not already there. Just hook up your old robocook to the integrator circuit and feed 'em in. I'll take care of that before I leave."

"And what about the—ah—special features?"

"The reducing monitors, you mean? Right over here. See? You just tape in the names of the members of the family and their present and desired weights, and the roboservitor takes care of the rest. Computes caloric intake, adjusts menus, and everything else."

Carmichael grinned at his wife. "Told you I was going to do something about our weight, Ethel. No more dieting for you, Myra—the robot does all the work." Catching a sour look on his son's face, he added, "And you're not so lean yourself, Buster."

"I don't think there'll be any trouble," Robinson said buoyantly. "But if there is, just buzz for me. I handle service and delivery for Marhew Stores in this area."

"Right."

"Now if you'll get me your obsolete robocook, I'll transfer the family recipes before I cart it away on the trade-in-deal."

There was a momentary tingle of nostalgia and regret when Robinson left, half an hour later, taking old Jemima with him. Carmichael had almost come to think of the battered '43

Madison as a member of the family. After all, he had bought her sixteen years before, only a couple of years after his marriage.

But she—*it*, he corrected in annoyance—was only a robot, and robots became obsolete. Besides, Jemima probably suffered all the aches and pains of a robot's old age and would be happier dismantled. Carmichael blotted Jemima from his mind.

The four of them spent most of the rest of that evening discovering things about their new roboservitor. Carmichael drew up a table of their weights (himself, 192; Ethel, 145; Myra, 139; Joey, 189) and the amount they proposed to weigh in three months' time (himself, 180; Ethel, 125; Myra, 120; Joey, 175). Carmichael then let his son, who prided himself on his knowledge of practical robotics, integrate the figures and feed them to the robot's programming bank.

"You wish this schedule to take effect immediately?" the roboservitor queried in a deep, mellow bass.

Startled, Carmichael said, "T-tomorrow morning, at breakfast. We might as well start right away."

"He speaks well, doesn't he?" Ethel asked.

"He sure does," Joey said. "Jemima always stammered and squeaked, and all she could say was, 'Dinner is served' and 'Be careful, sir, the soup plate is verry warrm.' "

Carmichael smiled. He noticed his daughter admiring the robot's bulky frame and sleek bronze limbs, and thought resignedly that a seventeen-year-old girl could find the strangest sorts of love objects. But he was happy to see that they were all evidently pleased with the robot. Even with the discount and the trade-in, it *had* been a little on the costly side.

But it would be worth it.

Carmichael slept soundly and woke early, anticipating the first breakfast under the new regime. He still felt pleased with himself.

Dieting had always been such a nuisance, he thought—but, on the other hand, he had never enjoyed the sensation of an annoying roll of fat pushing outward against his elastobelt. He exercised sporadically, but it did little good, and he never had the initiative to keep a rigorous dieting campaign going for long. Now, though, with the mathematics of reducing done effortlessly for him, all the calculating and cooking being handled by the new robot—now, for the first time since he had been Joey's age, he could look forward to being slim and trim once again.

He dressed, showered and hastily depilated. It was 0730. Breakfast was ready.

Ethel and the children were already at the table when he arrived. Ethel and Myra were munching toast; Joey was peering at a bowl of milkless dry cereal, next to which stood a full glass of milk. Carmichael sat down.

"Your toast, sir," the roboservitor murmured.

Carmichael stared at the single slice. It had already been buttered for him, and the butter had evidently been measured out with a micrometer. The robot proceeded to hand him a cup of black coffee.

He groped for the cream and sugar. They weren't anywhere on the table. The other members of his family were regarding him strangely, and they were curiously, suspiciously silent.

"I like cream and sugar in my coffee," he said to the hovering roboservitor. "Didn't you find that in Jemima's old recipe bank?"

"Of course, sir. But you must learn to drink your coffee without such things, if you wish to lose weight."

Carmichael chuckled. Somehow he had not expected the regimen to be quite like this—quite so, well, Spartan. "Oh, yes. Of course. Ah—are the eggs ready yet?" He considered a day incomplete unless he began it with soft-boiled eggs.

"Sorry, no sir. On Mondays, Wednesdays and Fridays, breakfast is to consist of toast and black coffee only, except for Master Joey, who gets cereal, fruit juice and milk."

"I—see."

Well, he had asked for it. He shrugged and took a bite of the toast. He sipped the coffee; it tasted like river mud, but he tried not to make a face.

Joey seemed to be going about the business of eating his cereal rather oddly. Carmichael noticed next. "Why don't you pour that glass of milk *into* the cereal?" he asked. "Won't it taste better that way?"

"Sure it will. But Bismark says I won't get another glass if I do, so I'm eating it this way."

"Bismark?"

Joey grinned. "It's the name of a famous 19th-Century German dictator. They called him the Iron Chancellor." He jerked his head toward the kitchen, to which the roboservitor had silently retreated. "Pretty good name for him, eh?"

"No," said Carmichael. "It's silly."

"It has a certain ring of truth, though," Ethel remarked.

Carmichael did not reply. He finished his toast and coffee somewhat glumly and signalled Clyde to get the car out of the garage. He felt depressed—dieting didn't seem to be so effortless after all, even with the new robot.

As he walked toward the door, the robot glided around him and handed him a small printed slip of paper. Carmichael stared at it. It said:

FRUIT JUICE
LETTUCE & TOMATO SALAD
(ONE) HARD-BOILED EGG
BLACK COFFEE

"What is this thing?"

"You are the only member of this family group who will not be eating three meals a day under my personal supervision. This is your luncheon menu. Please adhere to it," the robot said smoothly.

Repressing a sputter, Carmichael said, "Yes—yes. Of course."

He pocketed the menu and made his way uncertainly to the waiting car.

He was faithful to the robot's orders at lunchtime that day; even though he was beginning to develop resistance to the idea that had seemed so appealing only the night before, he was willing, at least, to give it a try.

But something prompted him to stay away from the restaurant where Normandy Trust employees usually lunched, and where there were human waiters to smirk at him and fellow executives to ask prying questions.

He ate instead at a cheap robocafeteria two blocks to the north. He slipped in surreptitiously with his collar turned up, punched out his order (it cost him less than a credit altogether) and wolfed it down. He still felt hungry when he had finished, but he compelled himself to return loyally to the office.

He wondered how long he was going to be able to keep up this iron self-control. Not very long, he realized dolefully. And if anyone from the company caught him eating at a robocafeteria, he'd be a laughing stock. Someone of executive status just *didn't* eat lunch by himself in mechanized cafeterias.

By the time he had finished his day's work, his stomach felt knotted and pleated. His hand was shaky as he punched out his destination on the car's autopanel, and he was thankful that it took less than an hour to get home from the office. Soon, he thought, he'd be tasting food again. Soon. Soon. He switched on the roof-mounted video, leaned back at the recliner and tried to relax as the car bore him homeward.

He was in for a surprise, though, when he stepped through the safety field into his home. Clyde was waiting as always, and, as always, took his hat and cloak. And, as always, Carmichael reached out for the cocktail that Clyde prepared nightly to welcome him home.

There was no cocktail.

"Are we out of gin, Clyde?"

"No, sir."

"How come no drink, then?"

The robot's rubberized metallic features seemed to drop. "Because, sir, a Martini's caloric content is inordinately high. Gin is rated at a hundred calories per ounce and—"

"Oh, no. You too!"

"Pardon, sir. The new roboservitor has altered my responsive circuits to comply with the regulations now in force in this household."

Carmichael felt his fingers starting to tremble. "Clyde, you've been my butler for almost twenty years."

"Yes, sir."

"You always make my drinks for me. You mix the best Martinis in the Western Hemisphere."

"Thank you, sir."

"And you're going to mix one for me right now! That's a direct order!"

"Sir! I—" The robutler staggered wildly and nearly careened into Carmichael. It seemed to have lost all control over its gyro-balance; it clutched agonizingly at its chest panel and started to sag.

Hastily, Carmichael barked, "Order countermanded! Clyde, are you all right?"

Slowly, and with a creak, the robot straightened up. It looked dangerously close to an overload. "Your direct order set up a first-level conflict in me, sir," Clyde whispered faintly. "I—came close to burning out just then, sir. May—may I be excused?"

"Of course. Sorry, Clyde." Carmichael balled his fists. There was such a thing as going too far! The roboservitor—Bismarck—had obviously placed on Clyde a flat prohibition against serving liquor to him. Reducing or no reducing, there were *limits*.

Carmichael strode angrily toward the kitchen.

His wife met him halfway. "I didn't hear you come in, Sam. I want to talk to you about—"

"Later. Where's that robot?"

"In the kitchen, I imagine. It's almost dinnertime."

He brushed past her and swept on into the kitchen, where Bismarck was moving efficiently from electrostove to magnetic worktable. The robot swivelled as Carmichael entered.

"Did you have a good day, sir?"

"No! I'm hungry!"

"The first days of a diet are always the most difficult Mr. Carmichael. But your body will adjust to the reduction in food intake before long."

"I'm sure of that. But what's this business of tinkering with Clyde?"

"The butler insisted on preparing an alcoholic drink for you. I was forced to adjust his programming. From now on, sir, you may indulge in cocktails on Tuesdays, Thursdays, and Saturdays. I beg to be excused from further discussion now, sir. The meal is almost ready."

Poor Clyde! Carmichael thought. *And poor me!* He gnashed his teeth impotently a few times, then gave up and turned away from the glistening, overbearing roboservitor. A light gleamed on the side of the robot's head, indicating that he had shut off his audio circuits and was totally engaged in his task.

Dinner consisted of steak and peas, followed by black coffee. The steak was rare; Carmichael preferred it well done. But Bismarck—the name was beginning to take hold—had had all the latest dietetic theories taped into him, and rare meat it was.

After the robot had cleared the table and tidied up the kitchen, it retired to its storage place in the basement, which gave the Carmichael family a chance to speak openly to each other for the first time that evening.

"Lord!" Ethel snorted. "Sam, I don't object to losing weight, but if we're going to be *tyrannized* in our own home—"

"Mom's right," Joey put in. "It doesn't seem fair for that thing to feed us whatever it pleases. And I didn't like the way it messed around with Clyde's circuits."

Carmichael spread his hands. "I'm not happy about it either. But we have to give it a try. We can always make readjustments in the programming if it turns out to be necessary."

"But how long are we going to keep this up?" Myra wanted to know. "I had three meals in this house today and I'm starved!"

"Me, too," Joey said. He elbowed himself from his chair and looked around. "Bismark's downstairs. I'm going to get a slice of lemon pie while the coast is clear."

"No!" Carmichael thundered.

"No?"

"There's no sense in my spending three thousand credits on a dietary robot if you're going to cheat, Joey. I forbid you to have any pie."

"But, Dad, I'm hungry! I'm a growing boy! I'm—"

"You're sixteen years old, and if you grow much more, you won't fit inside the house," Carmichael snapped, looking up at his six-foot-one son.

"Sam, we can't starve the boy," Ethel protested. "If he wants pie, let him have some. You're carrying this reduction fetish too far."

Carmichael considered that. Perhaps, he thought, I *am* being a little over severe. And the thought of lemon pie was a tempting one. He was pretty hungry himself.

"All right," he said with feigned reluctance. "I guess a bit of pie won't wreck the plan. In fact, I suppose I'll have some myself. Joey, why don't you—"

"Begging your pardon," a purring voice said behind him. Carmichael jumped half an inch. It was the robot, Bismarck. "It would be most unfortunate if you were to have pie now, Mr. Carmichael. My calculations are very precise."

Carmichael saw the angry gleam in his son's eye, but the robot seemed extraordinarily big at that moment, and it happened to stand between him and the kitchen.

He sighed weakly. "Let's forget the lemon pie, Joey."

After two full days of the Bismarckian diet, Carmichael discovered that his inner resources of will power were beginning to crumble. On the third day he tossed away the printed lunchtime diet and went out irresponsibly with MacDougal and Hennessey for a six-course lunch, complete with cocktails. It seemed to him that he hadn't tasted real food since the robot arrived.

That night, he was able to tolerate the seven-hundred-calorie dinner without any inward grumblings, being still well lined with lunch. But Ethel and Myra and Joey were increasingly irritable. It seemed that the robot had usurped Ethel's job of handling the daily marketing and had stocked in nothing but a huge supply of healthy low-calorie foods. The larder now bulged with wheat germ, protein bread, irrigated salmon, and other hitherto unfamiliar items. Myra had taken up biting her nails; Joey's mood was one of black sullen brooding, and Carmichael knew how that could lead to trouble quickly with a sixteen-year-old.

After the meager dinner, he ordered Bismarck to go to the basement and stay there until summoned.

The robot said, "I must advise you, sir, that I will detect indulgence in any forbidden foods in my absence and adjust for it in the next meals."

"You have my word," Carmichael said, thinking it was indeed queer to have to pledge on your honor to your own robot. He waited until the massive servitor had vanished below; then he turned to Joey and said, "Get the instruction manual, boy."

Joey grinned in understanding. Ethel said, "Sam, what are you going to do?"

Carmichael patted his shrunken waistline. "I'm going to take a can opener to that creature and adjust his programming. He's overdoing this diet business. Joey, have you found the instructions on how to reprogram the robot?"

"Page 167. I'll get the tool kit, Dad."

"Right." Carmichael turned to the robutler, who was standing by dumbly, in his usual forward-stooping posture of expectancy. "Clyde, go down below and tell Bismarck we want him right away."

Moments later, the two robots appeared. Carmichael said to the roboservitor, "I'm afraid it's necessary for us to change your program. We've overestimated our capacity for losing weight."

"I beg you to reconsider, sir. Extra weight is harmful to every vital organ in the body. I plead with you to maintain my scheduling unaltered."

"I'd rather cut my own throat. Joey, inactivate him and do your stuff."

Grinning fiercely, the boy stepped forward and pressed the stud that opened the robot's ribcage. A frightening assortment of gears, cams and translucent cables became visible inside the robot. With a small wrench in one hand and the open instruction book in the other, Joey prepared to make the necessary changes, while Carmichael held his breath and a pall of silence descended on the living room. Even old Clyde leaned forward to have a better view.

Joey muttered, "Lever F2, with the yellow indicia, is to be advanced one notch . . . umm. Now twist Dial B9 to the left, thereby opening the taping compartment and—oops!"

Carmichael heard the clang of a wrench and saw the bright flare of sparks; Joey leaped back, cursing with surprisingly mature skill. Ethel and Myra gasped simultaneously.

"What happened?" four voices—Clyde's coming in last demanded.

"Dropped the damn wrench," Joey said. "I guess I shorted out something in there."

The robot's eyes were whirling satanically and its voice box was emitting an awesome twelve-cycle rumble. The great metal creature stood stiffly in the middle of the living room; with brusque gestures of its big hands, it slammed shut the open chest plates.

"We'd better call Mr. Robinson," Ethel said worriedly. "A short-circuited robot is likely to explode, or worse."

"We should have called Robinson in the first place," Carmichael murmured bitterly. "It's my fault for letting Joey tinker with an expensive and delicate mechanism like that. Myra, get me the card Mr. Robinson left."

"Gee, Dad, this is the first time I've ever had anything like that go wrong," Joey insisted. "I didn't know—"

"You're darned right you didn't know." Carmichael took

the card from his daughter and started toward the phone. "I hope we can reach him at this hour. If we can't—"

Suddenly Carmichael felt cold fingers prying the card from his hand. He was so startled he relinquished it without a struggle. He watched as Bismarck efficiently ripped it into little fragments and shoved them into a wall disposal unit.

The robot said, "There will be no further meddling with my program tapes." Its voice was deep and strangely harsh.

"What—"

"Mr. Carmichael, today you violated the program I set down for you. My perceptors reveal that you consumed an amount far in excess of your daily lunchtime requirement."

"Sam, what—"

"Quiet, Ethel. Bismarck, I order you to shut yourself off at once."

"My apologies, sir. I cannot serve you if I am shut off."

"I don't *want* you to serve me. You're out of order. I want you to remain still until I can phone the repairman and get him to service you."

Then he remembered the card that had gone into the disposal unit. He felt a faint tremor of apprehension.

"You took Robinson's card and destroyed it."

"Further alteration of my circuits would be detrimental to the Carmichael family," said the robot. "I cannot permit you to summon the repairman."

"Don't get him angry, Dad," Joey warned. "I'll call the police. I'll be back in—"

"You will remain within this house," the robot said. Moving with impressive speed on its oiled treads, it crossed the room, blocking the door, and reached far above its head to activate the impassable privacy field that protected the house. Carmichael watched, aghast, as the inexorable robotic fingers twisted and manipulated the field controls.

"I have now reversed the polarity of the house privacy field," the robot announced. "Since you are obviously not to be trusted to keep to the diet I prescribe, I cannot allow you to leave the premises. You will remain within and continue to obey my beneficial advice."

Calmly, he uprooted the telephone. Next, the windows were opaqued and the stud broken off. Finally, the robot seized the instruction book from Joey's numbed hands and shoved it into the disposal unit.

"Breakfast will be served at the usual time," Bismarck said mildly. "For optimum purposes of health, you are all to be asleep by 2300 hours. I shall leave you now, until morning. Good night."

Carmichael did not sleep well that night, nor did he eat well the next day. He awoke late, for one thing—well past nine. He discovered that someone, obviously Bismarck, had neatly cancelled out the impulses from the housebrain that woke him at seven each morning.

The breakfast menu was toast and black coffee. Carmichael ate disgruntedly, not speaking, indicating by brusque scowls that he did not want to be spoken to. After the miserable meal had been cleared away, he surreptitiously tiptoed to the front door in his dressing gown and darted a hand toward the handle.

The door refused to budge. He pushed until sweat dribbled down his face. He heard Ethel whisper warningly, *"Sam—"* and a moment later cool metallic fingers gently disengaged him from the door.

Bismarck said, "I beg your pardon, sir. The door will not open. I explained this last night."

Carmichael gazed sourly at the gimmicked control box of the privacy field. The robot had them utterly hemmed in. The reversed privacy field made it impossible for them to leave the house; it cast a sphere of force around the entire detached dwelling. In theory, the field could be penetrated from outside, but nobody was likely to come calling without an invitation. Not here in Westley. It wasn't one of those neighborly subdivisions where everybody knew everybody else. Carmichael had picked it for that reason.

"Damn you," he growled, "you can't hold us *prisoners* in here!"

"My intent is only to help you," said the robot, in a

mechanical yet dedicated voice. "My function is to supervise your diet. Since you will not obey willingly, obedience must be enforced—for your own good."

Carmichael scowled and walked away. The worst part of it was that the roboservitor sounded so *sincere!*

Trapped. The phone connection was severed. The windows were darkened. Somehow, Joey's attempt at repairs had resulted in a short circuit of the robot's obedience filters, and had also exaggeratedly stimulated its sense of function. Now Bismarck was determined to make them lose weight if it had to kill them to do so.

And that seemed very likely.

Blockaded, the Carmichael family met in a huddled little group to whisper plans for a counterattack. Clyde stood watch, but the robutler seemed to be in a state of general shock since the demonstration of the servitor-robot's independent capacity for action, and Carmichael now regarded him as undependable.

"He's got the kitchen walled off with some kind of electronic-based force web," Joey said. "He must have built it during the night. I tried to sneak in and scrounge some food, and got nothing but a flat nose for trying."

"I know," Carmichael said sadly. "He built the same sort of doohickey around the bar. Three hundred credits of good booze in there and I can't even grab the handle!"

"This is no time to worry about drinking," Ethel said morosely. "We'll be skeletons any day."

"It isn't *that* bad, Mom!" Joey said.

"Yes, it is!" cried Myra. "I've lost five pounds in four days!"

"Is that so terrible?"

"I'm wasting away," she sobbed. "My figure—it's vanishing! And—"

"Quiet," Carmichael whispered. "Bismarck's coming!"

The robot emerged from the kitchen, passing through the force barrier as if it had been a cobweb. It seemed to have effect on humans only, Carmichael thought. "Lunch will be served in eight minutes," it said obsequiously, and returned to its lair.

Carmichael glanced at his watch. The time was 1230 hours. "Probably down at the office they're wondering where I am," he said. "I haven't missed a day's work in years."

"They won't care," Ethel said. "An executive isn't required to account for every day off he takes, you know."

"But they'll worry after three or four days, won't they?" Myra asked. "Maybe they'll try to phone—or even send a rescue mission!"

From the kitchen, Bismarck said coldly, "There will be no danger of that. While you slept this morning, I notified your place of employment that you were resigning."

Carmichael gasped. Then, recovering, he said: "You're lying! The phone's cut off—and you never would have risked leaving the house, even if we *were* asleep!"

"I communicated with them via a microwave generator I constructed with the aid of your son's reference books last night," Bismarck replied. "Clyde reluctantly supplied me with the number. I also phoned your bank and instructed them to handle for you all such matters as tax payments, investment decisions, etc. To forestall difficulties, let me add that a force web will prevent access on your part to the electronic equipment in the basement. I will be able to conduct such communication with the outside world as will be necessary for your welfare, Mr. Carmichael. You need have no worries on that score."

"No," Carmichael echoed hollowly. "No worries."

He turned to Joey. "We've got to get out of here. Are you sure there's no way of disconnecting the privacy field?"

"He's got one of his force fields rigged around the control box. I can't even get near the thing."

"If only we had an iceman, or an oilman, the way the oldtime houses did," Ethel said bitterly. "He'd show up and come inside and probably he'd know how to shut the field off. But not *here*. Oh no. We've got a shiny chrome-plated cryostat in the basement that dishes out lots of liquid helium to

run the fancy cryotronic supercooled power plant that gives us
heat and light, and we have enough food in the freezer to last
for at least a decade or two, and so we can live like this for
years, a neat little self-contained island in the middle of
civilization, with nobody bothering us, nobody wondering
about us, and Sam Carmichael's pet robot to feed us whenever and as little as it pleases—''

There was a cutting edge to her voice that was dangerously
close to hysteria.

"Ethel, please," said Carmichael.

"Please what? Please keep quiet? Please stay calm? Sam,
we're *prisoners* in here!"

"I know. You don't have to raise your voice."

"Maybe if I do, someone will hear us and come and get us
out," she replied more coolly.

"It's four hundred feet to the next home, dear. And in the
seven years we've lived here, we've had about two visits
from our neighbors. We paid a stiff price for seclusion and
now we're paying a stiffer one. But please keep under control, Ethel."

"Don't worry, Mom. I'll figure a way out of this," Joey
said reassuringly.

In one corner of the living room, Myra was sobbing quietly
to herself, blotching her makeup. Carmichael felt a faintly
claustrophobic quiver. The house was big, three levels and
twelve rooms, but even so he could get tired of it very
quickly.

"Luncheon is served," the roboservitor announced in
booming tones.

And tired of lettuce-and-tomato lunches, too, Carmichael
added silently, as he shepherded his family toward the dining
room for their meagre midday meal.

"You have to do *something* about this, Sam," Ethel
Carmichael said on the third day of their imprisonment.

He glared at her. "Have to, eh? And just what am I
supposed to do?"

"Daddy, don't get excited," Myra said.

He whirled on her. "Don't tell me what I should or shouldn't do!"

"She can't help it, dear. We're all a little overwrought. After all, cooped up here—"

"I know. Like lambs in a pen," he finished acidly. "Except that we're not being fattened for slaughter. We're—we're being *thinned*, and for our own alleged good!"

Carmichael subsided gloomily. Toast-and-black-coffee, lettuce-and-tomato, rare-steak-and-peas. Bismarck's channels seemed to have frozen permanently at that daily menu.

But what could he do?

Contact with the outside world was impossible. The robot had erected a bastion in the basement from which he conducted such little business with the world as the Carmichael family had. Generally, they were self-sufficient. And Bismarck's force fields insured the impossibility of any attempts to disconnect the outer sheath, break into the basement, or even get at the food supply or the liquor. It was all very neat, and the four of them were fast approaching a state of starvation.

"Sam?"

He lifted his head wearily. "What is it, Ethel?"

"Myra had an idea before. Tell him, Myra."

"Oh, it would never work," Myra said demurely.

"Tell *him!*"

"Well—Dad, you *could* try to turn Bismarck off."

"Huh?" Carmichael grunted.

"I mean if you or Joey could distract him somehow, then Joey or you could open him up again and—"

"No," Carmichael snapped. "That thing's seven feet tall and weighs three hundred pounds. If you think *I'm* going to wrestle with it—"

"We could let Clyde try," Ethel suggested.

Carmichael shook his head vehemently. "The carnage would be frightful."

Joey said, "Dad, it may be our only hope."

"You too?" Carmichael asked.

He took a deep breath. He felt himself speared by two

deadly feminine glances, and he knew there was no hope but to try it. Resignedly, he pushed himself to his feet and said, "Okay. Clyde, go call Bismarck. Joey, I'll try to hang onto his arms while you open up his chest. Yank anything you can."

"Be careful," Ethel warned. "If there's an explosion—"

"If there's an explosion, we're all free," Carmichael said testily. He turned to see the broad figure of the roboservitor standing at the entrance to the living room.

"May I be of service, sir?"

"You may," Carmichael said. "We're having a little debate here and we want your evidence. It's a matter of defannising the poozlestan and—*Joey, open him up!*"

Carmichael grabbed for the robot's arms, trying to hold them without getting hurled across the room, while his son clawed frantically at the stud that opened the robot's innards. Carmichael anticipated immediate destruction—but, to his surprise, he found himself slipping as he tried to grasp the thick arms.

"Dad, it's no use. I—he—"

Carmichael found himself abruptly four feet off the ground. He heard Ethel and Myra scream and Clyde's, "*Do* be careful, sir."

Bismarck was carrying them across the room, gently, cradling him in one giant arm and Joey in the other. It set them down on the couch and stood back.

"Such an attempt is highly dangerous," Bismarck said reprovingly. "It puts me in danger of harming you physically. Please avoid any such acts in the future."

Carmichael stared broodingly at his son. "Did you have the same trouble I did?"

Joey nodded. "I couldn't get within an inch of his skin. It stands to reason, though. He's built one of those damned force screens around *himself*, too!"

Carmichael groaned. He did not look at his wife and his children. Physical attack on Bismarck was now out of the question. He began to feel as if he had been condemned to life imprisonment—and that his stay in durance vile would not be extremely prolonged.

In the upstairs bathroom, six days after the beginning of the blockade, Sam Carmichael stared at his haggard fleshless face in the mirror before wearily climbing on the scale.

He weighed 180.

He had lost twelve pounds in less than two weeks. He was fast becoming a quivering wreck.

A thought occurred to him as he stared at the wavering needle on the scale, and sudden elation spread over him. He dashed downstairs. Ethel was doggedly crocheting in the living room; Joey and Myra were playing cards grimly, desperately now, after six solid days of gin rummy and honeymoon bridge.

"Where's that robot?" Carmichael roared. "Come out here!"

"In the kitchen," Ethel said tonelessly.

"Bismarck! Bismarck!" Carmichael roared. "Come out here!"

The robot appeared. "How may I serve you, sir?"

"Damn you, scan me with your superpower receptors and tell me how much I weigh!"

After a pause, the robot said gravely, "One hundred seventy-nine pounds eleven ounces, Mr. Carmichael."

"Yes! Yes! And the original program I had taped into you was supposed to reduce me from 192 to 180," Carmichael crowed triumphantly. "So I'm finished with you, as long as I don't gain any more weight. And so are the rest of us, I'll bet. Ethel! Myra! Joey! Upstairs and weigh yourselves!"

But the robot regarded him with a doleful glare and said, "Sir, I find no record within me of any limitation on your reduction of weight."

"What?"

"I have checked my tapes fully. I have a record of an order causing weight reduction, but that tape does not appear to specify a *terminus ad quem*."

Carmichael exhaled and took three staggering steps backward. His legs wobbled; he felt Joey supporting him. He mumbled, "But I thought—I'm sure we did—I *know* we instructed you—"

Hunger gnawed at his flesh. Joey said softly, "Dad, probably that part of his tape was erased when he short-circuited."

"Oh," Carmichael said numbly.

He tottered into the living room and collapsed heavily in what had once been his favorite armchair. It wasn't anymore. The entire house had become odious to him. He longed to see the sunlight again, to see trees and grass, even to see that excrescence of an ultramodern house that the left-hand neighbors had erected.

But now that would be impossible. He had hoped, for a few minutes at least, that the robot would release them from dietary bondage when the original goal was shown to be accomplished. Evidently that was to be denied him. He giggled, then began to laugh.

"What's so funny, dear?" Ethel asked. She had lost her earlier tendencies to hysteria, and after long days of complex crocheting now regarded the universe with quiet resignation.

"Funny? The fact that I weigh 180 now. I'm lean, trim, fit as a fiddle. Next month I'll weigh 170. Then 160. Then finally about 88 pounds or so. We'll all shrivel up. Bismarck will starve us to death."

"Don't worry, Dad. We're going to get out of this."

Somehow Joey's brash boyish confidence sounded forced now. Carmichael shook his head. "We won't. We'll never get out. And Bismarck's going to reduce us *ad infinitum.* He's got no *terminus ad quem!*"

"What's he saying?" Myra asked.

"It's Latin," Joey explained. "But listen, Dad—I have an idea that I think will work." He lowered his voice. "I'm going to try to adjust Clyde, see? If I can get a sort of multiple vibrating effect in his neural pathway, maybe I can slip him through the reversed privacy field. He can go get help, find someone who can shut the field off. There's an article on multiphase generators in last month's *Popular Electromagnetics* and it's in my room upstairs. I—"

His voice died away. Carmichael, who had been listening with the air of a condemned man hearing his reprieve, said impatiently, "Well? Go on. Tell me more."

"Didn't you hear that, Dad?"

"Hear what?"

"The front door. I thought I heard it open just now."

"We're all cracking up," Carmichael said dully. He cursed the salesman at Marhew, he cursed the inventor of cryotronic robots, he cursed the day he had first felt ashamed of good old Jemima and resolved to replace her with a new model.

"I hope I'm not intruding, Mr. Carmichael," a new voice said apologetically.

Carmichael blinked and looked up. A wiry, ruddy-cheeked figure in a heavy peajacket had materialized in the middle of the living room. He was clutching a green metal toolbox in one gloved hand. He was Robinson, the robot repairman.

Carmichael asked hoarsely, "How did *you* get in?"

"Through the front door. I could see a light on inside, but nobody answered the doorbell when I rang, so I stepped in. Your doorbell's out of order. I thought I'd tell you. I know it's rude—"

"Don't apologize," Carmichael muttered. "We're delighted to see you."

"I was in the neighborhood, you see, and I figured I'd drop in and see how things were working out with your new robot," Robinson said.

Carmichael told him crisply and precisely and quickly. "So we've been prisoners in here for six days," he finished. "And your robot is gradually starving us to death. We can't hold out much longer."

The smile abruptly left Robinson's cheery face. "I *thought* you all looked rather unhealthy. Oh, damn, now there'll be an investigation and all kinds of trouble. But at least I can end your imprisonment."

He opened his toolbox and selected a tubular instrument eight inches long, with a glass bulb at one end and a trigger attachment at the other. "Force-field damper," he explained.

He pointed it at the control box of the privacy field and nodded in satisfaction. "There. Great little gadget. That neutralizes the effects of what the robot did and you're no longer blockaded. And now, if you'll produce the robot—"

Carmichael sent Clyde off to get Bismarck. The robutler returned a few moments later, followed by the looming roboservitor. Robinson grinned gaily, pointed the neutralizer at Bismarck and squeezed. The robot froze in mid-glide, emitting a brief squeak.

"There. That should immobilize him. Let's have a look in that chassis now."

The repairman quickly opened Bismarck's chest and, producing a pocket flash, peered around in the complex interior of the servomechanism, making occasional clucking inaudible comments.

Overwhelmed with relief, Carmichael shakily made his way to a seat. Free! Free at last! His mouth watered at the thought of the meals he was going to have in the next few days. Potatoes and Martinis and warm buttered rolls and all the other forbidden foods!

"Fascinating," Robinson said, half to himself. "The obedience filters are completely shorted out, and the purpose nodes were somehow soldered together by the momentary high-voltage arc. I've never seen anything quite like this, you know."

"Neither had we," Carmichael said hollowly.

"Really, though—this is an utterly new breakthrough in robotic science! If we can reproduce this effect, it means we can build self-willed robots—and think of what *that* means to science!"

"We know already," Ethel said.

"I'd love to watch what happens when the power source is operating," Robinson went on. "For instance, is that feedback loop really negative or—"

"No!" five voices shrieked at once—with Clyde, as usual, coming in last.

It was too late. The entire event had taken no more than a

tenth of a second. Robinson had squeezed his neutralizer trigger again, activating Bismarck—and in one quick swoop the roboservitor seized neutralizer and toolbox from the stunned repairman, activated the privacy field once again, and exultantly crushed the fragile neutralizer between two mighty fingers.

Robinson stammered, "But—but—"

"This attempt at interfering with the well-being of the Carmichael family was ill-advised," Bismarck said severely. He peered into the toolbox, found a second neutralizer and neatly reduced it to junk. He clanged shut his chest plates.

Robinson turned and streaked for the door, forgetting the reactivated privacy field. He bounced back hard, spinning wildly around. Carmichael rose from his seat just in time to catch him.

There was a panicky, trapped look on the repairman's face. Carmichael was no longer able to share the emotion; inwardly he was numb, totally resigned, not minded for further struggle.

"He—he moved so *fast!*" Robinson burst out.

"He did indeed," Carmichael said tranquilly. He patted his hollow stomach and sighed gently. "Luckily, we have an unoccupied guest bedroom for you, Mr. Robinson. Welcome to our happy little home. I hope you like toast and black coffee for breakfast."

THE PRIZE OF PERIL

BY ROBERT SHECKLEY (1928-   )

THE MAGAZINE OF FANTASY AND SCIENCE FICTION
MAY

Robert Sheckley has always been a master of social science extrapolation combined with satire, and I fondly remember the impact his stories had on my then pliable mind in the 1950s. 1958 was a particularly important year for him, since it saw the publication of his first science fiction novel, the still-exciting Immortality Delivered *(later revised as* Immortality, Inc.*). Although he has published some ten novels in the field, it is his work at the shorter lengths for which he will be remembered.*

"The Prize of Peril" is a fine example of a good writer taking a trend to its logical conclusion. It is an idea that has been used by other writers, including Stephen King in The Running Man. *As I write these words* Variety *says that game shows featuring considerable physical danger are to appear among next year's television offerings.*

Thanks a lot, Bob. (MHG)

The proper way of doing a satire is to take some aspect of society that strikes you as particularly stupid and carry it to a logical extreme. The effect, when properly done, is to magnify the stupidity to so horrifying an extent that it can be missed by no one, however jaded.

For instance, we have all watched game shows on television where people are asked to perform difficult tasks in a short period of time and where failure subjects them to ridiculous and undignified postures and events while the studio audience (and, presumably, the home audience) laughs unfeelingly. Or where couples are asked to answer questions about each other that cannot help but make each of them look foolish, again to cries of merriment from the onlookers.

But why do people subject themselves to such indignities? —for money, of course (do you have to ask?). There's always the chance that they will get a brand-new automobile or a trip to Hawaii and then they scream in pretty joy as they wipe away the egg from their hair.

The idea that these shows teach is that people will sacrifice anything if it means getting something for nothing.

You may say, "What harm does it do? It's just fun."

—Well, I won't talk about the weakening of moral fiber, because I don't like to preach, but we might ask where it would stop. How exciting do we want to make it? To what extent can we deepen the level of humiliation? —Let Robert Scheckley tell you. (IA)

Raeder lifted his head cautiously above the window sill. He saw the fire escape, and below it a narrow alley. There was a weather-beaten baby carriage in the alley, and three garbage cans. As he watched, a black-sleeved arm moved from behind the furthest can, with something shiny in its fist. Raeder ducked down. A bullet smashed through the window above his head and punctured the ceiling, showering him with plaster.

Now he knew about the alley. It was guarded, just like the door.

He lay at full length on the cracked linoleum, staring at the bullet hole in the ceiling, listening to the sounds outside the door. He was a tall man with bloodshot eyes and a two-day stubble. Grime and fatigue had etched lines into his face. Fear had touched his features, tightening a muscle here and twitching a nerve there. The results were startling. His face had character now, for it was reshaped by the expectation of death.

There was a gunman in the alley and two on the stairs. He was trapped. He was dead.

Sure, Raeder thought, he still moved and breathed; but that was only because of death's inefficiency. Death would take care of him in a few minutes. Death would poke holes in his face and body, artistically dab his clothes with blood, arrange his limbs in some grotesque position of the graveyard ballet . . .

Raeder bit his lip sharply. He wanted to live. There had to be a way.

He rolled onto his stomach and surveyed the dingy cold-water apartment into which the killers had driven him. It was a perfect little one-room coffin. It had a door, which was watched, and a fire escape, which was watched. And it had a tiny windowless bathroom.

He crawled to the bathroom and stood up. There was a ragged hole in the ceiling, almost four inches wide. If he could enlarge it, crawl through into the apartment above . . .

He heard a muffled thud. The killers were impatient. They were beginning to break down the door.

He studied the hole in the ceiling. No use even considering it. He could never enlarge it in time.

They were smashing against the door, grunting each time they struck. Soon the lock would tear out, or the hinges would pull out of the rotting wood. The door would go down, and the two blank-faced men would enter, dusting off their jackets . . .

But surely someone would help him! He took the tiny television set from his pocket. The picture was blurred, and he didn't bother to adjust it. The audio was clear and precise.

He listened to the well-modulated voice of Mike Terry addressing his vast audience.

"*. . . terrible spot,*" Terry was saying. "*Yes folks, Jim Raeder is in a truly terrible predicament. He had been hiding, you'll remember, in a third-rate Broadway hotel under* *an assumed name. It seemed safe enough. But the bellhop recognized him, and gave that information to the Thompson gang."*

The door creaked under repeated blows. Raeder clutched the little television set and listened.

"Jim Raeder just managed to escape from the hotel! Closely pursued, he entered a brownstone at one fifty-six West End Avenue. His intention was to go over the roofs. And it might have worked, folks, it just might have worked. But the roof door was locked. It looked like the end. . . . But Raeder found that apartment seven was unoccupied and unlocked. He entered . . ."

Terry paused for emphasis, then cried: *"—and now he's trapped there, trapped like a rat in a cage! The Thompson gang is breaking down the door! The fire escape is guarded! Our camera crew, situated in a nearby building, is giving you a closeup now. Look, folks, just look! Is there no hope for Jim Raeder?"*

Is there no hope, Raider silently echoed, perspiration pouring from him as he stood in the dark, stifling little bathroom, listening to the steady thud against the door.

"Wait a minute!" Mike Terry cried. *"Hang on, Jim Raeder, hang on a little longer. Perhaps there is hope! I have an urgent call from one of our viewers, a call on the Good Samaritan Line! Here's someone who thinks he can help you, Jim. Are you listening, Jim Raeder?"*

Raeder waited, and heard the hinges tearing out of rotten wood.

"Go right ahead, sir," said Mike Terry. *"What is your name, sir?"*

"Er—Felix Bartholemow."

"Don't be nervous, Mr. Bartholemow. Go right ahead."

"Well, OK. Mr. Raeder," said an old man's shaking voice, *"I used to live at one five six West End Avenue. Same apartment you're trapped in, Mr. Raeder—fact! Look, that bathroom has got a window, Mr. Raeder. It's been painted over, but it has got a—"*

Raeder pushed the television set into his pocket. He located the outlines of the window and kicked. Glass shattered, and daylight poured startlingly in. He cleared the jagged sill and quickly peered down.

Below was a long drop to a concrete courtyard.

The hinges tore free. He heard the door opening. Quickly Raeder climbed through the window, hung by his fingertips for a moment, and dropped.

The shock was stunning. Groggily he stood up. A face appeared at the bathroom window.

"Tough luck," said the man, leaning out and taking careful aim with a snub-nosed .38.

At that moment a smoke bomb exploded inside the bathroom.

The killer's shot went wide. He turned, cursing. More smoke bombs burst in the courtyard, obscuring Raeder's figure.

He could hear Mike Terry's frenzied voice over the TV set in his pocket. *"Now run for it!"* Terry was screaming. *"Run, Jim Raeder, run for your life. Run now, while the killers' eyes are filled with smoke. And thank Good Samaritan Sarah Winters of three four one two Edgar Street, Brockton, Mass., for donating five smoke bombs and employing the services of a man to throw them!"*

In a quieter voice, Terry continued: *"You've saved a man's life today, Mrs. Winters. Would you tell our audience how it—"*

Raider wasn't able to hear any more. He was running through the smoke-filled courtyard, past clothes lines, into the open street.

He walked down 63d Street, slouching to minimize his height, staggering slightly from exertion, dizzy from lack of food and sleep.

"Hey you!"

Raeder turned. A middle-aged woman was sitting on the steps of a brownstone, frowning at him.

"You're Raeder, aren't you? The one they're trying to kill?"

Raeder started to walk away.

"Come inside here, Raeder," the woman said.

Perhaps it was a trap. But Raeder knew that he had to depend upon the generosity and good-heartedness of the people. He was their representative, a projection of themselves, an average guy in trouble. Without them, he was lost. With them, nothing could harm him.

Trust in the people, Mike Terry had told him. They'll never let you down.

He followed the woman into her parlor. She told him to sit down and left the room, returning almost immediately with a plate of stew. She stood watching him while he ate, as one would watch an ape in the zoo eat peanuts.

Two children came out of the kitchen and stared at him. Three overalled men came out of the bedroom and focused a television camera on him. There was a big television set in the parlor. As he gulped his food, Raeder watched the image of Mike Terry, and listened to the man's strong, sincere, worried voice.

"There he is folks," Terry was saying. *"There's Jim Raeder now, eating his first square meal in two days. Our camera crews have really been working to cover this for you! Thanks, boys. . . . Folks, Jim Raeder has been given a brief sanctuary by Mrs. Velma O'Dell, of three forty-three Sixty-Third Street. Thank you, Good Samaritan O'Dell! It's really wonderful, how people from all walks of life have taken Jim Raeder to their hearts!"*

"You better hurry," Mrs. O'Dell said.

"Yes ma'am," Raeder said.

"I don't want no gunplay in my apartment."

"I'm almost finished, ma'am."

One of the children asked. "Aren't they going to kill him?"

"Shut up," said Mrs. O'Dell.

"Yes Jim," chanted Mike Terry, *"you'd better hurry. Your killers aren't far behind. They aren't stupid men, Jim. Vi-*

*cious, warped, insane—yes! But not stupid. They're following
a trail of blood—blood from your torn hand, Jim!"*

Raeder hadn't realized until now that he'd cut his hand on
the window sill.

"Here, I'll bandage that," Mrs. O'Dell said. Raeder stood
up and let her bandage his hand. Then she gave him a brown
jacket and a gray slouch hat.

"My husband's stuff," she said.

"He has a disguise, folks!" Mike Terry cried delightedly.
*"This is something new! A disguise! With seven hours to go
until he's safe!"*

"Now get out of here," Mrs. O'Dell said.

"I'm going, ma'am," Raeder said. "Thanks."

"I think you're stupid," she said. "I think you're stupid to
be involved in this."

"Yes ma'am."

"It just isn't worth it."

Raeder thanked her and left. He walked to Broadway,
caught a subway to 59th Street, then an uptown local to 86th.
There he bought a newspaper and changed for the Manhasset
thru-express.

He glanced at his watch. He had six and a half hours to go.

The subway roared under Manhattan. Raeder dozed, his
bandaged hand concealed under the newspaper, the hat pulled
over his face. Had he been recognized yet? Had he shaken the
Thompson gang? Or was someone telephoning them now?

Dreamily he wondered if he had escaped death. Or was he
still a cleverly animated corpse, moving around because of
death's inefficiency? (My dear, death is so *laggard* these
days! Jim Raeder walked about for hours after he died, and
actually answered people's *questions* before he could be de-
cently buried!)

Raeder's eyes snapped open. He had dreamed something
. . . unpleasant. He couldn't remember what.

He closed his eyes again and remembered, with mild astonishment, a time when he had been in no trouble.

That was two years ago. He had been a big pleasant young man working as a truck driver's helper. He had no talents. He was too modest to have dreams.

The tight-faced little truck driver had the dreams for him. "Why not try for a television show, Jim? I would if I had your looks. They like nice average guys with nothing much on the ball. As contestants. Everybody likes guys like that. Why not look into it?"

So he had looked into it. The owner of the local television store had explained it further.

"You see, Jim, the public is sick of highly trained athletes with their trick reflexes and their professional courage. Who can feel for guys like that? Who can identify? People want to watch exciting things, sure, but not when some joker is making it his business for fifty thousand a year. That's why organized sports are in a slump. That's why the thrill shows are booming."

"I see," said Raeder.

"Six years ago, Jim, Congress passed the Voluntary Suicide Act. Those old senators talked a lot about free will and self-determinism at the time. But that's all crap. You know what the Act really mean? It means the amateurs can risk their lives for the big loot, not just professionals. In the old days you had to be a professional boxer or footballer or hockey player if you wanted your brains beaten out legally for money. But now that opportunity is open to ordinary people like you, Jim."

"I see," Raeder said again.

"It's a marvelous opportunity. Take you. You're no better than anyone, Jim. Anything you can do, anyone can do. You're *average*. I think the thrill shows would go for you."

Raeder permitted himself to dream. Television shows looked like a sure road to riches for a pleasant young fellow with no particular talent or training. He wrote a letter to a show called *Hazard* and enclosed a photograph of himself.

Hazard was interested in him. The JBC network investigated, and found that he was average enough to satisfy the wariest viewer. His parentage and affiliations were checked. At last he was summoned to New York, and interviewed by Mr. Moulian.

Moulian was dark and intense, and chewed gum as he talked. "You'll do," he snapped. "But not for *Hazard*. You'll appear on *Spills*. It's a half-hour daytime show on Channel Three."

"Gee," said Raeder.

"Don't thank me. There's a thousand dollars if you win or place second, and a consolation prize of a hundred dollars if you lose. But that's not important."

"No sir."

"*Spills* is a *little* show. The JBC network uses it as a testing ground. First- and second-place winners on *Spills* move on to *Emergency*. The prizes are much bigger on *Emergency*."

"I know they are, sir."

"And if you do well on *Emergency* there are the first-class thrill shows, like *Hazard* and *Underwater Perils*, with their nationwide coverage and enormous prizes. And then comes the really big time. How far you go is up to you."

"I'll do my best, sir," Raeder said.

Moulian stopped chewing gum for a moment and said, almost reverently, "You can do it, Jim. Just remember. You're *the people*, and *the people* can do anything."

The way he said it made Raeder feel momentarily sorry for Mr. Moulian, who was dark and frizzy-haired and pop-eyed, and was obviously not *the people*.

They shook hands. Then Raeder signed a paper absolving the JBC of all responsibility should he lose his life, limbs or reason during the contest. And he signed another paper exercising his rights under the Voluntary Suicide Act. The law required this, and it was a mere formality.

In three weeks, he appeared on *Spills*.

The program followed the classic form of the automobile race. Untrained drivers climbed into powerful American and European competition cars and raced over a murderous twenty-mile course. Raeder was shaking with fear as he slid his big Maserati into the wrong gear and took off.

The race was a screaming, tire-burning nightmare. Raeder stayed back, letting the early leaders smash themselves up on the counterbanked hairpin turns. He crept into third place when a Jaguar in front of him swerved against an Alfa-Romeo, and the two cars roared into a plowed field. Raeder gunned for second place on the last three miles, but couldn't find passing room. An S-curve almost took him, but he fought the car back on the road, still holding third. Then the lead driver broke a crankshaft in the final fifty yards, and Jim ended in second place.

He was now a thousand dollars ahead. He received four fan letters, and a lady in Oshkosh sent him a pair of argyles. He was invited to appear on *Emergency*.

Unlike the others, *Emergency* was not a competition-type program. It stressed individual initiative. For the show, Raeder was knocked out with a non-habit-forming narcotic. He awoke in the cockpit of a small airplane, cruising on autopilot at ten thousand feet. His fuel gauge showed nearly empty. He had no parachute. He was supposed to land the plane.

Of course, he had never flown before.

He experimented gingerly with the controls, remembering that last week's participant had recovered consciousness in a submarine, had opened the wrong valve, and had drowned.

Thousands of viewers watched spellbound as this average man, a man just like themselves, struggled with the situation just as they would do. Jim Raeder was *them*. Anything he could do, they could do. He was representative of *the people*.

Raeder managed to bring the ship down in some semblance of a landing. He flipped over a few times, but his seat belt held. And the engine, contrary to expectations, did not burst into flames.

He staggered out with two broken ribs, three thousand dollars, and a chance, when he healed, to appear on *Torero*.

At last, a first-class thrill show! *Torero* paid ten thousand dollars. All you had to do was kill a black Miura bull with a sword, just like a real trained matador.

The fight was held in Madrid, since bullfighting was still illegal in the United States. It was nationally televised.

Raeder had a good cuadrilla. They liked the big, slow-moving American. The picadors really leaned into their lances, trying to slow the bull for him. The banderilleros tried to run the beast off his feet before driving in their banderillas. And the second matador, a mournful man from Algiceras, almost broke the bull's neck with fancy capework.

But when all was said and done it was Jim Raeder on the sand, a red muleta clumsily gripped in his left hand, a sword in his right, facing a ton of black, blood-streaked, wide-horned bull.

Someone was shouting, "Try for the lung, *hombre*. Don't be a hero, stick him in the lung." But Jim only knew what the technical adviser in New York had told him: Aim with the sword and go in over the horns.

Over he went. The sword bounced off bone, and the bull tossed him over its back. He stood up, miraculously ungouged, took another sword and went over the horns again with his eyes closed. The god who protects children and fools must have been watching, for the sword slid in like a needle through butter, and the bull looked startled, stared at him unbelievingly, and dropped like a deflated balloon.

They paid him ten thousand dollars, and his broken collar bone healed in practically no time. He received twenty-three fan letters, including a passionate invitation from a girl in Atlantic City, which he ignored. And they asked him if he wanted to appear on another show.

He had lost some of his innocence. He was now fully aware that he had been almost killed for pocket money. The big loot lay ahead. Now he wanted to be almost killed for something worthwhile.

So he appeared on *Underwater Perils*, sponsored by Fairlady's Soap. In face mask, respirator, weighted belt, flippers and knife, he slipped into the warm waters of the

Caribbean with four other contestants, followed by a cage-protected camera crew. The idea was to locate and bring up a treasure which the sponsor had hidden there.

Mask diving isn't especially hazardous. But the sponsor had added some frills for public interest. The area was sown with giant clams, moray eels, sharks of several species, giant octopuses, poison coral, and other dangers of the deep.

It was a stirring contest. A man from Florida found the treasure in a deep crevice, but a moray eel found him. Another diver took the treasure, and a shark took him. The brilliant blue-green water became cloudy with blood, which photographed well on color TV. The treasure slipped to the bottom and Raeder plunged after it, popping an eardrum in the process. He plucked it from the coral, jettisoned his weighted belt and made for the surface. Thirty feet from the top he had to fight another diver for the treasure.

They feinted back and forth with their knives. The man struck, slashing Raeder across the chest. But Raeder, with the self-possession of an old contestant, dropped his knife and tore the man's respirator out of his mouth.

That did it. Raeder surfaced, and presented the treasure at the stand-by boat. It turned out to be a package of Fairlady's Soap—''The Greatest Treasure of All.''

That netted him twenty-two thousand dollars in cash and prizes, and three hundred and eight fan letters, and an interesting proposition from a girl in Macon, which he seriously considered. He received free hospitalization for his knife slash and burst eardrum, and injections for coral infection.

But best of all, he was invited to appear on the biggest of the thrill shows. *The Prize of Peril.*

And that was when the real trouble began. . . .

The subway came to a stop, jolting him out of his reverie. Raeder pushed back his hat and observed, across the aisle, a man staring at him and whispering to a stout woman. Had they recognized him?

He stood up as soon as the doors opened, and glanced at his watch. He had five hours to go.

*   *   *

At the Manhasset station he stepped into a taxi and told the driver to take him to New Salem.

"New Salem?" the driver asked, looking at him in the rear vision mirror.

"That's right."

The driver snapped on his radio. "Fare to New Salem. Yep, that's right. *New Salem*."

They drove off. Raeder frowned, wondering if it had been a signal. It was perfectly usual for taxi drivers to report to their dispatchers, of course. But something about the man's voice . . .

"Let me off here," Raeder said.

He paid the driver and began walking down a narrow country road that curved through sparse woods. The trees were too small and too widely separated for shelter. Raeder walked on, looking for a place to hide.

There was a heavy truck approaching. He kept on walking, pulling his hat low on his forehead. But as the truck drew near, he heard a voice from the television set in his pocket. It cried, *"Watch out!"*

He flung himself into the ditch. The truck careened past, narrowly missing him, and screeched to a stop. The driver was shouting, "There he goes! Shoot, Harry, shoot!"

Bullets clipped leaves from the trees as Raeder sprinted into the woods.

"It's happened again!" Mike Terry was saying, his voice high-pitched with excitement. *"I'm afraid Jim Raeder let himself be lulled into a false sense of security. You can't do that, Jim! Not with your life at stake! Not with killers pursuing you! Be careful, Jim, you still have four and a half hours to go!"*

The driver was saying, "Claude, Harry, go around with the truck. We got him boxed."

"They've got you boxed, Jim Raeder!" Mike Terry cried. *"But they haven't got you yet! And you can thank Good Samaritan Susy Peters of twelve Elm Street, South Orange,*

New Jersey, for that warning shout just when the truck was bearing down on you. We'll have little Susy on stage in just a moment. . . . Look, folks, our studio helicopter has arrived on the scene. Now you can see Jim Raeder running, and the killers pursuing, surrounding him . . ."

Raeder ran through a hundred yards of woods and found himself on a concrete highway, with open woods beyond. One of the killers was trotting through the woods behind him. The truck had driven to a connecting road, and was now a mile away, coming toward him.

A car was approaching from the other direction. Raeder ran into the highway, waving frantically. The car came to a stop.

"Hurry!" cried the blond young woman driving it.

Raeder dived in. The woman made a U-turn on the highway. A bullet smashed through the windshield. She stamped on the accelerator, almost running down the lone killer who stood in the way.

The car shrugged away before the truck was within firing range.

Raeder leaned back and shut his eyes tightly. The woman concentrated on her driving, watching for the truck in her rear-vision mirror.

"It's happened again!" cried Mike Terry, his voice ecstatic *"Jim Raeder has been plucked again from the jaws of death, thanks to Good Samaritan Janice Morrow of four three three Lexington Avenue, New York City. Did you ever see anything like it, folks? The way Miss Morrow drove through a fusillade of bullets and plucked Jim Raeder from the mouth of doom! Later we'll interview Miss Morrow and get her reactions. Now, while Jim Raeder speeds away—perhaps to safety, perhaps to further peril—we'll have a short announcement from our sponsor. Don't go away! Jim's got four hours and ten minutes until he's safe. Anything can happen!"*

"OK," the girl said. "We're off the air now. Raeder, what in the hell is the matter with you?"

"Eh?" Raeder asked. The girl was in her early twenties.

She looked efficient, attractive, untouchable. Raeder noticed that she had good features, a trim figure. And he noticed that she seemed angry.

"Miss," he said, "I don't know how to thank you for—"

"Talk straight," Janice Morrow said. "I'm no Good Samaritan. I'm employed by the JBC network."

"So the program had me rescued!"

"Cleverly reasoned," she said.

"But why?"

"Look, this is an expensive show, Raeder. We have to turn in a good performance. If our rating slips, we'll all be in the street selling candy apples. And you aren't co-operating."

"What? Why?"

"Because you're terrible," the girl said bitterly. "You're a flop, a fiasco. Are you trying to commit suicide? Haven't you learned *anything* about survival?"

"I'm doing the best I can."

"The Thompsons could have had you a dozen times by now. We told them to take it easy, stretch it out. But it's like shooting a clay pigeon six feet tall. The Thompsons are co-operating, but they can only fake so far. If I hadn't come along, they'd have had to kill you—air-time or not."

Raeder stared at her, wondering how such a pretty girl could talk that way. She glanced at him, then quickly looked back to the road.

"Don't give me that look!" she said. "*You* chose to risk your life for money, buster. And plenty of money! You knew the score. Don't act like some innocent little grocer who finds the nasty hoods are after him. That's a different plot."

"I know," Raeder said.

"If you can't live well, at least try to die well."

"You don't mean that," Raeder said.

"Don't be too sure. . . . You've got three hours and forty minutes until the end of the show. If you can stay alive, fine. The boodle's yours. But if you can't at least try to give them a run for the money."

Raeder nodded, staring intently at her.

"In a few moments we're back on the air. I develop engine trouble, let you off. The Thompsons go all out now. They kill you when and if they can, as soon as they can. Understand?"

"Yes," Raeder said. "If I make it, can I see you some time?"

She bit her lip angrily. "Are you trying to kid me?"

"No. I'd like to see you again. May I?"

She looked at him curiously. "I don't know. Forget it. We're almost on. I think your best bet is the woods to the right. Ready?"

"Yes. Where can I get in touch with you? Afterward, I mean."

"Oh, Raeder, you aren't paying attention. Go through the woods until you find a washed-out ravine. It isn't much, but it'll give you some cover."

"Where can I get in touch with you?" Raeder asked again.

"I'm in the Manhattan telephone book." She stopped the car. "OK, Raeder, start running."

He opened the door.

"Wait." She leaned over and kissed him on the lips. "Good luck, you idiot. Call me if you make it."

And then he was on foot, running into the woods.

He ran through birch and pine, past an occasional split-level house with staring faces at the big picture window. Some occupant of those houses must have called the gang, for they were close behind him when he reached the washed-out little ravine. Those quiet, mannerly, law-abiding people didn't want him to escape, Raeder thought sadly. They wanted to see a killing. Or perhaps they wanted to see him *narrowly escape* a killing.

It came to the same thing, really.

He entered the ravine, burrowed into the thick underbrush and lay still. The Thompsons appeared on both ridges, moving slowly, watching for any movement. Raeder held his breath as they came parallel to him.

He heard the quick explosion of a revolver. But the killer

had only shot a squirrel. It squirmed for a moment, then lay still.

Lying in the underbrush, Raeder heard the studio helicopter overhead. He wondered if any cameras were focused on him. It was possible. And if someone were watching, perhaps some Good Samaritan would help.

So looking upward, toward the helicopter, Raeder arranged his face in a reverent expression, clasped his hands and prayed. He prayed silently, for the audience didn't like religious ostentation. But his lips moved. That was every man's privilege.

And a real prayer was on his lips. Once, a lipreader in the audience had detected a fugitive *pretending* to pray, but actually just reciting multiplication tables. No help for that man!

Raeder finished his prayer. Glancing at his watch, he saw that he had nearly two hours to go.

And he didn't want to die! It wasn't worth it, no matter how much they paid! He must have been crazy, absolutely insane to agree to such a thing. . . .

Butt he knew that wasn't true. And he remembered just how sane he had been.

One week ago he had been on the *Prize of Peril* stage, blinking in the spotlight, and Mike Terry had shaken his hand.

"Now Mr. Raeder," Terry had said solemnly, "do you understand the rules of the game you are about to play?"

Raeder nodded.

"If you accept, Jim Raeder, you will be a *hunted man* for a week. *Killers* will follow you, Jim. *Trained* killers, men wanted by the law for other crimes, granted immunity for this single killing under the Voluntary Suicide Act. They will be trying to kill *you*, Jim. Do you understand?"

"I understand," Raeder said. He also understood the two hundred thousand dollars he would receive if he could live out the week.

"I ask you again, Jim Raeder. We force no man to play for stakes of death."

"I want to play," Raeder said.

Mike Terry turned to the audience. "Ladies and gentlemen, I have here a copy of an exhaustive psychological test which an impartial psychological testing firm made on Jim Raeder at our request. Copies will be sent to anyone who desires them for twenty-five cents to cover the cost of mailing. The test shows that Jim Raeder is sane, well-balanced, and fully responsible in every way." He turned to Raeder.

"Do you still want to enter the contest, Jim?"

"Yes, I do."

"Very well!" cried Mike Terry. "Jim Raeder, meet your would-be killers!"

The Thompson gang moved on stage, booed by the audience.

"Look at them, folks," said Mike Terry, with undisguised contempt. "Just look at them! Antisocial, thoroughly vicious, completely amoral. These men have no code but the criminal's warped code, no honor but the honor of the cowardly hired killer. They are doomed men, doomed by our society which will not sanction their activities for long, fated to an early and unglamorous death."

The audience shouted enthusiastically.

"What have you to say, Claude Thompson?" Terry asked.

Claude, the spokesman of the Thompsons, stepped up to the microphone. He was a thin, clean-shaven man, conservatively dressed.

"I figure," Claude Thompson said hoarsely, "I figure we're no worse than anybody. I mean, like soldiers in a war, *they* kill. And look at the graft in government, and the unions. Everybody's got their graft."

That was Thompson's tenuous code. But how quickly, with what precision Mike Terry destroyed the killer's rationalizations! Terry's questions pierced straight to the filthy soul of the man.

At the end of the interview Claude Thompson was perspiring, mopping his face with a silk handkerchief and casting quick glances at his men.

Mike Terry put a hand on Raeder's shoulder. "Here is the man who has agreed to become your victim—if you can catch him."

"We'll catch him," Thompson said, his confidence returning.

"Don't be too sure," said Terry. "Jim Raeder has fought wild bulls—now he battles jackals. He's an average man. He's *the people*—who mean ultimate doom to you and your kind."

"We'll get him," Thompson said.

"And one thing more," Terry said, very softly. "Jim Raeder does not stand alone. The folks of America are for him. Good Samaritans from all corners of our great nation stand ready to assist him. Unarmed, defenceless, Jim Raeder can count on the aid and good-heartedness of *the people*, whose representative he is. So don't be too sure, Claude Thompson! The average men are for Jim Raeder—and there are a lot of average men!"

Raeder thought about it, lying motionless in the underbrush. Yes, *the people* had helped him. But they had helped the killers, too.

A tremor ran through him. He had chosen, he reminded himself. He alone was responsible. The psychological test had proved that.

And yet, how responsible were the psychologists who had given him the test? How responsible was Mike Terry for offering a poor man so much money? Society had woven the noose and put it around his neck, and he was hanging himself with it, and calling it free will.

Whose fault?

"Aha!" someone cried.

Raeder looked up and saw a portly man standing near him. The man wore a loud tweed jacket. He had binoculars around his neck, and a cane in his hand.

"Mister," Raeder whispered, "please don't tell!"

"Hi!" shouted the portly man, pointing at Raeder with his cane. "Here he is!"

A madman, thought Raeder. The damned fool must think he's playing Hare and Hounds.

"Right over here!" the man screamed.

Cursing, Raeder sprang to his feet and began running. He came out of the ravine and saw a white building in the distance. He turned toward it. Behind him he could still hear the man.

"That way, over there. Look, you fools, can't you see him yet?"

The killers were shooting again. Raeder ran, stumbling over uneven ground, past three children playing in a tree house.

"Here he is!" the children screamed. "Here he is!"

Raeder groaned and ran on. He reached the steps of the building, and saw that it was a church.

As he opened the door, a bullet struck him behind the right kneecap.

He fell, and crawled inside the church.

The television set in his pocket was saying, *"What a finish, folks, what a finish! Raeder's been hit! He's been hit, folks, he's crawling now, he's in pain, but he hasn't given up! Not Jim Raeder!"*

Raeder lay in the aisle near the altar. He could hear a child's eager voice saying, "He went in there, Mr. Thompson. Hurry, you can still catch him!"

Wasn't a church considered a sanctuary, Raeder wondered.

Then the door was flung open, and Raeder realized that the custom was no longer observed. He gathered himself together and crawled past the altar, out the back door of the church.

He was in an old graveyard. He crawled past crosses and stars, past slabs of marble and granite, past stone tombs and rude wooden markers. A bullet exploded on a tombstone near his head, showering him with fragments. He crawled to the edge of an open grave.

They had received him, he thought. All of those nice

average normal people. Hadn't they said he was their representative? Hadn't they sworn to protect their own? But no, they loathed him. Why hadn't he seen it? Their hero was the cold, blank-eyed gunman, Thompson, Capone, Billy the Kid, Young Lochinvar, El Cid, Cuchulain, the man without human hopes or fears. They worshiped him, that dead, implacable robot gunman, and lusted to feel his foot in their face.

Raeder tried to move, and slid helplessly into the open grave.

He lay on his back, looking at the blue sky. Presently a black silhouette loomed above him, blotting out the sky. Metal twinkled. The silhouette slowly took aim.

And Raeder gave up all hope forever.

"*WAIT, THOMPSON!*" roared the amplified voice of Mike Terry.

The revolver wavered.

"*It is one second past five o'clock! The week is up!* JIM RAEDER HAS WON!"

There was a pandemonium of cheering from the studio audience.

The Thompson gang, gathered around the grave, looked sullen.

"*He's won, friends, he's won!*" Mike Terry cried. "*Look, look on your screen! The police have arrived, they're taking the Thompsons away from their victim—the victim they could not kill. And all this is thanks to you, Good Samaritans of America. Look folks, tender hands are lifting Jim Raeder from the open grave that was his final refuge. Good Samaritan Janice Morrow is there. Could this be the beginning of a romance? Jim seems to have fainted, friends, they're giving him a stimulant. He's won two hundred thousand dollars! Now we'll have a few words from Jim Raeder!*"

There was a short silence.

"*That's odd,*" said Mike Terry. "*Folks, I'm afraid we can't hear from Jim just now. The doctors are examining him. Just one moment . . .*"

There was a silence. Mike Terry wiped his forehead and smiled.

"It's the strain, folks, the terrible strain. The doctor tells me . . . Well, folks, Jim Raeder is temporarily not himself. But it's only temporary! JBC is hiring the best psychiatrists and psychoanalysts in the country. We're going to do everything humanly possible for this gallant boy. And entirely at our own expense."

Mike Terry glanced at the studio clock. *"Well, it's about time to sign off, folks. Watch for the announcement of our next great thrill show. And don't worry, I'm sure that very soon we'll have Jim Raeder back with us."*

Mike Terry smiled, and winked at the audience. *"He's bound to get well, friends. After all, we're all pulling for him!"*

OR ALL THE SEAS WITH OYSTERS

BY AVRAM DAVIDSON (1923–   )

GALAXY SCIENCE FICTION
MAY

Born in Yonkers, New York, Avram Davidson fought with the Israeli Army in 1947 and 1948 and is one of the science fiction and fantasy field's most unique writers. He has a wry sense of humor combined with the willingness to experiment and take chances. He edited (part of the time from Mexico) The Magazine of Fantasy and Science Fiction *from 1962 to 1964, and much of his best fiction has appeared there. His collections include* What Strange Seas and Shores *(1965),* The Best of Avram Davidson *(1979), and* The Collected Fantasies of Avram Davidson *(1973). Serious mystery readers know him as well, since he is a master of the form, and I would love to see him publish a novel in that* genre. *Now in his mid-sixties, he is still going strong and may yet achieve the fame that he deserves.*

"Or All the Seas with Oysters" is typical of his style, method, and concerns, and it won the Hugo Award for the best short fiction of 1958. (MHG)

Lives there a man who doesn't have dire suspicions of the inanimate world. I am being constantly thwarted by non-living objects from the most cosmic to the most petty.

When I'm driving, my dear wife Janet sees to it that I wear clip-on dark spectacles against the Solar glare. They're the kind that flip up and down at need. So when the Sun goes behind a cloud, I flip them up, and the Sun instantly emerges. So I flip them down and the Sun instantly scrabbles up a cloud from somewhere and gets behind it. This happens over and over—I call it the "spectacular law."

This is similar to the way it always rains when I am making a long auto trip—regardless of the weather forecast. When necessary, it rains out of a clear blue sky.

Those are cosmic examples. Now imagine yourself dropping a paper clip that you happen to need. Tell me the truth. Doesn't it invariably drop through a spacewarp? It is nowhere on the ground. You remember hearing the clank as it struck, but you can search with a microscope and you won't find it. Sometimes you do find it eventually (entirely by accident, and when you no longer need it, of course) and you then realize that by the operation of no conceivable law of physics could that paper clip, when dropped, have gone from your fingers to the place where you found it.

Anyway, if you think about these things you'll be in the proper mood for Avram Davidson's story. (IA)

When the man came into the F & O Bike Shop, Oscar greeted him with a hearty "Hi, there!" Then, as he looked closer at the middle-aged visitor with the eyeglasses and business suit, his forehead creased and he began to snap his thick fingers.

"Oh, say, I know you," he muttered. "Mr.—um—name's on the tip of my tongue, doggone it . . ." Oscar was a barrel-chested fellow. He had orange hair.

"Why, sure you do," the man said. There was a Lion's emblem in his lapel. "Remember, you sold me a girl's bicycle with gears, for my daughter? We got to talking about that red French racing bike your partner was working on—"

Oscar slapped his big hand down on the cash register. He raised his head and rolled his eyes up. "Mr. Whatney!" Mr. Whatney beamed. "Oh, *sure*. Gee, how could I forget?" And we went across the street afterward and had a couple of beers. Well, how you *been*, Mr. Whatney? I guess the bike—it was an English model, wasn't it? Yeah. It must of given satisfaction or you would of been back, huh?''

Mr. Whatney said the bicycle was fine, just fine. Then he said, ''I understand there's been a change, though. You're all by yourself now. Your partner . . .''

Oscar looked down, pushed his lower lip out, nodded. ''You heard, huh? Ee-up. I'm all by myself now. Over three months now.''

The partnership had come to an end three months ago, but it had been faltering long before then. Ferd liked books, long-playing records and high-level conversation. Oscar liked beer, bowling and women. Any women. Any time.

The shop was located near the park; it did a big trade in renting bicycles to picnickers. If a woman was barely old enough to be *called* a woman, and not quite old enough to be called an *old* woman, or if she was anywhere in between, and if she was alone, Oscar would ask, ''How does that machine feel to you? All right?''

''Why . . . I guess so.''

Taking another bicycle, Oscar would say, ''Well, I'll just ride along a little bit with you, to make sure. Be right back, Ferd.'' Ferd always nodded gloomily. He knew that Oscar would not be right back. Later, Oscar would say, ''Hope you made out in the shop as good as I did in the park.''

''Leaving me all alone here all that time,'' Ferd grumbled.

And Oscar usually flared up. ''Okay, then, next time *you* go and leave *me* stay here. See if I begrudge you a little fun.'' But he knew, of course, that Ferd—tall, thin, pop-eyed Ferd— would never go. ''Do you good,'' Oscar said, slapping his sternum. ''Put hair on your chest.''

Ferd muttered that he had all the hair on his chest that he needed. He would glance down covertly at his lower arms; they were thick with long black hair, though his upper arms were slick and white. It was already like that when he was in high school, and some of the others would laugh at him—call him "Ferdie the Birdie." They knew it bothered him, but they did it anyway. How was it possible—he wondered then; he still do now—for people deliberately to hurt someone else who hadn't hurt them? How was it possible?

He worried over other things. All the time.

"The Communists—" He shook his head over the newspaper. Oscar offered an advice about the Communists in two short words. Or it might be capital punishment. "Oh, what a terrible thing if an innocent man was to be executed," Ferd moaned. Oscar said that was the guy's tough luck.

"Hand me that tire-iron," Oscar said.

And Ferd worried even about other people's minor concerns. Like the time the couple came in with the tandem and the baby-basket on it. Free air was all they took; then the woman decided to change the diaper and one of the safety pins broke.

"Why are there never any safety pins?" the woman fretted, rummaging here and rummaging there. "There are *never* any safety pins."

Ferd made sympathetic noises, went to see if he had any; but, though he was sure there'd been some in the office, he couldn't find them. So they drove off with one side of the diaper tied in a clumsy knot.

At lunch, Ferd said it was too bad about the safety pins. Oscar dug his teeth into a sandwich, tugged, tore, chewed, swallowed. Ferd liked to experiment with sandwich spreads— the one he liked most was cream-cheese, olives, anchovy and avocado, mashed up with a little mayonnaise—but Oscar always had the same pink luncheon-meat.

"It must be difficult with a baby." Ferd nibbled. "Not just traveling, but raising it."

Oscar said, "Jeez, there's drugstores in every block, and if you can't read, you can at least reckernize them."

"Drugstores? Oh, to buy safety pins, you mean."

"Yeah. Safety pins."

"But . . . you know . . . it's true . . . there's never any safety pins when you look."

Oscar uncapped his beer, rinsed the first mouthful around. "Aha! Always plenty of clothes hangers, though. Throw 'em out every month, next month same closet's full of 'm again. Now whatcha wanna do in your spare time, you invent a device which it'll make safety pins outa clothes hangers."

Ferd nodded abstractedly. "But in my spare time I'm working on the French racer. . . ." It was a beautiful machine, light, low-slung, swift, red and shining. You felt like a bird when you rode it. But, good as it was, Ferd knew he could make it better. He showed it to everybody who came in the place until his interest slackened.

Nature was his latest hobby, or, rather, reading about Nature. Some kids had wandered by from the park one day with tin cans in which they had put salamanders and toads, and they proudly showed them to Ferd. After that, the work on the red racer slowed down and he spent his spare time on natural history books.

"Mimicry!" he cried to Oscar. "A wonderful thing!"

Oscar looked up interestedly from the bowling scores in the paper. "I seen Edie Adams on TV the other night, doing her imitation of Marilyn Monroe. Boy, oh, boy."

Ferd was irritated, shook his head. "Not that kind of mimicry. I mean how insects and arachnids will mimic the shapes of leaves and twigs and so on, to escape being eaten by birds or other insects and arachnids."

A scowl of disbelief passed over Oscar's heavy face. "You mean they change their *shapes?* What you giving me?"

"Oh, it's true. Sometimes the mimicry is for aggressive purposes, though—like a South African turtle that looks like a rock and so the fish swim up to it and then it catches them. Or that spider in Sumatra. When it lies on its back, it looks like a bird dropping. Catches butterflies that way."

Oscar laughed, a disgusted and incredulous noise. It died away as he turned back to the bowling scores. One hand groped at his pocket, came away, scratched absently at the orange thicket under the shirt, then went patting his hip pocket.

"Where's the pencil?" he muttered, got up, stomped into the office, pulled open drawers. His loud cry of "Hey!" brought Ferd into the tiny room.

"What's the matter?" Ferd asked.

Oscar pointed to a drawer. "Remember that time you claimed there were no safety pins here? Look—whole gahdamn drawer is full of 'em."

Ferd stared, scratched his head, said feebly that he was certain he'd looked there before. . . .

A contralto voice from outside asked, "Anybody here?"

Oscar at once forgot the desk and its contents, called, "Be right with you," and was gone. Ferd followed him slowly.

There was a young woman in the shop, a rather massively built young woman, with muscular calves and a deep chest. She was pointing out the seat of her bicycle to Oscar, who was saying, "Uh-huh" and looking more at her than at anything else. "It's just a little too far forward ("Uh-huh"), as you can see. A wrench is all I need ("Uh-huh"). It was silly of me to forget my tools."

Oscar repeated, "Uh-huh" automatically, then snapped to. "Fix it in a jiffy," he said, and—despite her insistence that she could do it herself—he did fix it. Though not quite in a jiffy. He refused money. He prolonged the conversation as long as he could.

"Well, thank *you*," the young woman said. "And now I've got to go."

"That machine feel all right to you now?"

"Perfectly. Thanks—"

"Tell you what, I'll just ride along with you a little bit, just—"

Pear-shaped notes of laughter lifted the young woman's bosom. "Oh, you couldn't keep up with me! My machine is a *racer!*"

The moment he saw Oscar's eye flit to the corner, Ferd knew what he had in mind. He stepped forward. His cry of "No" was drowned out by his partner's loud, "Well, I guess this racer here can keep up with yours!"

The young woman giggled richly, said, well, they would see about that, and was off. Oscar, ignoring Ferd's outstretched hand, jumped on the French bike and was gone. Ferd stood in the doorway, watching the two figures, hunched over their handlebars, vanish down the road into the park. He went slowly back inside.

It was almost evening before Oscar returned, sweaty but smiling. Smiling broadly. "Hey, what a babe!" he cried. He wagged his head, he whistled, he made gestures, noises like escaping steam. "Boy, oh, boy, what an afternoon!"

"Give me the bike," Ferd demanded.

Oscar said, yeah, sure; turned it over to him and went to wash. Ferd looked at the machine. The red enamel was covered with dust; there was mud spattered and dirt and bits of dried grass. It seemed soiled—degraded. He had felt like a swift bird when he rode it. . . .

Oscar came out wet and beaming. He gave a cry of dismay, ran over.

"Stand away," said Ferd, gesturing with the knife. He slashed the tires, the seat and seat cover, again and again.

"You crazy?" Oscar yelled. "You outa your mind? Ferd, no, don't, Ferd—"

Ferd cut the spokes, bent them, twisted them. He took the heaviest hammer and pounded the frame into shapelessness, and then he kept on pounding till his breath was gasping.

"You're not only crazy," Oscar said bitterly, "you're rotten jealous. You can go to hell." He stomped away.

Ferd, feeling sick and stiff, locked up, went slowly home. He had no taste for reading, turned out the light and fell into bed, where he lay awake for hours, listening to the rustling noises of the night and thinking hot, twisted thoughts.

They didn't speak to each other for days after that, except for the necessities of the work. The wreckage of the French racer lay behind the shop. For about two weeks, neither wanted to go out back where he'd have to see it.

One morning Ferd arrived to be greeted by his partner, who began to shake his head in astonishment even before he started speaking. "How did you *do* it, how did you *do* it, Ferd? Jeez, what a beautiful job—I gotta hand it to you—no more hard feelings, huh, Ferd?"

Ferd took his hand. "Sure, sure. But what are you talking about?"

Oscar led him out back. There was the red racer, all in one piece, not a mark or scratch on it, its enamel bright as ever. Ferd gaped. He squatted down and examined it. It *was* his machine. Every change, every improvement he had made, was there.

He straightened up slowly. "Regeneration . . ."

"Huh? What say?" Oscar asked. Then, "Hey, kiddo, you're all white. Whad you do, stay up all night and didn't get no sleep? Come on in and siddown. But I still don't see how you done it."

Inside, Ferd sat down. He wet his lips. He said, "Oscar—listen—"

"Yeah?"

"Oscar. You know what regeneration is? No? Listen. Some kinds of lizards, you grab them by the tail, the tail breaks off and they grow a new one. If a lobster loses a claw, it regenerates another one. Some kinds of worms—and hydras and starfish—you cut them into pieces, each piece will grow back the missing parts. Salamanders can regenerate lost hands, and frogs can grow legs back."

"No kidding, Ferd. But, uh, I mean: Nature. Very interesting. But to get back to the bike now—how'd you manage to fix it so good?"

"I never touched it. It regenerated. Like a newt. Or a lobster."

Oscar considered this. He lowered his head, looked up at Ferd from under his eyebrows. "Well, now, Ferd . . . Look . . . How come all broke bikes don't do that?"

"This isn't an ordinary bike. I mean it isn't a real bike." Catching Oscar's look, he shouted, "Well, it's *true!*"

The shout changed Oscar's attitude from bafflement to incredulity. He got up. "So for the sake of argument, let's say all that stuff about the bugs and the eels or whatever the hell you were talking about is true. But they're alive. A bike ain't.'' He looked down triumphantly.

Ferd shook his leg from side to side, looked at it. ''A crystal isn't, either, but a broken crystal can regenerate itself if the conditions are right. Oscar, go see if the safety pins are still in the desk. Please, Oscar?''

He listened as Oscar, muttering, pulled the desk drawers out, rummaged in them, slammed them shut, tramped back.

''Naa,'' he said. ''All gone. Like that lady said that time, and you said, there never are any safety pins when you want 'em. They disap— Ferd? What're—''

Ferd jerked open the closet door, jumped back as a shoal of clothes hangers clattered out.

''And like *you* say,'' Ferd said with a twist of his mouth, ''on the other hand, there are always plenty of clothes hangers. There weren't any here before.''

Oscar shrugged. ''I don't see what you're getting at. But anybody could of got in here and took the pins and left the hangers. *I* could of—but I didn't. Or *you* could of. Maybe—'' He narrowed his eyes. ''Maybe you walked in your sleep and done it. You better see a doctor. Jeez, you look rotten.''

Ferd went back and sat down, put his head in his hands. ''I *feel* rotten. I'm scared, Oscar. Scared of what?'' He breathed noisily. ''I'll tell you. Like I explained before, about how things that live in the wild places, they mimic other things there. Twigs, leaves . . . toads that look like rocks. Well, suppose there are . . . things . . . that live in people places. Cities. Houses. These things could imitate—well, other kinds of things you find in people places—''

''*People* places, for crise sake!''

''Maybe they're a different kind of life-form. Maybe they get their nourishment out of the elements in the air. You know what safety pins *are*—these other kinds of them? Oscar, the safety pins are the pupa-forms and then they, like, *hatch*. Into the larval-forms. Which look just like coat hangers. They feel like them, even, but they're not. Oscar, they're not, not really, not really, not . . .''

He began to cry into his hands. Oscar looked at him. He shook his head.

After a minute, Ferd controlled himself somewhat. He snuffled. "All these bicycles the cops find, and they hold them waiting for owners to show up, and then we buy them at the sale because no owners show up because there aren't any, and the same with the ones the kids are always trying to sell us, and they say they just found them, and they really did because they were never made in a factory. They grew. They grow. You smash them and throw them away, they regenerate."

Oscar turned to someone who wasn't there and waggled his head. "Hoo, boy," he said. Then, to Ferd: "You mean one day there's a safety pin and the next day instead there's a coat hanger?"

Ferd said, "One day there's a cocoon; the next day there's a moth. One day there's an egg; the next day there's a chicken. But with . . . these it doesn't happen in the open daytime where you can see it. But at night, Oscar—at night you can *hear* it happening. All the little noises in the nighttime, Oscar—"

Oscar said, "Then how come we ain't up to our belly-button in bikes? If I had a bike for every coat hanger—"

But Ferd had considered that, too. If every codfish egg, he explained, or every oyster spawn grew to maturity, a man could walk across the ocean on the backs of all the codfish or oysters there'd be. So many died, so many were eaten by predatory creatures, that Nature had to produce a maximum in order to allow a minimum to arrive at maturity. And Oscar's question was: then who, uh, eats the, uh, coat hangers?

Ferd's eyes focused through the wall, buildings, park, more buildings, to the horizon. "You got to get the picture. I'm not talking about real pins or hangers. I got a name for the others—'false friends,' I call them. In high school French, we had to watch out for French words that looked like English words, but really were different. *'Faux amis,'* they call them. False friends. Pseudo-pins. Pseudo-hangers . . . Who eats them? I don't know for sure. Pseudo-vacuum cleaners, maybe?"

His partner, with a loud groan, slapped his hands against his thighs. He said, "Ferd, Ferd, for crise sake. You know what's the trouble with you? You talk about oysters, but you forgot what they're good for. You forgot there's two kinds of people in the world. Close up them books, them bug books and French books. Get out, mingle, meet people. Soak up some brew. You know what? The next time Norma—that's this broad's name with the racing bike—the next time she comes here, *you* take the red racer and *you* go out in the woods with her. I won't mind. And I don't think she will, either. Not *too* much."

But Ferd said no. "I never want to touch the red racer again. I'm afraid of it."

At this, Oscar pulled him to his feet, dragged him protestingly out to the back and forced him to get on the French machine. "Only way to conquer your fear of it!"

Ferd started off, white-faced, wobbling. And in a moment was on the ground, rolling and thrashing, screaming.

Oscar pulled him away from the machine.

"It threw me!" Ferd yelled. "It tried to kill me! Look—blood!"

His partner said it was a bump that threw him—it was his own fear. The blood? A broken spoke. Grazed his cheek. And he insisted Ferd get on the bicycle again, to conquer his fear.

But Ferd had grown hysterical. He shouted that no man was safe—that mankind had to be warned. It took Oscar a long time to pacify him and to get him to go home and into bed.

He didn't tell all this to Mr. Whatney, of course. He merely said that his partner had gotten fed up with the bicycle business.

"It don't pay to worry and try to change the world," he pointed out. "I always say take things the way they are. If you can't lick 'em, join 'em."

Mr. Whatney said that was his philosophy, exactly. He asked how things were, since.

"Well . . . not *too* bad. I'm engaged, you know. Name's Norma. Crazy about bicycles. Everything considered, things aren't bad at all. More work, yes, but I can do things all my own way, so . . ."

Mr. Whatney nodded. He glanced around the shop. "I see they're still making drop-frame bikes," he said, "though, with so many women wearing slacks, I wonder they bother."

Oscar said, "Well, I dunno. I kinda like it that way. Ever stop to think that bicycles are like people? I mean, of all the machines in the world, only bikes come male and female."

Mr. Whatney gave a little giggle, said that was *right*, he had never thought of it like that before. Then Oscar asked if Mr. Whatney had anything in particular in mind—not that he wasn't always welcome.

"Well, I wanted to look over what you've got. My boy's birthday is coming up—"

Oscar nodded sagely. "Now here's a job," he said, "which you can't get it in any other place but here. Specialty of the house. Combines the best features of the French racer and the American standard, but it's made right here, and it comes in three models—Junior, Intermediate and Regular. Beautiful, ain't it?"

Mr. Whatney observed that, say, that might be just the ticket. "By the way," he asked, "what's become of the French racer, the red one, used to be here?"

Oscar's face twitched. Then it grew bland and innocent and he leaned over and nudged his customer. "Oh, *that* one. Old Frenchy? Why, I put *him* out to stud!"

And they laughed and they laughed, and after they told a few more stories they concluded the sale, and they had a few beers and they laughed some more. And then they said what a shame it was about poor Ferd, poor old Ferd, who had been found in his own closet with an unraveled coat hanger coiled tightly around his neck.

TWO DOOMS

BY C. M. KORNBLUTH (1923–1958)

VENTURE SCIENCE FICTION
JULY

On March 21, 1958 Cyril Kornbluth shoveled snow after a late-winter storm, ran to catch a train, collapsed at the station, and died. At the age of thirty-five, he had been a professional writer for almost twenty years (such were the possibilities in those far-off days). He was a unique man with a unique editorial voice and his death shocked the world of science fiction. It would be years until the effects of his loss would wear off, although many, including myself, believe he would have achieved great international fame if he had lived another thirty years—we will never know, of course.

1958 saw the publication of his excellent collection, A Mile Beyond The Moon. *The following year would see his last novel,* Wolfbane, *written with his friend Frederik Pohl, who would do much to keep his work alive.*

"Two Dooms" is an alternate history story, one of my favorite forms, and is arguably the best short fiction on the "What if Germany had won World War II?" theme, which for good and bad reasons continues to fascinate readers and writers. (MHG)

The ifs of history are always fascinating and many a science fiction story has been written to explore the byways that were never taken. We think, perhaps, of "Bring the Jubilee" by Ward Moore, as a classic example.

A ferocious recent if, of nightmare intensity, is that "What if the Germans and Japanese had won World War II?" It doesn't bear thinking of, if the concentration camp and prisoner of war camp mentality were to have been brought to a beaten United States by those victors. The result might well be what Cyril Kornbluth describes in "Two Dooms."

But, you know, it's an American writing the story, and (in my case) an American reading the story. Cyril's blood boiled when he wrote and my blood boiled when I read. —But it's my business, as a science fiction writer, to think sideways, so to speak, to follow different and less usual paths of thought.

Suppose a Black or an Indian read the story, and was immersed in the sufferings of Americans of European descent being brutalized, enslaved, and killed by carelessly cruel conquerors. I wonder if their blood would boil quite as readily as mine did. I wonder, in fact, if a small, grim smile might not rest on their faces as they read, and if, perhaps, the fugitive thought of "And how do they like it?" might not hover at the edge of their minds.

Just a thought—but it might broaden your perspective as you read. (IA)

It was May, not yet summer by five weeks, but the afternoon heat under the corrugated roofs of Manhattan Engineer District's Los Alamos Laboratory was daily less bearable. Young Dr. Edward Royland had lost fifteen pounds from an already meager frame during his nine-month hitch in the desert. He wondered every day while the thermometer crawled up to its 5:45 peak whether he had made a mistake he would regret the rest of his life in accepting work with the Laboratory rather than letting the local draft board have his carcass and do what they pleased with it. His University of Chicago classmates were glamorously collecting ribbons and wounds from Saipan to Brussels; one of them, a first-rate mathematician named Hatfield, would do no more first-rate mathematics. He had gone down, burning, in an Eighth Air Force Mitchell bomber ambushed over Lille.

"And what, Daddy, did you do in the war?"

"Well, kids, it's a little hard to explain. They had this stupid atomic bomb project that never came to anything, and they tied up a lot of us in a Godforsaken place in New Mexico. We figured and we calculated and we fooled with uranium and some of us got radiation burns and then the war was over and they sent us home."

Royland was not amused by this prospect. He had heat rash under his arms and he was waiting, not patiently, for the Computer Section to send him his figures on Phase 56c, which was the (god-damn childish) code designation for Element Assembly Time. Phase 56c was Royland's own particular baby. He was under Rotschmidt, supervisor of WEAPON DESIGN TRACK III, and Rotschmidt was under Oppenheimer, who bossed the works. Sometimes a General Groves came through, a fine figure of a man, and once from a window Royland had seen the venerable Henry L. Stimson, Secretary of War, walking slowly down their dusty street, leaning on a cane and surrounded by young staff officers. That's what Royland was seeing of the war.

Laboratory! It had sounded inviting, cool, bustling but quiet. So every morning these days he was blasted out of his cot in a barracks cubicle at seven by "Oppie's whistle," fought for a shower and shave with thirty-seven other bachelor scientists in eight languages, bolted a bad cafeteria breakfast, and went through the barbed-wire Restricted Line to his "office"—another matchboard-walled cubicle, smaller and hotter and noisier, with talking and typing and clack of adding machines all around him.

Under the circumstances he was doing good work, he supposed. He wasn't happy about being restricted to his one tiny problem, Phase 56c, but no doubt he was happier than Hatfield had been when his Mitchell got it.

Under the circumstances . . . they included a weird haywire arrangement for computing. Instead of a decent differential analyzer machine they had a human sea of office girls with Burroughs' desk calculators; the girls screamed "Banzai!" and charged on differential equations and swamped them by sheer volume; they clicked them to death with their little adding machines. Royland thought hungrily of Conant's huge, beautiful analog differentiator up at M.I.T.; it was probably tied up by whatever the mysterious "Radiation Laboratory" there was doing. Royland suspected that the "Radiation Laboratory" had as much to do with radiation as his own "Manhattan Engineer District" had to do with Manhattan engineering. And the world was supposed to be trembling on the edge these days of a New Dispensation of Computing that would obsolete even the M.I.T. machine—tubes, relays, and binary arithmetic at blinding speed instead of the suavely turning cams and the smoothly extruding rods and the elegant scribed curves of Conant's masterpiece. He decided that he wouldn't like that; he would like it even less than he liked the little office girls clacking away, pushing lank hair from their dewed brows with undistracted hands.

He wiped his own brow with a sodden handkerchief and permitted himself a glance at his watch and the thermometer. Five-fifteen and 103 Fahrenheit.

He thought vaguely of getting out, of fouling up just enough to be released from the project and drafted. No; there was the post-war career to think of. But one of the big shots, Teller, had been irrepressible; he had rambled outside of his assigned mission again and again until Oppenheimer let him go; now Teller was working with Lawrence at Berkeley on something that had reputedly gone sour at a reputed quarter of a billion dollars—

A girl in khaki knocked and entered. "Your material from the Computer Section, Dr. Royland. Check them and sign here, please." He counted the dozen sheets, signed the clipboarded form she held out, and plunged into the material for thirty minutes.

When he sat back in his chair, the sweat dripped into his eyes unnoticed. His hands were shaking a little, though he did not know that either. Phase 56c of WEAPON DESIGN TRACK III was finished, over, done, successfully accomplished. The answer to the question "Can U_{235} slugs be assembled into a critical mass within a physically feasible time?" was in. The answer was "Yes."

Royland was a theory man, not a Wheatstone or a Kelvin; he liked the numbers for themselves and had no special passion to grab for wires, mica, and bits of graphite so that what the numbers said might immediately be given flesh in a wonderful new gadget. Nevertheless he could visualize at once a workable atomic bomb assembly within the framework of Phase 56c. You have so many microseconds to assemble your critical mass without it boiling away in vapor; you use them by blowing the subassemblies together with shaped charges; lots of microseconds to spare by that method; practically foolproof. Then comes the Big Bang.

Oppie's whistle blew; it was quitting time. Royland sat still in his cubicle. He should go, of course, to Rotschmidt and tell him; Rotschmidt would probably clap him on the back and pour him a jigger of Bols Geneva from the tall clay bottle he kept in his safe. Then Rotschmidt would go to Oppenheimer. Before sunset the project would be redesigned! TRACK I, TRACK II, TRACK IV, and TRACK V would be shut down and their people crammed into TRACK III, the one with the paydirt! New excitement would boil through the project; it had been torpid and souring for three months. Phase 56c was the first good news in at least that long; it had been one damned blind alley after another. General Groves had looked sour and dubious last time around.

Desk drawers were slamming throughout the corrugated, sunbaked building; doors were slamming shut on cubicles; down the corridor, somebody roared with laughter, strained laughter. Passing Royland's door somebody cried impatiently: "—aber was kan Man tun?"

Royland whispered to himself: "You damned fool, what are you thinking of?"

But he knew—he was thinking of the Big Bang, the Big

Dirty Bang, and of torture. The judicial torture of the old days, incredibly cruel by today's lights, stretched the whole body, or crushed it, or burned it, or shattered the fingers and legs. But even that old judicial torture carefully avoided the most sensitive parts of the body, the generative organs, though damage to these, or a real threat of damage to these, would have produced quick and copious confessions. You have to be more or less crazy to torture somebody that way; the sane man does not think of it as a possibility.

An M.P. corporal tried Royland's door and looked in. "Quitting time, professor," he said

"Okay," Royland said. Mechanically he locked his desk drawers and his files, turned his window lock, and set out his waste-paper basket in the corridor. Click the door; another day, another dollar.

Maybe the project *was* breaking up. They did now and then. The huge boner at Berkeley proved that. And Royland's barracks was light two physicists now; their cubicles stood empty since they had been drafted to M.I.T. for some anti-submarine thing. Groves had *not* looked happy last time around; how did a general make up his mind anyway? Give them three months, then the ax? Maybe Stimson would run out of patience and cut the loss, close the District down. Maybe F.D.R. would say at a Cabinet meeting, "By the way, Henry, what ever became of—?" and that would be the end if old Henry could say only that the scientists appear to be optimistic of eventual success, Mr. President, but that as yet there seems to be nothing *concrete*—

He passed through the barbed wire of the Line under scrutiny of an M.P. lieutenant and walked down the barracks-edged company street of the maintenance troops to their motor pool. He wanted a jeep and a trip ticket; he wanted a long desert drive in the twilight; he wanted a dinner of *frijoles* and eggplant with his old friend Charles Miller Nahataspe, the medicine man of the adjoining Hopi reservation. Royland's hobby was anthropology; he wanted to get a little drunk on it—he hoped it would clear his mind.

*   *   *

Nahataspe welcomed him cheerfully to his hut; his million wrinkles all smiled. "You want me to play informant for a while?" he grinned. He had been to Carlisle in the 1880's and had been laughing at the white man ever since; he admitted that physics was funny, but for a real joke give him cultural anthropology every time. "You want some nice unsavory stuff about our institutionalized homosexuality? Should I cook us a dog for dinner? Have a seat on the blanket, Edward."

"What happened to your chairs? And the funny picture of McKinley? And—and everything?" The hut was bare except for cooking pots that simmered on the stone-curbed central hearth.

"I gave the stuff away," Nahataspe said carelessly. "You get tired of things."

Royland thought he knew what that meant. Nahataspe believed he would die quite soon; these particular Indians did not believe in dying encumbered by possessions. Manners, of course, forbade discussing death.

The Indian watched his face and finally said: "Oh, it's all right for *you* to talk about it. Don't be embarrassed."

Royland asked nervously: "Don't you feel well?"

"I feel terrible. There's a snake eating my liver. Pitch in and eat. You feel pretty awful yourself, don't you?"

The hard-learned habit of security caused Royland to evade the question. "You don't mean that literally about the snake, do you, Charles?"

"Of course I do," Miller insisted. He scooped a steaming gourd full of stew from the pot and blew on it. "What would an untutored child of nature know about bacteria, viruses, toxins, and neoplasms? What would I know about break-the-sky medicine?"

Royland looked up sharply; the Indian was blandly eating. "Do you hear any talk about break-the-sky medicine?" Royland asked.

"No talk, Edward. I've had a few dreams about it." He

pointed with his chin toward the Laboratory. "You fellows over there shouldn't dream so hard; it leaks out."

Royland helped himself to stew without answering. The stew was good, far better than the cafeteria stuff, and he did not *have* to guess the source of the meat in it.

Miller said consolingly: "It's only kid stuff, Edward. Don't get so worked up about it. We have a long dull story about a horned toad who ate some loco-weed and thought he was the Sky God. He got angry and he tried to break the sky but he couldn't so he slunk into his hole ashamed to face all the other animals and died. But they never knew he tried to break the sky at all."

In spite of himself Royland demanded: "Do you have any stories about anybody who did break the sky?" His hands were shaking again and his voice almost hysterical. Oppie and the rest of them were going to break the sky, kick humanity right in the crotch, and unleash a prowling monster that would go up and down by night and day peering in all the windows of all the houses in the world, leaving no sane man ever unterrified for his life and the lives of his kin. Phase 56c, God-damn it to blackest hell, made sure of that! Well done, Royland; you earned your dollar today!

Decisively the old Indian set his gourd aside. He said: "We have a saying that the only good paleface is a dead paleface, but I'll make an exception for you, Edward. I've got some strong stuff from Mexico that will make you feel better. I don't like to see my friends hurting."

"Peyote? I've tried it. Seeing a few colored lights won't make me feel better, but thanks."

"Not peyote, this stuff. It's God Food. I wouldn't take it myself without a month of preparation; otherwise the Gods would scoop me up in a net. That's because my people see clearly, and your eyes are clouded." He was busily rummaging through a clay-chinked wicker box as he spoke; he came up with a covered dish. "You people have your sight cleared just a little by the God Food, so it's safe for you."

Royland thought he knew what the old man was talking

about. It was one of Nahataspe's biggest jokes that Hopi children understood Einstein's relativity as soon as they could talk—and there was some truth to it. The Hopi language—and thought—had no tenses and therefore no concept of time-as-an-entity; it had nothing like the Indo-European speech's subjects and predicates, and therefore no built-in metaphysics of cause and effect. In the Hopi language and mind all things were frozen together forever into one great relationship, a crytalline structure of space–time events that simply were because they were. So much for Nahataspe's people "seeing clearly." But Royland gave himself and any other physicist credit for seeing as clearly when they were working a four-dimensional problem in the X Y Z space variables and the T time variable.

He could have spoiled the old man's joke by pointing that out, but of course he did not. No, no; he'd get a jag and maybe a bellyache from Nahataspe's herb medicine and then go home to his cubicle with his problem unresolved: to kick or not to kick?

The old man began to mumble in Hopi, and drew a tattered cloth across the door frame of his hut; it shut out the last rays of the setting sun, long and slanting on the desert, pink-red against the adobe cubes of the Indian settlement. It took a minute for Royland's eyes to accommodate to the flickering light from the hearth and the indigo square of the ceiling smoke hole. Now Nahataspe was "dancing," doing a crouched shuffle around the hut holding the covered dish before him. Out of the corner of his mouth, without interrupting the rhythm, he said to Royland: "Drink some hot water now." Royland sipped from one of the pots on the hearth; so far it was much like peyote ritual, but he felt calmer.

Nahataspe uttered a loud scream, added apologetically: "Sorry, Edward," and crouched before him whipping the cover off the dish like a headwaiter. So God Food was dried black mushrooms, miserable, wrinkled little things. "You swallow them all and chase them with hot water," Nahataspe said.

Obediently Royland choked them down and gulped from the jug; the old man resumed his dance and chanting.

A little old self-hypnosis, Royland thought bitterly. Grab some imitation sleep and forget about old 56c, as if you could. He could see the big dirty one now, a hell of a fireball, maybe over Munich, or Cologne, or Tokyo, or Nara. Cooked people, fused cathedral stone, the bronze of the big Buddha running like water, perhaps lapping around the ankles of a priest and burning his feet off so he fell prone into the stuff. He couldn't see the gamma radiation, but it would be there, invisible sleet doing the dirty unthinkable thing, coldly burning away the sex of men and women, cutting short so many fans of life at their points of origin. Phase 56c could snuff out a family of Bachs, or five generations of Bernoullis, or see to it that the great Huxley-Darwin cross did not occur.

The fireball loomed, purple and red and fringed with green—

The mushrooms were reaching him, he thought fuzzily. He could really see it. Nahataspe, crouched and treading, moved through the fireball just as he had the last time, and the time before that. Déjà vu, extraordinarily strong, stronger than ever before, gripped him. Royland knew all this had happened to him before, and remembered perfectly what would come next; it was on the very tip of his tongue, as they say—

The fireballs began to dance around him and he felt his strength drain suddenly out; he was lighter than a feather; the breeze would carry him away; he would be blown like a dust mote into the circle that the circling fireballs made. And he knew it was wrong. He croaked with the last of his energy, feeling himself slip out of the world: "Charlie! Help!"

Out of the corner of his mind as he slipped away he sensed that the old man was pulling him now under the arms, trying to tug him out of the hut, crying dimly into his ear: "You should have told me you did not see through smoke! You see clear; I never knew; I nev—"

And then he slipped through into blackness and silence.

Royland awoke sick and fuzzy; it was morning in the hut;

there was no sign of Nahataspe. Well. Unless the old man had gotten to a phone and reported to the Laboratory, there were now jeeps scouring the desert in search of him and all hell was breaking loose in Security and Personnel. He would catch some of that hell on his return, and avert it with his news about assembly time.

Then he noticed that the hut had been cleaned of Nahataspe's few remaining possessions, even to the door cloth. A pang went through him; had the old man died in the night? He limped from the hut and looked around for a funeral pyre, a crowd of mourners. They were not there; the adobe cubes stood untenanted in the sunlight, and more weeds grew in the single street than he remembered. And his jeep, parked last night against the hut, was missing.

There were no wheeltracks, and uncrushed weeds grew tall where the jeep had stood.

Nahataspe's God Food had been powerful stuff. Royland's hand crept uncertainly to his face. No; no beard.

He looked about him, looked hard. He made the effort necessary to see details. He did not glance at the hut and because it was approximately the same as it had always been, concluded that it was unchanged, eternal. He looked and saw changes everywhere. Once-sharp adobe corners were rounded; protruding roof beams were bleached bone-white by how many years of desert sun? The wooden framing of the deep fortress-like windows had crumbled; the third building from him had wavering soot stains above its window boles and its beams were charred.

He went to it, numbly thinking: Phase 56c at least is settled. Not old Rip's baby now. They'll know me from fingerprints, I guess. One year? Ten? I *feel* the same.

The burned-out house was a shambles. In one corner were piled dry human bones. Royland leaned dizzily against the doorframe; its charcoal crumbled and streaked his hand. Those skulls were Indian—he was anthropologist enough to know that. Indian men, women and children, slain and piled in a heap. Who kills Indians? There should have been some sign of clothes, burned rags, but there were none. Who strips Indians naked and kills them?

Signs of a dreadful massacre were everywhere in the house. Bullet-pocks in the walls, high and low. Savage nicks left by bayonets—and swords? Dark stains of blood; it had run two inches high and left its mark. Metal glinted in a ribcage across the room. Swaying, he walked to the boneheap and thrust his hand into it. The thing bit him like a razor blade; he did not look at it as he plucked it out and carried it to the dusty street. With his back turned to the burned house he studied his find. It was a piece of swordblade six inches long, hand-honed to a perfect edge with a couple of nicks in it. It had stiffening ribs and the usual blood gutters. It had a perceptible curve that would fit into only one shape: the Samurai sword of Japan.

However long it had taken, the war was obviously over.

He went to the village well and found it choked with dust. It was while he stared into the dry hole that he first became afraid. Suddenly it all was real; he was no more an onlooker but a frightened and very thirsty man. He ransacked the dozen houses of the settlement and found nothing to his purpose—a child's skeleton here, a couple of cartridge cases there.

There was only one thing left, and that was the road, the same earth track it had always been, wide enough for one jeep or the rump-sprung station wagon of the Indian settlement that once had been. Panic invited him to run; he did not yield. He sat on the well curb, took off his shoes to meticulously smooth wrinkles out of his khaki G.I. socks, put the shoes on, and retied the laces loosely enough to allow for swelling, and hesitated a moment. Then he grinned, selected two pebbles carefully from the dust and popped them in his mouth. "Beaver Patrol, forward march," he said, and began to hike.

Yes, he was thirsty; soon he would be hungry and tired; what of it? The dirt road would meet state-maintained blacktop in three miles and then there would be traffic and he'd hitch a ride. Let them argue with his fingerprints if they felt like it. The Japanese had got as far as New Mexico, had they? Then God help their home islands when the counterblow had come. Americans were a ferocious people when trespassed on. Conceivably, there was not a Japanese left alive . . .

He began to construct his story as he hiked. In large parts it was a repeated "I don't know." He would tell them: "I don't expect you to believe this, so my feelings won't be hurt when you don't. Just listen to what I say and hold everything until the F.B.I. has checked my fingerprints. My name is—" And so on.

It was midmorning then, and he would be on the highway soon. His nostrils, sharpened by hunger, picked up a dozen scents on the desert breeze: the spice of sage, a whiff of acetylene stink from a rattler dozing on the shaded side of a rock, the throat-tightening reek of tar suggested for a moment on the air. That would be the highway, perhaps a recent hotpatch on a chuckhole. Then a startling tang of sulfur dioxide drowned them out and passed on, leaving him stung and sniffling and groping for a handkerchief that was not there. What in God's name had that been, and where from? Without ceasing to trudge he studied the horizon slowly and found a smoke pall to the far west dimly smudging the sky. It looked like a small city's, or a fair-sized factory's, pollution. A city or a factory where "in his time"—he formed the thought reluctantly—there had been none.

Then he was at the highway. It had been improved; it was a two-laner still, but it was nicely graded now, built up by perhaps three inches of gravel and tar beyond its old level, and lavishly ditched on either side.

If he had a coin he would have tossed it, but you went for weeks without spending a cent at Los Alamos Laboratory; Uncle took care of everything, from cigarettes to tombstones. He turned left and began to walk westward toward that sky smudge.

I am a reasonable animal, he was telling himself, and I will accept whatever comes in a spirit of reason. I will control what I can and try to understand the rest—

A faint siren scream began behind him and built up fast. The reasonable animal jumped for the ditch and hugged it for dear life. The siren howled closer, and motors roared. At the ear-splitting climax Royland put his head up for one glimpse, then fell back into the ditch as if a grenade had exploded in his middle.

The convoy roared on, down the *center* of the two-lane highway, straddling the white line. First the three little recon cars with the twin-mount machine guns, each filled brimful with three helmeted Japanese soldiers. Then the high-profiled, armored car of state, six-wheeled, with a probably ceremonial gun turret astern—nickel-plated gunbarrels are impractical—and the Japanese admiral in the fore-and-aft hat taking his lordly ease beside a rawboned, hatchet-faced SS officer in gleaming black. Then, diminuendo, two more little recon jobs . . .

"We've lost," Royland said in his ditch meditatively. "Ceremonial tanks with glass windows—we lost a *long* time ago." Had there been a Rising Sun insignia or was he now imagining that?

He climbed out and continued to trudge westward on the improved blacktop. You couldn't say "I reject the universe," not when you were as thirsty as he was.

He didn't even turn when the put-putting of a westbound vehicle grew loud behind him and then very loud when it stopped at his side.

"Zeegail," a curious voice said. "What are you doing here?"

The vehicle was just as odd in its own way as the ceremonial tank. It was minimum motor transportation, a kid's sled on wheels, powered by a noisy little air-cooled outboard motor. The driver sat with no more comfort than a cleat to back his coccyx against, and behind him were two twenty-five pound flour sacks that took up all the remaining room the little buckboard provided. The driver had the leathery Southwestern look; he wore a baggy blue outfit that was obviously a uniform and obviously unmilitary. He had a nametape on his breast above an incomprehensible row of dull ribbons:

MARTFIELD, E., 1218824, P/7 NQOTD43. He saw Royland's eyes on the tape and said kindly: "My name is Martfield—Paymaster Seventh, but there's no need to use my rank here. Are you all right, my man?"

"Thirsty," Royland said. "What's the NQOTD43 for?"

"You can read!" Martfield said, astounded. "Those ches—"

"Something to drink, please," Royland said. For the moment nothing else mattered in the world. He sat down on the buckboard like a puppet with cut strings.

"See here, fellow!" Martfield snapped in a curious, strangled way, forcing the words through his throat with a stagy, conventional effect of controlled anger. "You can stand until I invite you to sit!"

"Have you any water?" Royland asked dully.

With the same bark: "Who do you think you are?"

"I happen to be a theoretical physicist—" tiredly arguing with a dim seventh-carbon-copy imitation of a drill sergeant.

"Oh-*hoh!*" Martfield suddenly laughed. His stiffness vanished; he actually reached into his baggy tunic and brought out a pint canteen that gurgled. He then forgot all about the canteen in his hand, roguishly dug Royland in the ribs and said: "I should have suspected. You scientists! Somebody was supposed to pick you up—but he was another scientist, eh? Ah-hah-hah-hah!"

Royland took the canteen from his hand and sipped. So a scientist was supposed to be an idiot-savant, eh? Never mind now; drink. People said you were not supposed to fill your stomach with water after great thirst; it sounded to him like one of those puritanical rules people make up out of nothing because they sound reasonable. He finished the canteen while Martfield, Paymaster Seventh, looked alarmed, and wished only that there were three or four more of them.

"Got any food?" he demanded.

Martfield cringed briefly. "Doctor, I regret extremely that

I have nothing with me. However if you would do me the honor of riding with me to my quarters—"

"Let's go," Royland said. He squatted on the flour sacks and away they chugged at a good thirty miles an hour; it was a fair little engine. The Paymaster Seventh continued deferential, apologizing over his shoulder because there was no windscreen, later dropped his cringing entirely to explain that Royland was seated on flour—"*white* flour, understand?" An over-the-shoulder wink. He had a friend in the bakery at Los Alamos. Several buckboards passed the other way as they traveled. At each encounter there was a peering examination of insignia to decide who saluted. Once they met a sketchily enclosed vehicle that furnished its driver with a low seat instead of obliging him to sit with legs straight out, and Paymaster Seventh Martfield almost dislocated his shoulder saluting first. The driver of that one was a Japanese in a kimono. A long curved sword lay across his lap.

Mile after mile the smell of sulfur and sulfides increased; finally there rose before them the towers of a Frasch Process layout. It looked like an oilfield, but instead of ground-laid pipelines and bass-drum storage tanks there were foothills of yellow sulfur. They drove between them—more salutes from baggily uniformed workers with shovels and yard-long Stilson wrenches. Off to the right were things that might have been Solvay Process towers for sulfuric acid, and a glittering horror of a neo-Roman administration-and-labs building. The Rising Sun banner fluttered from its central flagstaff.

Music surged as they drove deeper into the area; first it was a welcome counterirritant to the pop-pop of the two-cycle buckboard engine, and then a nuisance by itself. Royland looked, annoyed, for the loudspeakers, and saw them everywhere—on power poles, buildings, gateposts. Schmaltzy Strauss waltzes bathed them like smog, made thinking just a little harder, made communication just a little more blurry even after you had learned to live with the noise.

"I miss music in the wilderness," Martfield confided over his shoulder. He throttled down the buckboard until they were just rolling; they had passed some line unrecognized by Royland beyond which one did not salute everybody—just the occasional Japanese walking by in business suit with blueprint-roll and slide rule, or in kimono with sword. It was a German who nailed Royland, however: a classic jack-booted German in black broadcloth, black leather, and plenty of silver trim. He watched them roll for a moment after exchanging salutes with Martfield, made up his mind, and said: "Halt."

The Paymaster Seventh slapped on the brake, killed the engine, and popped to attention beside the buckboard. Royland more or less imitated him. The German said, stiffly but without accent: "Whom have you brought here, Paymaster?"

"A scientist, sir. I picked him up on the road returning from Los Alamos with personal supplies. He appears to be a minerals prospector who missed a rendezvous, but naturally I have not questioned the Doctor."

The German turned to Royland contemplatively. "So, Doctor. Your name and specialty."

"Dr. Edward Royland," he said. "I do nuclear power research." If there was no bomb he'd be damned if he'd invent it now for these people.

"So? That is very interesting, considering that there is no such thing as nuclear power research. Which camp are you from?" The German threw an aside to the Paymaster Seventh, who was literally shaking with fear at the turn things had taken. "You may go, Paymaster. Of course you will report yourself for harboring a fugitive."

"At once, sir," Martfield said in a sick voice. He moved slowly away pushing the little buckboard before him. The Strauss waltz oom-pah'd its last chord and instantly the loudspeakers struck up a hoppity-hoppity folk dance, heavy on the brass.

"Come with me," the German said, and walked off, not even looking behind to see whether Royland was obeying. This itself demonstrated how unlikely any disobedience was to succeed. Royland followed at his heels, which of course were garnished with silver spurs. Royland had not seen a horse so far that day.

A Japanese stopped them politely inside the administration building, a rimless-glasses, office-manager type in a gray suit. "How nice to see you again, Major Kappel! Is there anything I might do to help you?"

The German stiffened. "I didn't want to bother your people, Mr. Ito. This fellow appears to be a fugitive from one of our camps; I was going to turn him over to our liaison group for examination and return."

Mr. Ito looked at Royland and slapped his face hard. Royland, by the insanity of sheer reflex, cocked his fist as a red-blooded boy should, but the German's reflexes operated also. He had a pistol in his hand and pressed against Royland's ribs before he could throw the punch.

"All right," Royland said, and put down his hand.

Mr. Ito laughed. "You are at least partly right, Major Kappel; he certainly is not from one of *our* camps! But do not let me delay you further. May I hope for a report on the outcome of this?"

"Of course, Mr. Ito," said the German. He holstered his pistol and walked on, trailed by the scientist. Royland heard him grumble something that sounded like "Damned extraterritoriality!"

They descended to a basement level where all the door signs were in German, and in an office labeled WISSENSCHAFTSLICHESICHERHEITSLIAISON Royland finally told his story. His audience was the major, a fat officer deferentially addressed as Colonel Biederman, and a bearded old civilian, a Dr. Piqueron, called in from another office. Royland suppressed only the matter of bomb research, and did it easily with the old security habit. His improvised cover story made the Los Alamos Laboratory a research center only for the generation of electricity.

The three heard him out in silence. Finally, in an amused voice, the colonel asked: "Who was this Hitler you mentioned?"

For that Royland was not prepared. His jaw dropped.

Major Kappel said: "Oddly enough, he struck on a name which does figure, somewhat infamously, in the annals of the Third Reich. One Adolf Hitler was an early Party agitator, but as I recall it he intrigued against the Leader during the War of Triumph and was executed."

"An ingenious madman," the colonel said. "Sterilized, of course?"

"Why, I don't know. I suppose so. Doctor, would you—?"

Dr. Piqueron quickly examined Royland and found him all there, which astonished them. Then they thought of looking for his camp tattoo number on the left bicep, and found none. Then, thoroughly upset, they discovered that he had no birth number above his left nipple either.

"And," Dr. Piqueron stammered, "his shoes are odd, sir—I just noticed. Sir, how long since you've seen sewn shoes and braided laces?"

"You must be hungry," the colonel suddenly said. "Doctor, have my aide get something to eat for—for the doctor."

"Major," said Royland, "I hope no harm will come to the fellow who picked me up. You told him to report himself."

"Have no fear, er, doctor," said the major. "Such humanity! You are of German blood?"

"Not that I know of; it may be."

"It *must* be!" said the colonel.

A platter of hash and a glass of beer arrived on a tray. Royland postponed everything. At last he demanded: "Now. Do you believe me? There must be fingerprints to prove my story still in existence."

"I feel like a fool," the major said. "You still could be hoaxing us. Dr. Piqueron, did not a German scientist establish that nuclear power is a theoretical and practical impossibility, that one always must put more into it than one can take out?"

Piqueron nodded and said reverently: "Heisenberg. Nineteen fifty-three, during the War of Triumph. His group was then assigned to electrical weapons research and produced the blinding bomb. But this fact does not invalidate the doctor's story; he says only that his group was *attempting* to produce nuclear power."

"We've got to research this," said the colonel. "Dr. Piqueron, entertain this man, whatever he is, in your laboratory."

Piqueron's laboratory down the hall was a place of astounding simplicity, even crudeness. The sinks, reagents, and balance were capable only of simple qualitative and quantitative analyses; various works in progress testified that they were not even strained to their modest limits. Samples of sulfur and its compounds were analyzed here. It hardly seemed to call for a "doctor" of anything, and hardly even for a human being. Machinery should be continuously testing the products as they flowed out; variations should be scribed mechanically on a moving tape; automatic controls should at least stop the processes and signal an alarm when variation went beyond limits; at most it might correct whatever was going wrong. But here sat Piqueron every day, titrating, precipitating, and weighing, entering results by hand in a ledger and telephoning them to the works!

Piqueron looked about proudly. "As a physicist you wouldn't understand all this, of course," he said. "Shall I explain?"

"Perhaps later, doctor, if you'd be good enough. If you'd first help me orient myself—"

So Piqueron told him about the War of Triumph (1940–1955) and what came after.

In 1940 the realm of der Fuehrer (Herr Goebbels, of course—that strapping blond fellow with the heroic jaw and eagle's eye whom you can see in the picture there) was simultaneously and treacherously invaded by the misguided French, the sub-human Slavs, and the perfidious British. The attack, for which the shocked Germans coined the name *blitzkrieg*, was timed to coincide with an internal eruption of sabotage, well-poisoning, and assassination by the *Zigeunerjuden*, or Jewpsies, of whom little is now known; there seem to be none left.

TWO DOOMS

By Nature's ineluctable law, the Germans had necessarily to be tested to the utmost so that they might fully respond. Therefore Germany was overrun from East and West, and Holy Berlin itself was taken; but Goebbels and his court withdrew like Barbarossa into the mountain fastnesses to await their day. It came unexpectedly soon. The deluded Americans launched a million-man amphibious attack on the homeland of the Japanese in 1945. The Japanese resisted with almost Teutonic courage. Not one American in twenty reached shore alive, and not one in a hundred got a mile inland. Particularly lethal were the women and children, who lay in camouflaged pits hugging artillery shells and aircraft bombs, which they detonated when enough invaders drew near to make it worthwhile.

The second invasion attempt, a month later, was made up of second-line troops scraped up from everywhere, including occupation duty in Germany.

"Literally," Piqueron said, "the Japanese did not know how to surrender, so they did not. They could not conquer, but they could and did continue suicidal resistance, consuming manpower of the allies and their own womanpower and childpower—a shrewd bargain for the Japanese! The Russians refused to become involved in the Japanese war; they watched with apish delight while two future enemies, as they supposed, were engaged in mutual destruction.

"A third assault wave broke on Kyushu and gained the island at last. What lay ahead? Only another assault on Honshu, the main island, home of the Emperor and the principal shrines. It was 1946; the volatile, child-like Americans were war-weary and mutinous; the best of them were gone by then. In desperation the Anglo-American leaders offered the Russians an economic sphere embracing the China coast and Japan as the price of participation."

The Russians grinned and assented; they would take that—at *least* that. They mounted a huge assault for the spring of 1947; they would take Korea and leap off from there for northern Honshu while the Anglo-American forces struck in the south. Surely this would provide at last a symbol before which the Japanese might without shame bow down and admit defeat!

And then, from the mountain fastnesses, came the radio voice: "Germans! Your Leader calls upon you again!" Followed the Hundred Days of Glory during which the German Army reconstituted itself and expelled the occupation troops—by then, children without combat experience, and leavened by not-quite-disabled veterans. Followed the seizure of the airfields; the Luftwaffe in business again. Followed the drive, almost a dress parade, to the Channel Coast, gobbling up immense munition dumps awaiting shipment to the Pacific Theater, millions of warm uniforms, good boots, mountains of rations, piles of shells and explosives that lined the French roads for scores of miles, thousands of two-and-a-half-ton trucks, and lakes of gasoline to fuel them. The shipyards of Europe, from Hamburg to Toulon, had been turning out, furiously, invasion barges for the Pacific. In April of 1947 they sailed against England in their thousands.

Halfway around the world, the British Navy was pounding Tokyo, Nagasaki, Kobe, Hiroshima, Nara. Three quarters of the way across Asia the Russian Army marched stolidly on; let the decadent British pickle their own fish; the glorious motherland at last was gaining her long-sought, long-denied, warm-water seacoast. The British, tired women without their men, children fatherless these eight years, old folks deathly weary, deathly worried about their sons, were brave but they were not insane. They accepted honorable peace terms; they capitulated.

With the Western front secure for the first time in history, the ancient Drive to the East was resumed; the immemorial struggle of Teuton against Slav went on.

His spectacles glittering with rapture, Dr. Piqueron said: "We were worthy in those days of the Teutonic Knights who seized Prussia from the sub-men! On the ever-glorious Twenty-first of May, Moscow was ours!"

Moscow and the monolithic state machinery it controlled,

and all the roads and rail lines and communication wires which led only to—and from—Moscow. Detroit-built tanks and trucks sped along those roads in the fine, bracing spring weather; the Red Army turned one hundred and eighty degrees at last and countermarched halfway across the Eurasian landmass, and at Kazan it broke exhausted against the Frederik Line.

Europe at last was One and German. Beyond Europe lay the dark and swarming masses of Asia, mysterious and repulsive folk whom it would be better to handle through the non-German, but chivalrous, Japanese. The Japanese were reinforced with shipping from Birkenhead, artillery from the Putilov Works, jet fighters from Châteauroux, steel from the Ruhr, rice from the Po valley, herring from Norway, timber from Sweden, oil from Romania, laborers from India. The American forces were driven from Kyushu in the winter of 1948, and bloodily back across their chain of island stepping-stones that followed.

Surrender they would not; it was a monstrous affront that shield-shaped North America dared to lie there between the German Atlantic and the Japanese Pacific threatening both. The affront was wiped out in 1955.

For one hundred and fifty years now the Germans and the Japanese had uneasily eyed each other across the banks of the Mississippi. Their orators were fond of referring to that river as a vast frontier unblemished by a single fortification. There was even some interpenetration; a Japanese colony fished out of Nova Scotia on the very rim of German America; a sulfur mine which was part of the Farben system lay in New Mexico, the very heart of Japanese America—this was where Dr. Edward Royland found himself, being lectured to by Dr. Piqueron, Dr. Gaston Pierre Piqueron, true-blue German.

"Here, of course," Dr. Piqueron said gloomily, "we are so damned provincial. Little ceremony and less manners. Well, it would be too much to expect them to assign *German*

Germans to this dreary outpost, so we French Germans must endure it somehow.''

"You're all French?" Royland asked, startled.

"French *Germans*," Piqueron stiffly corrected him. "Colonel Biederman happens to be a French German also; Major Kappel is—hrrmph—an Italian German." He sniffed to show what he thought of that.

The Italian German entered at that point, not in time to shut off the question: "And you all come from Europe?"

They looked at him in bafflement. "My grandfather did," Dr. Piqueron said. Royland remembered; so Roman legions used to guard their empire—Romans born and raised in Britain, or on the Danube, Romans who would never in their lives see Italy or Rome.

Major Kappel said affably: "Well, this needn't concern us. I'm afraid, my dear fellow, that your little hoax has not succeeded." He clapped Royland merrily on the back. "I admit you've tricked us all nicely; now may we have the facts?"

Piqueron said, surprised: "His story is false? The shoes? The missing *geburtsnummer*? And he appears to understand some chemistry!"

"Ah-h-h—but he said his speciality was *physics*, doctor! Suspicious in itself!"

"Quite so. A discrepancy. But the rest—?"

"As to his birth number, who knows? As to his shoes, who cares? I took some inconspicuous notes while he was entertaining us and have checked thoroughly. There *was* no Manhattan Engineering District. There *was* no Dr. Oppenheimer, or Fermi, or Bohr. There *is* no theory of relativity, or equivalence of mass and energy. Uranium has one use only—coloring glass a pretty orange. There is such a thing as an isotope but it has nothing to do with chemistry; it is the name used in Race Science for a permissible variation within a subrace. And what have you to say to *that*, my dear fellow?"

Royland wondered first, such was the positiveness with which Major Kappel spoke, whether he had slipped into a universe of different physical properties and history entirely, one in which Julius Caesar discovered Peru and the oxygen molecule was lighter than the hydrogen atom. He managed to speak. "How did you find all that out, major?"

"Oh, don't think I did a skimpy job," Kappel smiled. "I looked it all up in the *big* encyclopedia."

Dr. Piqueron, chemist, nodded grave approval of the major's diligence and thorough grasp of the scientific method.

"You still don't want to tell us?" Major Kappel asked coaxingly.

"I can only stand by what I said."

Kappel shrugged. "It's not my job to persuade you; I wouldn't know how to begin. But I can and will ship you off forthwith to a work camp."

"What—is a work camp?" Royland unsteadily asked.

"Good heavens, man, a camp where one works! You're obviously an *ungleichgeschaltling* and you've got to be *gleichgeschaltet.*" He did not speak these words as if they were foreign; they were obviously part of the everyday American working vocabulary. *Gleichgeschaltet* meant to Royland something like "coordinated, brought into tune with." So he would be brought into tune—with what, and how?

The Major went on: "You'll get your clothes and your bunk and your chow, and you'll work, and eventually your irregular vagabondish habits will disappear and you'll be turned loose on the labor market. And you'll be damned glad we took the trouble with you." His face fell. "By the way, I was too late with your friend the Paymaster. I'm sorry. I sent a messenger to Disciplinary Control with a stop order. After all, if you took us in for an hour, why should you not have fooled a Pay-Seventh?"

"Too late? He's *dead?* For picking up a *hitchhiker?*"

"I don't know what that last word means," said the Major. "If it's dialect for 'vagabond,' the answer is ordinarily 'yes.' The man, after all, was a Pay-Seventh; he could read. Either you're keeping up your hoax with remarkable fidelity or you've been living in isolation. Could that be it? Is there a tribe of you somewhere? Well, the interrogators will find out; that's their job."

"The Dogpatch legend!" Dr. Piqueron burst out, thunderstruck. "He may be an Abnerite!"

"By Heaven," Major Kappel said slowly, "that might be it. What a feather in my cap to find a living Abernite."

"*Whose* cap?" demanded Dr. Piqueron coldly.

"I think I'll look the Dogpatch legend up," said Kappel, heading for the door and probably the big encyclopedia.

"So will I," Dr. Piqueron announced firmly. The last Royland saw of them they were racing down the corridor, neck and neck.

Very funny. And they had killed simple-minded Paymaster Martfield for picking up a hitchhiker. The Nazis always had been pretty funny—fat Hermann pretending he was young Seigfried. As blond as Hitler, as slim as Goering, and as tall as Goebbels. Immature guttersnipes who hadn't been able to hang a convincing frame on Dimitrov for the Reichstag fire; the world had roared at their bungling. Huge, corny party rallies with let's-play-detectives nonsense like touching the local flags to that hallowed banner on which the martyred Horst Wessel had had a nosebleed. And they had rolled over Europe, and they killed people . . .

One thing was certain: life in the work camp would at least bore him to death. He was supposed to be an illiterate simpleton, so things were excused him which were not excused an exalted Pay-Seventh. He poked through a closet in the corner of the laboratory—he and Piqueron were the same size—

He found a natty change of uniform and what must be a civilian suit: somewhat baggy pants and a sort of tunic with the neat, sensible Russian collar. Obviously it would be all right to wear it because here it was; just as obviously, it was all wrong for him to be dressed in chinos and a flannel shirt. He did not know exactly what this made him, but Martfield had been done to death for picking up a man in chinos and a flannel shirt. Royland changed into the civilian suit, stuffed his own shirt and pants far back on the top shelf of the closet;

this was probably concealment enough from those murderous clowns. He walked out, and up the stairs, and through the busy lobby, and into the industrial complex. Nobody saluted him and he saluted nobody. He knew where he was going—to a good, sound Japanese laboratory where there were no Germans.

Royland had known Japanese students at the University and admired them beyond words. Their brains, frugality, doggedness, and good humor made them, as far as he was concerned, the most sensible people he had ever known. Tojo and his warlords were not, as far as Royland was concerned, essentially Japanese but just more damnfool soldiers and politicians. The real Japanese would courteously listen to him, calmly check against available facts—

He rubbed his cheek and remembered Mr. Ito and his slap in the face. Well, presumably Mr. Ito was a damnfool soldier and politician—and demonstrating for the German's benefit in a touchy border area full of jurisdictional questions.

At any rate, he would *not* go to a labor camp and bust rocks or refinish furniture until those imbeciles decided he was *gleichgeschaltet;* he would go mad in a month.

Royland walked to the Solvay towers and followed the glass pipes containing their output of sulfuric acid along the ground until he came to a bottling shed where beetle-browed men worked silently filling great wicker-basketed carboys and heaving them outside. He followed other men who levered them up onto hand trucks and rolled them in one door of a storage shed. Out the door at the other end more men loaded them onto enclosed trucks which were driven up from time to time.

Royland settled himself in a corner of the storage shed behind a barricade of carboys and listened to the truck dispatcher swear at his drivers and the carboy handlers swear at their carboys.

"Get the god-damn Frisco shipment *loaded,* stupid! I don't *care* if you gotta go, we gotta get it out by *midnight!*"

So a few hours after dark Royland was riding west, without

much air, and in the dangerous company of one thousand gallons of acid. He hoped he had a careful driver.

A night, a day, and another night on the road. The truck never stopped except to gas up; the drivers took turns and ate sandwiches at the wheel and dozed off shift. It rained the second night. Royland, craftily and perhaps a little crazily, licked the drops that ran down the tarpaulin flap covering the rear. At the first crack of dawn, hunched between two wicker carcasses, he saw they were rolling through irrigated vegetable fields, and the water in the ditches was too much for him. He heard the transmission shift down to slow for a curve, swarmed over the tailgate, and dropped to the road. He was weak and limp enough to hit like a sack.

He got up, ignoring his bruises, and hobbled to one of the brimming five-foot ditches; he drank, and drank, and drank. This time puritanical folklore proved right; he lost it all immediately, or what had not been greedily absorbed by his shriveled stomach. He did not mind; it was bliss enough to *stretch*.

The field crop was tomatoes, almost dead ripe. He was starved for them; as he saw the rosy beauties he knew that tomatoes were the only thing in the world he craved. He gobbled one so that the juice ran down his chin; he ate the next two delicately, letting his teeth break the crispness of their skin and the beautiful taste ravish his tongue. There were tomatoes as far as the eye could see, on either side of the road, the green of the vines and the red dots of the ripe fruit graphed by the checkerboard of silvery ditches that caught the first light. Nevertheless, he filled his pockets with them before he walked on.

Royland was happy.

Farewell to the Germans and their sordid hash and murderous ways. *Look* at these beautiful fields! The Japanese are an innately artistic people who bring beauty to every detail of daily life. And they make damn good physicists, too. Confined in their stony home, cramped as he had been in the truck, they grew twisted and painful; why should they not have reached out for more room to grow, and what other way is there to reach but to make war? He could be very understanding about any people who had planted those beautiful tomatoes for him.

A dark blemish the size of a man attracted his attention. It lay on the margin of one of the swirling five-foot ditches out there to his right. And then it rolled slowly into the ditch with a splash, floundered a little, and proceeded to drown.

In a hobbling run Royland broke from the road and across the field. He did not know whether he was limber enough to swim. As he stood panting on the edge of the ditch, peering into the water, a head of hair surfaced near him. He flung himself down, stretched wildly, and grabbed the hair—and yet had detachment enough to feel a pang when the tomatoes in his tunic pocket smashed.

"Steady," he muttered to himself, yanked the head toward him, took hold with his other hand and lifted. A surprised face confronted him and then went blank and unconscious.

For half an hour Royland, weak as he was, struggled, cursed feebly, and sweated to get that body out of the water. At last he plunged in himself, found it only chest-deep, and shoved the carcass over the mudslick bank. He did not know by then whether the man was alive or dead or much care. He knew only that he couldn't walk away and leave the job half finished.

The body was that of a fat, middle-aged Oriental, surely Chinese rather than Japanese, though Royland could not say why he thought so. His clothes were soaked rags except for a leather wallet the size of a cigar box which he wore on a wide cloth belt. Its sole content was a handsome blue-glazed porcelain bottle. Royland sniffed at it and reeled. Some kind of super-gin! He sniffed again, and then took a conservative gulp of the stuff. While he was still coughing he felt the bottle being removed from his hand. When he looked he saw the Chinese, eyes still closed, accurately guiding the neck of the bottle to his mouth. The Chinese drank and drank and drank, then returned the bottle to the wallet and finally opened his eyes.

"Honorable sir," said the Chinese in flat, California American speech, "you have deigned to save my unworthy life. May I supplicate your honorable name?"

"Ah, Royland. Look, take it easy. Don't try to get up; you shouldn't even talk."

Somebody screamed behind Royland: "There has been thieving of tomatoes! There has been smasheeng and deestruction of thee vines Chil-dren you, will bee weet-ness be-fore the Jappa-neese!"

Christ, now what?

Now a skinny black man, not a Negro, in a dirty loincloth, and beside him like a pan-pipes five skinny black loinclothed offspring in decending order. All were capering, pointing, and threatening. The Chinese groaned, fished in his tattered robes with one hand, and pulled out a soggy wad of bills. He peeled one off, held it out, and said: "Begone, pestilential barbarians from beyond Tian-Shang. My master and I give you alms, not tribute."

The Dravidian, or whatever he was, grabbed the bill and keened: "Een-suffee-cient for the terrible dommage! The Jappa-neese—"

The Chinese waved them away boredly. He said: "If my master will condescend to help me arise?"

Royland uncertainly helped him up. The man was wobbly, whether from the near-drowning or the terrific belt of alcohol he'd taken there was no knowing. They proceeded to the road, followed by shrieks to be careful about stepping on the vines.

On the road, the Chinese said: "My unworthy name is Li Po. Will my master deign to indicate in which direction we are to travel?"

"What's this master business?" Royland demanded. "If you're grateful, swell, but I don't *own* you."

"My master is pleased to jest," said Li Po. Politely,

face-saving and third-personing Royland until hell wouldn't have it, he explained that Royland, having meddled with the Celestial decree that Li Po should, while drunk, roll into the irrigation ditch and drown, now had Li Po on his hands, for the Celestial Ones had washed theirs of him. "As my master of course will recollect in a moment or two." Understandingly, he expressed his sympathy with Royland's misfortune in acquiring him as an obligation, especially since he had a hearty appetite, was known to be dishonest, and suffered from fainting fits and spasms when confronted with work.

"I don't *know* about all this," Royland said fretfully. "Wasn't there another Li Po? A poet?"

"Your servant prefers to venerate his namesake as one of the greatest drunkards the Flowery Kingdom has ever known," the Chinese observed. And a moment later he bent over, clipped Royland behind the knees so that he toppled forward and bumped his head, and performed the same obeisance himself, more gracefully. A vehicle went sputtering and popping by on the road as they kowtowed.

Li Po said reproachfully: "I humbly observe that my master is unaware of the etiquette our noble overlords exact. Such negligence cost the head of my insignificant elder brother in his twelfth year. Would my master be pleased to explain how he can have reached his honorable years without learning what babes in their cradles are taught?"

Royland answered with the whole truth. Li Po politely begged clarification from time to time, and a sketch of his mental horizons emerged from his questioning. That "magic" had whisked Royland forward a century or more he did not doubt for an instant, but he found it difficult to understand why the proper *fung shui* precautions had not been taken to avert a disastrous outcome to the God Food experiment. He suspected, from a description of Nahataspe's hut, that a simple wall at right angles to the door would have kept all really important demons out. When Royland described his escape from German territory to Japanese, and why he had effected it, he was very bland and blank. Royland judged that Li Po privately thought him not very bright for having left *any* place to come here.

And Royland hoped he was not right. "Tell me what it's like," he said.

"This realm," said Li Po, "under our benevolent and noble overlords, is the haven of all whose skin is not the bleached-bone hue which indicates the undying curse of the Celestial Ones. Hither flock men of Han like my unworthy self, and the sons of Hind beyond the Tian-Shang that we may till new soil and raise up sons, and sons of sons to venerate us when we ascend."

"What was that bit," Royland demanded, "about the bleached bones? Do they shoot, ah, white men on sight here, or do they not?"

Li Po said evasively: "We are approaching the village where I unworthily serve as fortune teller, doctor of *fung shui*, occasional poet and storyteller. Let my master have no fear about his color. This humble one will roughen his master's skin, tell a circumstantial and artistic lie or two, and pass his master off as merely a leper."

After a week in Li Po's village Royland knew that life was good there. The place was a wattle-and-clay settlement of about two hundred souls on the bank of an irrigation ditch large enough to be dignified by the name of "canal." It was situated nobody knew just where; Royland thought it must be the San Fernando Valley. The soil was thick and rich and bore furiously the year round. A huge kind of radish was the principal crop. It was too coarse to be eaten by man; the villagers understood that it was feed for chickens somewhere up north. At any rate they harvested the stuff, fed it through a great hand-powered shredder, and shade-cured the shreds. Every few days a Japanese of low caste would come by in a truck, they would load tons of the stuff onto it, and wave their giant radish goodbye forever. Presumably the chickens ate it, and the Japanese then ate the chickens.

The villagers ate chicken too, but only at weddings and

funerals. The rest of the time they ate vegetables which they cultivated, a quarter-acre to a family, the way other craftsmen facet diamonds. A single cabbage might receive, during its ninety days from planting to maturity, one hundred work hours from grandmother, grandfather, son, daughter, eldest grandchild, and on down to the smallest toddler. Theoretically the entire family line should have starved to death, for there are not one hundred energy hours in a cabbage; somehow they did not. They merely stayed thin and cheerful and hard-working and fecund.

They spoke English by Imperial decree; the reasoning seemed to be that they were as unworthy to speak Japanese as to paint the Imperial Chrysanthemum Seal on their houses, and that to let them cling to their old languages and dialects would have been politically unwise.

They were a mixed lot of Chinese, Hindus, Dravidians, and, to Royland's surprise, low-caste and outcaste Japanese; he had not known there were such things. Village tradition had it that a *samurai* named Ugetsu long ago said, pointing at the drunk tank of a Hong Kong jail, "I'll have that lot," and "that lot" had been the ancestors of these villagers transported to America in a foul hold practically as ballast and settled here by the canal with orders to start making their radish quota. The place was at any rate called The Ugetsu Village, and if some of the descendants were teetotallers, others like Li Po gave color to the legend of their starting point.

After a week the cheerful pretense that he was a sufferer from Housen's disease evaporated and he could wash the mud off his face. He had merely to avoid the upper-caste Japanese and especially the *samurai*. This was not exactly a stigma; in general it was a good idea for *everybody* to avoid the *samurai*.

In the village Royland found his first love and his first religion both false.

He had settled down; he was getting used to the Oriental work rhythm of slow, repeated, incessant effort; it did not surprise him any longer that he could count his ribs. When he ate a bowl of artfully arranged vegetables, the red of pimiento played off against the yellow of parsnip, a slice of pickled beet adding visual and olfactory tang to the picture, he felt full enough; he *was* full enough for the next day's feeble work in the field. It was pleasant enough to play slowly with a wooden mattock in the rich soil; did not people once buy sand so their children might do exactly what he did, and envy their innocent absorption? Royland was innocently absorbed, then, and the radish truck had collected six times since his arrival, when he began to feel stirrings of lust. On the edge of starvation (but who knew this? For everybody was) his mind was dulled, but not his loins. They burned, and he looked about him in the fields, and the first girl he saw who was not repulsive he fell abysmally in love with.

Bewildered, he told Li Po, who was also Ugetsu Village's go-between. The storyteller was delighted; he waddled off to seek information and returned. "My master's choice is wise. The slave on whom his lordly eye deigned to rest is known as Vashti, daughter of Hari Bose, the distiller. She is his seventh child and so no great dowry can be expected (I shall ask for fifteen kegs toddy, but would settle for seven), but all this humble village knows that she is a skilled and willing worker in the hut as in the fields. I fear she has the customary lamentable Hindu talent for concocting curries, but a dozen good beatings at the most should cause her to reserve it to appropriate occasions, such as visits from her mother and sisters."

So, according to the sensible custom of Ugetsu, Vashti came that night to the hut which Royland shared with Li Po, and Li Po visited with cronies by his master's puzzling request. He begged humbly to point out that it would be dark in the hut, so this talk of lacking privacy was inexplicable to say the least. Royland made it an order, and Li Po did not really object, so he obeyed it.

It was a damnably strange night during which Royland learned all about India's national sport and most highly developed art form. Vashti, if she found him weak on the theory

144

side, made no complaints. On the contrary, when Royland woke she was doing something or other to his feet.

"More?" he thought incredulously. "With *feet?*" He asked what she was doing. Submissively she replied: "Worshipping my lord husband-to-be's big toe. I am a pious and old-fashioned woman."

So she painted his toe with red paint and prayed to it, and then she fixed breakfast—curry, and excellent. She watched him eat, and then modestly licked his leavings from the bowl. She handed him his clothes, which she had washed while he still slept, and helped him into them after she helped him wash. Royland thought incredulously: "It's not possible! It must be a show, to sell me on marrying her—as if I had to be sold!" His heart turned to custard as he saw her, without a moment's pause, turn from dressing him to polishing his wooden rake. He asked that day in the field, roundabout fashion, and learned that this was the kind of service he could look forward to for the rest of his life after marriage. If the woman got lazy he'd have to beat her, but this seldom happened more than every year or so. We have good girls here in Ugetsu Village.

So an Ugetsu Village peasant was in some ways better off than anybody from "his time" who was less than a millionaire!

His starved dullness was such that he did not realize this was true for only half the Ugetsu Village peasants.

Religion sneaked up on him in similar fashion. He went to the part-time Taoist priest because he was a little bored with Li Po's current after-dinner saga. He could have sat like all the others and listened passively to the interminable tale of the glorious Yellow Emperor, and the beautiful but wicked Princess Emerald, and the virtuous but plain Princess Moon Blossom; it just happened that he went to the priest of Tao and got hooked hard.

The kindly old man, a toolmaker by day, dropped a few pearls of wisdom which, in his foggy starvation-daze, Royland did not perceive to be pearls of undemonstrable nonsense, and showed Royland how to meditate. It worked the first time.

Royland bunged right smack through into a two-hundred-proof state of *samadhi*—the Eastern version of self-hypnotized Enlightenment—that made him feel wonderful and all-knowing and left him without a hangover when it wore off. He had despised, in college, the type of people who took psychology courses and so had taken none himself; he did not know a thing about self-hypnosis except as just demonstrated by this very nice old gentleman. For several days he was offensively religious and kept trying to talk to Li Po about the Eightfold Way, and Li Po kept changing the subject.

It took murder to bring him out of love and religion.

At twilight they were all sitting and listening to the story-teller as usual. Royland had been there just one month and for all he knew would be there forever. He soon would have his bride officially; he knew he had discovered The Truth About the Universe by way of Tao meditation; why should he change? Changing demanded a furious outburst of energy, and he did not have energy on that scale. He metered out his energy day and night; one had to save so much for tonight's love play, and then one had to save so much for tomorrow's planting. He was a poor man; he could not afford to change.

Li Po had reached a rather interesting bit where the Yellow Emperor was declaiming hotly: "Then she shall die! Whoever dare transgress Our divine will—"

A flashlight began to play over their faces. They perceived that it was in the hand of a *samurai* with kimono and sword. Everybody hastily kowtowed, but the *samurai* shouted irritably (all *samurai* were irritable, all the time): "Sit up, you fools! I want to see your stupid faces. I hear there's a peculiar one in this flea-bitten dungheap you call a village."

Well, by now Royland knew his duty. He rose and with downcast eyes asked: "Is the noble protector in search of my unworthy self?"

"Ha!" the *samurai* roared. "It's true! A big nose!" He hurled the flashlight away (all *samurai* were nobly contemptuous of the merely material), held his scabbard in his left hand, and swept out the long curved sword with his right.

Li Po stepped forward and said in his most enchanting voice: "If the Heaven-born would only deign to heed a word from this humble—" What he must have known would happen happened. With a contemptuous backhand sweep of the blade the *samurai* beheaded him and Li Po's debt was paid.

The trunk of the storyteller stood for a moment and then fell stiffly forward. The *samurai* stooped to wipe his blade clean on Li Po's ragged robes.

Royland had forgotten much, but not everything. With the villagers scattering before him he plunged forward and tackled the *samurai* low and hard. No doubt the *samurai* was a Brown Belt judo master; if so he had nobody but himself to blame for turning his back. Royland, not remembering that he was barefoot, tried to kick the *samurai's* face in. He broke his worshipful big toe, but its untrimmed horny nail removed the left eye of the warrior and after that it was no contest. He never let the *samurai* get up off the ground; he took out his other eye with the handle of a rake and then killed him an inch at a time with his hands, his feet, and the clownish rustic's traditional weapon, a flail. It took easily half an hour, and for the final twenty minutes the *samurai* was screaming for his mother. He died when the last light left the western sky, and in darkness Royland stood quite alone with the two corpses. The villagers were gone.

He assumed, or pretended, that they were within earshot and yelled at them brokenly: "I'm sorry, Vashti. I'm sorry, all of you. I'm gong. Can I make you understand?

"Listen. You aren't living. This isn't life. You're not making anything but babies, you're not changing, you're not growing up. That's not enough! You've got to read and write. You can't pass on anything but baby stories like the Yellow Emperor by word of mouth. The village is growing. Soon your fields will touch the fields of Sukoshi Village to the west, and then what happens? You won't know what to do, so you'll fight with Sukoshi Village.

"Religion. No! It's just getting drunk the way you do it. You're set up for it by being half-starved and then you go into *samadhi* and you feel better so you think you understand everything. No! You've got to *do* things. If you don't grow up, you die. All of you.

"Women. *That's* wrong. It's good for the men, but it's wrong. Half of you are slaves, do you understand? Women are people too, but you use them like animals and you've convinced them it's right for them to be old at thirty and discarded for the next girl. For God's sake, can't you try to think of yourselves in their place?

"The breeding, the crazy breeding—it's got to stop. You frugal Orientals! But you aren't frugal; you're crazy drunken sailors. You're squandering the whole world. Every mouth you breed has got to be fed by the land, and the land isn't infinite.

"I hope some of you understood. Li Po would have, a little, but he's dead.

"I'm going away now. You've been kind to me and all I've done is make trouble. I'm sorry."

He fumbled on the ground and found the *samurai's* flashlight. With it he hunted the village's outskirts until he found the Japanese's buckboard car. He started the motor with its crank and noisily rolled down the dirt track from the village to the highway.

Royland drove all night, still westward. His knowledge of southern California's geography was inexact, but he hoped to hit Los Angeles. There might be a chance of losing himself in a great city. He had abandoned hope of finding present-day counterparts of his old classmates like Jimmy Ichimura; obviously they had lost out. Why shouldn't they have lost? The soldier-politicians had won the war by happenstance, so all power to the soldier-politicians! Reasoning under the great natural law *post hoc ergo propter hoc*, Tojo and his crowd had decided: fanatic feudalism won the war; therefore fanatic feudalism is a good thing, and it necessarily follows that the more fanatical and feudal it is, the better a thing it is. So you had Sukoshi Village, and Ugetsu Village; Ichi Village, Ni

Village, San Village, Shi Village, dotting that part of Great Japan formerly known as North America, breeding with the good old fanatic feudalism and so feudally averse to new thought and innovations that it made you want to scream at them—which he had.

The single weak headlight of his buckboard passed few others on the road; a decent feudal village is self-contained.

Damn them and their suicidal cheerfulness! It was a pleasant trait; it was a fool in a canoe approaching the rapids saying: "Chin up! Everything's going to be all right if we just keep smiling."

The car ran out of gas when false dawn first began to pale the sky behind him. He pushed it into the roadside ditch and walked on; by full light he was in a tumble-down, planless, evil-smelling, paper-and-galvanized-iron city whose name he did not know. There was no likelihood of him being noticed as a "white" man by anyone not specifically looking for him. A month of outdoor labor had browned him, and a month of artistically composed vegetable plates had left him gaunt.

The city was carpeted with awakening humanity. Its narrow streets were paved with sprawled-out men, women, and children beginning to stir and hawk up phlegm and rub their rheumy eyes. An open sewer-latrine running down the center of each street was casually used, ostrich-fashion—the users hid their own eyes while in action.

Every mangled variety of English rang in Royland's ears as he trod between bodies.

There had to be something more, he told himself. This was the shabby industrial outskirts, the lowest marginal-labor area. Somewhere in the city there was beauty, science, learning!

He walked aimlessly plodding until noon, and found nothing of the sort. These people in the cities were food-handlers, food-traders, food-transporters. They took in one another's washing and sold one another chop suey. They made automobiles (Yes! There were one-family automobile factories which probably made six buckboards a year, filing all metal parts by hand out of bar stock!) and orange crates and baskets and coffins; abacuses, nails, and boots.

The Mysterious East has done it again, he thought bitterly. The Indians-Chinese-Japanese won themselves a nice sparse area. They could have laid things out neatly and made it pleasant for everybody instead of for a minute speck of aristocracy which he was unable even to detect in this human soup . . . but they had done it again. They had bred irresponsibly just as fast as they could until the land was *full*. Only famines and pestilence could "help" them now.

He found exactly one building which owned some clear space around it and which would survive an earthquake or a flicked cigarette butt. It was the German Consulate.

I'll give them the Bomb, he said to himself. Why not? None of this is mine. And for the Bomb I'll exact a price of some comfort and dignity for as long as I live. *Let* them blow one another up! He climbed the consulate steps.

To the black-uniformed guard at the swastika-trimmed bronze doors he said: *"Whenn die Lichtstärke der von einer Fläche kommenden Strahlung dem Cosinus des Winkels zwischen Strahlrichtung und Flächennormalen proportional ist, so nennen wir die Fläche eine volkommen streunde Fläche."* Lambert's Law, Optics I. All the Goethe he remembered happened to rhyme, which might have made the guard suspicious.

Naturally the German came to attention and said apologetically: "I don't speak German. What is it, sir?"

"You may take me to the consul," Royland said, affecting boredom.

"Yes, sir. At once, sir. Er, you're an *agent* of course, sir?"

Royland said witheringly: *"Sicherheit, bitte!"*

"Yessir. This way, sir!"

The consul was a considerate, understanding gentleman. He was somewhat surprised by Royland's true tale, but said from time to time: "I see; I see. Not impossible. Please go on."

Royland concluded: "Those people at the sulfur mine were, I hope, unrepresentative. One of them at least complained that it was a dreary sort of backwoods assignment. I am simply gambling that there is intelligence in your Reich. I ask you to get me a real physicist for twenty minutes of conversation. You, Mr. Consul, will not regret it. I am in a position to turn over considerable information on—atomic power." So he had not been able to say it after all; the Bomb was still an obscene kick below the belt.

"This has been very interesting, Dr. Royland," said the consul gravely. "You referred to your enterprise as a gamble. I too shall gamble. What have I to lose by putting you *en rapport* with a scientist of ours if you prove to be a plausible lunatic?" He smiled to soften it. "Very little indeed. On the other hand, what have I to gain if your extraordinary story is quite true? A great deal. I will go along with you, doctor. Have you eaten?"

The relief was tremendous. He had lunch in a basement kitchen with the Consulate guards—a huge lunch, a rather nasty lunch of stewed *lungen* with a floured gravy, and cup after cup of coffee. Finally one of the guards lit up an ugly little spindle-shaped cigar, the kind Royland had only seen before in the caricatures of George Grosz, and as an afterthought offered one to him.

He drank in the rank smoke and managed not to cough. It stung his mouth and cut the greasy aftertaste of the stew satisfactorily. One of the blessings of the Third Reich, one of its gross pleasures. They were just people, after all—a certain censorious, busybody type of person with altogether too much power, but they were human. By which he meant, he supposed, members of Western Industrial Culture like him.

After lunch he was taken by truck from the city to an airfield by one of the guards. The plane was somewhat bigger than a B-29 he had once seen, and lacked propellers. He presumed it was one of the "jets" Dr. Piqueron had mentioned. His guard gave his dossier to a Luftwaffe sergeant at the foot of the ramp and said cheerfully: "Happy landings, fellow. It's all going to be all right."

"Thanks," he said. "I'll remember you, Corporal Collins. You've been very helpful." Collins turned away.

Royland climbed the ramp into the barrel of the plane. A bucket-seat job, and most of the seats were filled. He dropped into one on the very narrow aisle. His neighbor was in rags; his face showed signs of an old beating. When Royland addressed him he simply cringed away and began to sob.

The Luftwaffe sergeant came up, entered, and slammed the door. The "jets" began to wind up, making an unbelievable racket; further conversation was impossible. While the plane taxied, Royland peered through the windowless gloom at his fellow-passengers. They all looked poor and poorly.

God, were they so quickly and quietly airborne? They were. Even in the bucket seat, Royland fell asleep.

He was awakened, he did not know how much later, by the sergeant. The man was shaking his shoulder and asking him: "Any joolery hid away? Watches? Got some nice fresh water to sell to people that wanna buy it."

Royland had nothing, and would not take part in the miserable little racket if he had. He shook his head indignantly and the man moved on with a grin. He would not last long! —petty chiselers were leaks in the efficient dictatorship; they were rapidly detected and stopped up. Mussolini made the trains run on time, after all. (But naggingly Royland recalled mentioning this to a Northwestern University English professor, one Bevans. Bevans had coldly informed him that from 1931 to 1936 he had lived under Mussolini as a student and tourist guide, and therefore had extraordinary opportunities for observing whether the trains ran on time or not, and could definitely state that they did not; that railway timetables under Mussolini were best regarded as humorous fiction.)

And another thought nagged at him, a thought connected with a pale, scarred face named Bloom. Bloom was a young refugee physical chemist working on WEAPONS DEVELOPMENT TRACK I, and he was somewhat crazy, perhaps. Royland, on

TRACK III, used to see little of him and could have done with even less. You couldn't say hello to the man without it turning into a lecture on the horrors of Nazism. He had wild stories about "gas chambers" and crematoria which no reasonable man could believe, and was a blanket slanderer of the German medical profession. He claimed that trained doctors, certified men, used human beings in experiments which terminated fatally. Once, to try and bring Bloom to reason, he asked what sort of experiments these were, but the monomaniac had heard that worked out: piffling nonsense about reviving mortally frozen men by putting naked women into bed with them! The man was probably sexually deranged to believe that; he naively added that one variable in the series of experiments was to use women immediately after sexual intercourse, one hour after sexual intercourse, et cetera. Royland had blushed for him and violently changed the subject.

But that was not what he was groping for. Neither was Bloom's crazy story about the woman who made lampshades from the tattooed skin of concentration camp prisoners; there were people capable of such things, of course, but under no regime whatever do they rise to positions of authority; they simply can't do the work required in positions of authority because their insanity gets in the way.

"Know your enemy," of course—but making up pointless lies? At least Bloom was not the conscious prevaricator. He got letters in Yiddish from friends and relations in Palestine, and these were laden with the latest wild rumors supposed to be based on the latest word from "escapees."

Now he remembered. In the cafeteria about three months ago Bloom had been sipping tea with a somewhat shaking hand and rereading a letter. Royland tried to pass him with only a nod, but the skinny hand shot out and held him.

Bloom looked up with tears in his eyes: "It's cruel, I'm tellink you, Royland, it's cruel. They're not givink them the right to scream, to strike a futile blow, to sayink prayers *Kiddush ha Shem* like a Jew should when he is dyink for

Consecration of the Name! They trick them, they say they go to farm settlements, to labor camps, so four-five of the stink-ink bastards can handle a whole trainload Jews. They trick the clothes off of them at the camps, they sayink they delouse them. They trick them into room says showerbath over the door and then it too late to sayink prayers; *then goes on the gas.*"

Bloom had let go of him and put his head on the table between his hands. Royland had mumbled something, patted his shoulder, and walked on, shaken. For once the neurotic little man might have got some straight facts. That was a very circumstantial touch about expediting the handling of prisoners by systematic lies—always the carrot and the stick.

Yes, everybody had been so god-damn agreeable since he climbed the Consulate steps! The friendly door guard, the Consul who nodded and remarked that his story was not an impossible one, the men he'd eaten with—all that quiet optimism. "Thanks. I'll remember you, Corporal Collins. You've been very helpful." He had felt positively benign toward the corporal, and now remembered that the corporal had turned around *very* quickly after he spoke. *To hide a grin?*

The guard was working his way down the aisle again and noticed that Royland was awake. "Changed your mind by now?" he asked kindly. "Got a good watch, maybe I'll find a piece of bread for you. You won't need a watch where you're going, fella."

"What do you mean?" Royland demanded.

The guard said soothingly: "Why, they got clocks all over them work camps, fella. Everybody knows what time it is in them work camps. You don't need no watches there. Watches just get in the way at them work camps." He went on down the aisle, quickly.

Royland reached across the aisle and, like Bloom, gripped the man who sat opposite him. He could not see much of him; the huge windowless plane was lit only by half a dozen stingy bulbs overhead. "What are you here for?" he asked.

The man said shakily: "I'm a Laborer Two, see? A Two. Well, my father he taught me to read, see, but he waited until I was ten and knew the score? See? So I figured it was a family tradition, so I taught my own kid to read because he was a pretty smart kid, ya know? I figured he'd have some fun reading like I did, no harm done, who's to know, ya know? But I should of waited a couple years, I guess, because the kid was too young and got to bragging he could read, ya know how kids do? I'm from St. Louis, by the way. I should of said first I'm from St. Louis a track maintenance man, see, so I hopped a string of returning empties for San Diego because I was scared like you get."

He took a deep sigh. "Thirsty," he said. "Got in with some Chinks, nobody to trouble ya, ya stay outta the way, but then one of them cops-like seen me and he took me to the Consul place like they do, ya know? Had me scared, they always tole me illegal reading they bump ya off, but they don't, ya know? Two years work camp, how about that?"

Yes, Royland wondered. How about it?

The plane decelerated sharply; he was thrown forward. Could they brake with those "jets" by reversing the stream or were the engines just throttling down? He heard gurgling and thudding; hydraulic fluid to the actuators letting down the landing gear. The wheels bumped a moment later and he braced himself; the plane was still and the motors cut off seconds later.

Their Luftwaffe sergeant unlocked the door and bawled through it: "Shove that goddam ramp, willya?" The sergeant's assurance had dropped from him; he looked like a very scared man. He must have been a very brave one, really, to have let himself be locked in with a hundred doomed men, protected only by an eight-shot pistol and a chain of systematic lies.

They were herded out of the plane onto a runway of what Royland immediately identified as the Chicago Municipal Airport. The same reek wafted from the stockyards; the row of airline buildings at the eastern edge of the field was ancient and patched but unchanged; the hangars, though, were now something that looked like inflated plastic bags. A good trick. Beyond the buildings surely lay the dreary red-brick and painted-siding wastes of Cicero, Illinois.

Luftwaffe men were yapping at them: "Form up, boys; make a line! Work means freedom! Look tall!" They shuffled and were shoved into columns of fours. A snappy majorette in shiny satin panties and white boots pranced out of an administration building twirling her baton; a noisy march blared from louvers in her tall fur hat. Another good trick.

"Forward march, boys," she shrilled at them. "Wouldn't y'all just like to follow me?" Seductive smile and a wiggle of the rump; a Judas ewe. She strutted off in time to the music; she must have been wearing earstopples. They shuffled after her. At the airport gate they dropped their blue-coated Luftwaffe boys and picked up a waiting escort of a dozen black-coats with skulls on their high-peaked caps.

They walked in time to the music, hypnotized by it, through Cicero. Cicero had been bombed to hell and not rebuilt. To his surprise Royland felt a pang for the vanished Poles and Slovaks of Al's old bailiwick. There were *German* Germans, French Germans, and even Italian Germans, but he knew in his bones that there were no Polish or Slovakian Germans . . . And Bloom had been right all along.

Deathly weary after two hours of marching (the majorette was indefatigable) Royland looked up from the broken pavement to see a cockeyed wonder before him. It was a Castle; it was a Nightmare; it was the Chicago Parteihof. The thing abutted Lake Michigan; it covered perhaps sixteen city blocks. It frowned down on the lake at the east and at the tumbled acres of bombed-out Chicago at the north, west, and south. It was made of steel-reinforced concrete grained and grooved to look like medieval masonry. It was walled, moated, portcullised, towered, ramparted, crenellated. The death's-head guards looked at it reverently and the prisoners with fright. Royland wanted

only to laugh wildly. It was a Disney production. It was as
funny as Hermann Goering in full fig, and probably as deadly.

With a mumbo-jumbo of passwords, heils, and salutes they
were admitted, and the majorette went away, no doubt to
take off her boots and groan.

The most bedecked of the death's-head lined them up and
said affably: "Hot dinner and your beds presently, my boys;
first a selection. Some of you, I'm afraid, aren't well and
should be in sick bay. Who's sick? Raise your hands, please."

A few hands crept up. Stooped old men.

"That's right. Step forward, please." Then he went down
the line tapping a man here and there—one fellow with
glaucoma, another with terrible varicose sores visible through
the tattered pants he wore. Mutely they stepped forward.
Royland he looked thoughtfully over. "You're thin, my boy,"
he observed. "Stomach pains? Vomit blood? Tarry stools in
the morning?"

"Nossir!" Royland barked. The man laughed and continued down the line. The "sick bay" detail was marched off.
Most of them were weeping silently; they knew. Everybody
knew; everybody pretended that the terrible thing would not,
might not, happen. It was much more complex than Royland
had realized.

"Now," said the death's-head affably, "we require some
competent cement workers—"

The line of remaining men went mad. They surged forward
almost touching the officer but never stepping over an invisible line surrounding him. "Me!" some yelled. "Me! Me!"
Another cried: "I'm good with my hands, I can learn, I'm a
machinist too, I'm strong and young, I can learn!" A heavy
middle-aged one waved his hands in the air and boomed:
"Grouting and tile-setting! Grouting and tile-setting!" Royland
stood alone, horrified. They knew. They knew this was an
offer of real work that would keep them alive for a while.

He knew suddenly how to live in a world of lies.

The officer lost his patience in a moment or two, and whips

came out. Men with their faces bleeding struggled back into line. "Raise your hands, you cement people, and no lying, please. But you wouldn't lie, would you?" He picked half a dozen volunteers after questioning them briefly, and one of his men marched them off. Among them was the grouting-and-tile man, who looked pompously pleased with himself; such was the reward of diligence and virtue, he seemed to be proclaiming; pooh to those grasshoppers back there who neglected to learn A Trade.

"Now," said the officer casually, "we require some laboratory assistants." The chill of death stole down the line of prisoners. Each one seemed to shrivel into himself, become poker-faced, imply that he wasn't really involved in all this.

Royland raised his hand. The officer looked at him in stupefaction and then covered up quickly. "Splendid," he said. "Step forward, my boy. You," he pointed at another man. "You have an intelligent forehead; you look as if you'd make a fine laboratory assistant. Step forward."

"Please, no!" the man begged. He fell to his knees and clasped his hands in supplication. "Please no!" The officer took out his whip meditatively; the man groaned, scrambled to his feet, and quickly stood beside Royland.

When there were four more chosen, they were marched off across the concrete yard into one of the absurd towers, and up a spiral staircase and down a corridor, and through the promenade at the back of an auditorium where a woman screamed German from the stage at an audience of women. And through a tunnel and down the corridor of an elementary school with empty classrooms full of small desks on either side. And into a hospital area where the fake-masonry walls yielded to scrubbed white tile and the fake flagstones underfoot to composition flooring and the fake pinewood torches in bronze brackets that had lighted their way to fluorescent tubes.

At the door marked RASSENWISSENSCHAFT the guard rapped and a frosty-faced man in a laboratory coat opened up. "You requisitioned a demonstrator, Dr. Kalten," the guard said. "Pick any one of these."

Dr. Kalten looked them over. "Oh, this one, I suppose," he said. Royland. "Come in, fellow."

The Race Science Laboratory of Dr. Kalten proved to be a decent medical setup with an operating table, intricate charts of the races of men and their anatomical, mental, and moral makeups. There was also a phrenological head diagram and a horoscope on the wall, and an arrangement of glittering crystals on wire which Royland recognized. It was a model of one Hans Hoerbiger's crackpot theory of planetary formation, the *Welteislehre*.

"Sit there," the doctor said, pointing to a stool. "First I've got to take your pedigree. By the way, you might as well know that you're going to end up dissected for my demonstration in Race Science III for the Medical School, and your degree of cooperation will determine whether the dissection is performed under anaesthesia or not. Clear?"

"Clear, doctor."

"Curious—no panic. I'll wager we find you're a proto-Hamitoidal hemi-Nordic of at *least* degree five . . . but let's get on. Name?"

"Edward Royland."

"Birthdate?"

"July second, nineteen twenty-three."

The doctor threw down his pencil. "If my previous explanation was inadequate," he shouted, "let me add that if you continue to be difficult I may turn you over to my good friend Dr. Herzbrenner. Dr. Herzbrenner happens to teach interrogation technique at the Gestapo School. *Do—you—now—understand?*"

"Yes, doctor. I'm sorry I cannot withdraw my answer."

Dr. Kalten turned elaborately sarcastic. "How then do you account for your remarkable state of preservation at your age of approximately a hundred and eighty years?"

"Doctor, I am twenty-three years old. I have traveled through time."

"Indeed?" Kalten was amused. "And how was this accomplished?"

Royland said steadily: "A spell was put on me by a satanic Jewish magician. It involved the ritual murder and desanguination of seven beautiful Nordic virgins."

Dr. Kalten gaped for a moment. Then he picked up his pencil and said firmly: "You will understand that my doubts were logical under the circumstances. Why did you not give me the sound scientific basis for your surprising claim at once? Go ahead; tell me all about it."

He was Dr. Kalten's prize; he was Dr. Kalten's treasure. His peculiarities of speech, his otherwise-inexplicable absence of a birth number over his left nipple, when they got around to it the gold filling in one of his teeth, his uncanny knowledge of Old America, all now had a simple scientific explanation. He was from 1944. What was so hard to grasp about that? Any sound specialist knew about the lost Jewish Cabala magic, golems and such.

His story was that he had been a student Race Scientist under the pioneering master William D. Pully. (A noisy whack who used to barnstorm, the chaw-and-gallus belt with the backing of Deutches Neues Buro; sure enough they found him in Volume VII of the standard *Introduction to a Historical Handbook of Race Science*.) The Jewish fiends had attempted to ambush his master on a lonely road; Royland persuaded him to switch hats and coats; in the darkness the substitution was not noticed. Later in their stronghold he was identified, but the Nordic virgins had already been ritually murdered and drained of their blood, and it wouldn't keep. The dire fate destined for the master had been visited upon the disciple.

Dr. Kalten loved that bit. It tickled him pink that the sub-men's "revenge" on their enemy had been to precipitate him into a world purged of the sub-men entirely, where a Nordic might breathe freely!

Kalten, except for discreet consultations with such people as Old America specialists, a dentist who was stupefied by the gold filling, and a dermatologist who established that there was not and never had been a *geburtsnummer* on the subject examined, was playing Royland close to his vest. After a week it became apparent that he was reserving Royland for a grand unveiling which would climax the reading of a paper. Royland did not want to be unveiled; there were too many holes in his story. He talked with animation about the beauties of Mexico in the spring, its fair mesas, castus, and mushrooms. Could they make a short trip there? Dr. Kalten said they could not. Royland was becoming restless? Let him study, learn, profit by the matchless arsenal of the sciences available here in Chicago Parteihof. Dear old Chicago boasted distinguished exponents of the World Ice Theory, the Hollow World Theory, Dowsing, Homeopathic Medicine, Curative Folk Botany—

This last did sound interesting. Dr. Kalten was pleased to take his prize to the Medical School and introduce him as a protégé to Professor Albiani, of Folk Botany.

Albiani was a bearded gnome out of the Arthur Rackham illustrations for *Das Rheingold*. He loved his subject. "Mother Nature, the all-bounteous one! Wander the fields, young man, and with a seeing eye in an hour's stroll you will find the ergot that aborts, the dill that cools fever, the tansy that strengthens the old, the poppy that soothes the fretful teething babe!"

"Do you have any hallucinogenic Mexican mushrooms?" Royland demanded.

"We may," Albiani said, surprised. They browsed through the Folk Botany museum and pored over dried vegetation under glass. From Mexico there were peyote, the buttons and the root, and there was marihuana, root, stem, seed, and stalk. No mushrooms.

"They may be in the storeroom," Albiani muttered.

All the rest of the day Royland mucked through the store-room where specimens were waiting for exhibit space on some rotation plan. He went to Albiani and said, a little wild-eyed: "They're not there."

Albiani had been interested enough to look up the mushrooms in question in the reference books. "See?" he said happily, pointing to a handsome color plate of the mushroom: growing, mature, sporing, and dried. He read: " '. . . superstitiously called *God Food*,' " and twinkled through his beard at the joke.

"They're not there," Royland said.

The professor, annoyed at last, said: "There might be some uncatalogued in the basement. Really, we don't have room for everything in our limited display space—just the *interesting* items."

Royland pulled himself together and charmed the location of the department's basement storage space out of him, together with permission to inspect it. And, left alone for a moment, ripped the color plate from the professor's book and stowed it away.

That night Royland and Dr. Kalten walked out on one of the innumerable tower-tops for a final cigar. The moon was high and full; its light turned the cratered terrain that had been Chicago into another moon. The sage and his disciple from another day leaned their elbows on a crenellated rampart two hundred feet above Lake Michigan.

"Edward," said Dr. Kalten, "I shall read my paper tomorrow before the Chicago Academy of Race Science." The words were a challenge; something was wrong. He went on: "I shall expect you to be in the wings of the auditorium, and to appear at my command to answer a few questions from me and, if time permits, from our audience."

"I wish it could be postponed," Royland said.

"No doubt."

"Would you explain your unfriendly tone of voice, doctor?" Royland demanded. "I think I've been completely cooperative and have opened the way for you to win undying fame in the annals of Race Science."

"Cooperative, yes. Candid—I wonder? You see, Edward, a dreadful thought struck me today. I have always thought it amusing that the Jewish attack on Reverend Pully should have been for the purpose of precipitating him into the future and that it should have misfired.'' He took something out of his pocket: a small pistol. He aimed it casually at Royland. ''Today I began to wonder *why* they should have done so. Why did they not simply murder him, as they did thousands, and dispose of him in their secret crematoria, and permit no mention in their controlled newspapers and magazines of the disappearance?

''Now, the blood of seven Nordic virgins can have been no cheap commodity. One pictures with ease Nordic men patrolling their precious enclaves of humanity, eyes roving over every passing face, noting who bears the stigmata of the sub-men, and following those who do most carefully indeed lest race-defilement be committed with a look or an 'accidental' touch in a crowded street. Nevertheless the thing was done; your presence here is proof of it. It must have been done at enormous cost; hired Slavs and Negroes must have been employed to kidnap the virgins, and many of them must have fallen before Nordic rage.

''This merely to silence one small voice crying in the wilderness? *I—think—not.* I think, Edward Royland, or whatever your real name may be, that Jewish arrogance sent you, a Jew yourself, into the future as a greeting from the Jewry of that day to what it foolishly thought would be the triumphant Jewry of this. At any rate, the public questioning tomorrow will be conducted by my friend Dr. Herzbrenner, whom I have mentioned to you. If you have any little secrets, they will not remain secrets long. No, no! Do not move toward me. I shall shoot you disablingly in the knee if you do.''

Royland moved toward him and the gun went off; there was an agonizing hammer blow high on his left shin. He picked up Kalten and hurled him, screaming, over the parapet two hundred feet into the water. And collapsed. The pain was horrible. His shinbone was badly cracked if not broken through. There was not much bleeding; maybe there would be later.

He need not fear that the shot and scream would rouse the castle. Such sounds were not rare in the Medical Wing.

He dragged himself, injured leg trailing, to the doorway of Kalten's living quarters; he heaved himself into a chair by the signal bell and threw a rug over his legs. He rang for the diener and told him very quietly: "Go to the medical storeroom for a leg U-brace and whatever is necessary for a cast, please. Dr. Kalten has an interesting idea he wishes to work out."

He should have asked for a syringe of morphine—no he shouldn't. It might affect the time distortion.

When the man came back he thanked him and told him to turn in for the night.

He almost screamed getting his shoe off; his trouser leg he cut away. The gauze had arrived just in time; the wound was beginning to bleed more copiously. Pressure seemed to stop it. He constructed a sloppy walking cast on his leg. The directions on the several five-pound cans of plaster helped.

His leg was getting numb; good. His cast probably pinched some major nerve, and a week in it would cause permanent paralysis; who cared about *that?*

He tried it out and found he could get across the floor inefficiently. With a strong-enough bannister he could get downstairs but not, he thought, up them. That was all right. He was going to the basement.

God-damning the medieval Nazis and their cornball castle every inch of the way, he went to the basement; there he had a windfall. A dozen drunken SS men were living it up in a corner far from the censorious eyes of their company commander; they were playing a game which might have been called Spin the Corporal. They saw Royland limping and wept sentimental tears for poor ol' doc with a bum leg; they carried him two winding miles to the storeroom he wanted, and shot the lock off for him. They departed, begging him to call on ol' Company K any time, bes' fellas in Chicago, doc. Ol' Bruno here can tear the arm off a Latvik shirker with his bare hands, honest, doc! Jus' the way you twist a drumstick off a turkey. You wan' us to get a Latvik an' show you?

He got rid of them at last, clicked on the light, and began his search. His leg was now ice cold, painfully so. He rummaged through the uncatalogued botanicals and found after what seemed like hours a crate shipped from Jalasca. Royland opened it by beating its corners against the concrete floor. It yielded and spilled plastic envelopes; through the clear material of one he saw the wrinkled black things. He did not even compare them with the color plate in his pocket. He tore the envelope open and crammed them into his mouth, and chewed and swallowed.

Maybe there had to be a Hopi dancing and chanting, maybe there didn't have to be. Maybe one had to be calm, if bitter, and fresh from a day of hard work at differential equations which approximated the Hopi mode of thought. Maybe you only had to fix your mind savagely on what you desired, as his was fixed now. Last time he had hated and shunned the Bomb; what he wanted was a world without the Bomb. He had got it, all right!

. . . his tongue was thick and the fireballs were beginning to dance around him, the circling circles . . .

Charles Miller Nahataspe whispered: "Close. Close. I was so frightened."

Royland lay on the floor of the hut, his leg unsplinted, unfractured, but aching horribly. Drowsily he felt his ribs; he was merely slender now, no longer gaunt. He mumbled: "You were working to pull me back from this side?"

"Yes. You, you were there?"

"I was there. God, let me sleep."

He rolled over heavily and collapsed into complete unconsciousness.

When he awakened it was still dark and his pains were gone. Nahataspe was crooning a healing song very softly. He stopped when he saw Royland's eyes open. "Now you know about break-the-sky medicine," he said.

"Better than anybody. What time is it?"

"Midnight."

"I'll be going then." They clasped hands and looked into each other's eyes.

The jeep started easily. Four hour earlier, or possibly two months earlier, he had been worried about the battery. He chugged down the settlement road and knew what would happen next. He wouldn't wait until morning; a meteorite might kill him, or a scorpion in his bed. He would go directly to Rotschmidt in his apartment, defy Vrouw Rotschmidt and wake her man up to tell him about 56c, tell him we have the Bomb.

We have a symbol to offer the Japanese now, something to which they can surrender, and will surrender.

Rotschmidt would be philosophical. He would probably sigh about the Bomb: "Ah, do we ever act responsibly? Do we ever know what the consequences of our decisions will be?"

And Royland would have to try to avoid answering him very sharply: "Yes. This once we damn well do."

THE BIG FRONT YARD

BY CLIFFORD D. SIMAK (1904–1988)

ASTOUNDING SCIENCE FICTION
OCTOBER

Clifford Simak left us in 1988—we sometimes forget just how recent is the genre of science fiction—the first sf magazine, Amazing Stories—appeared in 1926, which means that a good (but declining) number of the first generation of readers and writers are still alive, are coterminous with the field itself.

Most of the first generation of writers could not change with the times and with the field and are justly forgotten today. Cliff Simak was one of the exceptions; here was a man who published his first story "The World of the Red Sun" in 1931 and wrote evolving, quality sf until shortly before his death over fifty years later, winning a Nebula Award as late as 1980. The Science Fiction Writers of America honored him (and themselves) by awarding him a Grand Master Nebula in 1976.

He is perhaps best known for the group of stories that make up the book City (1952), one of which, "Desertion" (1944) has to be one of the ten greatest sf stories ever written, but he produced much excellent work in his long career.

He was a moral man whose values found clear expression in his writing, and he will be missed. (MHG)

* * *

It is impossible to look forward without looking back and our view of the future is bound to be affected by our experience of the past.

During the "Age of Exploration" that began in the early 1400s, Europeans brought their ships to the coasts of other continents and that meant trade. On the whole everyone profits by trading, provided one side is not so strong that it steals and enslaves rather than trades.

But aside from that, trade sometimes has its bad aspects. The Indians of the Americas got smallpox from the Europeans, and they gave us tobacco in exchange. On the whole, Europeans may have gotten the worse of it. Smallpox has been eradicated, but smoking has not, and the number of people killed by smoking, either through its direct effect on the body or through its propensity for starting fires, is enormous—even among those who, themselves, do not smoke.

One wonders what difficulties extraterrestrial gifts might give rise to. Suppose you could build houses of materials that are impervious to weather or any kind of damage; that essentially last forever. You end up with structures that can never change. How do you get rid of such a structure if you get tired of it. How do you enjoy novelty or change of fashion or taste.

When immortality brings about changelessness, surely that is too high a price to pay, whether we're talking about human evolution or the diversity of technology. (IA)

Hiram Taine came awake and sat up in his bed.

Towser was barking and scratching at the floor.

"Shut up," Taine told the dog.

Towser cocked quizzical ears at him and then resumed the barking and scratching at the floor.

Taine rubbed his eyes. He ran a hand through his rat's-nest head of hair. He considered lying down again and pulling up the covers.

But not with Towser barking.

"What's the matter with you, anyhow?" he asked Towser, with not a little wrath.

"*Whuff,*" said Towser, industriously proceeding with his scratching at the floor.

"If you want out," said Taine, "all you got to do is open the screen door. You know how it is done. You do it all the time."

Towser quit his barking and sat down heavily, watching his master getting out of bed.

Taine put on his shirt and pulled on his trousers, but didn't bother with his shoes.

Towser ambled over to a corner, put his nose down to the baseboard and snuffled moistly.

"You got a mouse?" asked Taine.

"*Whuff,*" said Towser, most emphatically.

"I can't ever remember you making such a row about a mouse," Taine said, slightly puzzled. "You must be off your rocker."

It was a beautiful summer morning. Sunlight was pouring through the open window.

Good day for fishing, Taine told himself, then remembered that there'd be no fishing, for he had to go out and look up that old four-poster maple bed that he had heard about up Woodman way. More than likely, he thought, they'd want twice as much as it was worth. It was getting so, he told himself, that a man couldn't make an honest dollar. Everyone was getting smart about antiques.

He got up off the bed and headed for the living room.

"Come on," he said to Towser.

Tower came along, pausing now and then to snuffle into corners and to whuffle at the floor.

"You got it bad," said Taine.

Maybe it's a rat, he thought. The house was getting old.

He opened the screen door and Towser went outside.

"Leave that woodchuck be today," Taine advised him. "It's a losing battle. You'll never dig him out."

Towser went around the corner of the house.

Taine noticed that something had happened to the sign that hung on the post beside the driveway. One of the chains had become unhooked and the sign was dangling.

He padded out across the driveway slab and the grass, still wet with dew, to fix the sign. There was nothing wrong with it—just the unhooked chain. Might have been the wind, he thought, or some passing urchin. Although probably not an urchin. He got along with kids. They never bothered him, like they did some others in the village. Banker Stevens, for example. They were always pestering Stevens.

He stood back a way to be sure the sign was straight.

It read, in big letters:

HANDY MAN

And under that, in smaller lettering:

I fix anything

And under that:

ANTIQUES FOR SALE

What have you got to trade?

Maybe, he told himself, he'd ought to have two signs, one for his fix-it shop and one for antiques and trading. Some day, when he had the time, he thought, he'd paint a couple of new ones. One for each side of the driveway. It would look neat that way.

He turned around and looked across the road at Turner's Woods. It was a pretty sight, he thought. A sizable piece of woods like that right at the edge of town. It was a place for birds and rabbits and woodchucks and squirrels and it was full of forts built through generations by the boys of Willow Bend.

Some day, of course, some smart operator would buy it up

and start a housing development or something equally objectionable and when that happened a big slice of his own boyhood would be cut out of his life.

Towser came around the corner of the house. He was sidling along, sniffing at the lowest row of siding and his ears were cocked with interest.

"That dog is nuts," said Taine and went inside.

He went into the kitchen, his bare feet slapping on the floor.

He filled the teakettle, set it on the stove and turned the burner on underneath the kettle.

He turned on the radio, forgetting that it was out of kilter.

When it didn't make a sound, he remembered and, disgusted, snapped it off. That was the way it went, he thought. He fixed other people's stuff, but never got around to fixing any of his own.

He went into the bedroom and put on his shoes. He threw the bed together.

Back in the kitchen the stove had failed to work again. The burner beneath the kettle was still cold.

Taine hauled off and kicked the stove. He lifted the kettle and held his palm above the burner. In a few seconds he could detect some heat.

"Worked again," he told himself.

Some day, he knew, kicking the stove would fail to work. When that happened, he'd have to get to work on it. Probably wasn't more than a loose connection.

He put the kettle back onto the stove.

There was a clatter out in front and Taine went out to see what was going on.

Beasly, the Horton's yardboy-chauffeur-gardener-et cetera was backing a rickety old truck up the driveway. Beside him sat Abbie Horton, the wife of H. Henry Horton, the village's most important citizen. In the back of the truck, lashed on with ropes and half-protected by a garish red and purple quilt, stood a mammoth television set. Taine recognized it from of old. It was a good ten years out of date and still, by any

171

standard, it was the most expensive set ever to grace any home in Willow Bend.

Abbie hopped out of the truck. She was an energetic, bustling, bossy woman.

"Good morning, Hiram," she said. "Can you fix this set again?"

"Never saw anything that I couldn't fix," said Taine, but nevertheless he eyed the set with something like dismay. It was not the first time he had tangled with it and he knew what was ahead.

"It might cost you more than it's worth," he warned her. "What you really need is a new one. This set is getting old and—"

"That's just what Henry said," Abbie told him, tartly. "Henry wants to get one of the color sets. But I won't part with this one. It's not just TV, you know. It's a combination with radio and a record player and the wood and style are just right for the other furniture, and besides—"

"Yes, I know," said Taine, who'd heard it all before.

Poor old Henry, he thought. What a life the man must lead. Up at the computer plant all day long, shooting off his face and bossing everyone, then coming home to a life of petty tyranny.

"Beasly," said Abbie, in her best drill-sergeant voice, "you get right up there and get that thing untied."

"Yes'm," Beasly said. He was a gangling, loose-jointed man who didn't look too bright.

"And see you be careful with it. I don't want it all scratched up."

"Yes'm," said Beasly.

"I'll help," Taine offered.

The two climbed into the truck and began unlashing the old monstrosity.

"It's heavy," Abbie warned. "You two be careful of it."

"Yes'm," said Beasly.

It was heavy and it was an awkward thing to boot, but Beasly and Taine horsed it around to the back of the house and up the stoop and through the back door and down the basement stairs, with Abbie following eagle-eyed behind them, alert to the slightest scratch.

The basement was Taine's combination workshop and display room for antiques. One end of it was filled with benches and with tools and machinery and boxes full of odds and ends and piles of just plain junk were scattered everywhere. The other end housed a collection of rickety chairs, sagging bedposts, ancient highboys, equally ancient lowboys, old coal scuttles painted gold, heavy iron fireplace screens and a lot of other stuff that he had collected from far and wide for as little as he could possibly pay for it.

He and Beasly set the TV down carefully on the floor. Abbie watched them narrowly from the stairs.

"Why, Hiram," she said, excited, "you put a ceiling in the basement. It looks a whole lot better."

"Huh?" asked Taine.

"The ceiling. I said you put in a ceiling."

Taine jerked his head up and what she said was true. There was a ceiling there, but he'd never put it in.

He gulped a little and lowered his head, then jerked it quickly up and had another look. The ceiling was still there.

"It's not that block stuff," said Abbie with open admiration. "You can't see any joints at all. How did you manage it?"

Taine gulped again and got back his voice. "Something I thought up," he told her weakly.

"You'll have to come over and do it to our basement. Our basement is a sight. Beasly put the ceiling in the amusement room, but Beasly is all thumbs."

"Yes'm," Beasly said contritely.

"When I get the time," Taine promised, ready to promise anything to get them out of there.

"You'd have a lot more time," Abbie told him acidly, "if you weren't gadding around all over the country buying up that broken-down old furniture that you call antiques. Maybe you can fool the city folks when they come driving out here, but you can't fool me.''

"I make a lot of money out of some of it," Taine told her calmly.

"And lose your shirt on the rest of it," she said.

"I got some old china that is just the kind of stuff you are looking for," said Taine. "Picked it up just a day or two ago. Made a good buy on it. I can let you have it cheap."

"I'm not interested," she said and clamped her mouth tight shut.

She turned around and went back up the stairs.

"She's on the prod today," Beasly said to Taine. "It will be a bad day. It always is when she starts early in the morning."

"Don't pay attention to her," Taine advised.

"I try not to, but it ain't possible. You sure you don't need a man? I'd work for you cheap."

"Sorry, Beasly. Tell you what—come over some night soon and we'll play some checkers."

"I'll do that, Hiram. You're the only one who ever asks me over. All the others ever do is laugh at me or shout."

Abbie's voice came bellowing down the stairs. "Beasly, are you coming? Don't go standing there all day. I have rugs to beat."

"Yes'm," said Beasly, starting up the stairs.

At the truck, Abbie turned on Taine with determination: "You'll get that set fixed right away? I'm lost without it."

"Immediately," said Taine.

He stood and watched them off, then looked around for Towser, but the dog had disappeared. More than likely he was at the woodchuck hole again, in the woods across the road. Gone off, thought Taine, without his breakfast, too.

The teakettle was boiling furiously when Taine got back to the kitchen. He put coffee in the maker and poured in the water. Then he went downstairs.

The ceiling was still there.

He turned on all the lights and walked around the basement, staring up at it.

It was a dazzling white material and it appeared to be translucent—up to a point, that is. One could see into it, but he could not see through it. And there were no signs of seams. It was fitted neatly and tightly around the water pipes and the ceiling lights.

Taine stood on a chair and rapped his knuckles against it sharply. It gave out a bell-like sound, almost exactly as if he'd rapped a fingernail against a thinly-blown goblet.

He got down off the chair and stood there, shaking his head. The whole thing was beyond him. He had spent part of the evening repairing Banker Stevens' lawn mower and there'd been no ceiling then.

He rummaged in a box and found a drill. He dug out one of the smaller bits and fitted it in the drill. He plugged in the cord and climbed on the chair again and tried the bit against the ceiling. The whirling steel slid wildly back and forth. It didn't make a scratch. He switched off the drill and looked closely at the ceiling. There was not a mark upon it. He tired again, pressing against the drill with all his strength. The bit went *ping* and the broken end flew across the basement and hit the wall.

Taine stepped down off the chair. He found another bit and fitted it in the drill and went slowly up the stairs, trying to think. But he was too confused to think. That ceiling should not be up there, but there it was. And unless he went stark, staring crazy and forgetful as well, he had not put it there.

In the living room, he folded back one corner of the worn and faded carpeting and plugged in the drill. He knelt and started drilling in the floor. The bit went smoothly through the old oak flooring, then stopped. He put on more pressure and the drill spun without getting any bite.

And there wasn't supposed to be anything underneath that wood! Nothing to stop a drill. Once through the flooring, it should have dropped into the space between the joists.

Taine disengaged the drill and laid it to one side.

He went into the kitchen and the coffee now was ready. But before he poured it, he pawed through a cabinet drawer and found a pencil flashlight. Back in the living room he shone the light into the hole that the drill had made.

There was something shiny at the bottom of the hole.

He went back to the kitchen and found some day-old doughnuts and poured a cup of coffee. He sat at the kitchen table, eating doughnuts and wondering what to do.

There didn't appear, for the moment at least, much that he could do. He could putter around all day trying to figure out what had happened to his basement and probably not be any wiser than he was right now.

His money-making Yankee soul rebelled against such a horrid waste of time.

There was, he told himself, that maple four-poster that he should be getting to before some unprincipled city antique dealer should run afoul of it. A piece like that, he figured, if a man had any luck at all, should sell at a right good price. He might turn a handsome profit on it if he only worked it right.

Maybe, he thought, he could turn a trade on it. There was the table model TV set that he had traded a pair of ice skates for last winter. Those folks out Woodman way might conceivably be happy to trade the bed for a reconditioned TV set, almost like brand new. After all, they probably weren't using the bed and, he hoped fervently, had no idea of the value of it.

He ate the doughnuts hurriedly and gulped down an extra cup of coffee. He fixed a plate of scraps for Towser and set it outside the door. Then he went down into the basement and got the table TV set and put it in the pickup truck. As an afterthought, he added a reconditioned shotgun which would be perfectly all right if a man were careful not to use these far-reaching, powerful shells, and a few other odds and ends that might come in handy on a trade.

He got back late, for it had been a busy and quite satisfactory day. Not only did he have the four-poster loaded on the truck, but he had as well a rocking chair, a fire screen, a bundle of ancient magazines, an old-fashioned barrel churn, a walnut highboy and a Governor Winthrop on which some half-baked, slap-happy decorator had applied a coat of apple-green paint. The television set, the shotgun and five dollars had gone into the trade. And what was better yet, he'd managed it so well that the Woodman family probably was dying of laughter at this very moment about how they'd taken him.

He felt a little ashamed of it—they'd been such friendly people. They had treated him so kindly and had him stay for dinner and had sat and talked with him and shown him about the farm and even asked him to stop by if he went through that way again.

He'd wasted the entire day, he thought, and he rather hated that, but maybe it had been worth it to build up his reputation out that way as the sort of character who had softening of the head and didn't know the value of a dollar. That way, maybe some other day, he could do some more business in the neighborhood.

He heard the television set as he opened the back door, sounding loud and clear, and he went clattering down the basement stairs in something close to a panic. For now that he'd traded off the table model, Abbie's set was the only one downstairs and Abbie's set was broken.

It was Abbie's set, all right. It stood just where he and Beasly had put it down that morning and there was nothing wrong with it—nothing wrong at all. It was even televising color.

Televising color!

He stopped at the bottom of the stairs and leaned against the railing for support.

The set kept right on televising color.

Taine stalked the set and walked around behind it.

The back of the cabinet was off, leaning against a bench that stood behind the set, and he could see the innards of it glowing cheerily.

He squatted on the basement floor and squinted at the lighted innards and they seemed a good deal different from the way that they should be. He'd repaired the set many times before and he thought he had a good idea of what the working parts would look like. And now they all seemed different, although just how he couldn't tell.

A heavy step sounded on the stairs and a hearty voice came booming down to him.

"Well, Hiram, I see you got it fixed."

Taine jackknifed upright and stood there slightly frozen and completely speechless.

Henry Horton stood foursquarely and happily on the stairs, looking very pleased.

"I told Abbie that you wouldn't have it done, but she said for me to come over anyway— Hey, Hiram, it's in color! How did you do it, man?"

Taine grinned sickly. "I just got fiddling around," he said.

Henry came down the rest of the stairs with a stately step and stood before the set, with his hands behind his back, staring at it fixedly in his best executive manner.

He slowly shook his head. "I never would have thought," he said, "that it was possible."

"Abbie mentioned that you wanted color."

"Well, sure. Of course I did. But not on this old set. I never would have expected to get color on this set. How did you do it, Hiram?"

Taine told the solemn truth. "I can't rightly say," he said.

Henry found a nail keg standing in front of one of the benches and rolled it out in front of the old-fashioned set. He sat down warily and relaxed into solid comfort.

"That's the way it goes," he said. "There are men like you, but not very many of them. Just Yankee tinkerers. You keep messing around with things, trying one thing here and another there and before you know it you come up with something."

He sat on the nail keg, staring at the set.

"It's sure a pretty thing," he said. "It's better than the

color they have in Minneapolis. I dropped in at a couple of the places the last time I was there and looked at the color sets. And I tell you honest, Hiram, there wasn't one of them that was as good as this.''

Taine wiped his brow with his shirt sleeve. Somehow or other, the basement seemed to be getting warm. He was fine sweat all over.

Henry found a big cigar in one of his pockets and held it out to Taine.

"No, thanks. I never smoke."

"Perhaps you're wise," said Henry. "It's a nasty habit."

He stuck the cigar into his mouth and rolled it east to west.

"Each man to his own," he proclaimed expansively. "When it comes to a thing like this, you're the man to do it. You seem to think in mechanical contraptions and electronic circuits. Me, I don't know a thing about it. Even in the computer game, I still don't know a thing about it; I hire men who do. I can't even saw a board or drive a nail. But I can organize. You remember, Hiram, how everybody snickered when I started up the plant?''

"Well, I guess some of them did, at that."

"You're darn tooting they did. They went around for weeks with their hands up to their faces to hide smart-aleck grins. They said, what does Henry think he's doing, starting up a computer factory out here in the sticks; he doesn't think he can compete with those big companies in the east, does he? And they didn't stop their grinning until I sold a couple of dozen units and had orders for a year or two ahead.''

He fished a lighter from his pocket and lit the cigar carefully, never taking his eyes off the television set.

"You got something there," he said, judiciously, "that may be worth a mint of money. Some simple adaptation that will fit on any set. If you can get color on this old wreck, you can get color on any set that's made.''

He chuckled moistly around the mouthful of cigar. "If RCA knew what was happening here this minute, they'd go out and cut their throats.''

179

"But I don't know what I did," protested Taine.

"Well, that's all right," said Henry, happily. "I'll take this set up to the plant tomorrow and turn loose some of the boys on it. They'll find out what you have here before they're through with it."

He took the cigar out of his mouth and studied it intently, then popped it back in again.

"As I was saying, Hiram, that's the difference in us. You can do the stuff, but you miss the possibilities. I can't do a thing, but I can organize it once the thing is done. Before we get through with this, you'll be wading in twenty dollar bills clear up to your knees."

"But I don't have—"

"Don't worry. Just leave it all to me. I've got the plant and whatever money we may need. We'll figure out a split."

"That's fine of you," said Taine mechanically.

"Not at all," Henry insisted, grandly. "It's just my aggressive, grasping sense of profit. I should be ashamed of myself, cutting in on this."

He sat on the keg, smoking and watching the TV perform in exquisite color.

"You know, Hiram," he said, "I've often thought of this, but never got around to doing anything about it. I've got an old computer up at the plant that we will have to junk because it's taking up room that we really need. It's one of our early models, a sort of experimental job that went completely sour. It sure is a screwy thing. No one's ever been able to make much out of it. We tried some approaches that probably were wrong—or maybe they were right, but we didn't know enough to make them quite come off. It's been standing in a corner all these years and I should have junked it long ago. But I sort of hate to do it. I wonder if you might not like it—just to tinker with."

"Well, I don't know," said Taine.

Henry assumed an expansive air. "No obligation, mind you. You may not be able to do a thing with it—I'd frankly be surprised if you could, but there's no harm in trying.

Maybe you'll decide to tear it down for the salvage you can get. There are several thousand dollars worth of equipment in it. Probably you could use most of it one way or another.''

"It might be interesting," conceded Taine, but not too enthusiastically.

"Good," said Henry, with an enthusiasm that made up for Taine's lack of it. "I'll have the boys cart it over tomorrow. It's a heavy thing. I'll send along plenty of help to get it unloaded and down into the basement and set up."

Henry stood up carefully and brushed cigar ashes off his lap.

"I'll have the boys pick up the TV set at the same time," he said. "I'll have to tell Abbie you haven't got it fixed yet. If I ever let it get into the house, the way it's working now, she'd hold onto it."

Henry climbed the stairs heavily and Taine saw him out the door into the summer night.

Taine stood in the shadow, watching Henry's shadowed figure go across the Widow Taylor's yard to the next street behind his house. He took a deep breath of the fresh night air and shook his head to try to clear his buzzing brain, but the buzzing went right on.

Too much had happened, he told himself. Too much for any single day—first the ceiling and now the TV set. Once he had a good night's sleep he might be in some sort of shape to try to wrestle with it.

Towser came around the corner of the house and limped slowly up the steps to stand beside his master. He was mud up to his ears.

"You had a day of it, I see," said Taine. "And, just like I told you, you didn't get the woodchuck."

"Whoof," said Towser, sadly.

"You're just like a lot of the rest of us," Taine told him, severely. "Like me and Henry Horton and all the rest of us. You're chasing something and you think you know what you're chasing, but you really don't. And what's even worse, you have no faint idea of why you're chasing it.''

Towser thumped a tired tail upon the stoop.

Taine opened the door and stood to one side to let Towser in, then went in himself.

He went through the refrigerator and found part of a roast, a slice or two of luncheon meat, a dried-out slab of cheese and half a bowl of cooked spaghetti. He made a pot of coffee and shared the food with Towser.

Then Taine went back downstairs and shut off the television set. He found a trouble lamp and plugged it in and poked the light into the innards of the set.

He squatted on the floor, holding the lamp, trying to puzzle out what had been done to the set. It was different, of course, but it was a little hard to figure out in just what ways it was different. Someone had tinkered with the tubes and had them twisted out of shape and there were little white cubes of metal tucked here and there in what seemed to be an entirely haphazard and illogical manner—although, Taine admitted to himself, there probably was no haphazardness. And the circuit, he saw, had been rewired and a good deal of wiring had been added.

But the most puzzling thing about it was that the whole thing seemed to be just jury-rigged—as if someone had done no more than a hurried, patch-up job to get the set back in working order on an emergency and temporary basis.

Someone, he thought!

And who had that someone been?

He hunched around and peered into the dark corners of the basement and he felt innumerable and many-legged imaginary insects running on his body.

Someone had taken the back off the cabinet and leaned it against the bench and had left the screws which held the back laid neatly in a row upon the floor. Then they had jury-rigged the set and jury-rigged it far better than it had ever been before.

If this was a jury-job, he wondered, just what kind of job

would it have been if they had had the time to do it up in style?

They hadn't had the time, of course. Maybe they had been scared off when he had come home—scared off even before they could get the back on the set again.

He stood up and moved stiffly away.

First the ceiling in the morning—and now, in the evening, Abbie's television set.

And the ceiling, come to think of it, was not a ceiling only. Another liner, if that was the proper term for it, of the same material as the ceiling, had been laid beneath the floor, forming a sort of boxed-in area between the joists. He had struck that liner when he had tried to drill into the floor.

And what, he asked himself, if all the house were like that, too?

There was just one answer to it all: *There was something in the house with him!*

Towser had heard that *something* or smelled it or in some other manner sensed it and had dug frantically at the floor in an attempt to dig it out, as if it were a woodchuck.

Except that this, whatever it might be, certainly was no woodchuck.

He put away the trouble light and went upstairs.

Towser was curled up on a rug in the living room beside the easy chair and beat his tail in polite decorum in greeting to his master.

Taine stood and stared down at the dog. Towser looked back at him with satisfied and sleepy eyes, then heaved a doggish sigh and settled down to sleep.

Whatever Towser might have heard or smelled or sensed this morning, it was quite evident that as of this moment he was aware of it no longer.

Then Taine remembered something else.

He had filled the kettle to make water for the coffee and had set it on the stove. He had turned on the burner and it had worked the first time.

He hadn't had to kick the stove to get the burner going.

183

He woke in the morning and someone was holding down his feet and he sat up quickly to see what was going on.

But there was nothing to be alarmed about; it was only Towser who had crawled into bed with him and now lay sprawled across his feet.

Towser whined softly and his back legs twitched as he chased dream rabbits.

Taine eased his feet from beneath the dog and sat up, reaching for his clothes. It was early, but he remembered suddenly that he had left all of the furniture he had picked up the day before out there in the truck and should be getting downstairs where he could start reconditioning it.

Towser went on sleeping.

Taine stumbled to the kitchen and looked out of the window and there, squatted on the back stoop, was Beasly, the Horton man-of-all-work.

Taine went to the back door to see what was going on.

"I quit them, Hiram," Beasly told him. "She kept on pecking at me every minute of the day and I couldn't do a thing to please her, so I up and quit."

"Well, come on in," said Taine. "I suppose you'd like a bite to eat and a cup of coffee."

"I was kind of wondering if I could stay here, Hiram. Just for my keep until I can find something else."

"Let's have breakfast first," said Taine, "then we can talk about it."

He didn't like it, he told himself. He didn't like it at all. In another hour or so Abbie would show up and start stirring up a ruckus about how he'd lured Beasly off. Because, no matter how dumb Beasly might be, he did a lot of work and took a lot of nagging and there wasn't anyone else in town who would work for Abbie Horton.

"Your ma used to give me cookies all the time," said Beasly. "Your ma was a real good woman, Hiram."

"Yes, she was," said Taine.

"My ma used to say that you folks were quality, not like the rest in town, no matter what kind of airs they were always putting on. She said your family was among the first settlers. Is that really true, Hiram?''

"Well, not exactly first settlers, I guess, but this house has stood here for almost a hundred years. My father used to say there never was a night during all those years that there wasn't at least one Taine beneath its roof. Things like that, it seems, meant a lot to father.''

"It must be nice,'' said Beasly, wistfully, "to have a feeling like that. You must be proud of this house, Hiram.''

"Not really proud; more like belonging. I can't imagine living in any other house.''

Taine turned on the burner and filled the kettle. Carrying the kettle back, he kicked the stove. But there wasn't any need to kick it; the burner was already beginning to take on a rosy glow.

Twice in a row, Taine thought. This thing is getting better!

"Gee, Hiram,'' said Beasly, "this is a dandy radio.''

"It's no good,'' said Taine. "It's broke. Haven't had the time to fix it.''

"I don't think so, Hiram. I just turned it on. It's beginning to warm up.''

"It's beginning to— Hey, let me see!'' yelled Taine.

Beasly told the truth. A faint hum was coming from the tubes.

A voice came in, gaining in volume as the set warmed up. It was speaking gibberish.

"What kind of talk is that?'' asked Beasly.

"I don't know,'' said Taine, close to panic now.

First the television set, then the stove and now the radio!

He spun the tuning knob and the pointer crawled slowly across the dial face instead of spinning across as he remembered it, and station after station sputtered and went past.

He tuned in the next station that came up and it was strange lingo, too—and he knew by then exactly what he had.

Instead of a $39.50 job, he had here on the kitchen table an all-band receiver like they advertised in the fancy magazines.

He straightened up and said to Beasly: "See if you can get someone speaking English. I'll get on with the eggs."

He turned on the second burner and got out the frying pan. He put it on the stove and found eggs and bacon in the refrigerator.

Beasly got a station that had band music playing.

"How's that?" he asked.

"That's fine," said Taine.

Towser came out from the bedroom, stretching and yawning. He went to the door and showed he wanted out.

Taine let him out.

"If I were you," he told the dog, "I'd lay off that woodchuck. You'll have all the woods dug up."

"He ain't digging after any woodchuck, Hiram."

"Well, a rabbit, then."

"Not a rabbit, either. I snuck off yesterday when I was supposed to be beating rugs. That's what Abbie got so sore about."

Taine grunted, breaking eggs into the skillet.

"I snuck away and went over to where Towser was. I talked with him and he told me it wasn't a woodchuck or a rabbit. He said it was something else. I pitched in and helped him dig. Looks to me like he found an old tank of some sort buried out there in the woods."

"Towser wouldn't dig up any tank," protested Taine. "He wouldn't care about anything except a rabbit or a woodchuck."

"He was working hard," insisted Beasly. "He seemed to be excited."

"Maybe the woodchuck just dug his hole under this old tank or whatever it might be."

"Maybe so," Beasly agreed. He fiddled with the radio some more. He got a disk jockey who was pretty terrible.

Taine shoveled eggs and bacon onto plates and brought them to the table. He poured big cups of coffee and began buttering the toast.

"Dive in," he said to Beasly.

"This is good of you, Hiram, to take me in like this. I won't stay no longer than it takes to find a job."

"Well, I didn't exactly say—"

"There are times," said Beasly, "when I get to thinking I haven't got a friend and then I remember your ma, how nice she was to me and all—"

"Oh, all right," said Taine.

He knew when he was licked.

He brought the toast and a jar of jam to the table and sat down, beginning to eat.

"Maybe you got something I could help you with," suggested Beasly, using the back of his hand to wipe egg off his chin.

"I have a load of furniture out in the driveway. I could use a man to help me get it down into the basement."

"I'll be glad to do that," said Beasly. "I am good and strong. I don't mind work at all. I just don't like people jawing at me."

They finished breakfast and then carried the furniture down into the basement. They had some trouble with the Governor Winthrop, for it was an unwieldy thing to handle.

When they finally horsed it down, Taine stood off and looked at it. The man, he told himself, who slapped paint onto that beautiful cherrywood had a lot to answer for.

He said to Beasly: "We have to get the paint off that thing there. And we must do it carefully. Use paint remover and a rag wrapped around a spatula and just sort of roll it off. Would you like to try it?"

"Sure, I would. Say, Hiram, what will we have for lunch?"

"I don't know," said Taine. "We'll throw something together. Don't tell me you're hungry."

"Well, it was sort of hard work, getting all that stuff down here."

"There are cookies in the jar on the kitchen shelf," said Taine. "Go and help yourself."

When Beasly went upstairs, Taine walked slowly around

the basement. The ceiling, he saw, was still intact. Nothing else seemed to be disturbed.

Maybe that television set and the stove and radio, he thought, was just their way of paying rent to me. And if that were the case, he told himself, whoever they might be, he'd be more than willing to let them stay right on.

He looked around some more and could find nothing wrong.

He went upstairs and called to Beasly in the kitchen.

"Come on out to the garage, where I keep the paint. We'll hunt up some remover and show you how to use it."

Beasly, a supply of cookies clutched in his hand, trotted willingly behind him.

As they rounded the corner of the house they could hear Towser's muffled barking. Listening to him, it seemed to Taine that he was getting hoarse.

Three days, he thought—or was it four?

"If we don't do something about it," he said, "that fool dog is going to get himself wore out."

He went into the garage and came back with two shovels and a pick.

"Come on," he said to Beasly. "We have to put a stop to this before we have any peace."

Towser had done himself a noble job of excavation. He was almost completely out of sight. Only the end of his considerably bedraggled tail showed out of the hole he had clawed in the forest floor.

Beasly had been right about the tanklike thing. One edge of it showed out of one side of the hole.

Towser backed out of the hole and sat down heavily, his whiskers dripping clay, his tongue hanging out of the side of his mouth.

"He says that it's about time that we showed up," said Beasly.

Taine walked around the hole and knelt down. He reached down a hand to brush the dirt off the projecting edge of

Beasly's tank. The clay was stubborn and hard to wipe away, but from the feel of it the tank was heavy metal.

Taine picked up a shovel and rapped it against the tank. The tank gave out a clang.

They got to work, shoveling away a foot or so of topsoil that lay above the object. It was hard work and the thing was bigger than they had thought and it took some time to get it uncovered, even roughly.

"I'm hungry," Beasly complained.

Taine glanced at his watch. It was almost one o'clock.

"Run on back to the house," he said to Beasly. "You'll find something in the refrigerator and there's milk to drink."

"How about you, Hiram? Ain't you ever hungry?"

"You could bring me back a sandwich and see if you can find a trowel."

"What you want a trowel for?"

"I want to scrape the dirt off this thing and see what it is."

He squatted down beside the thing they had unearthed and watched Beasly disappear into the woods.

"Towser," he said, "this is the strangest animal you ever put to ground."

A man, he told himself, might better joke about it—if to do no more than keep his fear away.

Beasly wasn't scared, of course. Beasly didn't have the sense to be scared of a thing like this.

Twelve feet wide by twenty long and oval shaped. About the size, he thought, of a good-size living room. And there never had been a tank of that shape or size in all of Willow Bend.

He fished his jackknife out of his pocket and started to scratch away the dirt at one point on the surface of the thing. He got a square inch of free dirt and it was no metal such as he had ever seen. It looked for all the world like glass.

He kept on scraping at the dirt until he had a clean place as big as an outstretched hand.

It wasn't any metal. He'd almost swear to that. It looked

like cloudy glass—like the milk-glass goblets and bowls he was always on the lookout for. There were a lot of people who were plain nuts about it and they'd pay fancy prices for it.

He closed the knife and put it back into his pocket and squatted, looking at the oval shape that Towser had discovered.

And the conviction grew: Whatever it was that had come to live with him undoubtedly had arrived in the same contraption. From space or time, he thought, and was astonished that he thought it, for he'd never thought such a thing before.

He picked up his shovel and began to dig again, digging down this time, following the curving side of this alien thing that lay within the earth.

And as he dug, he wondered. What should he say about this—or should he say anything? Maybe the smartest course would be to cover it again and never breathe a word about it to a living soul.

Beasly would talk about it, naturally. But no one in the village would pay attention to anything that Beasly said. Everyone in Willow Bend knew Beasly was cracked.

Beasly finally came back. He carried three inexpertly-made sandwiches wrapped in an old newspaper and a quart bottle almost full of milk.

"You certainly took your time," said Taine, slightly irritated.

"I got interested," Beasly explained.

"Interested in what?"

"Well, there were three big trucks and they were lugging a lot of heavy stuff down into the basement. Two or three big cabinets and a lot of other junk. And you know Abbie's television set? Well, they took the set away. I told them that they shouldn't, but they took it anyway."

"I forgot," said Taine. "Henry said he'd send the computer over and I plumb forgot."

Taine ate the sandwiches, sharing them with Towser, who was very grateful in a muddy way.

Finished, Taine rose and picked up his shovel.

"Let's get to work," he said.

"But you got all that stuff down in the basement."

"That can wait," said Taine. "This job we have to finish."

It was getting dusk by the time they finished.

Taine leaned wearily on his shovel.

Twelve feet by twenty across the top and ten feet deep—and all of it, every bit of it, made of the milk-glass stuff that sounded like a bell when you whacked it with a shovel.

They'd have to be small, he thought, if there were many of them, to live in a space that size, especially if they had to stay there very long. And that fitted in, of course, for if they weren't small they couldn't now be living in the space between the basement joists.

If they were really living there, thought Taine. If it wasn't all just a lot of supposition.

Maybe, he thought, even if they had been living in the house, they might be there no longer—for Towser had smelled or heard or somehow sensed them in the morning, but by that very night he'd paid them no attention.

Taine slung his shovel across his shoulder and hoisted the pick.

"Come on," he said, "let's go. We've put in a long, hard day."

They tramped out through the brush and reached the road. Fireflies were flickering off and on in the woody darkness and the street lamps were swaying in the summer breeze. The stars were hard and bright.

Maybe they still were in the house, thought Taine. Maybe when they found out what Towser had objected to them, they had fixed it so he'd be aware of them no longer.

They probably were highly adaptive. It stood to good reason they would have to be. It hadn't taken them too long, he told himself grimly, to adapt to a human house.

He and Beasly went up the gravel driveway in the dark to put the tools away in the garage and there was something funny going on, for there was no garage.

There was no garage and there was no front on the house and the driveway was cut off abruptly and there was nothing but the curving wall of what apparently had been the end of the garage.

They came up to the curving wall and stopped, squinting unbelieving in the summer dark.

There was no garage, no porch, no front of the house at all. It was as if someone had taken the opposite corners of the front of the house and bent them together until they touched, folding the entire front of the building inside the curvature of the bent-together corners.

Taine now had a curved-front house. Although it was, actually, not as simple as all that, for the curvature was not in proportion to what actually would have happened in case of such a feat. The curve was long and graceful and somehow not quite apparent. It was as if the front of the house had been eliminated and an illusion of the rest of the house had been summoned to mask the disappearance.

Taine dropped the shovel and the pick and they clattered on the driveway gravel. He put his hand up to his face and wiped it across his eyes, as if to clear his eyes of something that could not possibly be there.

And when he took the hand away it had not changed a bit.

There was no front to the house.

Then he was running around the house, hardly knowing he was running, and there was a fear inside of him at what had happened to the house.

But the back of the house was all right. It was exactly as it had always been.

He clattered up the stoop with Beasly and Towser running close behind him. He pushed open the door and burst into the entry and scrambled up the stairs into the kitchen and went across the kitchen in three strides to see what had happened to the front of the house.

At the door between the kitchen and the living room he stopped and his hands went out to grasp the door jamb as he stared in disbelief at the windows of the living room.

It was night outside. There could be no doubt of that. He

had seen the fireflies flickering in the brush and weeds and the street lamps had been lit and the stars were out.

But a flood of sunlight was pouring through the windows of the living room and out beyond the windows lay a land that was not Willow Bend.

"Beasly," he gasped, "look out there in front!"

Beasly looked.

"What place is that?" he asked.

"That's what I'd like to know."

Towser had found his dish and was pushing it around the kitchen floor with his nose, by way of telling Taine that it was time to eat.

Taine went across the living room and opened the front door. The garage, he saw, was there. The pickup stood with its nose against the open garage door and the car was safe inside.

There was nothing wrong with the front of the house at all.

But if the front of the house was all right, that was all that was.

For the driveway was chopped off just a few feet beyond the tail end of the pickup and there was no yard or woods or road. There was just a desert—a flat, far-reaching desert, level as a floor, with occasional boulder piles and haphazard clumps of vegetation and all of the ground covered with sand and pebbles. A big blinding sun hung just above a horizon that seemed much too far away and a funny thing about it was that the sun was in the north, where no proper sun should be. It had a peculiar whiteness, too.

Beasly stepped out on the porch and Taine saw that he was shivering like a frightened dog.

"Maybe," Taine told him, kindly, "you'd better go back in and start making us some supper."

"But, Hiram—"

"It's all right," said Taine. "It's bound to be all right."

"If you say so, Hiram."

He went in and the screen door banged behind him and in a minute Taine heard him in the kitchen.

He didn't blame Beasly for shivering, he admitted to himself. It was a sort of shock to step out of your front door into an unknown land. A man might eventually get used to it, of course, but it would take some doing.

He stepped down off the porch and walked around the truck and around the garage corner and when he rounded the corner he was half prepared to walk back into familiar Willow Bend—for when he had gone in the back door the village had been there.

There was no Willow Bend. There was more of the desert, a great deal more of it.

He walked around the house and there was no back to the house. The back of the house now was just the same as the front had been before—the same smooth curve pulling the sides of the house together.

He walked on around the house to the front again and there was desert all the way. And the front was still all right. It hadn't changed at all. The truck was there on the chopped-off driveway and the garage was open and the car inside.

Taine walked out a way into the desert and hunkered down and scooped up a handful of the pebbles and the pebbles were just pebbles.

He squatted there and let the pebbles trickle through his fingers.

In Willow Bend there was a back door and there wasn't any front. Here, wherever here might be, there was a front door, but there wasn't any back.

He stood up and tossed the rest of the pebbles away and wiped his dusty hands upon his breeches.

Out of the corner of his eye he caught a sense of movement on the porch and there they were.

A line of tiny animals, if animals they were, came marching down the steps, one behind another. They were four inches high or so and they went on all four feet, although it was plain to see that their front feet were really hands, not feet.

They had ratlike faces that were vaguely human, with noses long and pointed. They looked as if they might have scales instead of hide, for their bodies glistened with a rippling motion as they walked. And all of them had tails that looked very much like the coiled-wire tails one finds on certain toys and the tails stuck straight up above them, quivering as they walked.

They came down the steps in single file, in perfect military order, with half a foot or so of spacing between each one of them.

They came down the steps and walked out into the desert in a straight, undeviating line as if they knew exactly where they might be bound. There was something deadly purposeful about them and yet they didn't hurry.

Taine counted sixteen of them and he watched them go out into the desert until they were almost lost to sight.

There go the ones, he thought, who came to live with me. They are the ones who fixed up the ceiling and who repaired Abbie's television set and jiggered up the stove and radio. And more than likely, too, they were the ones who had come to Earth in the strange milk-glass contraption out there in the woods.

And if they had come to Earth in that deal out in the woods, then what sort of place was this?

He climbed the porch and opened the screen door and saw the neat, six-inch circle his departing guests had achieved in the screen to get out of the house. He made a mental note that some day, when he had the time, he would have to fix it.

He went in and slammed the door behind him.

"Beasly," he shouted.

There was no answer.

Towser crawled from beneath the love seat and apologized.

"It's all right, pal," said Taine. "That outfit scared me, too."

He went into the kitchen. The dim ceiling light shone on the overturned coffee pot, the broken cup in the center of the

195

floor, the upset bowl of eggs. One broken egg was a white and yellow gob on the linoleum.

He stepped down on the landing and saw that the screen door in the back was wrecked beyond repair. Its rusty mesh was broken—exploded might have been a better word—and a part of the frame was smashed.

Taine looked at it in wondering admiration.

"The poor fool," he said. "He went straight through it without opening it at all."

He snapped on the light and went down the basement stairs. Halfway down he stooped in utter wonderment.

To his left was a wall—a wall of the same sort of material as had been used to put in the ceiling.

He stooped and saw that the wall ran clear across the basement, floor to ceiling, shutting off the workshop area.

And inside the workshop, what?

For one thing, he remembered, the computer that Henry had sent over just this morning. Three trucks, Beasly had said—three truckloads of equipment delivered straight into their paws!

Taine sat down weakly on the steps.

They must have thought, he told himself, that he was co-operating! Maybe they had figured that he knew what they were about and so went along with them. Or perhaps they thought he was paying them for fixing up the TV set and the stove and radio.

But to tackle first things first, why had they repaired the TV set and the stove and radio? As a sort of rental payment? As a friendly gesture? Or as a sort of practice run to find out what they could about this world's technology? To find, perhaps, how their technology could be adapted to the materials and conditions on this planet they had found?

Taine raised a hand and rapped with his knuckles on the wall beside the stairs and the smooth white surface gave out a pinging sound.

He laid his ear against the wall and listened closely and it seemed to him he could hear a low-key humming, but if so it was so faint he could not be absolutely sure.

Banker Stevens' lawn mower was in there, behind the wall, and a lot of other stuff waiting for repair. They'd take the hide right off him, he thought, especially Banker Stevens. Stevens was a tight man.

Beasly must have been half-crazed with fear, he thought. When he had seen those things coming up out of the basement, he'd gone clean off his rocker. He'd gone straight through the door without even bothering to try to open it and now he was down in the village yapping to anyone who'd stop to listen to him.

No one ordinarily would pay Beasly much attention, but if he yapped long enough and wild enough, they'd probably do some checking. They'd come storming up here and they'd give the place a going over and they'd stand goggle-eyed at what they found in front and pretty soon some of them would have worked their way around to sort of running things.

And it was none of their business, Taine stubbornly told himself, his ever-present business sense rising to the fore. There was a lot of real estate lying around out there in his front yard and the only way anyone could get to it was by going through the house. That being the case, it stood to reason that all that land out there was his. Maybe it wasn't any good at all. There might be nothing there. But before he had other people overrunning it, he'd better check and see.

He went up the stairs and out into the garage.

The sun was still just above the northern horizon and there was nothing moving.

He found a hammer and some nails and a few short lengths of plank in the garage and took them in the house.

Towser, he saw, had taken advantage of the situation and was sleeping in the gold-upholstered chair. Taine didn't bother him.

Taine locked the back door and nailed some planks across it. He locked the kitchen and the bedroom windows and nailed planks across them, too.

That would hold the villagers for a while, he told himself, when they came tearing up here to see what was going on.

He got his deer rifle, a box of cartridges, a pair of binoculars and an old canteen out of a closet. He filled the canteen at the kitchen tap and stuffed a sack with food for him and Towser to eat along the way, for there was no time to wait and eat.

Then he went into the living room and dumped Towser out of the gold-upholstered chair.

"Come on, Tows," he said. "We'll go and look things over."

He checked the gasoline in the pickup and the tank was almost full.

He and the dog got in and he put the rifle within easy reach. Then he backed the truck and swung it around and headed out, north, across the desert.

It was easy traveling. The desert was as level as a floor. At times it got a little rough, but no worse than a lot of the back roads he traveled hunting down antiques.

The scenery didn't change. Here and there were low hills, but the desert itself kept on mostly level, unraveling itself into that far-off horizon. Taine kept on driving north, straight into the sun. He hit some sandy stretches, but the sand was firm and hard and he had no trouble.

Half an hour out he caught up with the band of things—all sixteen of them—that had left the house. They were still traveling in line at their steady pace.

Slowing down the truck, Taime traveled parallel with them for a time, but there was no profit in it; they kept on traveling their course, looking neither right nor left.

Speeding up, Taine left them behind.

The sun stayed in the north, unmoving, and that certainly was queer. Perhaps, Taine told himself, this world spun on its axis far more slowly than the Earth and the day was longer. From the way the sun appeared to be standing still, perhaps a good deal longer.

Hunched above the wheel, staring out into the endless stretch of desert, the strangeness of it struck him for the first time with its full impact.

This was another world—there could be no doubt of that—another planet circling another star, and where it was in actual space no one on Earth could have the least idea. And yet, through some machination of those sixteen things walking straight in line, it also was lying just outside the front door of his house.

Ahead of him a somewhat larger hill loomed out of the flatness of the desert. As he drew nearer to it, he made out a row of shining objects lined upon its crest. After a time he stopped the truck and got out with the binoculars.

Through the glasses, he saw that the shining things were the same sort of milk-glass contraptions as had been in the woods. He counted eight of them, shining in the sun, perched upon some sort of rock-gray cradles. And there were other cradles empty.

He took the binoculars from his eyes and stood there for a moment, considering the advisability of climbing the hill and investigating closely. But he shook his head. There'd be time for that later on. He'd better keep on moving. This was not a real exploring foray, but a quick reconnaissance.

He climbed into the truck and drove on, keeping watch upon the gas gauge. When it came close to half full he'd have to turn around and go back home again.

Ahead of him he saw a faint whiteness above the dim horizon line and he watched it narrowly. At times it faded away and then came in again, but whatever it might be was so far off he could make nothing of it.

He glanced down at the gas gauge and it was close to the halfway mark. He stopped the pickup and got out with the binoculars.

As he moved around to the front of the machine he was puzzled at how slow and tired his legs were and then remembered—he should have been in bed many hours ago. He looked at his watch and it was two o'clock and that meant, back on Earth, two o'clock in the morning. He had been awake for more than twenty hours and much of that time he had been engaged in the backbreaking work of digging out the strange thing in the woods.

He put up the binoculars and the elusive white line that he had been seeing turned out to be a range of mountains. The great, blue, craggy mass towered up above the desert with the gleam of snow on its peaks and ridges. They were a long way off, for even the powerful glasses brought them in as little more than a misty blueness.

He swept the glasses slowly back and forth and the mountains extended for a long distance above the horizon line.

He brought the glasses down off the mountains and examined the desert that stretched ahead of him. There was more of the same that he had been seeing—the same floorlike levelness, the same occasional mounds, the self-same scraggy vegetation.

And a house!

His hands trembled and he lowered the glasses, then put them up to his face again and had another look. It was a house, all right. A funny-looking house standing at the foot of one of the hillocks, still shadowed by the hillock so that one could not pick it out with the naked eye.

It seemed to be a small house. Its roof was like a blunted cone and it lay tight against the ground, as if it hugged or crouched against the ground. There was an oval opening that probably was a door, but there was no sign of windows.

He took the binoculars down again and stared at the hillock. Four or five miles away, he thought. The gas would stretch that far and even if it didn't he could walk the last few miles into Willow Bend.

It was queer, he thought, that a house should be all alone out here. In all the miles he'd traveled in the desert he'd seen no sign of life beyond the sixteen little ratlike things that marched in single file, no sign of artificial structure other than the eight milk-glass contraptions resting in their cradles.

He climbed into the pickup and put it into gear. Ten

minutes later he drew up in front of the house, which still lay within the shadow of the hillock.

He got out of the pickup and hauled his rifle after him. Towser leaped to the ground and stood with his hackles up, a deep growl in his throat.

"What's the matter, boy?" asked Taine.

Towser growled again.

The house stood silent. It seemed to be deserted.

The walls were built, Taine saw, of rude, rough masonry crudely set together, with a crumbling, mudlike substance used in lieu of mortar. The roof originally had been of sod and that was queer, indeed, for there was nothing that came close to sod upon this expanse of desert. But now, although one could see the lines where the sod strips had been fitted together, it was nothing more than earth baked hard by the desert sun.

The house itself was featureless, entirely devoid of any ornament, with no attempt at all to soften the harsh utility of it as a simple shelter. It was the sort of thing that a shepherd people might have put together. It had the look of age about it; the stone had flaked and crumbled in the weather.

Rifle slung beneath his arm, Taine paced toward it. He reached the door and glanced inside and there was darkness and no movement.

He glanced back for Towser and saw that the dog had crawled beneath the truck and was peering out and growling.

"You stick around," said Taine. "Don't go running off."

With the rifle thrust before him, Taine stepped through the door into the darkness. He stood for a long moment to allow his eyes to become accustomed to the gloom.

Finally he could make out the room in which he stood. It was plain and rough, with a rude stone bench along one wall and queer unfunctional niches hollowed in another. One rickety piece of wooden furniture stood in a corner, but Taine could not make out what its use might be.

An old and deserted place, he thought, abandoned long ago. Perhaps a shepherd people might have lived here in some long-gone age, when the desert had been a rich and grassy plain.

There was a door into another room and as he stepped through it he heard the faint, far-off booming sound and something else as well—the sound of pouring rain! From the open door that led out through the back he caught a whiff of salty breeze and he stood there frozen in the center of that second room.

Another one!

Another house that led to another world!

He walked slowly forward, drawn toward the outer door, and he stepped out into a cloudy, darkling day with the rain streaming down from wildly racing clouds. Half a mile away, across a field of jumbled broken, iron-gray boulders, lay a pounding sea that raged upon the coast, throwing great spumes of angry spray high into the air.

He walked out from the door and looked up at the sky, and the rain drops pounded at his face with a stinging fury. There was a chill and a dampness in the air and the place was eldritch—a world jerked straight from some ancient Gothic tale of goblin and of sprite.

He glanced around and there was nothing he could see, for the rain blotted out the world beyond this stretch of coast, but behind the rain he could sense or seemed to sense a presence that sent shivers down his spine. Gulping in fright, Taine turned around and stumbled back again through the door into the house.

One world away, he thought, was far enough; two worlds away was more than one could take. He trembled at the sense of utter loneliness that tumbled in his skull and suddenly this long-forsaken house became unbearable and he dashed out of it.

Outside the sun was bright and there was welcome warmth. His clothes were damp from rain and little beads of moisture lay on the rifle barrel.

He looked around for Towser and there was no sign of the dog. He was not underneath the pickup; he was nowhere in sight.

Taine called and there was no answer. His voice sounded lone and hollow in the emptiness and silence.

He walked around the house, looking for the dog, and there was no back door to the house. The rough rock walls of the sides of the house pulled in with that funny curvature and there was no back to the house at all.

But Taine was not interested; he had known how it would be. Right now he was looking for his dog and he felt the panic rising in him. Somehow it felt a long way from home.

He spent three hours at it. He went back into the house and Towser was not there. He went into the other world again and searched among the tumbled rocks and Towser was not there. He went back to the desert and walked around the hillock and then he climbed to the crest of it and used the binoculars and saw nothing but the lifeless desert, stretching far in all directions.

Dead-beat with weariness, stumbling, half asleep even as he walked, he went back to the pickup.

He leaned against it and tried to pull his wits together.

Continuing as he was would be a useless effort. He had to get some sleep. He had to go back to Willow Bend and fill the tank and get some extra gasoline so that he could range farther afield in his search for Towser.

He couldn't leave the dog out here—that was unthinkable. But he had to plan, he had to act intelligently. He would be doing Towser no good by stumbling around in his present shape.

He pulled himself into the truck and headed back for Willow Bend, following the occasional faint impressions that his tires had made in the sandy places, fighting a half-dead drowsiness that tried to seal his eyes shut.

Passing the higher hill on which the milk-glass things had stood, he stopped to walk around a bit so he wouldn't fall asleep behind the wheel. And now, he saw, there were only seven of the things resting in their cradles.

But that meant nothing to him now. All that meant anything was to hold off the fatigue that was closing down upon him, to cling to the wheel and wear off the miles, to get back to Willow Bend and get some sleep and then come back again to look for Towser.

Slightly more than halfway home he saw the other car and watched it in numb befuddlement, for this truck that he was driving and the car at home in his garage were the only two vehicles this side of his house.

He pulled the pickup to a halt and tumbled out of it.

The car drew up and Henry Horton and Beasly and a man who wore a star leaped quickly out of it.

"Thank God we found you, man!" cried Henry, striding over to him.

"I wasn't lost," protested Taine. "I was coming back."

"He's all beat out," said the man who wore the star.

"This is Sheriff Hanson," Henry said. "We were following your tracks."

"I lost Towser," Taine mumbled. "I had to go and leave him. Just leave me be and go hunt for Towser. I can make it home."

He reached out and grabbed the edge of the pickup's door to hold himself erect.

"You broke down the door," he said to Henry. "You broke into my house and you took my car—"

"We had to do it, Hiram. We were afraid that something might have happened to you. The way that Beasly told it, it stood your hair on end."

"You better get him in the car," the sheriff said. "I'll drive the pickup back."

"But I have to hunt for Towser!"

"You can't do anything until you've had some rest."

Henry grabbed him by the arm and led him to the car and Beasly held the rear door open.

"You got any idea what this place is?" Henry whispered conspiratorially.

"I don't positively know," Taine mumbled. "Might be some other—"

Henry chuckled. "Well, I guess it doesn't really matter. Whatever it may be, it's put us on the map. We're in all the newscasts and the papers are plastering us in headlines and the town is swarming with reporters and cameramen and there are big officials coming. Yes, sir, I tell you, Hiram, this will be the making of us—"

Taine heard no more. He was fast asleep before he hit the seat.

He came awake and lay quietly in the bed and he saw the shades were drawn and the room was cool and peaceful.

It was good, he thought, to wake in a room you knew—in a room that one had known for his entire life, in a house that had been the Taine house for almost a hundred years.

Then memory clouted him and he sat bolt upright.

And now he heard it—the insistent murmur from outside the window.

He vaulted from the bed and pulled one shade aside. Peering out, he saw the cordon of troops that held back the crowd that overflowed his back yard and the back yards back of that.

He let the shade drop back and started hunting for his shoes, for he was fully dressed. Probably Henry and Beasly, he told himself, had dumped him into bed and pulled off his shoes and let it go at that. But he couldn't remember a single thing of it. He must have gone dead to the world the minute Henry had bundled him into the back seat of the car.

He found the shoes on the floor at the end of the bed and sat down upon the bed to pull them on.

And his mind was racing on what he had to do.

He'd have to get some gasoline somehow and fill up the truck and stash an extra can or two into the back and he'd have to take some food and water and perhaps his sleeping bag. For he wasn't coming back until he found his dog.

He got on his shoes and tied them, then went out into the living room. There was no one there, but there were voices in the kitchen.

He looked out the window and the desert lay outside, unchanged. The sun, he noticed, had climbed higher in the sky, but out in his front yard it was still forenoon.

He looked at his watch and it was six o'clock and from the way the shadows had been falling when he'd peered out of the bedroom window, he knew that it was 6:00 P.M. He realized with a guilty start that he must have slept almost around the clock. He had not meant to sleep that long. He hadn't meant to leave Towser out there that long.

He headed for the kitchen and there were three persons there—Abbie and Henry Horton and a man in military garb.

"There you are," cried Abbie merrily. "We were wondering when you would wake up."

"You have some coffee cooking, Abbie?"

"Yes, a whole pot full of it. And I'll cook up something else for you."

"Just some toast," said Taine. "I haven't got much time. I have to hunt for Towser."

"Hiram," said Henry, "this is Colonel Ryan, National Guard. He has his boys outside."

"Yes, I saw them through the window."

"Necessary," said Henry. "Absolutely necessary. The sheriff couldn't handle it. The people came rushing in and they'd have torn the place apart. So I called the governor."

"Taine," the colonel said, "sit down. I want to talk with you."

"Certainly," said Taine, taking a chair. "Sorry to be in such a rush, but I lost my dog out there."

"This business," said the colonel, smugly, "is vastly more important than any dog could be."

"Well, colonel, that just goes to show that you don't know Towser. He's the best dog I ever had and I've had a lot of them. Raised him from a pup and he's been a good friend all these years—"

"All right," the colonel said, "so he is a friend. But still I have to talk with you."

"You just sit and talk," Abbie said to Taine. "I'll fix up some cakes and Henry brought over some of that sausage that we get out on the farm."

The back door opened and Beasly staggered in to the accompaniment of a terrific metallic banging. He was carrying three empty five-gallon gas cans in one hand and two in the other hand and they were bumping and banging together as he moved.

"Say," yelled Taine, "what's going on here?"

"Now, just take it easy," Henry said. "You have no idea the problems that we have. We wanted to get a big gas tank moved through here, but we couldn't do it. We tried to rip out the back of the kitchen to get it through, but we couldn't—"

"You did what!"

"We tried to rip out the back of the kitchen," Henry told him calmly. "You can't get one of those big storage tanks through an ordinary door. But when we tried, we found that the entire house is boarded up inside with the same kind of material that you used down in the basement. You hit it with an ax and it blunts the steel—"

"But, Henry, this is my house and there isn't anyone who has the right to start tearing it apart."

"Fat chance," the colonel said. "What I would like to know, Taine, what is that stuff that we couldn't break through?"

"Now you take it easy, Hiram," cautioned Henry. "We have a big new world waiting for us out there—"

"It isn't waiting for you or anyone," yelled Taine.

"And we have to explore it and to explore it we need a stockpile of gasoline. So since we can't have a storage tank, we're getting together as many gas cans as possible and then we'll run a hose through here—"

"But, Henry—"

"I wish," said Henry sternly, "that you'd quit interrupting me and let me have my say. You can't even imagine the logistics that we face. We're bottlenecked by the size of a regulation door. We have to get supplies out there and we have to get transport. Cars and trucks won't be so bad. We can disassemble them and lug them through piecemeal, but a plane will be a problem.''

''You listen to me, Henry. There isn't anyone going to haul a plane through here. This house has been in my family for almost a hundred years and I own it and I have a right to it and you can't come in highhanded and start hauling stuff through it.''

''But,'' said Henry plaintively, ''we need a plane real bad. You can cover so much more ground when you have a plane.''

Beasly went banging through the kitchen with his cans and out into the living room.

The colonel sighed. ''I had hoped, Mr. Taine, that you would understand how the matter stood. To me it seems very plain that it's your patriotic duty to co-operate with us in this. The government, of course, could exercise the right of eminent domain and start condemnation action, but it would rather not do that. I'm speaking unofficially, of course, but I think it's safe to say the government would much prefer to arrive at an amicable agreement.''

''I doubt,'' Taine said, bluffing, not knowing anything about it, ''that the right to eminent domain would be applicable. As I understand it, it applies to buildings and to roads—''

''This is a road,'' the colonel told him flatly. ''A road right through your house to another world.''

''First,'' Taine declared, ''the government would have to show it was in the public interest and that refusal of the owner to relinquish title amounted to an interference in government procedure and—''

''I think,'' the colonel said, ''that the government can prove it is in the public interest.''

''I think,'' Taine said angrily, ''I better get a lawyer.''

''If you really mean that,'' Henry offered, ever helpful, ''and you want to get a good one—and I presume you do—I would be pleased to recommend a firm that I am sure would represent your interests most ably and be, at the same time, fairly reasonable in cost."

The colonel stood up, seething. "You'll have a lot to answer, Taine. There'll be a lot of things the government will want to know. First of all, they'll want to know just how you engineered this. Are you ready to tell that?"

"No," said Taine, "I don't believe I am."

And he thought with some alarm: They think that I'm the one who did it and they'll be down on me like a pack of wolves to find out just how I did it. He had visions of the FBI and the state department and the Pentagon and, even sitting down, he felt shaky in the knees.

The colonel turned around and marched stiffly from the kitchen. He went out the back and slammed the door behind him.

Henry looked at Taine speculatively.

"Do you really mean it?" he demanded. "Do you intend to stand up to them?"

"I'm getting sore," said Taine. "They can't come in here and take over without even asking me. I don't care what anyone may think, this is my house. I was born here and I've lived here all my life and I like the place and—"

"Sure," said Henry. "I know just how you feel."

"I suppose it's childish of me, but I wouldn't mind so much if they showed a willingness to sit down and talk about what they meant to do once they'd taken over. But there seems no disposition to even ask me what I think about it. And I tell you, Henry, this is different than it seems. This isn't a place where we can walk in and take over, no matter what Washington may think. There's something out there and we better watch our step—"

"I was thinking," Henry interrupted, "as I was sitting here, that your attitude is most commendable and deserving of support. It has occurred to me that it would be most unneighborly of me to go on sitting here and leave you in the fight alone. We could hire ourselves a fine array of legal talent and we could fight the case and in the meantime we could form a land and development company and that way we could make sure that this new world of yours is used the way it should be used.

"It stands to reason, Hiram, that I am the one to stand beside you, shoulder to shoulder, in this business since we're already partners in this TV deal."

"What's this about TV?" shrilled Abbie, slapping a plate of cakes down in front of Taine.

"Now, Abbie," Henry said patiently, "I have explained to you already that your TV set is back of that partition down in the basement and there isn't any telling when we can get it out."

"Yes, I know," said Abbie, bringing a platter of sausages and pouring a cup of coffee.

Beasly came in from the living room and went bumbling out the back.

"After all," said Henry, pressing his advantage, "I would suppose I had some hand in it. I doubt you could have done much without the computer I sent over."

And there it was again, thought Taine. Even Henry thought he'd been the one who did it.

"But didn't Beasly tell you?"

"Beasly said a lot, but you know how Beasly is."

And that was it, of course. To the villagers it would be no more than another Beasly story—another whopper that Beasly had dreamed up. There was no one who believed a word that Beasly said.

Taine picked up the cup and drank his coffee, gaining time to shape an answer and there wasn't any answer. If he told the truth, it would sound far less believable than any lie he'd tell.

"You can tell me, Hiram. After all, we're partners."

He's playing me for a fool, thought Taine. Henry thinks he can play anyone he wants for a fool and sucker.

"You wouldn't believe me if I told you, Henry."

210

"Well," Henry said, resignedly, getting to his feet, "I guess that part of it can wait."

Beasly came tramping and banging through the kitchen with another load of cans.

"I'll have to have some gasoline," said Taine, "if I'm going out for Towser."

"I'll take care of that right away," Henry promised smoothly. "I'll send Ernie over with his tank wagon and we can run a hose through here and fill up those cans. And I'll see if I can find someone who'll go along with you."

"That's not necessary. I can go alone."

"If we had a radio transmitter. Then you could keep in touch."

"But we haven't any. And, Henry, I can't wait. Towser's out there somewhere—"

"Sure, I know how much you thought of him. You go out and look for him if you think you have to and I'll get started on this other business. I'll get some lawyers lined up and we'll draw up some sort of corporate papers for our land development—"

"And, Hiram," Abbie said, "will you do something for me, please?"

"Why, certainly," said Taine.

"Would you speak to Beasly. It's senseless the way he's acting. There wasn't any call for him to up and leave us. I might have been a little sharp with him, but he's so simpleminded he's infuriating. He ran off and spent half a day helping Towser at digging out that woodchuck and—"

"I'll speak to him," said Taine.

"Thanks, Hiram. He'll listen to you. You're the only one he'll listen to. And I wish you could have fixed my TV set before all this came about. I'm just lost without it. It leaves a hole in the living room. It matched my other furniture, you know."

"Yes, I know," said Taine.

"Coming, Abbie?" Henry asked, standing at the door.

He lifted a hand in a confidential farewell to Taine. "I'll see you later, Hiram. I'll get it all fixed up."

I just bet you will, thought Taine.

He went back to the table, after they were gone, and sat down heavily in a chair.

The front door slammed and Beasly came panting in, excited.

"Towser's back!" he yelled. "He's coming back and he's driving in the biggest woodchuck you ever clapped your eyes on."

Taine leaped to his feet.

"Woodchuck! That's an alien planet. It hasn't any woodchucks."

"You come and see," yelled Beasly.

He turned and raced back out again, with Taine following close behind.

It certainly looked considerably like a woodchuck—a sort of man-size woodchuck. More like a woodchuck out of a children's book, perhaps, for it was walking on its hind legs and trying to look dignified even while it kept a weather eye on Towser.

Towser was back a hundred feet or so, keeping a wary distance from the massive chuck. He had the pose of a good sheepherding dog, walking in a crouch, alert to head off any break that the chuck might make.

The chuck came up close to the house and stopped. Then it did an about-face so that it looked back across the desert and it hunkered down.

It swung its massive head to gaze at Beasly and Taine and in the limpid brown eyes Taine saw more than the eyes of an animal.

Taine walked swiftly out and picked up the dog in his arms and hugged him tight against him. Towser twisted his head around and slapped a sloppy tongue across his master's face.

Taine stood with the dog in his arms and looked at the man-size chuck and felt a great relief and an utter thankfulness.

Everything was all right now, he thought. Towser had come back.

He headed for the house and out into the kitchen.

He put Towser down and got a dish and filled it at the tap. He placed it on the floor and Towser lapped at it thirstily, slopping water all over the linoleum.

"Take it easy, there," warned Taine. "You don't want to overdo it."

He hunted in the refrigerator and found some scraps and put them in Towser's dish.

Towser wagged his tail with doggish happiness.

"By rights," said Taine, "I ought to take a rope to you, running off like that."

Beasly came ambling in.

"That chuck is a friendly cuss," he announced. "He's waiting for someone."

"That's nice," said Taine, paying no attention.

He glanced at the clock.

"It's seven-thirty," he said. "We can catch the news. You want to get it, Beasly?"

"Sure. I know right where to get it. That fellow from New York."

"That's the one," said Taine.

He walked into the living room and looked out the window. The man-size chuck had not moved. He was sitting with his back to the house, looking back the way he'd come.

Waiting for someone, Beasly had said, and it looked as if he might be, but probably it was all just in Beasly's head.

And if he were waiting for someone, Taine wondered, who might that someone be? *What* might that someone be? Certainly by now the word had spread out that there was a door into another world. And how many doors, he wondered, had been opened through the ages?

Henry had said that there was a big new world out there waiting for Earthmen to move in. And that wasn't it at all. It was the other way around.

The voice of the news commentator came blasting from the radio in the middle of a sentence:

". . . finally got into the act. Radio Moscow said this evening that the Soviet delegate will make representations in the U.N. tomorrow for the internationalization of this other world and the gateway to it.

"From that gateway itself, the home of a man named Hiram Taine, there is no news. Complete security had been clamped down and a cordon of troops form a solid wall around the house, holding back the crowds. Attempts to telephone the residence are blocked by a curt voice which says that no calls are being accepted for that number. And Taine himself has not stepped from the house."

Taine walked back into the kitchen and sat down.

"He's talking about you," Beasly said importantly.

"Rumor circulated this morning that Taine, a quiet village repair man and dealer in antiques, and until yesterday a relative unknown, had finally returned from a trip which he made out into this new and unknown land. But what he found, if anything, no one yet can say. Nor is there any further information about this other place beyond the fact that it is a desert and, to the moment, lifeless.

"A small flurry of excitement was occasioned late yesterday by the finding of some strange object in the woods across the road from the residence, but this area likewise was swiftly cordoned off and to the moment Colonel Ryan, who commands the troops, will say nothing of what actually was found.

"Mystery man of the entire situation is one Henry Horton, who seems to be the only unofficial person to have entry to the Taine house. Horton, questioned earlier today, had little to say, but managed to suggest an air of great conspiracy. He hinted he and Taine were partners in some mysterious venture and left hanging in midair the half impression that he and Taine had collaborated in opening the new world.

"Horton, it is interesting to note, operates a small computer plant and it is understood on good authority that only recently he delivered a computer to Taine, or at least some sort of machine to which considerable mystery is attached. One story is that this particular machine had been in the process of development for six or seven years.

"Some of the answers to the matter of how all this did happen and what actually did happen must wait upon the findings of a team of scientists who left Washington this evening after an all-day conference at the White House, which was attended by representatives from the military, the state department, the security division and the special weapons section.

"Throughout the world the impact of what happened yesterday at Willow Bend can only be compared to the sensation of the news, almost twenty years ago, of the dropping of the first atomic bomb. There is some tendency among many observers to believe that the implications of Willow Bend, in fact, may be even more earth-shaking than were those at Hiroshima.

"Washington insists, as is only natural, that this matter is of internal concern only and that it intends to handle the situation as it best affects the national welfare.

"But abroad there is a rising storm of insistence that this is not a matter of national policy concerning one nation, but that it necessarily must be a matter of worldwide concern.

"There is an unconfirmed report that a U.N. observer will arrive in Willow Bend almost momentarily. France, Britain, Bolivia, Mexico and India have already requested permission of Washington to send observers to the scene and other nations undoubtedly plan to file similar requests.

"The world sits on edge tonight, waiting for the word from Willow Bend and—"

Taine reached out and clicked the radio to silence.

"From the sound of it," said Beasly, "we're going to be overrun by a batch of foreigners."

Yes, thought Taine, there might be a batch of foreigners,

but not exactly in the sense that Beasly meant. The use of the word, he told himself, so far as any human was concerned, must be outdated now. No man of Earth ever again could be called a foreigner with alien life next door—literally next door. What were the people of the stone house?

And perhaps not the alien life of one planet only, but the alien life of many. For he himself had found another door into yet another planet and there might be many more such doors and what would these other worlds be like, and what was the purpose of the doors?

Someone, *something*, had found a way of going to another planet short of spanning light-years of lonely space—a simpler and a shorter way than flying through the gulfs of space. And once the way was open, then the way stayed open and it was as easy as walking from one room to another.

But one thing—one ridiculous thing—kept puzzling him and that was the spinning and the movement of the connected planets, of all the planets that must be linked together. You could not, he argued, establish solid, factual links between two objects that move independently of one another.

And yet, a couple of days ago, he would have contended just as stolidly that the whole idea on the face of it was fantastic and impossible. Still it had been done. And once one impossibility was accomplished, what logical man could say with sincerity that the second could not be?

The doorbell rang and he got up to answer it.

It was Ernie, the oil man.

"Henry said you wanted some gas and I came to tell you I can't get it until morning."

"That's all right," said Taine. "I don't need it now."

And swiftly slammed the door.

He leaned against it, thinking: I'll have to face them sometime. I can't keep the door locked against the world. Sometime, soon or late, the Earth and I will have to have this out.

And it was foolish, he thought, for him to think like this, but that was the way it was.

He had something here that the Earth demanded; something that Earth wanted or thought it wanted. And yet, in the last analysis, it was his responsibility. It had happened on his land, it had happened in his house; unwittingly, perhaps, he'd even aided and abetted it.

And the land and house are mine, he fiercely told himself, and that world out there was an extension of his yard. No matter how far or where it went, an extension of his yard.

Beasly had left the kitchen and Taine walked into the living room. Towser was curled up and snoring gently in the gold-upholstered chair.

Taine decided he would let him stay there. After all, he thought, Towser had won the right to sleep anywhere he wished.

He walked past the chair to the window and the desert stretched to its far horizon and there before the window sat the man-size woodchuck and Beasly side by side, with their backs turned to the window and staring out across the desert.

Somehow it seemed natural that the chuck and Beasly should be sitting there together—the two of them, it appeared to Taine, might have a lot in common.

And it was a good beginning—that a man and an alien creature from this other world should sit down companionably together.

He tried to envision the setup of these linked worlds, of which Earth was now a part, and the possibilities that lay inherent in the fact of linkage rolled thunder through his brain.

There would be contact between the Earth and these other worlds and what would come of it?

And come to think of it, the contact had been made already, but so naturally, so undramatically, that it failed to register as a great, important meeting. For Beasly and the chuck out there were contact and if it all should go like that, there was absolutely nothing for one to worry over.

This was no haphazard business, he reminded himself. It had been planned and executed with the smoothness of long practice. This was not the first world to be opened and it would not be the last.

The little ratlike things had spanned space—how many light-years of space one could not even guess—in the vehicle which he had unearthed out in the woods. They then had buried it, perhaps as a child might hide a dish by shoving it into a pile of sand. Then they had come to this very house and had set up the apparatus that had made this house a tunnel between one world and another. And once that had been done, the need of crossing space had been canceled out forever. There need be but one crossing and that one crossing would serve to link the planets.

And once the job was done the little ratlike things had left, but not before they had made certain that this gateway to their planet would stand against no matter what assault. They had sheathed the house inside the studdings with a wonder-material that would resist an ax and that, undoubtedly, would resist much more than a simple ax.

And they had marched in drill-order single file out to the hill where eight more of the space machines had rested in their cradles. And now there were only seven there, in their cradles on the hill, and the ratlike things were gone and, perhaps, in time to come, they'd land on another planet and another doorway would be opened, a link to yet another world.

But more, Taine thought, than the linking of mere worlds. It would be, as well, the linking of the peoples of those worlds.

The little ratlike creatures were the explorers and the pioneers who sought out other Earthlike planets and the creature waiting with Beasly just outside the window must also serve its purpose and perhaps in time to come there would be a purpose which man would also serve.

He turned away from the window and looked around the

room and the room was exactly as it had been ever since he could remember it. With all the change outside, with all that was happening outside, the room remained unchanged.

This is the reality, thought Taine, this is all the reality there is. Whatever else may happen, this is where I stand—this room with its fireplace blackened by many winter fires, the bookshelves with the old thumbed volumes, the easy-chair, the ancient worn carpet—worn by beloved and unforgotten feet through the many years.

And this also, he knew, was the lull before the storm.

In just a little while the brass would start arriving—the team of scientists, the governmental functionaries, the military, the observers from the other countries, the officials from the U.N.

And against all these, he realized, he stood weaponless and shorn of his strength. No matter what a man might say or think, he could not stand off the world.

This was the last day that this would be the Taine house. After almost a hundred years, it would have another destiny.

And for the first time in all those years there'd be no Taine asleep beneath its roof.

He stood looking at the fireplace and the shelves of books and he sensed the old, pale ghosts walking in the room and he lifted a hesitant hand as if to wave farewell, not only to the ghosts but to the room as well. But before he got it up, he dropped it to his side.

What was the use, he thought.

He went out to the porch and sat down on the steps.

Beasly heard him and turned around.

"He's nice," he said to Taine, patting the chuck upon the back. "He's exactly like a great big teddy bear."

"Yes, I see," said Taine.

"And best of all, I can talk with him."

"Yes, I know," said Taine, remembering that Beasly could talk with Towser, too.

He wondered what it would be like to live in the simple world of Beasly. At times, he decided, it would be comfortable.

The ratlike things had come in the spaceship, but why had they come to Willow Bend, why had they picked this house, the only house in all the village where they would have found the equipment that they needed to build their apparatus so easily and so quickly? For there was no doubt that they had cannibalized the computer to get the equipment they needed. In that, at least, Henry had been right. Thinking back on it, Henry, after all, had played quite a part in it.

Could they have foreseen that on this particular week in this particular house the probability of quickly and easily doing what they had come to do had stood very high?

Did they, with all their other talents and technology, have clairvoyance as well?

"There's someone coming," Beasly said.

"I don't see a thing."

"Neither do I," said Beasly, "but Chuck told me that he saw them."

"Told you!"

"I told you we been talking. There, I can see them too."

They were far off, but they were coming fast—three dots rode rapidly out of the desert.

He sat and watched them come and he thought of going in to get the rifle, but he didn't stir from his seat upon the steps. The rifle would do no good, he told himself. It would be a senseless thing to get it; more than that, a senseless attitude. The least that man could do, he thought, was to meet these creatures of another world with clean and empty hands.

They were closer now and it seemed to him that they were sitting in invisible chairs that traveled very fast.

He saw that they were humanoid, to a degree at least, and there were only three of them.

They came in with a rush and stopped very suddenly a hundred feet or so from where he sat upon the steps.

He didn't move or say a word—there was nothing he could say. It was too ridiculous.

They were, perhaps, a little smaller than himself, and black as the ace of spades, and they wore skin tight shorts and vests that were somewhat oversize and both the shorts and vests were the blue of April skies.

But that was not the worst of it.

They sat on saddles, with horns in front and stirrups and a sort of bedroll tied on the back, but they had no horses.

The saddles floated in the air, with the stirrups about three feet above the ground and the aliens sat easily in the saddles and stared at him and he stared back at them.

Finally he got up and moved forward a step or two and when he did that the three swung from the saddles and moved forward, too, while the saddles hung there in the air, exactly as they'd left them.

Taine walked forward and the three walked forward until they were no more than six feet apart.

"They say hello to you," said Beasly. "They say welcome to you."

"Well, all right, then, tell them— Say, how do you know all this!"

"Chuck tells me what they say and I tell you. You tell me and I tell him and he tells them. That's the way it works. That is what he's here for."

"Well, I'll be—" said Taine. "So you can really talk to him."

"I told you that I could," stormed Beasly. "I told you that I could talk to Towser, too, but you thought that I was crazy."

"Telepathy!" said Taine. And it was worse than ever now. Not only had the ratlike things known all the rest of it, but they'd known of Beasly, too.

"What was that you said, Hiram?"

"Never mind," said Taine. "Tell that friend of yours to tell them I'm glad to meet them and what can I do for them?"

He stood uncomfortably and stared at the three and he saw that their vests had many pockets and that the pockets were crammed, probably with their equivalent of tobacco and handkerchiefs and pocket knives and such.

"They say," said Beasly, "that they want to dicker."

"Dicker?"

"Sure, Hiram. You know, trade."

Beasly chuckled thinly. "Imagine them laying themselves open to a Yankee trader. That's what Henry says you are. He says you can skin a man on the slickest—"

"Leave Henry out of this," snapped Taine. "Let's leave Henry out of something."

He sat down on the ground and the three sat down to face him.

"Ask them what they have in mind to trade."

"Ideas," Beasly said.

"Ideas! That's a crazy thing—"

And then he saw it wasn't.

Of all the commodities that might be exchanged by an alien people, ideas would be the most valuable and the easiest to handle. They'd take no cargo room and they'd upset no economies—not immediately, that is—and they'd make a bigger contribution to the welfare of the cultures than trade in actual goods.

"Ask them," said Taine, "what they'll take for the idea back of those saddles they are riding."

"They say, what have you to offer?"

And that was the stumper. That was the one that would be hard to answer.

Automobiles and trucks, the internal gas engine—well, probably not. Because they already had the saddles. Earth was out of date in transportation from the viewpoint of these people.

222

Housing architecture—no, that was hardly an idea and, anyhow, there was that other house, so they knew of houses.

Cloth? No, they had cloth.

Paint, he thought. Maybe paint was it.

"See if they are interested in paint," Taine told Beasly.

"They say, what is it? Please explain yourself."

"O.K., then. Let's see. It's a protective device to be spread over almost any surface. Easily packaged and easily applied. Protects against weather and corrosion. It's decorative, too. Comes in all sorts of colors. And it's cheap to make."

"They shrug in their mind," said Beasly. "They're just slightly interested. But they'll listen more. Go ahead and tell them."

And that was more like it, thought Taine.

That was the kind of language that he could understand.

He settled himself more firmly on the ground and bent forward slightly, flicking his eyes across the three deadpan, ebony faces, trying to make out what they might be thinking.

There was no making out. Those were three of the deadest pans he had ever seen.

It was all familiar. It made him feel at home. He was in his element.

And in the three across from him, he felt somehow subconsciously, he had the best dickering opposition he had ever met. And that made him feel good too.

"Tell them," he said, "that I'm not quite sure. I may have spoken up too hastily. Paint, after all, is a mighty valuable idea."

"They say, just as a favor to them, not that they're really interested, would you tell them a little more."

Got them hooked, Taine told himself. If he could only play it right—

He settled down to dickering in earnest.

Hours later Henry Horton showed up. He was accompanied by a very urbane gentleman, who was faultlessly turned out and who carried beneath his arm an impressive attaché case.

Henry and the man stopped on the steps in sheer astonishment.

Taine was squatted on the ground with a length of board and he was daubing paint on it while the aliens watched. From the daubs here and there upon their anatomies, it was plain to see the aliens had been doing some daubing of their own. Spread all over the ground were other lengths of half-painted boards and a couple of dozen old cans of paint.

Taine looked up and saw Henry and the man.

"I was hoping," he said, "that someone would show up."

"Hiram," said Henry, with more importance than usual, "may I present Mr. Lancaster. He is a special representative of the United Nations."

"I'm glad to meet you, sir," said Taine. "I wonder if you would—"

"Mr. Lancaster," Henry explained grandly, "was having some slight difficulty getting through the lines outside, so I volunteered my services. I've already explained to him our joint interest in this matter."

"It was very kind of Mr. Horton," Lancaster said. "There was this stupid sergeant—"

"It's all in knowing," Henry said, "how to handle people."

The remark, Taine noticed, was not appreciated by the man from the U.N.

"May I inquire, Mr. Taine," asked Lancaster, "exactly what you're doing?"

"I'm dickering," said Taine.

"Dickering. What a quaint way of expressing—"

"An old Yankee word," said Henry quickly, "with certain connotations of its own. When you trade with someone you are exchanging goods, but if you're dickering with him you're out to get his hide."

"Interesting," said Lancaster. "And I suppose you're out to skin these gentlemen in the sky-blue vests—"

"Hiram," said Henry proudly, "is the sharpest dickerer in

these parts. He runs an antique business and he has to dicker hard—"

"And may I ask," said Lancaster, ignoring Henry finally, "what you might be doing with these cans of paint? Are these gentlemen potential customers for paint or—"

Taine threw down the board and rose angrily to his feet.

"If you'd both shut up!" he shouted. "I've been trying to say something ever since you got here and I can't get in a word. And I tell you, it's important—"

"Hiram!" Henry exclaimed in horror.

"It's quite all right," said the U.N. man. "We *have* been jabbering. And now, Mr. Taine?"

"I'm backed into a corner," Taine told him, "and I need some help. I've sold these fellows on the idea of paint, but I don't know a thing about it—the principle back of it or how it's made or what goes into it or—"

"But, Mr. Taine, if you're selling them the paint, what difference does it make—"

"I'm not selling them the paint," yelled Taine. "Can't you understand that? They don't want the paint. They want the *idea* of paint, the principle of paint. It's something that they never thought of and they're interested. I offered them the paint idea for the idea of their saddles and I've almost got it—"

"Saddles? You mean those things over there, hanging in the air?"

"That is right. Beasly, would you ask one of our friends to demonstrate a saddle?"

"You bet I will," said Beasly.

"What," demanded Henry, "has Beasly got to do with this?"

"Beasly is an interpreter. I guess you'd call him a telepath. You remember how he always claimed he could talk with Towser?"

"Beasly was always claiming things."

"But this time he was right. He tells Chuck, that funny-looking monster, what I want to say and Chuck tells these aliens. And these aliens tell Chuck and Chuck tells Beasly and Beasly tells me.''

"Ridiculous!" snorted Henry. "Beasly hasn't got the sense to be . . . what did you say he was?''

"A telepath," said Taine.

One of the aliens had gotten up and climbed into a saddle. He rode it forth and back. Then he swung out of it and sat down again.

"Remarkable," said the U.N. man. "Some sort of antigravity unit, with complete control. We could make use of that, indeed.''

He scraped his hand across his chin.

"And you're going to exchange the idea of paint for the idea of that saddle?''

"That's exactly it," said Taine, "but I need some help. I need a chemist or a paint manufacturer or someone to explain how paint is made. And I need some professor or other who'll understand what they're talking about when they tell me the idea of the saddle.''

"I see," said Lancaster. "Yes, indeed, you have a problem. Mr. Taine, you seem to me a man of some discernment—''

"Oh, he's all of that," interrupted Henry. "Hiram's quite astute.''

"So I suppose you'll understand," said the U.N. man, "that this whole procedure is quite irregular—''

"But it's not," exploded Taine. "That's the way they operate. They open up a planet and then they exchange ideas, They've been doing that with other planets for a long, long time. And ideas are all they want, just the new ideas, because that is the way to keep on building a technology and culture. And they have a lot of ideas, sir, that the human race can use.''

"That is just the point," said Lancaster. "This is perhaps the most important thing that has ever happened to us humans. In just a short year's time we can obtain data and ideas that will put ahead—theoretically, at least—by a thousand years. And in a thing that is so important, we should have experts on the job—''

"But," protested Henry, "you can't find a man who'll do a better dickering job than Hiram. When you dicker with him your back teeth aren't safe. Why don't you leave him be? He'll do a job for you. You can get your experts and your planning groups together and let Hiram front for you. These folks have accepted him and have proved they'll do business with him and what more do you want? All he needs is a little help."

Beasly came over and faced the U.N. man.

"I won't work with no one else," he said. "If you kick Hiram out of here, then I go with him. Hiram's the only person who ever treated me like a human—''

"There, you see!" Henry said, triumphantly.

"Now, wait a second, Beasly," said the U.N. man. "We could make it worth your while. I should imagine that an interpreter in a situation such as this could command a handsome salary."

"Money don't mean a thing to me," said Beasly. "It won't buy me friends. People still will laugh at me."

"He means it, mister," Henry warned. "There isn't anyone who can be as stubborn as Beasly. I know; he used to work for us."

The U.N. man looked flabbergasted and not a little desperate.

"It will take you quite some time," Henry pointed out, "to find another telepath—leastwise one who can talk to these people here."

The U.N. man looked as if he were strangling. "I doubt," he said, "there's another one on Earth."

"Well, all right," said Beasly, brutally, "let's make up our minds. I ain't standing here all day."

"All right," cried the U.N. man. "You two go ahead. Please, will you go ahead? This is a chance we can't let slip through our fingers. Is there anything you want? Anything I can do for you?"

"Yes, there is," said Taine. "There'll be the boys from

Washington and bigwigs from other countries. Just keep them off my back.''

''I'll explain most carefully to everyone. There'll be no interference.''

''And I need that chemist and someone who'll know about the saddles. And I need them quick. I can stall these boys a little longer, but not for too much longer.''

''Anyone you need,'' said the U.N. man. ''Anyone at all. I'll have them here in hours. And in a day or two there'll be a pool of experts waiting for whenever you may need them—on a moment's notice.''

''Sir,'' said Henry, unctuously, ''that's most co-operative. Both Hiram and I appreciate it greatly. And now, since this is settled, I understand that there are reporters waiting. They'll be interested in your statement.''

The U.N. man, it seemed, didn't have it in him to protest. He and Henry went tramping up the stairs.

Taine turned around and looked out across the desert.

''It's a big front yard,'' he said.

THE BURNING OF THE BRAIN

BY CORDWAINER SMITH (PAUL M. A. LINEBARGER; (1913–1966)

IF
OCTOBER

The amazing "Cordwainer Smith" was one of the least likely individuals to make an impact in science fiction. A Professor of Asiatic Politics at the School of Advanced International Studies at John Hopkins University for twenty years until his untimely death, he had from 1942 until 1966 also served as an officer in U.S. Army intelligence, where he was instrumental in the establishment of the Office of War Information (he was a world authority on propaganda warfare). Part of his service was spent in China, which may account for what many feel is the "Oriental" flavor and mood of his stories. Among his nonfiction books are such titles as Government in Republican China *(1938) and* Far Eastern Governments and Politics *(1952). The great bulk of his sf writing was set in his "Instrumentality of Mankind," which must rank as one of the great creations of modern science fiction.*

"The Burning of the Brain" is a different view of space travel, a subject which can be found in a number of his stories, and which would be worked with similar success and distinctiveness by Barry N. Malzberg. (MHG)

Cordwainer Smith has written a number of stories on the psychopathology of space travel, which shows how useful it is

229

to have large numbers of science fiction writers with different points of view.

I do not like to travel so I pay no attention to the minutiae of the phenomenon. When I simply must go from here to there, I walk, or take a taxi, or drive, and in every case it is a pain in the neck that must be gone through simply to change my position in the Universe. Naturally, I change it as infrequently as I can and to as small a degree as possible.

For that reason when I write a story in which space travel is involved, I tend to shrug it off. You get into the spaceship, turn on the ignition switch, put it into gear and drive away with your hands firmly on the steering wheel. The important thing is to get to the destination and get on with the story. (All right, I'm exaggerating.)

However, the fact is that each form of transportation has its own mystique. To be the captain of a sailing vessel in a storm is entirely different from being behind the steering wheel in a traffic jam, or flying in circles over an airport waiting to be given the word to descend.

It's nice, then, that Cordwainer Smith makes of spaceflight something completely different from any other form of transportation and lets us imagine a pilot's life that is totally different from anything we know. (IA)

I.
DOLORES OH

I tell you, it is sad, it is more than sad, it is fearful—for it is a dreadful thing to go into the Up-and-Out, to fly without flying, to move between the stars as a moth may drift among the leaves on a summer night.

Of all the men who took the great ships into planoform none was braver, none stronger, than Captain Magno Taliano.

Scanners had been gone for centuries and the jonasoidal effect had become so simple, so manageable, that the traversing of light-years was no more difficult to most of the passengers of the great ships than to go from one room to the other.

THE BURNING OF THE BRAIN

Passengers moved easily

Not the crew.

Least of all the captain.

The captain of a jonasoidal ship which had embarked on an interstellar journey was a man subject to rare and overwhelming strains. The art of getting past all the complications of space was far more like the piloting of turbulent waters in ancient days than like the smooth seas which legendary men once traversed with sails alone.

Go-Captain on the *We-Feinstein*, finest ship of its class, was Magno Taliano.

Of him it was said, "He could sail through hell with the muscles of his left eye alone. He could plow space with his living brain if the instruments failed . . ."

Wife to the Go-Captain was Dolores Oh. The name was Japonical, from some nation of the ancient days. Dolores Oh had been once beautiful, so beautiful that she took men's breath away, made wise men into fools, made young men into nightmares of lust and yearning. Wherever she went men had quarreled and fought over her.

But Dolores Oh was proud beyond all common limits of pride. She refused to go through the ordinary rejuvenescence. A terrible yearning a hundred or so years back must have come over her. Perhaps she said to herself, before that hope and terror which a mirror in a quiet room becomes to anyone:

"Surely I am me. There must be a *me* more than the beauty of my face; there must be a something other than the delicacy of skin and the accidental lines of my jaw and my cheekbone.

"What have men loved if it wasn't me? Can I ever find out who I am or what I am if I don't let beauty perish and live on in whatever flesh age gives me?"

She had met the Go-Captain and had married him in a romance that left forty planets talking and half the ship lines stunned.

Magno Taliano was at the very beginning of his genius. Space, we can tell you, is rough—rough like the wildest of storm-driven waters, filled with perils which only the most sensitive, the quickest, the most daring of men can surmount.

Best of them all, class for class, age for age, out of class, beating the best of his seniors, was Magno Taliano.

For him to marry the most beautiful beauty of forty worlds was a wedding like Heloise and Abelard's or like the unforgettable romance of Helen America and Mr. Grey-no-more.

The ships of the Go-Captain Magno Taliano became more beautiful year by year, century by century.

As ships became better he always obtained the best. He maintained his lead over the other Go-Captains so overwhelmingly that it was unthinkable for the finest ship of mankind to sail out amid the roughness and uncertainties of two-dimensional space without himself at the helm.

Stop-Captains were proud to sail space beside him. (Though the Stop-Captains had nothing more to do than to check the maintenance of the ship, its loading and unloading when it was in normal space, they were still more than ordinary men in their own kind of world, a world far below the more majestic and adventurous universe of the Go-Captains.)

Magno Taliano had a niece who in the modern style used a place instead of a name: she was called "Dita from the Great South House."

When Dita came aboard the *Wu-Feinstein* she had heard much of Dolores Oh, her aunt by marriage who had once captivated the men in many worlds. Dita was wholly unprepared for what she found.

Dolores greeted her civilly enough, but the civility was a sucking pump of hideous anxiety, the friendliness was the driest of mockeries, the greeting itself an attack.

What's the matter with the woman? thought Dita.

As if to answer her thought, Dolores said aloud and in words: "It's nice to meet a woman who's not trying to take Taliano from me. I love him. Can you believe that? Can you?"

"Of course," said Dita. She looked at the ruined face of

Dolores Oh, at the dreaming terror in Dolores' eyes, and she realized that Dolores had passed all limits of nightmare and had become a veritable demon of regret, a possessive ghost who sucked the vitality from her husband, who dreaded companionship, hated friendship, rejected even the most casual of acquaintances, because she feared forever and without limit that there was really nothing to herself, and feared that without Magno Taliano she would be more lost than the blackest of whirlpools in the nothing between the stars.

Magno Taliano came in.

He saw his wife and niece together.

He must have been used to Dolores Oh. In Dita's eyes Dolores was more frightening than a mud-caked reptile raising its wounded and venomous head with blind hunger and blind rage. To Magno Taliano the ghastly woman who stood like a witch beside him was somehow the beautiful girl he had wooed and had married one hundred sixty-four years before.

He kissed the withered cheek, he stroked the dried and stringy hair, he looked into the greedy terror-haunted eyes as though they were the eyes of a child he loved. He said, lightly and gently, "Be good to Dita, my dear."

He went on through the lobby of the ship to the inner sanctum of the planoforming room.

The Stop-Captain waited for him. Outside on the world of Sherman the scented breezes of that pleasant planet blew in through the open windows of the ship.

Wu-Feinstein, the finest ship of its class, had no need for metal walls. It was built to resemble an ancient, prehistoric estate named Mount Vernon, and when it sailed between the stars it was encased in its own rigid and self-renewing field of force.

The passengers went through a few pleasant hours of strolling on the grass, enjoying the spacious rooms, chatting beneath a marvelous simulacrum of an atmosphere-filled sky.

Only in the planoforming room did the Go-Captain know

what happened. The Go-Captain, his pinlighters sitting beside him, took the ship from one compression to another, leaping hotly and frantically through space, sometimes one light-year, sometimes a hundred light-years, jump, jump, jump, jump until the ship, the light touches of the captain's mind guiding it, passed the perils of millions upon millions of worlds, came out at its appointed destination, and settled as lightly as one feather resting upon others, settled into an embroidered and decorated countryside where the passengers could move as easily away from their journey as if they had done nothing more than to pass an afternoon in a pleasant old house by the side of a river.

II.
THE LOST LOCKSHEET

Magno Taliano nodded to his pinlighters. The Stop-Captain bowed obsequiously from the doorway of the planoforming room. Taliano looked at him sternly, but with robust friendliness. With formal and austere courtesy he asked, "Sir and colleague, is everything ready for the jonasoidal effect?"

The Stop-Captain bowed even more formally. "Truly ready, sir and master."

"The locksheets in place?"

"Truly in place, sir and master."

"The passengers secure?"

"The passengers are secure, numbered, happy, and ready, sir and master."

Then came the last and most serious of questions. "Are my pinlighters warmed with their pin-sets and ready for combat?"

"Ready for combat, sir and master." With these words the Stop-Captain withdrew. Magno Taliano smiled to his pinlighters. Through the minds of all of them were passed the same thought.

How could a man that pleasant stay married all those years to a hag like Dolores Oh? How could that witch, that horror, have ever been a beauty? How could that beast have ever been a woman, particularly the divine and glamorous Dolores Oh whose image we still see in four-di every now and then?

Yet pleasant he was, though long he may have been married to Dolores Oh. Her loneliness and greed might suck at him like a nightmare, but his strength was more than enough strength for two.

Was he not the captain of the greatest ship to sail between the stars?

Even as the pinlighters smiled their greetings back to him, his right hand depressed the golden ceremonial lever of the ship. This instrument alone was mechanical. All other controls in the ship had long since been formed telepathically or electronically.

Within the planoforming room the black skies became visible and the tissue of space shot up around them like boiling water at the base of a waterfall. Outside that one room the passengers still walked sedately on scented lawns.

From the wall facing him, as he sat rigid in his Go-Captain's chair, Magno Taliano sensed the forming of a pattern which in three or four hundred milliseconds would tell him where he was and would give him the next clue as to how to move.

He moved the ship with the impulses of his own brain, to which the wall was a superlative complement.

The wall was a living brickwork of locksheets, laminated charts, one hundred thousand charts to the inch, the wall preselected and preassembled for all imaginable contingencies of the journey which, each time afresh, took the ship across half-unknown immensities of time and space. The ship leapt, as it had before.

The new star focused.

Magno Taliano waited for the wall to show him where he was, expecting (in partnership with the wall) to flick the ship back into the pattern of stellar space, moving it by immense skips from source to destination.

This time nothing happened.

Nothing?

For the first time in a hundred years his mind knew panic.

It couldn't be nothing. Not *nothing*. Something had to focus. The locksheets always focused.

His mind reached into the locksheets and he realized with a devastation beyond all limits of ordinary human grief that they were lost as no ship had ever been lost before. By some error never before committed in the history of mankind, the entire wall was made of duplicates of the same locksheet.

Worst of all, the Emergency Return sheet was lost. They were amid stars none of them had ever seen before, perhaps as little as five hundred million miles, perhaps as far as forty parsecs.

And the locksheet was lost.

And they would die.

As the ship's power failed coldness and blackness and death would crush in on them in a few hours at the most. That then would be all, all of the *Wu-Feinstein*, all of Dolores Oh.

III.
THE SECRET OF THE OLD DARK BRAIN

Outside of the planoforming room of the *Wu-Feinstein* the passengers had no reason to understand that they were marooned in the nothing-at-all.

Dolores Oh rocked back and forth in an ancient rocking chair. Her haggard face looked without pleasure at the imaginary river that ran past the edge of the lawn. Dita from the Great South House sat on a hassock by her aunt's knees.

Dolores was talking about a trip she had made when she was young and vibrant with beauty, a beauty which brought trouble and hate wherever it went.

". . . so the guardsman killed the captain and then came to my cabin and said to me, 'You've got to marry me now. I've given up everything for your sake,' and I said to him, 'I never said that I loved you. It was sweet of you to get into a fight, and in a way I suppose it is a compliment to my beauty, but it doesn't mean that I belong to you the rest of my life. What do you think I am, anyhow?' ''

Dolores Oh sighed a dry, ugly sigh, like the crackling of subzero winds through frozen twigs. 'So you see, Dita, being beautiful the way you are is no answer to anything. A woman has got to be herself before she finds out what she is. I know that my lord and husband, the Go-Captain, loves me because my beauty is gone, and with my beauty gone there is nothing but *me* to love, is there?''

An odd figure came out on the verandah. It was a pinlighter in full fighting costume. Pinlighters were never supposed to leave the planoforming room, and it was most extraordinary for one of them to appear among the passengers.

He bowed to the two ladies and said with the utmost courtesy:

"Ladies, will you please come into the planoforming room? We have need that you should see the Go-Captain now."

Dolores' hand leapt to her mouth. Her gesture of grief was as automatic as the striking of a snake. Dita sensed that her aunt had been waiting a hundred years and more for disaster, that her aunt had craved ruin for her husband the way that some people crave love and others crave death.

Dita said nothing. Neither did Dolores, apparently at second thought, utter a word.

They followed the pinlighter silently into the planoforming room.

The heavy door closed behind them.

Magno Taliano was still rigid in his Captain's chair.

He spoke very slowly, his voice sounding like a record played too slowly on an ancient parlophone.

"We are lost in space, my dear," said the frigid, ghostly

voice of the Captain, still in his Go-Captain's trance. *"We are lost in space and I thought that perhaps if your mind aided mine we might think of a way back."*

Dita started to speak.

A pinlighter told her: "Go ahead and speak, my dear. Do you have any suggestion?"

"Why don't we just go back? It would be humiliating, wouldn't it? Still it would be better than dying. Let's use the Emergency Return Locksheet and go on right back. The world will forgive Magno Taliano for a single failure after thousands of brilliant and successful trips."

The pinlighter, a pleasant enough young man, was as friendly and calm as a doctor informing someone of a death or of a mutilation. "The impossible has happened, Dita from the Great South House. All the locksheets are wrong. They are all the same one. And not one of them is good for emergency return."

With that the two women knew where they were. They knew that space would tear into them like threads being pulled out of a fiber so that they would either die bit by bit as the hours passed and as the material of their bodies faded away a few molecules here and a few there. Or, alternatively, they could die all at once in a flash if the Go-Captain chose to kill himself and the ship rather than to wait for a slow death. Or, if they believed in religion, they could pray.

The pinlighter said to the rigid Go-Captain, "We think we see a familiar pattern at the edge of your own brain. May we look in?"

Taliano nodded very slowly, very gravely.

The pinlighter stood still.

The two women watched. Nothing visible happened, but they knew that beyond the limits of vision and yet before their eyes a great drama was being played out. The minds of the pinlighters probed deep into the mind of the frozen Go-Captain, searching amid the synapses for the secret of the faintest clue to their possible rescue.

Minutes passed. They seemed like hours.

At last the pinlighter spoke. "We can see into your mid-brain, Captain. At the edge of your paleocortex there is a star pattern which resembles the upper left rear of our present location."

The pinlighter laughed nervously. "We want to know can you fly the ship home on your brain?"

Magno Taliano looked with deep tragic eyes at the inquirer. His slow voice came out at them once again since he dared not leave the half-trance which held the entire ship in stasis. *"Do you mean can I fly the ship on a brain alone? It would burn out my brain and the ship would be lost anyhow. . . ."*

"But we're lost, lost, lost," screamed Dolores Oh. Her face was alive with hideous hope, with a hunger for ruin, with a greedy welcome of disaster. She screamed at her husband, "Wake up, my darling, and let us die together. At least we can belong to each other that much, that long, forever!"

"Why die?" said the pinlighter softly. "You tell him, Dita."

Said Dita, "Why not try, sir and uncle?"

Slowly Magno Taliano turned his face toward his niece. Again his hollow voice sounded. *"If I do this I shall be a fool or a child or a dead man but I will do it for you."*

Dita had studied the work of the Go-Captains and she knew well enough that if the paleocortex was lost the personality became intellectually sane, but emotionally crazed. With the most ancient part of the brain gone the fundamental controls of hostility, hunger, and sex disappeared. The most ferocious of animals and the most brilliant of men were reduced to a common level—a level of infantile friendliness in which lust and playfulness and gentle, unappeasable hunger became the eternity of their days.

Magno Taliano did not wait.

He reached out a slow hand and squeezed the hand of Dolores Oh. *"As I die you shall at last be sure I love you."*

Once again the women saw nothing. They realized they had been called in simply to give Magno Taliano a last glimpse of his own life.

A quiet pinlighter thrust a beam-electrode so that it reached square into the paleocortex of Captain Magno Taliano.

The planoforming room came to life. Strange heavens swirled about them like milk being churned in a bowl.

Dita realized that her partial capacity of telepathy was functioning even without the aid of a machine. With her mind she could feel the dead wall of the locksheets. She was aware of the rocking of the *Wu-Feinstein* as it leapt from space to space, as uncertain as a man crossing a river by leaping from one ice-covered rock to the other.

In a strange way she even knew that the paleocortical part of her uncle's brain was burning out at last and forever, that the star patterns which had been frozen in the locksheets lived on in the infinitely complex pattern of his own memories, and that with the help of his own telepathic pinlighters he was burning out his brain cell by cell in order for them to find a way to the ship's destination. This indeed was his last trip.

Dolores Oh watched her husband with a hungry greed surpassing all expression.

Little by little his face became relaxed and stupid.

Dita could see the midbrain being burned blank, as the ship's controls with the help of the pinlighters searched through the most magnificent intellect of its time for a last course into harbor.

Suddenly Dolores Oh was on her knees, sobbing by the hand of her husband.

A pinlighter took Dita by the arm.

"We have reached destination," he said.

"And my uncle?"

The pinlighter looked at her strangely.

She realized he was speaking to her without moving his lips—speaking mind-to-mind with pure telepathy.

"Can't you see it?"

She shook her head dazedly.

The pinlighter thought his emphatic statement at her once again.

"As your uncle burned out his brain, you picked up his skills. Can't you sense it? You are a Go-Captain yourself and one of the greatest of us."

"And he?"

The pinlighter thought a merciful comment at her.

Magno Taliano had risen from his chair and was being led from the room by his wife and consort, Dolores Oh. He had the amiable smile of an idiot, and his face for the first time in more than a hundred years trembled with shy and silly love.

THE YELLOW PILL

BY ROG PHILLIPS
(ROGER PHILLIPS GRAHAM; 1909–1965)

ASTOUNDING SCIENCE FICTION
OCTOBER

"Rog Phillips" was a journeyman writer who produced a great amount of decent commercial copy. He was a mainstay of the Ziff-Davis group of science fiction publications from his debut in 1945 until the mid-1950s. As the author of "The Club House" feature in Amazing *and later other magazines, he was something of an influential force within fandom of the period. His four novels in the field were all slight efforts, with* The Involuntary Immortals *(1959) the only one of continuing interest.*

This is not to say that there were not gems buried among the numerous stories he published under a large group of pseudonyms, because there were—two excellent examples are "Game Preserve" (1957) and the following story.

"The Yellow Pill" is simply one of the best perception stories ever written, and perception or "reality" stories have a rich and distinguished history in science fiction. It is also evidence of what "Rog Phillips" could have accomplished if he had a more demanding editor and/or greater motivation. (MHG)

One of the most disturbing questions ever posed was that of Pontius Pilate. "What is truth?" he asked, wearily.

There is also the story of the Chinese sage, who said,

"Last night I dreamed I was a butterfly. But am I a human being who dreamed last night I was a butterfly, or am I a butterfly who is dreaming right now that I am a human being?"

We all tend to lean at least slightly toward solipsism. What do you know that you don't gather through your senses? How do you know your senses are telling you the truth?

In fact, is everything your senses tell you a lie? How do you know anyone or anything else exists? Are you only an isolated and solitary patch of existence who has created a whole Universe about yourself to avoid being alone? Mark Twain ends his bitter The Mysterious Stranger *by describing the narrator of the story as being just that.*

Does Rangoon, Burma exist—really exist—if you have never been there? Or, for that matter, Charleston, South Carolina? Did the Universe exist before you were born? Will it exist after you die? How can you possibly know *anything about such basic questions concerning existence.*

The fortunate thing is that we don't spend much time thinking about these things, or we might go into a tailspin. We just accept the Universe and everything about us at face value. Science fiction, however, doesn't necessarily deal with face value—so read on. (IA)

Dr. Cedric Elton slipped into his office by the back entrance, shucked off his topcoat and hid it in the small, narrow-doored closet, then picked up the neatly piled patient cards his receptionist Helena Fitzroy had placed on the corner of his desk. There were only four, but there could have been a hundred if he accepted everyone who asked to be his patient, because his successes had more than once been spectacular and his reputation as a psychiatrist had become so great because of this that his name had become synonymous with psychiatry in the public mind.

His eyes flicked over the top card. He frowned, then went to the small square of one-way glass in the reception-room door and looked through it. There were four police officers and a man in a strait jacket.

THE YELLOW PILL

The card said the man's name was Gerald Bocek, and that he had shot and killed five people in a supermarket, and had killed one officer and wounded two others before being captured.

Except for the strait jacket, Gerald Bocek did not have the appearance of being dangerous. He was about twenty-five, with brown hair and blue eyes. There were faint wrinkles of habitual good nature about his eyes. Right now he was smiling, relaxed, and idly watching Helena, who was pretending to study various cards in her desk file but was obviously conscious of her audience.

Cedric returned to his desk and sat down. The card for Jerry Bocek said more about the killings. When captured, Bocek insisted that the people he had killed were not people at all, but blue-scaled Venusian lizards who had boarded his spaceship, and that he had only been defending himself.

Dr. Cedric Elton shook his head in disapproval. Fantasy fiction was all right in its place, but too many people took it seriously. Of course, it was not the fault of the fiction. The same type of person took other types of fantasy seriously in earlier days, burning women as witches, stoning men as devils—

Abruptly Cedric deflected the control on the intercom and spoke into it. "Send Gerald Bocek in, please," he said.

A moment later the door to the reception room opened. Helena flashed Cedric a scared smile and got out of the way quickly. One police officer led the way, followed by Gerald Bocek, closely flanked by two officers with the fourth one in the rear, who carefully closed the door. It was impressive, Cedric decided. He nodded toward a chair in front of his desk and the police officers sat the straight-jacketed man in it, then hovered near by, ready for anything.

"You're Jerry Bocek?" Cedric asked.

The strait-jacketed man nodded cheerfully.

"I'm Dr. Cedric Elton, a psychiatrist," Cedric said. "Do you have any idea at all why you have been brought to me?"

"Brought to you?" Jerry echoed, chuckling. "Don't kid

me. You're my old pal, Gar Castle. Brought to you? How could I get *away* from you in this stinking tub?''

''Stinking tub?'' Cedric said.

''Spaceship,'' Jerry said. ''Look, Gar. Untie me, will you? This nonsense has gone far enough.''

''My name is Dr. Cedric Elton,'' Cedric enunciated. ''You are not on a spaceship. You were brought to my office by the four policemen standing in back of you, and—''

Jerry Bocek turned his head and studied each of the four policemen with frank curiosity. ''What policemen?'' he interrupted. ''You mean these four gear lockers?'' He turned his head back and looked pityingly at Dr. Elton. ''You'd better get hold of yourself, Gar,'' he said. ''You're imagining things.''

''My name is Dr. Cedric Elton,'' Cedric said.

Gerald Bocek leaned forward and said with equal firmness, ''Your name is Gar Castle. I refuse to call you Dr. Cedric Elton because your name is Gar Castle, and I'm going to keep on calling you Gar Castle because we have to have at least one peg of rationality in all this madness or you will be cut completely adrift in this dream world you've cooked up.''

Cedric's eyebrows shot halfway up to his hairline.

''Funny,'' he mused, smiling. ''That's exactly what I was just going to say to you!''

Cedric continued to smile. Jerry's serious intenseness slowly faded. Finally an answering smile tugged at the corners of his mouth. When it became a grin, Cedric laughed, and Jerry began to laugh with him. The four police officers looked at one another uneasily.

''Well!'' Cedric finally gasped. ''I guess that puts us on an even footing! You're nuts to me and I'm nuts to you!''

''An equal footing is right!'' Jerry shouted in high glee. Then he sobered. ''Except,'' he said gently, ''I'm tied up.''

''In a strait jacket,'' Cedric corrected.

''Ropes,'' Jerry said firmly.

''You're dangerous,'' Cedric said. ''You killed six people, one of them a police officer, and wounded two other officers.''

"I blasted five Venusian lizard pirates who boarded our ship," Jerry said, "and melted the door off of one gear locker, and seared the paint on two others. You know as well as I do, Gar, how space madness causes you to personify everything. That's why they drill into you that the minute you think there are more people on board the ship than there were at the beginning of the trip you'd better go to the medicine locker and take a yellow pill. They can't hurt anything but a delusion."

"If that is so," Cedric said, "why are *you* in a strait jacket?"

"I'm tied up with ropes," Jerry said patiently. "You tied me up. Remember?"

"And those four police officers behind you are gear lockers?" Cedric said. "OK, if one of those gear lockers comes around in front of you and taps you on the jaw with his fist, would you still believe it's a gear locker?"

Cedric nodded to one of the officers, and the man came around in front of Gerald Bocek and, quite carefully, hit him hard enough to rock his head but not hurt him. Jerry's eyes blinked with surprise, then he looked at Cedric and smiled. "Did you feel that?" Cedric said quietly.

"Feel what?" Jerry said. "Oh!" He laughed. "You imagined that one of the gear lockers—a police officer in your dream world—came around in front of me and hit me?" He shook his head in pity. "Don't you understand, Gar, that it didn't really happen? Untie me and I'll prove it. Before your very eyes I'll open the door on your *Policeman* and take out the pressure suit, or magnetic grapple, or whatever is in it. Or are you afraid to? You've surrounded yourself with all sorts of protective delusions. I'm tied with ropes, but you imagine it to be a strait jacket. You imagine yourself to be a psychiatrist named Dr. Cedric Elton, so that you can convince yourself that you're sane and I'm crazy. Probably you imagine yourself a very *famous* psychiatrist that everyone would like to come to for treatment. World famous, no doubt. Probably you even think you have a beautiful receptionist. What is her name?"

"Helena Fitzroy," Cedric said.

Jerry nodded. "It figures," he said resignedly. "Helena Fitzroy is the expediter at Mars Port. You try to date her every time we land there, but she won't date you."

"Hit him again," Cedric said to the officer. While Jerry's head was still rocking from the blow, Cedric said, "Now! Is it *my* imagination that your head is still rocking from the blow?"

"What blow?" Jerry said, smiling. "I felt no blow."

"Do you mean to say," Cedric said incredulously, "that there is no corner of your mind, no slight residue of rationality, that tries to tell you your rationalizations aren't reality?"

Jerry smiled ruefully. "I have to admit," he said, "when you seem so absolutely certain you're right and I'm nuts, it almost makes me doubt. Untie me, Gar, and let's try to work this thing out sensibly." He grinned. "You know, Gar, *one* of us has to be nuttier than a fruit cake."

"If I had the officers take off your strait jacket, what would you do?" Cedric asked. "Try to grab a gun and kill some more people?"

"That's one of the things I'm worried about," Jerry said. "If those pirates came back, with me tied up, you're just space crazy enough to welcome them aboard. That's why you *must* untie me. Our lives may depend on it, Gar."

"Were would you get a gun?" Cedric asked.

"Where they're always kept," Jerry said. "In the gear lockers."

Cedric looked at the four policemen, at their holstered revolvers. One of them grinned feebly at him.

"I'm afraid we can't take your strait jacket off just yet," Cedric said. "I'm going to have the officers take you back now. I'll talk with you again tomorrow. Meanwhile I want you to think seriously about things. Try to get below this level of rationalization that walls you off from reality. Once you make a dent in it the whole delusion will vanish." He looked up at the officers. "All right, take him away. Bring him back the same time tomorrow."

The officers urged Jerry to his feet. Jerry looked down at Cedric, a gentle expression on his face. "I'll try to do that, Gar," he said. "And I hope you do the same thing. I'm much encouraged. Several times I detected genuine doubt in your eyes. And—" Two of the officers pushed him firmly toward the door. As they opened it Jerry turned his head and looked back. "*Take* one of those yellow pills in the medicine locker, Gar," he pleaded. "It can't hurt you."

At a little before five-thirty Cedric tactfully eased his last patient all the way across the reception room and out, then locked the door and leaned his back against it.

"Today was rough," he sighed.

Helena glanced up at him briefly, then continued typing. "I only have a little more on this last transcript," she said.

A minute later she pulled the paper from the typewriter and placed it on the neat stack beside her.

"I'll sort and file them in the morning," she said. "It was rough, wasn't it, Doctor? That Gerald Bocek is the most unusual patient you've had since I've worked for you. And poor Mr. Potts. A brilliant executive, making half a million a year, and he's going to have to give it up. He seems so normal."

"He is normal," Cedric said. "People with above normal blood pressure often have very minor cerebral hemorrhages so small that the affected area is no larger than the head of a pin. All that happens is that they completely forget things that they knew. They can relearn them, but a man whose judgment must always be perfect can't afford to take the chance. He's already made one error in judgment that cost his company a million and a half. That's why I consented to take him on as a—Gerald Bocek really upset me, Helena. I *consent* to take a five hundred thousand dollar a year executive as a patient."

"He was frightening, wasn't he?" Helena said. "I don't mean so much because he's a mass murderer as—"

"I know. I know," Cedric said. "Let's prove him wrong. Have dinner with me."

Rog Phillips

"We agreed—"

"Let's break the agreement this once."

Helena shook her head firmly. "Especially not now," she said. "Besides, it wouldn't prove anything. He's got you boxed in on that point. If I went to dinner with you, it would only show that a wish fulfillment entered your dream world."

"Ouch," Cedric said, wincing. "That's a dirty word. I wonder how he knew about the yellow pills? I can't get out of my mind the fact that *if* we had spaceships and *if* there were a type of space madness in which you began to personify objects, a yellow pill would be the right thing to stop that."

"How?" Helena said.

"They almost triple the strength of nerve currents from end organs. What results is that reality practically shouts down any fantasy insertions. It's quite startling. I took one three years ago when they first became available. You'd be surprised how little you actually see of what you look at, especially of people. You look at symbol inserts instead. I had to cancel my appointments for a week. I found I couldn't work without my professionally built symbol inserts about people that enable me to see them—not as they really are—but as a complex of normal and abnormal symptoms."

"I'd like to take one sometime," Helena said.

"That's a twist," Cedric said laughing. "One of the characters in a dream world takes a yellow pill and discovers it doesn't exist at all except as a fantasy."

"Why don't we both take one?" Helena said.

"Uh uh," Cedric said firmly. "I couldn't do my work."

"You're afraid you might wake up on a spaceship?" Helena said, grinning.

"Maybe I am," Cedric said. "Crazy, isn't it? But there is one thing today that stands out as a serious flaw in my reality. It's so glaring that I actually am afraid to ask you about it."

"Are you serious?" Helena said.

"I am." Cedric nodded. "How does it happen that the police brought Gerald Bocek here to my office instead of holding him in the psychiatric ward at City Hospital and having me go there to see him? How does it happen the D.A.

250

didn't get in touch with me beforehand and discuss the case with me?''

"I . . . I don't know!'' Helena said. "I received no call. They just showed up, and I assumed they wouldn't have without your knowing about it and telling them to. Mrs. Fortesque was your first patient and I called her at once and caught her just as she was leaving the house, and told her an emergency case had come up." She looked at Cedric with round, startled eyes.

"Now we know how the patient must feel," Cedric said, crossing the reception room to his office door. "Terrifying, isn't it, to think that if I took a yellow pill all this might *vanish*—my years of college, my internship, *my fame as the world's best known psychiatrist*, and you. Tell me, Helena, are you sure you aren't an expediter at Mars Port?''

He leered at her mockingly as he slowly closed the door, cutting off his view of her.

Cedric put his coat away and went directly to the small square of one-way glass in the reception-room door. Gerald Bocek, still in strait jacket, were there, and so were the same four police officers.

Cedric went to his desk and, without sitting down, deflected the control on the intercom.

"Helena," he said, "before you send in Gerald Bocek get me the D.A. on the phone."

He glanced over the four patient cards while waiting. Once he rubbed his eyes gently. He had had a restless night.

When the phone rang he reached for it. "Hello? Dave?" he said. "About this patient, Gerald Bocek—"

"I was going to call you today," the District Attorney's voice sounded. "I called you yesterday morning at ten, but no one answered, and I haven't had time since. Our police psychiatrist, Walters, says you might be able to snap Bocek out of it in a couple of days—at least long enough so that we can get some sensible answers out of him. Down underneath his delusion of killing lizard pirates from Venus, there has to be some reason for that mass killing, and the press is after us on this.''

"But why bring him to my office?'' Cedric said. "It's OK, of course, but . . . that is . . . I didn't think you could! Take a patient out of the ward at City Hospital and transport him around town.''

"I thought that would be less of an imposition on you,'' the D.A. said. "I'm in a hurry on it.''

"Oh,'' Cedric said. "Well, OK, Dave. He's out in the waiting room. I'll do my best to snap him back to reality for you.''

He hung up slowly, frowning. *"Less of an imposition!''* His whispered words floated into his ears as he snapped into the intercom, "Send Gerald Bocek in, please.''

The door from the reception room opened, and once again the procession of patient and police officers entered.

"Well, well, good morning, Gar,'' Jerry said. "Did you sleep well? I could hear you talking to yourself most of the night.''

"I am Dr. Cedric Elton,'' Cedric said firmly.

"Oh, yes,'' Jerry said. "I promised to try to see things your way, didn't I? I'll try to co-operate with you, Dr. Elton.'' Jerry turned to the four officers. "Let's see now, these gear lockers are policemen, aren't they? How do you do, officers.'' He bowed to them, then looked around him. "And,'' he said, "this is your office, Dr. Elton. A very impressive office. That thing you're sitting behind is not the chart table but your desk, I gather.'' He studied the desk intently. "All metal, with a gray finish, isn't it.''

"All wood,'' Cedric said. "Walnut.''

"Yes of course,'' Jerry murmured. "How stupid of me. I really want to get into your reality, Gar . . . I mean Dr. Elton. Or get you into mine. I'm the one who's at a disadvantage, though. Tied up, I can't get into the medicine locker and take a yellow pill like you can. Did you take one yet?''

"Not yet,'' Cedric said.

"Uh, why don't you describe your office to me, Dr. Elton?'' Jerry said. "Let's make a game of it. Describe parts of things and then let me see if I can fill in the rest. Start with your desk. It's genuine walnut? An executive style desk. Go on from there.''

"All right," Cedric said. "Over here to my right is the intercom, made of gray plastic. And directly in front of me is the telephone.''

"Stop," Jerry said. "Let me see if I can tell you your telephone number.'' He leaned over the desk and looked at the telephone, trying to keep his balance in spite of his arms being encased in the strait jacket. "Hm-m-m," he said, frowning. "Is the number Mulberry five dash nine oh three seven?''

"No," Cedric said. "It's Cedar sev—''

"Stop!" Jerry said. "Let me say it. It's Cedar seven dash four three nine nine.''

"So you did read it and were just having your fun," Cedric snorted.

"If you say so," Jerry said.

"What other explanation can you have for the fact that it is my number, if you're unable to actually see reality?'' Cedric said.

"You're absolutely right, Dr. Elton," Jerry said. "I think I understand the tricks my mind is playing on me now. I read the number on your phone, but it didn't enter my conscious awareness. Instead, it cloaked itself with the pattern of my delusion, so that consciously I pretended to look at a phone that I couldn't see, and I thought, 'His phone number will obviously be one he's familiar with.' The most probable is the home phone of Helena Fitzroy in Mars Port, so I gave you that, but it wasn't it. When you said Cedar I knew right away it was your own apartment phone number.''

Cedric sat perfectly still. Mulberry 5-9037 was actually Helena's apartment phone number. He hadn't recognized it until Gerald Bocek told him.

"Now you're beginning to understand," Cedric said after a moment. "Once you realize that your mind has walled off your consciousness from reality, and is substituting a rationalized pattern of symbology in its place, it shouldn't be long until you break through. Once you manage to see one thing as it really is, the rest of the delusion will disappear."

"I understand now," Jerry said gravely. "Let's have some more of it. Maybe I'll catch on."

They spent an hour at it. Toward the end Jerry was able to finish the descriptions of things with very little error.

"You are definitely beginning to get through," Cedric said with enthusiasm.

Jerry hesitated. "I suppose so," he said. "I must. But on the conscious level I have the idea—a rationlization, of course— that I am beginning to catch on to the pattern of your imagination so that when you give me one or two key elements I can fill in the rest. But I'm going to try, really try—Dr. Elton."

"Fine," Cedric said heartily. "I'll see you tomorrow, same time. We should make the breakthrough then."

When the four officers had taken Gerald Bocek away, Cedric went into the outer office.

"Cancel the rest of my appointments," he said.

"But why?" Helena protested.

"Because I'm upset!" Cedric said. "How did a madman whom I never knew until yesterday know your phone number?"

"He could have looked it up in the phone book."

"Locked in a room in the psychiatric ward at City Hospital?" Cedric said. "How did he know your name yesterday?"

"Why," Helena said, "all he had to do was read it on my desk here."

Cedric looked down at the brass name plate.

"Yes," he grunted. "Of course. I'd forgotten about that. I'm so accustomed to it being there that I never see it."

He turned abruptly and went back into his office.

He sat down at his desk, then got up and went into the sterile whiteness of his compact laboratory. Ignoring the impressive battery of electronic instruments he went to the medicine cabinet. Inside, on the top shelf, was the glass stopped bottle he wanted. Inside it were a hundred vivid yellow pills. He shook out one and put the bottle away, then went back into his office. He sat down, placing the yellow pill in the center of the white note pad.

There was a brief knock on the door to the reception room and the door opened. Helena came in.

"I've canceled all your other appointments for today," she said. "Why don't you go out to the golf course? A change will do you—" She saw the yellow pill in the center of the white note pad and stopped.

"Why do you look so frightened?" Cedric said. "Is it because, if I take this little yellow pill, you'll cease to exist?"

"Don't joke," Helena said.

"I'm not joking," Cedric said. "Out there, when you mentioned about your brass name plate on your desk, when I looked down it was blurred for just a second, then became sharply distinct and solid. And into my head popped the memory that the first thing I do when I have to get a new receptionist is get a brass name plate for her, and when she quits I make her a present of it."

"But that's the truth," Helena said. "You told me all about it when I started working for you. You also told me that while you still had your reason about you I was to solemnly promise that I would never accept an invitation from you for dinner or anything else, because business could not mix with pleasure. Do you remember that?"

"I remember," Cedric said. "A nice pat rationalization in any man's reality to make the rejection be my own before you could have time to reject me yourself. Preserving the ego is the first principle of madness."

"But it isn't!" Helena said. "Oh, darling, I'm *here!* This is *real!* I don't care if you fire me or not. I've loved you forever, and you mustn't let that mass murderer get you down. I actually think he isn't insane at all, but has just figured out a way to seem insane so he won't have to pay for his crime."

"You think so?" Cedric said, interested. "It's a possibility. But he would have to be as good a psychiatrist as I am— You see? Delusions of grandeur."

"Sure," Helena said, laughing thinly. "Napoleon was obviously insane because he thought he was Napoleon."

"Perhaps," Cedric said. "But you must admit that if you are real, my taking this yellow pill isn't going to change that, but only confirm the fact."

"And make it impossible for you to do your work for a week," Helena said.

"A small price to pay for sanity," Cedric said. "No, I'm going to take it."

"You aren't!" Helena said, reaching for it.

Cedric picked it up an instant before she could get it. As she tried to get it away from him, he evaded her and put it his mouth. A loud gulp showed he had swallowed it.

He sat back and looked up at Helena curiously.

"Tell me, Helena," he said gently. "Did you know all the time that you were only a creature of my imagination? The reason I want to know is—"

He closed his eyes and clutched his head in his hands.

"God!" he groaned. "I feel like I'm dying! I didn't feel like this the other time I took one." Suddenly his mind steadied, and his thoughts cleared. He opened his eyes.

On the chart table in front of him the bottle of yellow pills lay on its side, pills scattered all over the table. On the other side of the control room lay Jerry Bocek, his back propped against one of the four gear lockers, sound asleep, with so many ropes wrapped around him that it would probably be impossible for him to stand up.

Against the far wall were three other gear lockers, two of them with their paint badly scorched, the third with its door half melted off.

And in various positions about the control room were the half-charred bodies of five blue-scaled Venusian lizards.

A dull ache rose in Gar's chest. Helena Fitzroy was gone. Gone, when she had just confessed she loved him.

Unbidden, a memory came into Gar's mind. Dr. Cedric Elton was the psychiatrist who had examined him when he got his pilot's license for third-class freighters—

"God!" Gar groaned again. And suddenly he was sick. He made a dash for the washroom, and after a while he felt better.

When he straightened up from the wash basin he looked at his reflection in the mirror for a long time, clinging to his hollow cheeks and sunken eyes. He must have been out of his head for two or three days.

The first time. Awful! Somehow, he had never quite believed in space madness.

Suddenly he remembered Jerry. Poor Jerry!

Gar lurched from the washroom back into the control room. Jerry was awake. He looked up at Gar, forcing a smile to his lips. "Hello, Dr. Elton," Jerry said.

Gar stopped as though shot.

"It's happened, Dr. Elton, just as you said it would," Jerry said, his smile widening.

"Forget that," Gar growled. "I took a yellow pill. I'm back to normal again."

Jerry's smile vanished abruptly. "I know what I did now," he said. "It's terrible. I killed six people. But I'm sane now. I'm willing to take what's coming to me."

"Forget that!" Gar snarled. "You don't have to humor me now. Just a minute and I'll untie you."

"Thanks, Doctor," Jerry said. "It will sure be a relief to get out of this strait jacket."

Gar knelt beside Jerry and untied the knots in the ropes and unwound them from around Jerry's chest and legs.

"You'll be all right in a minute," Gar said, massaging Jerry's limp arms. The physical and nervous strain of sitting there immobilized had been rugged.

Slowly he worked circulation back into Jerry, then helped him to his feet.

"You don't need to worry, Dr. Elton," Jerry said. "I

don't know why I killed those people, but I know I would never do such a thing again. I must have been insane.''

"Can you stand now?" Gar said, letting go of Jerry.

Jerry took a few steps back and forth, unsteadily at first, then with better co-ordination. His resemblance to a robot decreased with exercise.

Gar was beginning to feel sick again. He fought it.

"You OK now, Jerry boy?" he asked worriedly.

"I'm fine now, Dr. Elton," Jerry said. "And thanks for everything you've done for me."

Abruptly Jerry turned and went over to the air-lock door and opened it.

"Good-by now, Dr. Elton," he said.

"Wait!" Gar screamed, leaping toward Jerry.

But Jerry had stepped into the air lock and closed the door. Gar tried to open it, but already Jerry had turned on the pump that would evacuate the air from the lock.

Screaming Jerry's name senselessly in horror, Gar watched through the small square of thick glass in the door as Jerry's chest quickly expanded, then collapsed as a mixture of phlegm and blood dribbled from his nostrils and lips, and his eyes enlarged and glazed over, then one of them ripped open and collapsed, its fluid draining down his cheek.

He watched as Jerry glanced toward the side of the air lock and smiled, then spun the wheel that opened the air lock to the vacuum of space, and stepped out.

And when Gar finally stopped screaming and sank to the deck, sobbing, his knuckles were broken and bloody from pounding on bare metal.

UNHUMAN SACRIFICE

BY KATHERINE MACLEAN (1925–   )

ASTOUNDING SCIENCE FICTION
NOVEMBER

Katherine MacLean is not nearly as well known as she deserves to be, partly because her career has been marked by long periods of comparative silence and partly because she has produced only a handful of novels—most notably Cosmic Checkmate *(1962) and* Missing Man *(1975).*

*It is in her three collections—*The Diploids and Other Flights of Fancy *(1962),* Trouble With Treaties *(1975), and* The Trouble With You Earth People *(1980) that her finest work can be found. She debuted with "Defense Mechanism" in 1949, and that story, like most of her work, is concerned primarily with the social sciences, especially anthropology and psychology. Her story "Missing Man" the basis of the above mentioned novel, won a Nebula Award in 1971.*

"Unhuman Sacrifice" is an outstanding example of what a talented science fiction writer can do with the subject of social customs. (MHG)

Knowing the absolute truth (or, to be more accurate, thinking you do) is a dangerous and hateful thing. When the Puritans settled in New England, they established Sunday as a day of rest. It was a cosmic affair, ordained by God for the whole world, as anyone could plainly see if they read the beginning of the book of Genesis.

The Puritan judges fined those misguided inhabitants of the colony who violated the Sabbath by engaging in profane activities. They also fined the Indians who had never heard of the Sabbath, and told the poor, confused aborigines that on a particular day of the week they shouldn't go hunting.

It works the other way around, too. There are factories in the United States that are now owned by Japanese gentlemen, and the Japanese owners may tell American underlings how to behave in accordance with Japanese notions of politeness.

At least, I watched on television once, as a Japanese gentleman explained that drinking from a glass of water is a rather gross thing. It is unpleasant to watch the lips open, and slobber over the rim of the glass, and water cascading into the mouth and, therefore, the thing to do when you must drink (and what a pity Nature compels us to do so ugly a thing), is to hold the glass in one hand and raise the other to hide the sight from the world. And behold, we have invented a brand-new embarrassment.

Words cannot express my indignation over this. I'm going to drink as I please, I am, and I think Katherine MacLean would agree with me. (IA)

"Damn! He's actually doing it. Do you hear that?"

A ray of sunlight and a distant voice filtered down from the open arch in the control room above. The distant voice talked and paused, talked and paused. The words were blurred, but the tone was recognizable.

"He's outside preaching to the natives."

The two engineers were overhauling the engines but paused to look up towards the voice.

"Maybe not," said Charlie, the junior engineer. "After all, he doesn't know their language."

"He'd preach anyway," said Henderson, senior engineer and navigator. He heaved with a wrench on a tight bolt, the wrench slipped, and Henderson released some words that made Charlie shudder.

On the trip, Charlie had often dreamed apprehensively that Henderson had strangled the passenger. And once he had dreamed that he himself had strangled the passenger and Henderson, too.

When awake the engineers carefully avoided irritating words or gestures, remained cordial towards each other and the passenger no matter what the temptation to snarl, and tried to keep themselves in a tolerant good humor.

It had not been easy.

Charlie said, "How do you account for the missionary society giving him a ship of his own? A guy like that, who just gets in your hair when he's trying to give you advice, a guy with a natural born talent for antagonizing people?"

"Easy," Henderson grunted, spinning the bolt. He was a stocky, square-built man with a brusque manner and a practised tolerance of other people's oddities. "The missionary society was trying to get rid of him. You can't get any farther away than they sent us!"

The distant voice filtered into the control room from the unseen sunlit landscape outside the ship. It sounded resonant and confident. "The poor jerk thinks it was an honor," Henderson added. He pulled out the bolt and dropped it on the padded floor with a faint thump.

"Anyhow," Charlie said, loosening bolt heads in a circle as the manual instructed, "he can't use the translator machine. It's not ready yet, not until we get the rest of their language. He won't talk to them if they can't understand."

"Won't he?" Henderson fitted his wrench to another bolt and spun it angrily. "Then, what is he doing?"

Without waiting for an answer he replied to his own question. "*Preaching,* that's what he is doing!"

It seemed hot and close in the engine room, and the sunlight from outside beckoned.

Charlie paused and wiped the back of his arm against his

forehead. "Preaching won't do him any good. If they can't understand him, they won't listen."

"We didn't listen, and that didn't stop him from preaching to *us!*" Henderson snapped. "He's lucky we found a landing planet so soon, he's lucky he didn't drive us insane first. A man like that is a danger to a ship." Henderson, like Charlie, knew the stories of ships which had left with small crews, and returned with a smaller crew of one or two red-eyed maniacs and a collection of corpses. Henderson was a conservative. He preferred the regular shipping runs, the ships with a regular sized crew and a good number of passengers. Only an offer of triple pay and triple insurance indemnity had lured him from the big ships to be co-engineer on this odd three-man trip.

"Oh . . . I didn't mind being preached at," Charlie's tone was mild, but he stared upwards in the direction of the echoing voice with a certain intensity in his stance.

"Come off it, you twerp. We only have to be sweet to each other on a trip when we're cabin-bound. Don't kid old Harry, you didn't like it."

"No," said Charlie dreamily, staring upwards with a steady intensity. "Can't say that I did. He's not such a good preacher. I've met better in bars." The echoing voice from outside seemed to be developing a deeper echo. "He's got the translator going, Harry. I think we ought to stop him."

Charlie was a lanky redhead with a mild manner, about the same age as the preacher, but Henderson, who had experience, laid a restraining hand on his shoulder.

"I'll do it," said Henderson, and scrambled up the ladder to the control room.

The control room was a pleasant shading of greys, brightly lit by the sunlight that streamed in through the open archway. The opening to the outside was screened only by a billowing curtain of transparent sarantype plastic film, ion-coated to allow air to pass freely, but making a perfect and aseptic filter against germs and small insects. The stocky engineer hung a clear respirator box over a shoulder, brought the tube up to his mouth, and walked through the plastic film. It folded over him and wrapped him in an intimate tacky embrace, and gripped to its own surface behind him, sealing itself around him like a loose skin. Just past the arch he walked through a frame of metal like a man-sized croquet wicket and stopped while it tightened a noose around the trailing films of plastic behind him, cutting him free of the doorway curtain and sealing the break with heat.

Without waiting for the plastic to finish wrapping and tightening itself around him, the engineer went down the ramp, trailing plastic film in gossamer veils, like ghostly battle flags.

They could use this simple wrapping of thin plastic as an airsuit air lock, for the air of the new world was rich and good, and the wrapping was needed only to repel strange germs or infections. They were not even sure that there were any such germs; but the plastic was a routine precaution for ports in quarantine, and the two engineers were accustomed to wearing it. It allowed air to filter by freely, so that Henderson could feel the wind on his skin, only slightly diminished. He was wearing uniform shorts, and the wind felt cool and pleasant.

Around the spaceship stretched grassy meadow and thin forest, and beyond that in one direction lay the blue line of the sea, and in another the hazy blue-green of distant low mountains. It was so like the southern United States of Charlie's boyhood that the young engineer had wept with excitement when he first looked out of the ship. Harry Henderson did not weep, but he paused in his determined stride and looked around, and understood again how incredibly lucky they had been to find an Earth-type planet of such perfection. He was a firm believer in the hand of fate, and he wondered what fate planned for the living things of this green planet, and why it had chosen him as its agent.

Down in the green meadow, near the foot of the ramp sat the translator machine, still in its crate and on a wheeled dolly but with one side opened to expose the controls. It looked like a huge box, and it was one of the most expensive of the new inductive language analysers, brought along by their passengers in the hope and expectation of finding a planet with natives.

Triumphant in his success, the passenger, the Revent Winton, sat cross-legged on top of the crate, like a small king on a large throne. He was making a speech, using the mellow round tones of a trained elocutonist, with all the transparent plastic around his face hardly muffling his voice at all.

And the natives were listening. They sat around the translator box in a wide irregular circle, and stared. They were bald, with fur in tufts about their knees and elbows. Occasionally one got up, muttering to the others, and hurried away; and occasionally one came into the area and sat down to listen.

"Do not despair," called Revent Winton, in bell-like tones. "Now that I have shown you the light, you know that you have lived in darkness and sin all your lives, but do not despair. . . ."

The translator machine was built to assimilate a vast number of words and sentences in any tongue, along with fifty or so words in direct translation, and from that construct or find a grammatical pattern and print a handbook of the native language. Meanwhile, it would translate any word it was sure of. Henderson figured out the meaning of a few native words the day before and recorded them in, and the machine was industriously translating those few words whenever they appeared, like a deep bell, tolling the antiphony to the preacher's voice. The machine spoke in an enormous bass that was Henderson's low tones recorded through a filter and turned up to twenty times normal volume.

"I . . . LIGHT . . . YOU . . . YOU . . . LIVED . . . DARK . . . LIFE . . ."

The natives sat on the green grass and listened with an air of patient wonder.

"Revent Winton," Harry tried to attract his attention.

Winton leaned towards the attentive natives, his face softened with forgiveness. "No, say to yourselves merely—I have lived in error. Now I will learn the true path of a righteous life."

The machine in the box below him translated words into its voice of muted thunder. "SAY YOU . . . I . . . LIVED . . . I . . . PATH . . . LIFE. . . ."

The natives moved. Some got up and came closer, staring at the box, and others clustered and murmured to each other, and went away in small groups, talking.

Henderson decided not to tell the Revent what the machine had said. But this had to be stopped.

"Revent Winton!"

The preacher leaned over and looked down at him benevolently. "What is it, my son?" He was younger than the engineer, dark, intense and sure of his own righteousness.

"MY SON," said the translator machine in its voice of muted thunder. The sound rolled and echoed faintly back from the nearby woods, and the natives stared at Henderson.

Henderson muttered a bad word. The natives would think he was Winton's son! Winton did not know what it had said.

"Don't curse," Winton said patiently. "What is it, Harry?"

"Sorry," Henderson apologized, leaning his arms on the edge of the crate. "Switch off the translator, will you?"

"WILL YOU . . ." thundered the translator. The preacher switched it off.

"Yes?" he asked, leaning forward. He was wearing a conservative suit of knitted dark grey tights and a black shirt. Henderson felt badly dressed in his shorts and bare hairy chest.

"Revent, do you think it's the right thing to do, to preach to these people? The translator isn't finished, and we don't know anything about them yet. Anthropologists don't even make a suggestion to a native about his customs without studying the whole tribe and the way it lives for a couple of generations. I mean, you're going off half cocked. It's too soon to give them advice."

"I came to give them advice," Winton said gently. "They need my spiritual help. An anthropologist comes to observe.

They don't meddle with what they observe, for meddling would change it. But I am not here to observe, I am here to help them. Why should I wait?''

Winton had a remarkable skill with syllogistic logic. He always managed to sound as if his position were logical, somehow, in spite of Henderson's conviction that he was almost always entirely wrong. Henderson often, as now, found himself unable to argue.

"How do you know they need help?" he asked uncertainly. "Maybe their way of life is all right."

"Come now," said the preacher cheerfully, swinging his hand around the expanse of green horizon. "These are just primitives, not angels. I'd be willing to guess that they eat their own kind, or torture, or have human sacrifices."

"Humanoid sacrifices," Henderson muttered.

Winton's ears were keen. "Don't quibble. You know they will have some filthy primitive custom or other. Tribes on Earth used to have orgies and sacrifices in the spring. It's spring here—the Great Planner probably intended us to find this place in time to stop them."

"Oye," said Henderson and turned away to strike his forehead with the heel of his hand. His passenger was planning to interfere with a spring fertility ceremony. If these natives held such a ceremony—and it was possible that they might—they would be convinced that the ceremony insured the fertility of the earth, or the health of the sun, or the growth of the crops, or the return of the fish. They would be convinced that without the ceremony, summer would never return, and they would all starve. If Winton interfered, they would try to kill him.

Winton watched him, scowling at the melodrama of this gesture.

Henderson turned back to try to explain.

"Revent, I appeal to you, tampering is dangerous. Let us go back and report this planet, and let the government send a survey ship. When the scientists arrive, if they find that we have been tampering with the natives' customs without waiting for advice, they will consider it a crime. We will be notorious in scientific journals. We'll be considered responsible for any damage the natives sustain.''

The preacher glared. "Do you think that I am a coward, afraid of the anger of atheists?" He again waved a hand, indicating the whole sweep of the planet's horizon around them. "Do you think we found this place by accident? The Great Planner sent me here for a purpose. I am responsible to Him, not to you, or your scientist friends. I will fulfill His purpose." He leaned forward, staring at Henderson with dark fanatical eyes. "Go weep about your reputation somewhere else.''

Henderson stepped back, getting a clearer view of the passenger, feeling as if he had suddenly sprouted fangs and claws. He was still as he had appeared before, an intense, brunet young man, wearing dark tights and dark shirt, sitting cross-legged on top of a huge box, but now he looked primitive somehow, like a prehistoric naked priest on top of an altar.

"Anthropology is against this kind of thing," Henderson said.

Winton looked at him malevolently from his five foot elevation on the crate and the extra three feet of his own seated height. "You aren't an anthropologist, are you, Harry? You're an engineer?"

"That's right," Henderson admitted, hating him for the syllogism.

Wintons said sweetly: "Then why don't you go back to the ship and work on the engine?"

"There will be trouble," Henderson said softly.

"I am prepared for trouble," the Revent Winton said equally softly. He took a large old-fashioned revolver out of his carry case, and rested it on his knee.

The muzzle pointed midway between the engineer and the natives.

Henderson shrugged and went back up the ramp.

* * *

"What did he do?" Charlie was finishing his check of the fuel timers, holding a coffee cup in his free hand.

Angrily silent, Harry cut an exit slit from the plastic coating. He ripped off the gossamer films of plastic, wadded them up together and tossed them in a salvage hopper.

"He told me to mind my own business. And that's what I am going to do."

The preacher's impressive voice began to ring again from the distance outside, and, every so often, like a deep gong, the translator machine would speak a word in the native dialect.

"The translator is still going," Charlie pointed out.

"Let it. He doesn't know what it is saying." Sulkily, Henderson turned to a library shelf, and pulled out a volume: *The E.T. Planet, a manual of observation and behavior on extra-terrestrial planets, with examples.*

"What is it saying?"

"Almost nothing at all. All it translated out of a long speech the creep made was 'I life path.' "

The younger engineer lost his smile. "That was good enough for others. Winton doesn't know what the box is saying?"

"He thinks it's saying what he is saying. He's giving out with his usual line of malarky."

"We've got to stop it!" Charlie began to climb the ladder.

Henderson shrugged. "So go out and tell him the translator isn't working right. I should have told him. But if I get close to him now, I'd strangle him."

Charlie returned later, grinning. "It's O.K. The natives are scared of Winton, and they like the box; so they must think that the box is talking sense for itself, and Winton is gibbering in a strange language."

"He is. And it is," Henderson said sourly. "They are right."

"You're kind of hard on him." Charlie started searching the shelves for another copy of the manual of procedure for survey teams. "But I can see what you mean. Anyhow, I told Winton that he was making a bad impression on the natives. It stopped him. It stopped him cold. He said he would put off preaching for a week and study the natives a little. But he said we ought to fix up the translator, so that it translates what he says." Charlie turned, smiling, with a book in one hand, "That gives us time."

"Time for what?" Henderson growled without looking up from his book. "Do you think we can change Winton's mind? That bonehead believes that butting into people's lives is a sacred duty. Try talking any bonehead out of a sacred duty! He'd butt into a cannibal banquet! I hope he does. I hope they eat him!"

"Long pig," Charlie mused, temporarily diverted by the picture. "Tastes good to people, probably would taste foul to these natives, they're not the same species."

"He says he's planning to stop their spring festival. If it has sacrifices or anything he doesn't like, he says he'll stop it."

Charlie placed his fists on the table and leaned across towards Henderson, lowering his voice. "Look, we don't know even if the natives are going to have any spring festival. Maybe if we investigate we'll find out that there won't be one, or maybe we'll find out that Winton can't do them any harm. Maybe we don't have to worry. Only let's go out and investigate. We can write up reports on whatever we find, in standard form, and the journals will print them when we get back. Glory and all like that." He added, watching Henderson's expression: "Maybe, if we have to, we can break the translator."

It was the end of the season of dry. The river was small and ran in a narrow channel, and there were many fish near the surface. Spet worked rapidly, collecting fish from the fish traps, returning the empty traps to the water, salting the fish.

He was winded, but pleased with the recollection of last night's feast, and hungry in anticipation of the feast of the evening to come. This was the season of the special meals, cooking herbs and roots and delicacies with the fish. Tonight's feast might be the last he would ever have, for a haze was thickening over the horizon, and tomorrow the rains might come.

One of the strangers came and watched him. Spet ignored him politely and salted the fish without looking at him directly. It was dangerous to ignore a stranger, but to make the formal peace gestures and agreements would be implying that the stranger was from a tribe of enemies, when he might already be a friend. Spet preferred to be polite, so he pretended not to be concerned that he was being watched.

The haze thickened in the sky, and the sunlight weakened. Spet tossed the empty trap back to its place in the river with a skillful heave of his strong short arms. If he lived through the next week, his arms would not be strong and short, they would be weak and long. He began to haul in another trap line, sneaking side glances at the stranger as he pulled.

The stranger was remarkably ugly. His features were all misfit sizes. Reddish brown all over like a dead leaf, and completely bald of hair at knees and elbows, he shone as if he were wet, covered all over with a transparent shininess, like water, but the water never dripped. He was thick and sturdy and quick moving, like a youngling, but did not work. Very strange, unlike reality, he stood quietly watching, without attacking Spet, although he could have attacked without breaking a peace gesture. So he was probably not of any enemy tribe.

It was possible that the undripping water was an illusion, meant to indicate that the stranger was really the ghost of someone who had drowned.

The stranger continued to watch. Spet braced his feet against the grass of the bank and heaved on the next trap line, wanting to show his strength. He heaved too hard, and a strand of the net gave way. The stranger waded out into the water, and pulled in the strand, so that no fish escaped.

It was the act of a friend. And yet when the net trap was

safely drawn up on the bank, the brown stranger stepped back without comment or gesture, and watched exactly as before—as if his help was the routine of one kinfolk to another.

That showed that the brown one was his kin and a member of his family. But Spet had seen all of his live kinfolk, and none of them looked so strange. It followed reasonably that the brown one was a ghost, a ghost of a relative who had drowned.

Spet nodded at the ghost and transferred the fish from the trap to the woven baskets and salted them. He squatted to repair the broken strand of the net.

The brown ghost squatted beside him. It pointed at the net and made an inquiring sound.

"I am repairing the trap, Grandfather," Spet explained, using the most respectful name for the brown ghost relative.

The ghost put a hand over his own mouth, then pointed at the ground and released its mouth to make another inquiring noise.

"The ground is still dry, Grandfather," Spet said cordially, wondering what he wanted to know. He rose and flung the trap net out on its line into the river, hoping that the brown ghost would admire his strength. Figures in dreams often came to tell you something, and often they could not speak, but the way they looked and the signs they made were meant to give you a message. The brown ghost was shaped like a youngling, like Spet, as if he had drowned before his adult hanging ceremony. Perhaps this one came in daylight instead of dreams, because Spet was going to die and join the ghosts soon, before he became an adult.

The thought was frightening. The haze thickening on the horizon looked ominous.

The brown ghost repeated what Spet had said, almost in Spet's voice, blurring the words slightly. *The ground is still dry Grandfather.* He pointed at the ground and made an inquiring noise.

"Ground," said Spet thinking about death, and every song he had heard about it. Then he heard the ghost repeat the word, and saw the satisfaction of his expression, and realized that the ghost had forgotten how to talk, and wanted to be taught all over again, like a newborn.

That made courtesy suddenly a simple and pleasant game. As Spet worked, he pointed at everything, and said the word, he described what he was doing, and sometimes he sang the childhood work songs, that described the work.

The ghost followed and helped him with the nets, and listened and pointed at things he wanted to learn. Around his waist coiled a blind silver snake that Spet had not noticed at first, and the ghost turned the head of the snake towards Spet when he sang, and sometimes the ghost talked to the snake himself, with explanatory gestures.

It was very shocking to Spet that anyone would explain things to a snake, for snakes are wise, and a blind snake is the wise one of dreams——he who knows everything. The blind snake did not need to be explained to. Spet averted his eyes and would not look at it.

The ghost and he worked together, walking up the river bank, hauling traps, salting fish, and throwing the traps back, and Spet told what he was doing, and the ghost talked down to the snake around his waist, explaining something about what they were doing.

Once the brown ghost held the blind silver snake out towards Spet, indicating with a gesture that he should speak to it.

Terrified and awed, Spet fell to his knees. "Tell me, Wisest One, if you wish to tell me, will I die in the hanging?"

He waited, but the snake lay with casual indifference in the ghost's hand, and did not move or reply.

Spet rose from his knees and backed away. "Thank you, oh Wise One."

The ghost spoke to the snake, speaking very quietly, with apologetic gestures and much explanation, then wrapped it again around his waist, and helped Spet carry the loads of salted fish, without speaking again, or pointing at anything.

It was almost sundown.

*   *   *

On the way back to his family hut, Spet passed the Box That Speaks. The black gibbering spirit sat on top of it and gibbered as usual, but this time the Box stopped him and spoke to him, and called him by his own name, and asked questions about his life.

Spet was carrying a heavy load of salted fish in two baskets hung on a yoke across one sturdy shoulder. He was tired. He stood in the midst of the green meadow that in other seasons had been a river, with the silver hut of the ghosts throwing a long shadow across him. His legs were tired from wading in the river, and his mind was tired from the brown ghost asking him questions all day; so he explained the thing that was uppermost in his mind, instead of discussing fishing and weather. He explained that he was going to die. The ceremony of Hanging, by which the almost-adults became adults, was going to occur at the first rain, five younglings were ready, usually most of them lived, but he thought he would die.

The box fell silent, and the ghost on top stopped gibbering, so Spet knew that it was true, for people fall silent at a truth that they do not want to say aloud.

He made a polite gesture of leave-taking to the box, and went towards his family hut, feeling very unhappy. During the feast of that evening all the small ones ate happily of fish and roots and became even fatter, and the thin adults picked at the roots and herbs. Spet was the only youngling of adult-beginning age, and he should have been eating well to grow fat and build up his strength, but instead he went outside and looked at the sky and saw that it was growing cloudy. He did not go back in to the feast again, instead he crouched against the wall of the hut and shivered without sleeping. Before his eyes rested the little flat-bottomed boats of the family, resting in the dust behind the hut for the happy days of the rain. He would never travel in those boats again.

Hanging upside down was a painful way to become an

273

adult, but worth it, if you lived. It was going to be a very bad way to die.

Hurrying and breathless with his news, Revent Winton came upon the two engineers crouched at the river bank.

"I found out . . ." he began.

"*Shhh,*" one said without turning.

They were staring at a small creature at the edge of the water.

Winton approached closer and crouched beside them. "I have news that might interest you." He held his voice to a low murmur, but the triumph sounded in it like a rasp cutting through glass, a vibration that drew quick speculative glances from the engineers. They turned their attention back to the water's edge.

"Tell us when this is over. Wait."

The young preacher looked at what they were staring at, and saw a little four-legged creature with large eyes and bright pointed teeth struggling feebly in the rising water. The younger engineer, Charlie, was taking pictures of it.

"Its feet are stuck," Winton whispered. "Why don't you help it?"

"It's rooting itself," Henderson murmured back. "We're afraid that loud noises might make it stop."

"Rooting itself?" Winton was confused.

"The animal has two life stages, like a barnacle. You know, a barnacle is a little fish that swims around before it settles down to being just kind of a lump of rock. This one has a rooted stage that's coming on it now. When the water gets up to its neck it rolls up underwater and sticks its front legs out and starts acting like a kind of seaweed. Its hind feet are growing roots. This is the third one we've watched."

Winton looked at the struggling little creature. The water was rising towards its neck. The large bright eyes and small bared teeth looked frightened and uncomprehending. Winton shuddered.

"Horrible," he murmured. "Does it know what is happening?"

Henderson shrugged, "At least it knows the water is rising, and it knows it must not run away. It has to stand there and dig its feet in." He looked at Winton's expression and looked away. "Instinct comes as a powerful urge to do something. You can't fight instinct. Usually it's a pleasure to give in. It's not so bad."

Revent Paul Winton had always been afraid of drowning. He risked another glance at the little creature that was going to turn into a seaweed. The water had almost reached its neck, and it held its head high and panted rapidly with a thin whimpering sound.

"Horrible," Winton turned his back to it and pulled Henderson farther up the bank away from the river. "Mr. Henderson, I just found something."

He was very serious, but now he had trouble phrasing what he had to say. Henderson urged him, "Well, go on."

"I found it out from a native. The translator is working better today."

"Charlie and I just recorded about four hundred words and phrases into it by distance pickup. We've been interviewing natives all day." Henderson's face suddenly grew cold and angry. "By the way, I thought you said that you weren't going to use the translator until it is ready."

"I was just checking it." Winton actually seemed apologetic. "I didn't say anything, just asked questions."

"All right," Henderson nodded grudgingly. "Sorry I complained. What happened? You're all upset, man!"

Winton evaded his eyes and turned away, he seemed to be looking at the river, with its banks of bushes and trees. Then he turned and looked in the direction of the inland hills, his expression vague. "Beautiful green country. It looks so peaceful. God is lavish with beauty. It shows His goodness. When we think that God is cruel, it is only because we do not understand. God is not really cruel."

"All right, so God is not really cruel," Henderson repeated cruelly. "So what's new?"

Winton winced and pulled his attention back to Henderson.

"Henderson, you've noticed that there are two kinds of natives, tall, thin ones that are slow, and quick, sturdy, short ones that do all the hard work. The sturdy ones we see in all ages, from child size up. Right?"

"I noticed."

"What did you think it meant?"

"Charlie and I talked about it." Henderson was puzzled. "Just a guess, but we think that the tall ones are aristocrats. They probably own the short ones, and the short ones do all the work."

Thick clouds were piled up over the far hills, accounting for the slow rise in the river level.

"The short ones are the children of the tall thin ones. The tall thin ones are the adults. The adults are all sick, that is why the children do all the work."

"What . . ." Henderson began, but Winton overrode his voice, continuing passionately, his eyes staring ahead at the hills.

"They are sick because of something they do to themselves. The young ones, strong and healthy, when they are ready to become adults they . . . they are hung upside down. For days, Henderson, maybe for more than a week, the translator would not translate how long. Some of them die. Most of them . . . most of them are stretched, and become long and thin. He stopped, and started again with an effort. "The native boy could not tell me why they do this, or how it started. It has been going on for so long that they cannot remember."

Abruptly, and, to Henderson, shockingly, the preacher dropped to his knees and put his hands together. He tilted his head back with shut eyes and burst into prayer.

"Oh Lord, I do not know why You waited so long to help them to the true light, but I thank You that You sent me to stop this horrible thing."

Quickly he stood up and brushed his knees. "You'll help me, won't you?" he asked Henderson.

"How do we know it's true?" Henderson scowled. "It doesn't seem reasonable."

"Not reasonable?" Winton recovered his poise in sudden anger. "Come now Harry, you've been talking as if you knew some anthropology. Surely you remember the puberty ceremonies. Natives often have initiation ceremonies for the young males. It's to test their manhood. They torture the boys, and the ones who can take it without whimpering are considered to be men, and graduated. Filthy cruelty! The authorities have always made them stop."

"No one around here has any authority to order anyone else to stop," Harry grunted. He was shaken by Winton's description of the puberty ceremony, and managed to be sarcastic only from a deep conviction that Winton had been always wrong, and therefore would continue to be wrong. It was not safe to agree with the man. It would mean being wrong along with Winton.

"No authority? What of God?"

"Well, what *of* God?" Henderson asked nastily. "If He is everywhere. He was here before you arrived here. And He never did anything to stop them. You've only known them a week. How long has God known them?"

"You don't understand." The dark-haired young man spoke with total conviction, standing taller, pride straightening his spine. "It was more than mere luck that we found this planet. It is my destiny to stop these people from their ceremony. God sent me."

Henderson was extremely angry, in a white-faced way. He had taken the preacher's air of superiority in the close confine of a spaceship for two months, and listened patiently to his preaching without letting himself be angry, for the sake of peace in the spaceship. But now he was out in the free air again, and he had had his fill of arrogance, and wanted no more.

"Is that so?" he asked nastily. "Well, I'm on this expedition, too. How do you know that God did not send *me*, to stop *you?*"

Charlie finished taking pictures of the little animal under water as it changed, and came back up the bank, refolding the underwater lens. He was in time to see Winton slap the chief engineer in the face, spit out some profanity that would have started him on an hour of moral lecture, if he had heard either of them emit such words. He saw Winton turn and run, not as if he were running away, but as if he were running to do something, in sudden impatience.

Ten minutes later Henderson had finished explaining what was bothering the preacher. They lay on the bank lazily looking down into the water, putting half attention into locating some other interesting life form, and enjoying the reflection of sunset in the ripples.

"I wish I could chew grass," Henderson said. "It would make it just like watching a river when I was a kid. But the plastic stuff on my face keeps me from putting anything into my mouth."

"The leaves would probably be poisonous anyhow," Charlie brushed a hand through the pretty green of the grass. It was wiry and tough with thin round blades, like marsh grass. "This isn't really grass. This isn't really Earth, you know."

"I know, I wish I could forget it. I wonder what that creep, Winton, is doing now." Henderson rolled on his back and looked lazily at the sky. "I've got one up on him now. I got him to act like a creep right out in the open. He won't be giving me that superior, fatherly bilge. He might even call me Henderson now instead of Harry."

"Don't ask too much," Charlie clipped a piece of leaf from a weed and absently tried to put it into his mouth. It was stopped by the transparent plastic film that protected him from local germs and filtered the air he breathed.

He flicked the leaf away, "How did that creep get to be a missionary? Nothing wrong with him, except he can't get on with people. Doesn't help in his line of work to be like that."

"Easy, like I said," said Henderson, staring into the darkening pink and purple of the sky. "They encouraged him to be a missionary so he would go far far away. Don't ever tell him. He thinks that he was chosen for his eloquence." Henderson rolled back on to his stomach and looked at the river. It was a chilly purple now, with silver ripples. "More clouds over the mountains. And those little clouds overhead might thicken up and rain. If the river keeps rising, there might be a flood. We might have to move the ship."

"Winton said the native mentioned a flood." Charlie got up lazily and stretched. "Getting dark out here anyhow. We'll have to find out more about that interview."

They went in search of the preacher.

What he told them was disturbing, and vague.

"That was Spet," Henderson said. "That was the one I was learning words from all afternoon. And he told you he was going to die?"

Winton was earnest and pale. He sat crouched over the chart table as if his resolution to act had frightened him. "Yes. He said he was going to die. He said that they were going to hang him upside down in a tree as soon as the next rain starts. Because he is old enough."

"But he said that other young males live through it? Maybe he's wrong about dying. Maybe it's not as tough as it sounds."

"He said that many die," Winton said tonelessly. His hands lay motionless on the table. He was moved to a sudden flare of anger. "Oh those stupid savages. Cruel, cruel!" He turned his head to Henderson, looking up at him without the usual patronizing expression. "You'll fix the translator so that it translates me exactly, won't you? I don't want to shoot them to stop them from doing it. I'll just stop them by explaining that God doesn't want them to do this thing. They will have to understand me."

He turned his head to Charlie, standing beside him. "The savages call me Enaxip. What does that mean? Do they think I'm a god?"

"It means Big Box," Henderson cut in roughly. "They still think that the box is talking. I see them watch the box when they answer, they don't watch you. I don't know what they think you are.''

That night it did not rain. Winton allowed himself to fall asleep near dawn.

To Spet also it made a difference that it did not rain.

The next day he fished in the river as he always had.

The river was swollen and ran high and swiftly between its banks and fishing was not easy at first, but the brown ghost returned, bringing another one like himself, and they both helped Spet with pulling in the fish traps. The new ghost also wanted to be told how to talk, like a small one, and they all had considerable amusement as the two ghosts acted out ordinary things that often happened, and Spet told them the right words and songs to explain what they were doing.

One of them taught him a word in ghost language, and he knew that he was right to learn, because he would soon be a ghost.

When Spet carried the fish back along the path to his family hut that evening, he passed the Box That Talks. It spoke to him again, and again asked him questions.

The spirit covered with black that usually gibbered on top of the box was not there. Nothing was on top of the box, but the brown ghost who had just been helping him fish stood beside the box and spoke to it softly each time it asked Spet a question. The box spoke softly back to the ghost after Spet answered, discussing his answers, as if they had a problem concerning him.

Spet answered the questions politely, although some of them were difficult questions, asking reasons for things he had never thought needed a reason, and some were questions it was not polite to ask. He did not know why they discussed him, but it was their business and they would tell him if they chose.

When he left them, the brown ghost made a gesture of respect and mutual aid in work, and Spet returned, warmed and pleased by the respect of the ghost-relative.

He did not remember to be afraid until he was almost home.

It began to rain.

Charlie came up the ramp and into the spaceship, and found Henderson pacing up and down, his thick shoulders hunched, his fists clenched, and his face wrinkled with worry.

"Hi." Charlie did not expect an answer. He kicked the lever that tightened the noose on the curtain plastic behind him, watched the hot wire cut him loose from the curtain and seal the curtain in the same motion. He stood carefully folding and smoothing his new wrapping of plastic around himself, to make sure that the coating he had worn outside was completely coated by the new wrapping. All outside dust and germs had to be trapped between the two layers of sterile germproof plastic.

He stood mildly smoothing and adjusting the wrappings, watching Henderson pace with only the very dimmest flicker of interest showing deep in his eyes. He could withdraw his attention so that a man working beside him could feel completely unwatched and as if he had the privacy of a cloak of invisibility. Charlie was well mannered and courteous, and this was part of his courtesy.

"How're things?" he asked casually, slitting open his plastic cocoon and stepping out.

Henderson stopped pacing and took a cigar from a box on the table with savage impatience in his motions. "Very bad," he said. "Winton was right."

"Eh?" Charlie wadded up the plastic and tossed it into the disposal hopper.

"The natives, they actually do it." Henderson clenched the cigar between his teeth and lit it with savage jerky motions. "I asked Spet. No mistake in the translator this time. He said, yes, they hang the young men upside down in the trees after the first spring rain. And yes, it hurt, and yes sometimes one died, and no he didn't know why they had to do this or what it was for. Ha!'' Henderson threw the cigar away and began to pace again, snarling.

"Oh yes, the translator was working fine! Generations of torturing their boys with this thing, and the adults can't remember how it started, or why, and they go on doing it anyway. . . .''

Charlie leaned back against the chart table, following his pacing with his eyes. "Maybe," he said mildly, "there's some good reason for the custom."

"A good reason to hang upside down for a week? Name one!''

Charlie did not answer.

"I just came from the native village," he said conversationally as though changing the subject. "Winton has started. He's got the translator box right in the center of their village now, and he's sitting on top of it telling them that God is watching them, and stuff like that. I tried to reason with him, and he just pointed a gun at me. He said he'd stop the hanging ceremony even if he had to kill both of us and half the natives to do it.''

"So let him try to stop them, just by talking." Henderson, who had stopped to listen, began to pace again, glowering at the floor. "That flapping mouth! Talking won't do it. Talking by itself never does anything. I'm going to do it the easy way. I'm going to kidnap Spet, and keep them from getting him.

"Charlie, tribes only do things at the right season, what they call the right season. We'll turn Spet loose after the week is up, and they won't lay a hand on him. They'll just wait until next year. Meanwhile they'll be seeing that the trees aren't angry at them or any of that malarky. When they see that Spet got away with it, they'll have a chance to see a young male who's becoming a healthy adult without being all stretched out and physically wrecked.

"And maybe next year, Spet will decide to get lost by himself. Maybe after looking at how Spet looks compared with an adult who was hanged, some of the kids due for hanging next year would duck into the forest and get lost when it's due."

"It's a good dream," Charlie said, lounging, following Henderson's pacing with his eyes. "I won't remind you that we swore off dreaming. But I'm with you in this, man. How do we find Spet?"

Henderson sat down, smiling. "We'll see him at the stream tomorrow. We don't need to do anything until it starts raining."

Charlie started rummaging in the tool locker. "Got to get a couple of flashlights. We have to move fast. Have to find Spet in a hurry. It's already raining, been raining almost an hour."

Darkness and rain, and it was very strange being upside down. Not formal and ceremonial, like a story-song about it, but real, like hauling nets and thatching huts, and eating with his brothers. The world seemed to be upside down. The tree trunk was beside him, strong and solid, and the ground was above him like a roof being held up by the tree, and the sky was below his feet and very far away . . . and looking down at the clouds swirling in the depth of the sky he was afraid of falling into it. The sky was a lake, and he would fall through it like a stone falling through water. If one fell into the sky, one would fall and fall for a long time, it looked so very deep.

Rain fell upwards out of the sky and hit him under the chin. His ankles and wrists were tightly bound, but did not hurt, for the elders had used a soft rope of many strands tied in a way that would not stop circulation. His arms were at his sides, his wrists bound to the same strand that pulled at his ankles, and the pull on his arms was like standing upright, carrying a small weight of something. He was in a standing position, but upside down. It was oddly comfortable. The elders had many generations of experience to guide them, and they had chosen a tall tree with a high branch that was above the flood. They had seemed wise and certain, and he had felt confidence in them as they had bound and hung him up with great gentleness, speaking quietly to each other.

Then they had left him, towing their little flat-boats across the forest floor that was now a roof above his head, walking tall and stork-like across the dim lit glistening ground, which looked so strangely like a rough, wet ceiling supported by the trunks of trees.

The steady rain drummed against the twigs and small spring leaves, splashing in the deepening trickles of water that ran along the ground. Spet knew that somewhere the river was overflowing its banks and spreading into the forest and across meadows to meet and deepen the rain water. In the village the street would be muddy, and the children would be shouting, trying already to pole the boats in the street, wild with impatience for the rising of the river, to see again the cold swift flow of water and watch the huts of the town sag and flow downwards, dissolve and vanish beneath the smooth surface.

For a month in the time of floods everyone would live in boats. His tribe would paddle and pole up the coast, meeting other tribes, trading baskets and fishhooks, salt fish for salt meat, and swapping the old stories and songs with new variations brought from far places. Last time they had been lucky enough to come upon a large animal caught in the flood, swimming and helpless to resist the hunters. The men of the enemy tribe had traded skin for half the roast meat on a raft, and sang a long story song that no one had heard before. That was the best feast of all.

Then the horde of small boats would come home to the lakes that were draining meadows and forest, and take down the sick and dying young men who had been hanging in the trees, and tend and feed them and call them ''elder.'' They would then travel again for food, to fight through storms to salt the meat of drowned animals and hunt the deep sea fish caught in the dwindling lakes.

When the rains had stopped and the land began to dry, they

would return to the damp and drying land to sing and work and build a village of the smooth fresh clay left by the flood.

But Spet would not see those good times again. He hung in his tree upside down with the rain beating coolly against his skin. It was growing too dark to see more than the dim light of the sky. He shut his eyes, and behind his shut eyes were pictures and memories, and then dreams.

Here he is. How do we get him down. Did you bring a knife. How do we get up to him. It's slippery. I can't climb this thing. Wait, I'll give you a boost.

A flash of light, too steady for lightning, lasting a full second. Spet awoke fully, staring into the darkness, looking for the light which now was gone, listening to the mingled voices in the strange language.

"Don't use the flashlight, it will frighten him."

"Going to try to explain to him what we're doing?"

"No, not right away. He'll come along. Spet's a pal of mine already."

"Man, do these trees have roots. As big as the branches!"

"Like mangroves?"

"You're always claiming the South has everything. What are mangroves?"

"Florida swamp trees. They root straight into deep water. Give a hand here."

"Keeps raining like this and they're going to need their roots. How high can we climb just on the roots anyhow?"

"Think you're kidding? Why else would they have roots like this? This territory must be underwater usually, deep water. This flat land must be delta country. We're just in the dry season."

"What do you mean delta country? I'm a city boy, define your terms."

"I mean, we're at the mouth of one of those big wandering rivers like the Mississippi or the Yellow River that doesn't know where it's going to run next, and splits up into a lot of little rivers at the coast, and moves its channel every spring. I

noticed that grass around the ship looked like salt water grass. Should have thought about it.''

A dark figure appeared beside Spet and climbed past him toward the branch where the rope was tied. The next voice was distant. *''You trying to tell me we landed the ship in a riverbed? Why didn't you say something when we were landing?''*

''Didn't think of it, then.'' That voice was loud and close.

''It's a fine time to think of it now. I left the ship wide open. You up there yet?''

''Uh huh. I'm loosening the rope. Going to lower him slow. Catch him and keep him from landing on his head, will you?''

''Ready. Lower away.''

The voices stopped and the world began to spin, and the bole of the tree began to move past Spet's face.

Suddenly a pair of wet arms gripped him, and the voice of the brown ghost called, *''Got him.''*

Immediately the rope ceased to pull at Spet's ankles, and he fell against the brown ghost head-first and they both tumbled against the slippery high roots and slid down from one thick root to another until they stopped at the muddy ground. The ghost barked a few short words and began to untie the complex knots from Spet's ankles and wrists.

It was strange sitting on the wet ground with its coating of last year's leaves. Even right-side up the forest looked strange, and Spet knew that this was because of death, and he began to sing his death song.

The brown ghost helped him to his feet, and said clearly in ordinary words, *''Come on, boy, you can sing when we get there.''*

His friend dropped down from a low branch to the higher roots of the tree, slipped and fell on the ground beside them.

In Spet's language the standing one said to the other, *''No time for resting, Charlie, let's go.''*

It was very dark now, and the drips from the forest branches poured more heavily, beating against the skin.

The ghost on the ground barked a few of the same words the relative-ghost had made when he had fallen, and got up.

The two started off through the forest, beckoning Spet to follow. He wondered if he were a ghost already. Perhaps the ghosts had taken him to be a ghost without waiting for him to die. That was nice of them, and a favor, possibly because they were kinfolk. He followed them.

The rain had lightened, and become the steady, light falling spray that it would be for the next several days. Walking was difficult, for the floor of the forest was slippery with wet leaves, and the mud underneath was growing soft again, remembering the time it had been part of the water of the river, remembering that the river had left it there only a year ago. The ghosts with him made sputtering words in ghost talk, sometimes tripped and floundered and fell, helped each other up and urged him on.

The forest smelled of the good sweet odors of damp earth and growing green leaves. The water and mud were cooling against his hurting feet, and Spet unaccountably wanted to linger in the forest, and sit, and perhaps sleep.

The floods were coming, and the ghosts had no boats with them.

"Come on, Spet. We go to big boat. Come on, Spet."

Why did they stumble and flounder through the forest without a boat? And why were they afraid? Could ghosts drown? These ghosts, with their perpetually wet appearance—if they had drowned once, would they be forced to relive the drowning, and be caught in the floods every year? A bad thing that happened once, had to happen again and again in dreams. And your spirit self in the dream lived it each time as something new. There is no memory in the dream country. These ghosts were dream people, even though they chose to be in the awake world. They were probably bound by the laws of the dream world.

They would have to re-enact their drowning. Their boat was far away, and they were running towards the water course where the worst wave of the flood would come.

Spet understood suddenly that they wanted him to drown. He could not become a ghost, like these friendly brown ghosts, and live in their world, without first dying.

He remembered his first thought of them, that they carried the illusion of water over them because they had once drowned. They wanted him to be like them. They were trying to lure him through waters where he would stumble and drown as they had.

Naturally as they urged him on their gestures were nervous and guilty. It is not easy to urge a friend onwards to his death. But to be shaped like a young one, merry, brown, and covered with water, obviously he had to be drowned as they were drowned, young and merry, before the hanging had made a sad adult of him.

He would not let them know that he had guessed their intention. Running with them towards the place where the flood would be worst, he tried to remember at what verse he had stopped singing his death song, and began again from that verse, singing to stop the fear-thoughts. The rain beat coolly against his face and chest as he ran.

Each man in his own panic, they burst from the forest into the clearing. The engineers saw with a wave of relief that the spaceship was still there, a pale shaft upright in the midst of water. Where the meadow had been was a long narrow lake, reflecting the faint light of the sky, freckled with drifting spatters of rain.

"How do we get to it?" Charlie turned to them.

"How high is the water? Is the ramp covered?" Henderson asked practically, squinting through the rain.

"Ramp looks the same. I see grass sticking up in the water. It's not deep."

Charlie took a careful step and then another out into the silvery surface. Spongy grass met his feet under the surface, and the water lapped above his ankles, but no higher.

"It's shallow."

They started out towards the ship. It took courage to put their feet down into a surface that suggested unseen depth.

The shallow current of water tugged at their ankles, and grew deeper and stronger.

"Henderson, wait!"

The three stopped and turned at the call. The path to the village was close, curving away from the forest towards the distant river bank, a silvery road of water among dark bushes. A dark figure came stumbling along the path, surrounded by the silvery shine of the rising water. Ripples spread from his ankles as he ran.

He came to the edge where the bushes stopped and the meadow began, saw the lake-appearance of it, and stopped. The others were already thirty feet away.

"Henderson! Charlie!"

"Walk, it's not deep yet. Hurry up." Charlie gestured urgently for him to follow them. They were still thirty feet out, standing in the smooth silver of the rising water. It was almost to their knees.

Winton did not move. He looked across the shining shallow expanse of water, and his voice rose shrilly. "It's a lake, we need boats."

"It's shallow," Charlie called. The rain beat down on the water, specking it in small vanishing pockmarks. The two engineers hesitated, looking back at Winton, sensing something wrong.

Winton's voice was low, but the harshness of desperation made it clear as if he had screamed.

"Please. I can't swim—"

"Go get him," Henderson told Charlie. "He's got a phobia. I'll herd Spet to the ship, and then head back to help you."

Charlie was already splashing in long strides back to the immobile figure of the preacher. He started to shout when he got within earshot.

"Why didn't you say so, man? We almost left you behind!" He crouched down before the motionless fear-dazed figure. "Get on, man. You're getting taxi service."

"What?" asked Winton in a small distant voice. The water lapped higher.

"Get on my back," Charlie snapped impatiently. "You're getting transportation."

"The houses dissolved, and they went off in boats and left me alone. They said that I was an evil spirit. I think they did the hangings anyway, even though I told them it was wrong." Winton's voice was vague, but he climbed on Charlie's back. "The *houses* dissolved."

"Speak up, stop mumbling," muttered Charlie.

The spaceship stood upright ahead in the center of the shallow silver lake that had been a meadow. Its doors were open, and the bottom of the ramp was covered by water. Water tugged against Charlie's lower legs as he ran, and the rain beat against their faces and shoulders in a cool drumming.

It would have been pleasant, except that the fear of drowning was growing even in Charlie, and the silver of the shallow new lake seemed to threaten an unseen depth ahead.

"There seems to be a current," Winton said with an attempt at casual remarks. "Funny, this water looks natural here, as if the place were a river, and those trees look like the banks."

Charlie said nothing. Winton was right, but it would not be wise to tell a man with phobia about drowning that they were trying to walk across the bed of a river while the water returned to its channel.

"Why are you running?" asked the man he carried.

"To catch up with Henderson."

Once they were inside the spaceship with the door shut they could ignore the water level outside. Once inside, they would not have to tell Winton anything about how it was outside. A spaceship made a good submarine.

The water level was almost to Charlie's knees and he ran now in a difficult lurching fashion. Winton pulled up his feet nervously to keep them from touching the water. The plastic which they wore was semi-permeable to water and both of them were soaked.

"Who is that up ahead with Henderson?"

"Spet, the native boy."

"How did you persuade him to stay away from the ceremony?"

"We found him hanging and cut him down."

"Oh," Winton was silent a moment trying to absorb the fact that the engineers had succeeded in rescuing someone. "It's a different approach. I talked, but they wouldn't listen." He spoke apologetically, hanging on to Charlie's shoulders, his voice jolting and stopping as Charlie tripped over a concealed tuft of grass or small bush under the water. "They didn't even answer—or look at me. When the water got deep they went off in little boats and didn't leave a boat for me." Charlie tripped again and staggered to one knee. They both briefly floundered waist deep in the water, and then Charlie was up again, still with a grip on his passenger's legs, so that Winton was firmly on his back.

When he spoke again Winton's tone was casual, but his voice was hysterically high in pitch. "I asked them for a boat, but they wouldn't look at me."

Charlie did not answer. He respected Winton's attempt to conceal his terror. The touch of water can be a horrifying thing to a man with a phobia of drowning. He could think of nothing to distract Winton's attention from his danger, but he hoped desperately that the man would not notice that the water had deepened. It is not possible to run in water over knee height. There was no way to hurry now. The rain had closed in in veiling curtains, but he thought he saw the small figures of Henderson and the native in the distance reach the ramp which led to the spaceship.

If the flood hit them all now, Henderson and Spet could get inside, but how would he himself get this man with a phobia against water off his back and into the water to swim? He could visualize the bony arms tightening around his throat in an hysterical stranglehold. If a drowning man gets a clutch on you, you are supposed to knock him out and tow him. But how could he get this non-swimming type off his back and out where he could be hit?

If Winton could not brace himself to walk in water up to his ankles, he was not going to let go and try to swim in water up to his neck. He'd flip, for sure! Charlie found no logical escape from the picture. The pressure of the strong bony arms around his throat and shoulders and the quick irregular breathing of the man he was carrying made him feel trapped.

The water rose another inch or so, and the drag of it against his legs became heavier. The current was pulling sidewise.

"You're going slowly." Winton's voice had the harsh rasp of fear.

"No hurry." With difficulty, Charlie found breath to speak in a normal tone. "Almost there."

The curtain of rain lifted for a moment and he saw the spaceship, dark against the sky, and the ramp leading to its open door. The ramp was very shrunken, half covered by the rising water. It seemed a long way ahead.

As he watched, a light came on.

In the archway of the spaceship, Henderson flipped a switch and the lights went on.

Spet was startled. Sunlight suddenly came from the interior of the hut and shone against the falling rain in a great beam. Rain glittered through the beam in falling drops like sparks of white fire. It was very unlike anything real, but in dreams sunlight could be in one place and rain another at the same time, and no one in the dream country was surprised. And these were people who usually lived in the dream country, so apparently they had the power to do it in the real world also.

Nevertheless, Spet was afraid, for the sunlight did not look right as it was, coming out in a great widening beam across the rippling rain-pocked water. Sunlight did not mix well with rain.

"Sunlight," Spet said apologetically to his relative-ghost.

The brown ghost nodded and led him down the slope of the

ramp through the strange sparkling sunlight, with the ramp strange and hard underfoot.

"Don't go inside until I return," the ghost said, mouthing the words with difficulty. The ghost placed his hands around the railing of the ramp. "You hang on here and wait for me," said the brown ghost of someone in his family, and waded down into the water.

Spet followed him down into the comfortable water until his sore feet were off the end of the ramp and in the cooling soft mud, and then he gripped the rail obediently and waited. The water lapped at his waist like an embrace, and the wind sang a death song for him.

The bright glare of the strange sunlight on dancing water was beautiful, but it began to hurt his eyes. He closed them, and then heard a sound other than the wind. Two sounds.

One sound he recognized as the first flood crest crashing through the trees to the north, approaching them, and he knew he must hurry and drown before it arrived, because it was rough and hurtful.

The other sound was the strange voice of the black spirit which usually gibbered on top of the Box That Talks. Spet opened his eyes, and saw that the gibbering spirit was riding on the shoulders of the brown ghost, as he and his friend, the other brown ghost, moved through the waist-deep water towards Spet and the ramp.

The black spirit gibbered at him as they passed, and Spet felt a dim anger, wondering if it would bring bad luck to him with its chants, for its intentions could not be the same as the friendly ghosts.

"Spet, come up the ramp with us. It's dry inside. Don't look like that, there's nothing to be afraid of now, we'll go inside and shut the door, it will keep the water away, it won't get in . . . Come along, Spet."

The black spirit suddenly leaped down on the ramp with a strange scream. *"Aaaaiiii . . . He's turning into a seaweed. Quick, get him out of the water! Help!"*

The spirit with the black skin and white face possibly

wanted him for his own dark spirit world. He was coming down the ramp at Spet, screaming. He was too late though, Spet knew that he was safe for the dim land of the drowned with the friendly ghosts who had come for him. He felt his feet sending roots down into the mud, moving and rooting downward, and a wild joy came over him, and he knew that this was the right thing for him, much more right and natural than it would have been to become a tall sad adult.

He had been feeling a need for air, panting and drawing the cold air into his lungs. Just as the clawed hands of the dark spirit caught hold of his neck, Spet had enough air, and he leaned over into the dark and friendly water, away from the painful beauty of the bright lights and moving forms. The water closed around him, and the sound of voices was lost.

He could still feel the grip of the spirit's bony arms around his neck, pulling upwards, but he had seen the brown ghosts running towards them, and they would stop it from doing him any harm . . . so he dismissed the fear from his mind, and bent deeper into the dark, and plunged his hands with spread fingers deep into the mud, and gripped his ankles, as if he had always known just how to do this thing. His hands locked and became unable to unfold. They would never unfold again.

He felt the soft surge that was the first flood wave arriving and passing above him, and ignored it, and, with a mixture of terror and the certainty of doing right, he opened his mouth and took a deep breath of cold water.

All thought stopped. As the water rushed into his lungs, the rooted sea creature that was the forgotten adult stage of Spet's species began its thoughtless pseudo-plant existence, forgetting everything that had ever happened to it. Its shape changed.

The first wave of the flood did not quite reach up to the edge of the ship's entrance. It caught the two engineers as they dragged a screaming third human up the ramp towards the entrance, but it did not quite reach into the ship, and when it passed the three humans were still there. One of them struck the screaming one, and they carried him in.

*   *   *

Winton was hysterical for some time, but Henderson seemed quite normal. He worked well and rationally in compiling a good short survey report to carry to the planetary survey agency, and when the waters dried around the spaceship he directed the clearing of mud from the jets and the overhaul of the firing chambers without a sign of warp in his logic.

He did not want to speak to any native, and went into the ship when they appeared.

Winton was still slightly delirious when they took off from the planet, but, once in space, he calmed down and made a good recovery. He just did not talk about it. Henderson still seemed quite normal, and Charlie carefully did not tell Winton that Henderson kept a large bush in a glass enclosure in the engine room.

Ever since that time Henderson has been considered a little peculiar. He is a good enough risk for the big liners, for they have other engineers on board to take over if he ever cracks.

He has no trouble getting jobs, but wherever he goes he brings with him an oversized potted plant and puts it in the engine room and babies it with water and fertilizer. His fellow officers never kid him about it, for it is not a safe subject.

When Henderson is alone, or thinks he is alone, he talks to the potted bush. His tone is coaxing. But the bush never answers.

Charlie runs into him occasionally when their ships happen to dock at the same space port around the same planet. They share a drink and enjoy a few jokes together, but Charlie takes care not to get signed on to the same ship as Henderson. The sight of Henderson and his potted bush together make him nervous.

It's the wrong bush, but he'll never tell Henderson that.

THE IMMORTALS

BY JAMES E. GUNN (1923–   )

STAR SCIENCE FICTION
NO. 4

James Gunn is a professor of English at the University of Kansas, a noted scholar in the science fiction academic world, and has probably done as much as anyone to promote sf as serious literature. His most recent major work is The New Encyclopedia Of Science Fiction *(1988). Among his many honors and awards are service as President of the Science Fiction Research Association; President of the Science Fiction Writers of America (a rare double); and the Pilgrim Award given by the former organization.*

He is also a talented and careful writer of science fiction, whose body of work can stand with some of the biggest names in the field. From This Fortress World *in 1955 to* The Dreamers *in 1980, his novels have enriched the field, especially* Kampus, *which if it had been published in 1967 instead of 1977 would have received the attention it deserves (perhaps it still will). His story collections, which include* Future Imperfect *(1964),* Some Dreams Are Nightmares *(1974), and* The End Of The Dream *(1975) are even better, and a definitive ''Best of'' book is long overdue.*

''The Immortals'' became the novel The Immortals *of 1962 and (sort of) later the novelization* The Immortal *in 1975, but*

*is best known for the television series it led to—it should also
be known for the excellent story it is. (MHG)*

Science fiction writers have an affinity toward "dystopias."

*You know what a "utopia" is (from Greek words meaning
"good place"). It's a place where everything works perfectly
and everyone is happy, and goodness and niceness reign
supreme. Stories about utopias are inherently dull. Where's
the danger? Where's the suspense? Where's the doubt?*

*A "dystopia" ("bad place") is, of course, something where
everything is nightmarish and impossibly bad. Cyril Kornbluth
in "Two Dooms" described a dystopia, but that one was the
result of a military conquest that didn't really happen.*

*Jim Gunn described one that might conceivably happen
simply through the continuing development of medical technology.*

*The story first appeared thirty years ago, of course, but it
seems all the more horrifying for that since, in the thirty
years that have gone by, medical advance hasn't reassured
us. The expense continues to rise considerably faster than
inflation and new techniques are continually being introduced.*

*Since 1958, we have had organ transplants, and coronary
bypass operations, and CATscans and magnetic resonance
and test-tube babies and artificial hearts and so on.*

*One thing Jim Gunn didn't allow for was genetic engineer-
ing which might prevent some of the deformations and mal-
formations he speaks of, but never mind—it's an exciting and
very grisly story. (IA)*

The first patient was a young woman—an attractive enough
creature, with blond hair worn long around her shoulders and
a ripe body—if you could forgive the dirt and the odor.

Dr. Harry Elliott refrained from averting his nose. It would
do no good. He was a physician with a sacred trust—even
though (or perhaps especially because) he was only eighteen
years old. Even a citizen was entitled to his care—even a

citizen, without a chance at immortality, without even the prospect of a reprieve!

He looked her over thoughtfully. There was very little of interest in her case, no matter what disgusting ailment she might possess. The interesting areas of medicine—the research, say, that might synthesize the elixir of immortality—they had nothing to do with citizens or clinics. Harry Elliott's greatest interest in the clinic was in getting done with it. Once his residency was complete, then research loomed ahead.

"Hello, doc-tor," she said cheerfully. He muttered something, it didn't matter what. Outside in the waiting room there were fifty like her. In the halls beyond, where the Blood Bank was handing out its $5 bills for guaranteed germ-ridden citizen blood, there were hundreds more. Well, they were essential; he had to remember that. The blood they sold so cheerfully for five dollars (which instantly they took and ran with to some shover of illicit antibiotics and nostrums) was a great pool of immunities. Out of filth came health. It was a great lesson, and one which young Harry Elliott tried to keep in mind.

"I don't feel good, Doc-tor," she said sadly. "I'm always tired, like."

He grunted and resisted an impulse to have her disrobe. Not because of any danger involved—what was a citizen's chastity? A mythical thing like the unicorn. Besides, they expected it. From the stories the other doctors told, he thought they must come to the clinic for that purpose. But there was no use tempting himself. He would feel unclean for days.

She babbled as they always did. She had sinned against nature. She had not been getting enough sleep. She had not been taking her vitamins regularly. She had bought illicit terramycin from a shover for a kidney infection. It was all predictable and boring.

"I see," he kept muttering. And then, "I'm going to take a diagnosis now. Don't be frightened."

He switched on the diagnostic machine. A sphygmomanometer crept up snakelike from beneath the Freudian couch and squeezed her arm. A mouthpiece inserted itself between her lips. A stethoscope kissed her breast. A skull cap cupped her head. Metal caps pressed her fingertips. Bracelets caressed her ankles. A band embraced her hips. The machine punctured, sampled, counted, measured, listened, compared, correlated . . . .

In a moment it was over. Harry had his diagnosis. She was anemic; they all were. They couldn't resist that five dollars.

"Married?" he asked.

"Nah?" she said hesitantly.

"Better not waste any time. You're pregnant."

"Prag-nant?" she repeated.

"You're going to have a baby."

A joyful light broke across her face. "Aw! Is that all! I thought maybe it was a too-more. A baby I can take care of nicely. Tell me, Doctor, will it be a boy or girl?"

"A boy," Harry said wearily. The slut! Why did it always irritate him so?

She got up from the couch with lithe, careless grace. "Thank you, Doctor. I will go tell Georgie. He will be angry for a little, but I know how to make him glad."

There were others waiting in their consultation rooms, contemplating their symptoms. Harry checked the panel: a woman with pleurisy, a man with cancer, a child with rheumatic fever. . . . But Harry stepped out into the clinic to see if the girl dropped anything into the donation box as she passed. She didn't. Instead she paused by the shover hawking his wares just outside the clinic door.

"Get your aureomycin here," he chanted, "your penicillin, your terramycin. A hypodermic with every purchase. Good health! Good health! Stop those sniffles before they lay you low, low, low. Don't let that infection cost you your job, your health, your life. Get your filters, your antiseptics, your vitamins. Get your amulets, your good luck charms. I have here a radium needle which has already saved thirteen lives.

And here is an ampule of elixir vitae. Get your ilotycin here. . . .''

The girl bought an amulet and hurried off to Georgie. A lump of anger burned in Harry's throat.

The throngs were still marching silently in the street. In the back of the clinic a woman was kneeling at the operating table. She took a vitamin pill and a paper cup of tonic from the dispensary.

Behind the walls the sirens started. Harry turned toward the doorway. The gate in the Medical Center wall rolled up.

First came the outriders on their motorcycles. The people in the street scattered to the walls on either side, leaving a lane down the center of the street. The outriders brushed carelessly close to them—healthy young squires, their nose filters in place, their goggled eyes haughty, their guns slung low on their hips.

That would have been something, Harry thought enviously, to have been a company policeman. There was a dash to them, a hint of violence. They were hell on wheels. And if they were one-tenth as successful with women as they were reputed to be, there was no woman—from citizen through technician and nurse up to their suburban peers—who was immune to them.

Well, let them have the glamour and the women. He had taken the safer and more certain route to immortality. Few company policemen made it.

After the outriders came an ambulance, its armored ports closed, its automatic 40-millimeter gun roaming restlessly for a target. More outriders covered the rear. Above the convoy a helicopter swooped low.

"Raid!" somebody screamed—too late.

Something glinted in the sunlight, became a line of small, round objects beneath the helicopter, dropping in an arc toward the street. One after another they broke with fragile, popping sounds. They moved forward through the convoy.

Like puppets when the puppeteer has released the strings,

the outriders toppled to the street, skidding limply as their motorcycles slowed and stopped on their single wheels.

The ambulance could not stop. It rolled over one of the fallen outriders and crashed into a motorcycle, bulldozing it out of the way. The 40-millimeter gun had jerked erratically to fix its radar sight on the helicopter, but the plane was skimming the rooftops. Before the gun could get the range the plane was gone.

Harry smelled something sharply penetrating. His head felt swollen and light. The street tilted and then straightened.

In the midst of the crowd beyond the ambulance an arm swung up. Something dark sailed through the air and smashed against the top of the ambulance. Flames splashed across it. They dripped down the sides, ran into gun slits and observation ports, were drawn into the air intake.

A moment followed in which nothing happened. The scene was like a frozen tableau—the ambulance and the motorcycles balanced in the street, the outriders and some of the nearest citizens crumpled and twisted on the pavement, the citizens watching, the flames licking up toward greasy, black smoke.

Then the side door of the ambulance fell open.

A medic staggered out, clutching something in one hand, beating at flames on his white jacket with the other.

The citizens watched silently, not moving to help or hinder. From among them stepped a dark-haired man. His hand went up. It held something limp and dark. The hand came down against the medic's head.

No sound came to Harry over the roar of the idling motorcycles and ambulance. The pantomime continued, and he was part of the frozen audience as the medic fell and the man stooped, patted out the flames with his bare hands, picked the object out of the medic's hand, and looked at the ambulance door.

There was a girl standing there, Harry noticed. From this distance Harry could tell little more than that she was dark-haired and slender.

The flames on the ambulance had burned themselves out. The girl stood in the doorway, not moving. The man beside the fallen medic looked at her, started to hold out a hand, and, letting it drop, turned and faded back into the crowd.

Less than two minutes had passed since the sirens began.

Silently the citizens pressed forward. The girl turned and went back into the ambulance. The citizens stripped the outriders of their clothing and weapons, looted the ambulance of its black bag and medical supplies, picked up their fallen fellows, and disappeared.

It was like magic. One moment the street was full of them. The next moment they were gone. The street was empty of life.

Behind the Medical Center walls the sirens began again.

It was like a release. Harry began running down the street, his throat swelling with wordless shouts.

Out of the ambulance came a young boy. He was slim and small—no more than seven. He had blond hair, cut very short, and dark eyes in a tanned face. He wore a ragged T-shirt that once might have been white and a pair of blue jeans cut off above the knees.

He reached an arm back into the ambulance. A yellowed claw came out to meet it and then an arm. The arm was a gnarled stick encircled with ropy blue veins like lianas. Attached to it was a man on stiff, stiltlike legs. He was very old. His hair was thin, white silk. His scalp and face were wrinkled parchment. A tattered tunic fell from bony shoulders, around his permanently bent back, and was caught in folds around his loins.

The boy led the old man slowly and carefully into the ruined street, because the old man was blind, his eyelids flat and dark over empty sockets. The old man bent painfully over the fallen medic. His fingers explored the medic's skull. Then he moved to the outrider who had been run over by the ambulance. The man's chest was crushed; a pink froth edged his lips as punctured lungs gasped for breath.

He was as good as dead. Medical science could do nothing for injuries that severe, that extensive.

Harry reached the old man, grabbed him by one bony shoulder. "What do you think you're doing?"

The old man didn't move. He held to the outrider's hand for a moment and then creaked to his feet. "Healing," he answered in a voice like the whisper of sandpaper

"That man's dying," Harry said.

"So are we all," said the old man.

Harry glanced down at the outrider. Was he breathing easier or was that illusion?

It was then the stretcher bearers reached them.

Harry had a difficult time finding the Dean's office. The Medical Center covered hundreds of city blocks, and it had grown under a strange stimulus of its own. No one had ever planned for it to be so big, but it had sprouted an arm here when demand for medical care and research outgrew the space available, a wing there, and arteries through and under and around.

He followed the glowing guidestick through the unmarked corridors, and tried to remember the way. But it was useless. He inserted the stick into the lock on the armored door. The door swallowed the stick and opened. As soon as Harry had entered, the door swung shut and locked.

He was in a bare anteroom. On a metal bench bolted to the floor along one wall sat the boy and the old man from the ambulance. The boy looked up at Harry curiously and then his gaze returned to his folded hands. The old man rested against the wall.

A little farther along the bench was a girl. She looked like the girl who had stood in the doorway of the ambulance, but she was smaller than he had thought and younger. Her face was pale. Only her blue eyes were vivid as they looked at him with a curious appeal and then faded. His gaze dropped to her figure; it was boyish and unformed, clad in a simple, brown dress belted at the waist. She was no more than twelve or thirteen, he thought.

The reception box had to repeat the question twice: "Name?"

"Dr. Harry Elliott," he said.

"Advance for confirmation."

He went to the wall beside the far door and put his right hand against the plate set into it. A light flashed into his right eye, comparing retinal patterns.

"Deposit all metal objects in the receptable," the box said.

Harry hesitated and then pulled his stethoscope out of his jacket pocket, removed his watch, emptied his pants pockets of coins and pocket knife and hypospray.

Something clicked. "Nose filters," the box said.

Harry put those into the receptacle, too. The girl was watching him, but when he looked at her, her eyes moved away. The door opened. He went through the doorway. The door closed behind him.

Dean Mock's office was a magnificent room, twenty feet long and thirty feet wide, was decorated in a dark, mid-Victorian style. The furnishings all looked like real antiques, especially the yellow-oak rolltop desk and the mahogany instrument cabinet.

It looked rich and impressive. Personally, though, Harry preferred Twentieth Century Modern. Clean chromium-and-glass lines were esthetically pleasing; moreover, they were from the respectable first days of medical science—that period when mankind first began to realize that good health was not merely an accident, that it could be bought if men were willing to pay the price.

Harry had seen Dean Mock before, but never to speak to. His parents couldn't understand that. They thought he was the peer of everyone in the Medical Center because he was a doctor. He kept telling them how big the place was, how many people it contained: 75,000—100,000—only the statisticians knew how many. It didn't do any good; they still couldn't understand. Harry had given up trying.

The Dean didn't know Harry. He sat behind the rolltop

desk in his white jacket and studied Harry's record cast up on the frosted glass insert. He was good at it, but you couldn't deceive a man who had studied like that for ten years in this Center alone.

The Dean's black hair was thinning. He was almost eighty years old, of course. He didn't look it. He came of good stock, and he had the best of medical care. He was good for another twenty years, Harry estimated, without longevity shots. By that time, surely, with his position and his accomplishments, he would be voted a reprieve.

Once, in the confusion when a bomb had exploded in the power room, some of the doctors had whispered in the safe darkness that Mock's youthful appearance had a more reasonable explanation than heredity, but they were wrong. Harry had searched the lists, and Mock's name wasn't on them.

Mock looked up suddenly and caught Harry staring at him. Harry glanced away quickly but not before he had seen in Mock's eyes a look of—what—fright? desperation?

Harry couldn't understand it. The raid had been daring, this close to the Center walls, but nothing new. There had been raids before; there would be raids again. Any time something is valuable, lawless men will try to steal it. In Harry's day it happened to be medicine.

Mock said abruptly, "Then you saw the man? You could recognize him if you saw him again or if you had a good solidograph?"

"Yes, sir," Harry said. Why was Mock making such a production out of it? He had already been over this with the head resident and the chief of the company police.

"Do you know Governor Weaver?" Mock asked.

"An Immortal!"

"No, no," Mock said impatiently. "Do you know where he lives?"

"In the governor's mansion. Forty miles from here, almost due west."

"Yes, yes," Mock said. "You're going to carry a message

to him. The shipment has been hijacked. Hijacked." Mock had a nervous habit of repeating words. "It will be a week before another shipment is ready. A week. How we will get it to him I don't know." The last was muttered to himself.

Harry tried to make sense out of it. Carry a message to the governor? "Why don't you call him?" he said, unthinking.

But the question only roused Mock out of his introspection. "The underground cables are cut! No use repairing them. Repair men get shot. And even if they're fixed, they're only cut again next night. Radio and television are jammed. Jammed. Get ready. You'll have to hurry to get out the southwest gate before curfew."

"Curfew is for citizens," Harry said, uncomprehending. Was Mock going insane?

"Didn't I tell you?" Mock passed the back of his hand across his forehead as if to clear away cobwebs. "You're going alone, on foot, dressed as a citizen. A convoy would be cut to pieces. We've tried. We've been out of touch with the governor for three weeks. Three weeks! He must be getting impatient. Never make the governor impatient. It isn't healthy."

For the first time Harry really understood what the Dean was asking him to do. The governor! He had it in his power to cut half a lifetime off Harry's search for immortality. "But my residency——"

Mock looked wise. "The governor can do you more good than a dozen boards. More good."

Harry caught his lower lip between his teeth and counted off on his fingers. "I'll need nose filters, a small medical kit, a gun——"

Mock was shaking his head. "None of those. Out of character. If you reach the governor's mansion, it will be because you pass as a citizen, not because you defend yourself well or heal up your wounds afterward. And a day or two without filters won't reduce your life expectancy appreciably. Well, Doctor? Will you get through?"

"As I hope for immortality!" Harry said earnestly.

"Good, good. One more thing. You must deliver the people you saw in the anteroom. The boy's name is Christopher; the old man calls himself Pearce. He's some kind of neighborhood leech. The governor has asked for him."

"A leech?" Harry said incredulously.

Mock shrugged. His expression said that he considered the exclamation impertinent, but Harry could not restrain himself. "If we made an example of a few of these quacks——"

"The clinics would be more crowded than they are now. They serve a good purpose. Besides, what can we do? He doesn't claim to be a physician. He calls himself a healer. He doesn't drug, operate, advise, or manipulate. Sick people come to him and he touches them, touches them. Is that practicing medicine?"

Harry shook his head.

"If the sick people claim to be helped? Pearce claims nothing. He charges nothing. If the sick people are grateful, if they want to give him something, who is to stop them? Besides," he muttered, frowning, "that outrider is going to live. Anyway, the Governor insists on seeing him."

Harry sighed. "They'll get away. I'll have to sleep."

Mock jeered, "A feeble old man and a boy?"

"The girl's lively enough."

"Marna?" Mock reached into a drawer and brought out a hinged silver circle. He tossed it to Harry. Harry caught it and looked at it.

"It's a bracelet. Put it on."

It looked like nothing more. Harry shrugged, slipped it over his wrist, and clamped it shut. It seemed too big for a moment, and then it tightened. His wrist tingled where it rested.

"It's tuned to the one on the girl's wrist, tuned. When the girl moves away from you, her wrist will tingle. The farther she goes, the more it will hurt. After a little she will come back. I'd put bracelets on the boy and the old man, but they only work in pairs. If someone tries to remove the bracelet forcibly the girl will die. Die. It links itself to the nervous system. The governor has the only key. You'll tell him the girl is fertile."

Harry stared at Mock. "What about this bracelet?"

"The same. That way it's a warning device, too."

Harry took a deep breath and looked down at his wrist. The silver gleamed now like a snake's flat eyes.

"Why didn't you have one on the medic?"

"We did. We had to amputate his arm to get it off." Mock turned to his desk and started the microfilmed reports flipping past the window again. In a moment he looked up and seemed startled that Harry had not moved. "Still here? Get started. Wasted too much time now if you're going to beat curfew."

Harry turned and started toward the door through which he had come.

"One more thing," Dean Mock said. "Watch out for ghouls, ghouls. And headhunters. Headhunters."

Shortly after they set out, Harry had evolved a method of progress for his little group that was mutually unsatisfactory.

"Hurry up," he would say. "There's only a few minutes left before curfew."

The girl would look at him once and look away. Pearce, already moving more rapidly than Harry had any reason to expect, would say, "Patience. We'll get there."

None of them would speed up although it was vital to reach the City Gate before curfew. Harry would walk ahead rapidly, outdistancing the others. His wrist would begin to tingle, then to smart, to burn, and to hurt actively. The farther he left Marna behind, the worse the pain grew. Only the thought that her wrist felt just as bad sustained him.

After a little the pain would begin to ebb. He knew, then, without looking, that she had broken. When he would turn, she would be twenty feet behind him, no closer, willing to accept that much pain to keep from approaching him.

Then he would have to stop and wait for the old man.

Once, she walked on past, but after a little she could stand the pain no more, and she returned. After that she stopped when he did.

It was a small triumph for Harry, but something to strengthen him when he started thinking about the deadly thing on his wrist and the peculiar state of the world in which the Medical Center had been out of touch with the governor's mansion for three weeks, in which a convoy could not get through, in which a message had to be sent by a foot messenger.

Under other conditions, Harry might have thought Marna a lovely thing. She was slim and graceful, her skin was clear and unblemished, her features were regular and pleasing, and the contrast between her dark hair and her blue eyes was striking. But she was young and spiteful and linked to him by a hateful condition. They had been thrown together too intimately too soon and, besides! she was only a child.

They reached the City Gate with only a minute to spare.

On either side of them the chain link double fence stretched as far as Harry could see. There was no end to it, really. It completely encircled the town. At night it was electrified, and savage dogs roamed the space between the fences.

Somehow citizens still got out. They formed outlaw bands that attacked defenseless travelers. That would be one of the dangers.

The head guard at the gate was a dark-skinned, middle-aged squire. At sixty he had given up any hopes for immortality; he intended to get what he could out of this life. That included bullying his inferiors.

He looked at the blue, daylight-only pass and then at Harry. "Topeka? On foot." He chuckled. It made his big belly shake until he had to cough. "If the ghouls don't get you, the headhunters will. The bounty on heads is twenty dollars now. Outlaw heads only, but then heads don't talk. Not if they're detached from bodies. Of course, that's what you're figuring on doing—joining a wolf pack." He spat on the sidewalk beside Harry's foot.

Harry jerked back his foot in revulsion. The guard's eyes brightened.

"Are you going to let us through?" Harry asked.

"Let you through?" Slowly the guard looked at his wrist-watch. "Can't do that. Past curfew. See?"

Automatically Harry bent over to look. "But we got here before curfew——" he began. The guard's fist hit him just above the left ear and sent him spinning away.

"Get back in there and stay in there, you filthy citizens!" the guard shouted.

Harry's hand went to his pocket where he kept the hypospray, but it was gone. Words that would blast the guard off his post and into oblivion trembled on his lips, but he didn't dare utter them. He wasn't Dr. Elliott anymore, not until he reached the governor's mansion. He was Harry Eliott, citizen, fair game for any man's fist, who should consider himself lucky it was only a fist.

"Now," the guard said suggestively, "if you were to leave the girl as security——" He coughed.

Marna shrank back. She touched Harry accidentally. It was the first time they had touched, in spite of a more intimate linkage that joined them in pain and release, and something happened to Harry. His body recoiled automatically from the touch, as it would from a burning-hot sterilizer. Marna stiffened, aware of him.

Harry, disturbed, saw Pearce shuffling toward the guard, guided by his voice. Pearce reached out, his hand searching. He touched the guard's tunic, then his arm, and worked his way down the arm to the hand. Harry stood still, his hand doubled into a fist at his side, waiting for the guard to hit the old man. But the guard gave Pearce the instinctive respect due age and only looked at him curiously.

"Weak lungs," Pearce whispered. "Watch them. Pneumonia might kill before antibiotics could help. And in the lower left lobe, a hint of cancer——"

"Aw, now!" The guard jerked his hand away, but his voice was frightened.

"X-ray," Pearce whispered. "Don't wait."

"There ain't nothing wrong with me," the guard stammered. "You—you're trying to scare me." He coughed.

"No exertion. Sit down. Rest."

"Why, I'll—I'll——" He began coughing violently. He jerked his head at the gate. "Go on," he said, choking. "Go out there and die."

The boy, Christopher, took the old man's hand and led him through the open gateway. Harry caught Marna's upper arm—again the contact—and half helped her, half pushed her through the gate, keeping his eye warily on the guard. But the man's eyes were turned inward toward something far more vital.

As soon as they were through, the gate slammed down behind them and Harry released Marna's arm as if it were distasteful to hold. Fifty yards beyond, down the right-hand lanes of the disused six-lane divided highway, Harry said, "I suppose I ought to thank you."

Pearce whispered, "That would be polite."

Harry rubbed his head where the guard had hit him. It was swelling. He wished for a medical kit. "How can I be polite to a charlatan?"

"Politeness is cheap."

"Still—to lie to the man about his condition. To say—cancer——" Harry had a hard time saying it. It was a dirty word, the one disease, aside from death itself, for which medical science had found no final cure.

"Was I lying?"

Harry stared sharply at the old man and then shrugged. He looked at Marna. "We're all in this together. We might as well make it as painless as possible. If we try to get along, we might even all make it alive."

"Get along?" Marna said. Harry heard her speak for the first time; her voice was low and melodious even in anger. "With this?" She held up her arm. The silver bracelet gleamed in the last red rays of the sun.

Harry said harshly, raising his wrist, "You think it's any better for me?"

Pearce whispered, "We will cooperate, Christopher and I—I, Dr. Elliott, because I am too old to do anything else and Christopher because he is young and discipline is good for the young."

Christopher grinned. "Grampa used to be a doctor before he learned how to be a healer."

"Pride dulls the senses and warps the judgment," Pearce whispered.

Harry held back a comment. Now was no time to argue about medicine and quackery.

The road was deserted. The once-magnificent pavement was cracked and broken. Grass sprouted tall and thick in the cracks. The weeds stood like young trees along both edges, here and there the big, brown faces of sunflowers, fringed in yellow, nodding peacefully.

To either side were the ruins of what had once been called the suburbs. Then the distinction between that and the city had been only a line drawn on a map; there had been no fences. But when these had gone up, the houses outside had soon crumbled.

The real suburbs were far out. First it was turnpike time to the city that had become more important than distance, then helicopter time. Finally time had run out for the city. It had become so obviously a sea of carcinogens and disease that the connection to the suburbs had been broken. Shipments of food and raw materials went in and shipments of finished materials came out, but nobody went there any more—except to the medical centers. They were located in the cities because their raw material was there: the blood, the organs, the diseases, the bodies for experiment. . . .

Harry walked beside Marna, ahead of Christopher and Pearce, but the girl didn't look at him. She walked with her eyes straight ahead, as if she were alone. Harry said finally, "Look, it's not my fault. I didn't ask for this. Can't we be friends?"

She glanced at him just once. "No!"

His lips tightened, and he dropped back. He let his wrist tingle. What did he care if a thirteen-year-old girl disliked him?

The western horizon was fading from scarlet into lavender and purple. Nothing moved in the ruins or along the road. They were alone in an ocean of desolation. They might have been the last people on a ruined earth.

Harry shivered. Soon it would be hard to keep to the road. "Hurry!" he snapped at Pearce, "if you don't want to spend the night out here with the ghouls and the headhunters."

"There are worse companions," Pearce whispered.

By the time they reached the motel, the moonless night was completely upon them and the old suburbs were behind. The sprawling place was dark except for a big neon sign that said "M TEL," a smaller sign that said "Vacancy," and, at the gate in the fence that surrounded the whole place, a mat that said "Welcome," and a frosted glass plate that said, "Push button."

Harry was about to push the button when Christopher said urgently, "Dr. Elliott. Look!" He pointed toward the fence at the right with a stick he had picked up half a mile back.

"What?" Harry snapped. He was tired and nervous and dirty. He peered into the darkness. "A dead rabbit."

"Christopher means the fence is electrified," Marna said, "and the mat you're standing on is made out of metal. I don't think we should go in there."

"Nonsense!" Harry said sharply. "Would you rather stay out here at the mercy of whatever roams the night? I've stopped at these motels before. There's nothing wrong with them."

Christopher held out his stick. "Maybe you'd better push the button with this."

Harry frowned, took the stick, and stepped off the mat. "Oh, all right," he said ungraciously. At the second try, he pushed the button.

The frosted glass plate became a television eye. "Who rings?"

"Four travelers bound for Topeka," Harry said. He held up the pass in front of the eye. "We can pay."

"Welcome," said the speaker. "Cabins thirteen and fourteen will open when you deposit the correct amount of money. What time do you wish to be awakened?"

Harry looked at his companions. "Sunrise," he said.

"Good night," said the speaker. "Sleep tight."

The gate rolled up. Christopher led Pearce around the Welcome mat and down the driveway beyond. Marna followed. Irritated, Harry jumped over the mat and caught up with them.

A single line of glass bricks along the edge of the driveway glowed fluorescently to point out the direction they should go. They passed a tank trap and a machine-gun emplacement, but the place was deserted.

When they reached cabin thirteen, Harry said, "We won't need the other one. We'll stay together." He put three twenty-dollar uranium pieces into the coin slot.

"Thank you," the door said. "Come in."

As the door opened, Christopher darted inside. The small room held a double bed, a chair, a desk, and a floor lamp. In the corner was a small, partioned bathroom with an enclosed shower, a lavatory, and a toilet. The boy went immediately to the desk, found a plastic menu card, returned to the door. He helped Pearce into the room and then waited by the door until Harry and Marna were inside. He cracked the menu into two pieces. As the door swung shut, he slipped one of the pieces between the door and the jamb. He started back toward Pearce, stumbled against the lamp and knocked it over. It crashed and went out. They were left with only the illumination from the bathroom light.

"Clumsy little fool!" Harry said sharply.

Marna was at the desk, writing. She turned and handed the paper to Harry. Impatiently he edged toward the light and looked at it. It said:

Christopher has broken the eye, but the room is still bugged. We can't break that without too much suspicion. Can I speak to you outside?

"That is the most ridiculous——" Harry began.

"This seems adequate." Pearce's voice was noticeably penetrating. "You two can sleep in fourteen." His blind face was turned intently toward Harry.

Harry sighed. If he didn't humor them, he would get no rest at all. He opened the door and stepped into the night with Marna. The girl moved close to him, put her arms around his neck and her cheek against his. Without his volition, his arms went around her waist. Her lips moved against his ear; a moment later he realized that she was speaking.

"I do not like you, Dr. Elliott, but I do not want us all killed. Can you afford another cabin?"

"Of course, but—I'm not going to leave those two alone."

"That's beside the point. Naturally it would be foolish for us not to stick together. Please, now. Ask no questions. When we go in fourteen, take off your jacket and throw it casually over the lamp. I'll do the rest."

Harry let himself be led to the next cabin. He fed the door. It greeted them and let them in. The room was identical with thirteen. Marna slipped a piece of plastic between the door and the jamb as the door closed. She looked at Harry expectantly.

He shrugged, took off his jacket, and tossed it over the lamp. The room took on a shadowy and sinister appearance. Marna knelt, rolled up a throw rug, and pulled down the covers on the bed. She went to the wall phone, gave it a little tug, and the entire flat vision plate swung out on hinges. She reached into it, grabbed something, and pulled it out. There seemed to be hundreds of turns of copper wire on a spool.

Marna went to the shower enclosure, unwinding wire as she went. She stood outside the enclosure and fastened one end of the wire to the hot water faucet. Then she strung it around the room like a spider's web, broke it off, and fastened the free end to the drain in the shower floor. This she threaded through the room close to but not touching the first wire.

She tiptoed her way out between the wires, picked up the throw rug, and tossed it on the bed.

"Well, 'night," she said, motioning Harry toward the door and to be careful of the wires. When Harry reached it without mishap, Marna turned off the lamp, removed the jacket, and slipped over to join him.

She let the door slam behind them and sighed a big sigh.

"Now you've fixed it," Harry whispered savagely. "Neither of the showers will work, and I'll have to sleep on the floor."

"You shouldn't want to take a shower anyway," Marna said. "It would be your last one. They're wired." Resentfully, and feeling foolish, Harry returned with Marna to cabin thirteen, where he dumped the boy in with the old man, and aggressively occupied one entire bed for himself.

Harry couldn't sleep. First it had been the room, shadowed and silent, and then the harsh breathing of the old man and the softer breaths of Christopher and Marna. As a resident, he was not used to sleeping in the same room with other persons.

Then his arm had tingled—not much but just enough to keep him awake. He had got out of bed and crawled to where Marna was lying on the floor. She, too, had been awake. Silently he had urged her to share the bed with him, gesturing that he would not touch her, he had no desire to touch her, and if he had, he swore by Hippocrates that he would restrain himself. He only wanted to ease the tingling under the bracelet so that he could go to sleep.

She motioned that he could lie on the floor beside her, but he shook his head. Finally she relented enough to move to the floor beside the bed. By lying on his stomach and letting his arm dangle, Harry relieved the tingling and fell into an uneasy sleep.

He had dreams. He was performing a long and difficult lung resection. The microsurgical controls slipped in his sweaty fingers; the scalpel sliced through the aorta. The patient started up on the operating table, the blood spurting from her heart. It was Marna. She began to chase him down long hospital halls.

The overhead lights kept getting farther and farther apart until Harry was running in complete darkness through warm, sticky blood that kept rising higher and higher until it closed over his head.

Harry woke up, smothering, fighting against something that enveloped him completely, relentlessly. There was a sound of scuffling nearby. Something spat and crackled. Someone cursed.

Harry fought, futilely. Something ripped. Again. Harry caught a glimpse of a grayer darkness, struggled toward it, and came out through a long rip in the taut blanket, which had been pulled under the bed on all four sides.

"Quick!" Christopher said, folding up his pocket knife. He headed for the door where Pearce was already standing patiently.

Marna picked up a metal leg which had been unscrewed from the desk. Christopher slipped the chair out from under the doorknob and silently opened the door. He led Pearce outside. Marna followed. Dazedly, Harry followed her.

In cabin fourteen someone screamed. Something flashed blue. A body fell. Harry smelled the odor of burning flesh.

Marna ran ahead of them toward the gate. She rested the ferule of the desk leg on the ground and let the metal bar fall toward the fence. The fence spat blue flame. It ran, crackling, down the leg. The leg glowed redly and sagged. Then everything went dark, including the neon sign above them and the light at the gate.

"Help me!" Marna panted.

She was trying to lift the gate. Harry put his hands underneath and lifted. The gate moved a foot and stuck.

Up the drive someone yelled hoarsely, without words. Harry strained at the gate. It yielded, rolled up silently. Harry put up his hand to hold it while Marna got through and then Pearce and the boy. Harry edged through and let it drop.

A moment later the electricity flickered on again. The desk leg melted through and dropped away.

Harry looked back. Coming toward them was a motorized wheelchair. In it was something lumpy and monstrous, a nightmarish menace—until Harry recognized it for what it was: a basket case, a quadruple amputee complicated by a heart condition. An artificial heart-and-lung machine rode on the back of the wheelchair like a second head. Behind galloped a gangling scarecrow creature with hair that flowed out behind. It wore a dress in imitation of a woman. . . .

Harry stood there watching, fascinated, while the wheelchair stopped beside the gun emplacement. Wires reached out from one of the chair arms like medusan snakes, inserted themselves into control plugs. The machine gun started to chatter. Something plucked at Harry's sleeve.

The spell was broken. He turned and ran into the darkness.

Half an hour later he was lost. Marna, Pearce, and the boy were gone. All he had left was a tired body, an arm that burned, and a wrist that hurt worse than anything he could remember.

He felt his upper arm. His sleeve was wet. He brought his fingers to his nose. Blood. The bullet had creased him.

He sat disconsolately on the edge of the turnpike, the darkness as thick as soot around him. He looked at the fluorescent dial of his watch. Three-twenty. A couple of hours until sunrise. He sighed and tried to ease the pain in his wrist by rubbing around the bracelet. It seemed to help. In a few minutes it dropped to a tingle.

"Dr. Elliott," someone said softly.

He turned. Relief and something like joy flooded through his chest. There, outlined against the dim starlight, were Christopher, Marna and Pearce.

"Well," Harry said gruffly, "I'm glad you didn't try to escape."

"We wouldn't do that, Dr. Elliott," Christopher said.

"How did you find me?" Harry asked.

Marna silently held up her arm.

The bracelet. Of course. He had given them too much credit, Harry thought sourly. Marna sought him out because she could not help herself, and Christopher, because he was out here alone with a senile old man to take care of and he needed help.

Although, honesty forced him to admit, it had been himself and not Christopher and Pearce who had needed help back there a mile or two. If they had depended on him, their heads would be drying in the motel's dry-storage room, waiting to be turned in for the bounty. Or their still-living bodies would be on their way to some organ bank somewhere.

"Christopher," Harry said to Pearce, "must have been apprenticed to a bad-debt evader."

Pearce accepted it for what it was: a compliment and an apology. "Dodging the collection agency traps and keeping out of the way of the health inspector," he whispered, "make growing up in the city a practical education. You're hurt."

Harry started. How did the old man know? Even with eyes, it was too dark to see more than silhouettes. Harry steadied himself. It was an instinct, perhaps. Diagnosticians got it, sometimes, he was told. After they had been practicing for years. They could smell disease before the patient lay down on the couch. From the gauges they got only confirmation.

Or maybe it was simpler than that. Maybe the old man smelled the blood with a nose grown keen to compensate for his blindness.

The old man's fingers were on his arm, surprisingly gentle. Harry pulled his arm away roughly. "It's only a crease."

The charlatan's fingers found his arm again. "It's bleeding. Find some dry grass, Christopher."

Marna was close. She had made a small, startled movement toward him when Pearce had discovered his wound. Harry could not accept her actions for sympathy; her hate was too tangible. Perhaps she was wondering what she would do if he were to die.

Peace ripped the sleeve away.

"Here's the grass, Grampa," Christopher said.

How did the boy find the dry grass in the dark? "You aren't going to put that on the wound!" Harry said quickly.

"It will stop the bleeding," Pearce whispered.

"But the germs——"

"Germs can't hurt you, unless you want them to."

He put the grass on the wound and bound it with the sleeve. "That will be better soon."

He would take it off, Harry told himself, as soon as they started walking. Somehow, though, it was easier to let it alone now that the harm was done. Then he forgot about it.

When they started walking again, Harry found himself beside Marna. "I suppose you got your education dodging health inspectors in the city, too?" he said drily.

She shook her head. "No. There's never been much else to do. Ever since I can remember I've been trying to escape. I got free once." Her voice was filled with remembered happiness. "I was free for twenty-four hours, and then they found me."

"But I thought——" Harry began. "Who are you?"

"Me? I'm the governor's daughter." She said it so bitterly that Harry recoiled.

Sunrise found them on the turnpike. They had outdistanced the last ruined motel. Now, on either side of the turnpike, were rolling, grassy hills, valleys filled with trees, and the river winding muddily beside them, sometimes so close they could throw a rock into it, sometimes turning beyond the hills out of sight.

The day was warm. Above them the sky was blue with only a trace of fleecy cloud on the western horizon. Occasionally a rabbit would hop across the road in front of them and vanish into the brush on the other side. Once they saw a deer lift its head beside the river and stare at them curiously.

Harry stared back with hunger in his eyes.

"Dr. Elliott," Christopher said.

Harry looked at him. In the boy's soiled hand was an irregular lump of solidifed brown sugar. It was speckled with lint and other unidentifiable accretions, but at the moment it was the most desirable object Harry could think of. His mouth watered and he swallowed hard. "Give it to Pearce and the girl. They'll need their strength. And you, too."

"That's all right," Christopher said. "I have more." He held up three other pieces in his left hand. He gave one to Marna and one to Pearce. The old man bit into his with the brown stubs that served him as teeth.

Harry picked off the largest pieces of foreign matter and then could restrain his hunger no more. Breakfast was unusually satisfying.

They kept walking, not moving rapidly but steadily. Pearce never complained. He kept his bent old legs tottering forward, and Harry gave up trying to move him faster.

They passed a hydroponic farm with an automated canning factory close behind it. No one moved around either building. Only the belts turned, carrying the tanks toward the factory to be harvested or away from it refilled with nutrients, replanted with new crops.

"We should pick up something for lunch," Harry said. It would be theft but in a good cause. He could get his pardon directly from the governor.

"Too dangerous," Christopher said.

"Every possible entrance," Marna said, "is guarded by spy beams and automatic weapons."

"Christopher will get us a good supper," Pearce whispered.

They saw a suburban villa on a distant hill, but there was no one around it. They plodded on along the grass-grown double highway toward Lawrence.

Suddenly Christopher said, "Down! In the ditch beside the road!"

This time Harry moved quickly, without questions. He helped Pearce down the slope—the old man was very light—and threw himself down into the ditch beside Marna. A minute later motors raced by not far away. As the sound dwindled, Harry risked a glance above the top of the ditch. A group of motorcycles was disappearing on the road toward the city. "What was that?" Harry asked, shaken.

"Wolfpack!" Marna said, hatred and disgust mingled in her voice.

"But they looked like company police," Harry objected.

"When they grow up they will be company policemen," Marna said.

"I thought the wolfpacks were made up of escaped citizens," Harry said.

Marna looked at him scornfully. "Is that what they tell you?"

"A citizen," Pearce whispered, "is lucky to stay alive when he's alone. A group of them wouldn't last a week."

They got back up on the turnpike and started walking again. Christopher was nervous as he led Pearce. He kept turning to look behind them and glancing from side to side. Soon Harry was edgy too.

"Down!" Christopher shouted.

Something whistled. A moment later Harry was struck a solid blow in the middle of the back. It knocked him hard to the ground. Marna screamed.

Harry rolled over, feeling as if his back were broken. Christopher and Pearce were on the pavement beside him, but Marna was gone.

A rocket blasted a little ahead and above. Then another. Pearce looked up. A powered glider zoomed toward the sky. Marna was dangling from it, her body twisting and struggling to get free. From a second glider swung empty talons—padded hooks like those which had closed around Marna and had almost swooped up Harry.

Harry got to his knees, clutching his wrist. It was beginning to send stabs of pain up his arm like a prelude to a symphony of anguish. The only thing that kept him from falling to the pavement in writhing torment was the black anger that surged through his veins. He shook his fist at the turning gliders, climbing on smoking jets.

"Dr. Elliott!" Christopher said urgently.

With blurred eyes Harry looked for the voice. The boy was in the ditch again. So was the old man.

"They'll be back! Get down!" the boy said.

"But they've got Marna!" Harry said.

"It won't help if you get killed."

One glider swooped like a hawk toward a mouse. The other, carrying Marna, continued to circle as it climbed. Harry rolled toward the ditch. A line of chattering bullets chipped at the pavement where he had been.

"I thought," he gasped, "they were trying to take us alive."

"They hunt heads, too," Christopher said.

"Anything for a thrill," Pearce whispered.

"I never did anything like that," Harry moaned. "I never knew anyone who did."

"You were busy," Pearce said.

It was true. Since four years old he had been in school constantly, most of that time in medical school. He had been home only for a brief day now and then; he scarcely knew his parents any more. What would he know of the pastimes of young squires? But this—this wolfpack business!

The first glider was a small cross in the sky; Marna, a speck hanging from it. It straightened and glided toward Lawrence. The second followed.

Suddenly Harry began beating the ground with his aching arm. "Why did I dodge? I should have let myself be captured with her. She'll die."

"She's strong," Pearce whispered, "stronger than you or Christopher, stronger than almost anyone. But sometimes strength is the cruelest thing. Follow her. Get her away.''

Harry looked at the bracelet from which pain lanced up his arm and through his body. Yes, he could follow her. As long as he could move he could find her. But feet were so slow against glider wings.

"The motorcycles will be coming back," Christopher said. "The gliders will have radioed them."

"But how do we capture a motorcycle?" Harry asked. The pain wouldn't let him think clearly.

Christopher had already pulled up his T-shirt. Around his thin waist was wrapped turn after turn of nylon cord. "Sometimes we fish," he said. He stretched the cord across the two-lane pavement in the concealment of grass grown tall in a crack. He motioned Harry to lie flat on the other side. "Let them pass, all but the last one," he said. "Hope that he's a straggler, far enough behind so that the others won't notice when we stand up. Wrap the cord around your waist. Get it up where it will catch him around the chest."

Harry lay beside the pavement while his left arm felt as though it were a swelling balloon, and the balloon was filled with pain. He looked at it once, curiously, but it was still the same size.

After an eternity came the sound of motors, many of them. As the first passed, Harry cautiously lifted his head. There was a straggler. He was about a hundred feet behind the others; he was speeding now to catch up.

The others passed. As the straggler got within twenty feet Harry jumped up, bracing himself against the impact. Christopher sprang up at the same instant. The young squire had no time to move; he had time only to look surprised before he hit the cord. The cord pulled Harry out into the middle of the pavement, his heels skidding. Christopher had tied his end to the trunk of a young tree.

The squire smashed into the pavement—but the motorcycle slowed and heeled over into the bank of weeds. Beyond, far down the road, the others didn't look back.

Harry untangled himself from the cord and ran to the squire. He was as old as Harry and as big. He had a harelip and a withered leg. His skull was crushed. He was dead.

Harry closed his eyes. He had seen men die before, but he had never been the cause of it. It was like breaking his Hippocratic Oath.

"Some must die," Pearce whispered. "It is better for the evil to die young."

Harry stripped quickly and got into the squire's clothes and goggles. He strapped the pistol down on his hip and turned to Christopher and Pearce. "What about you?"

"We won't try to escape," Pearce said.

"I don't mean that. Will you be all right?"

Pearce put a hand on the boy's shoulder. "Christopher will take care of me. And he will find you after you have rescued Marna."

The confidence in Pearce's voice strengthened Harry. He did not pause to question that confidence. He mounted the motorcycle, settled himself into the saddle seat, and turned the throttle. The motorcycle took off violently.

It was tricky, riding on one wheel, but he had had experience on similar vehicles in the Subterranean Medical Center thoroughfares.

His arm hurt, but it was not like it had been before when he was helpless. Now it was a guidance system. As he rode, he could feel the pain lessen. That meant he was getting closer to Marna.

It was night before he found her. The other motorcycles had completely outdistanced him, and he had swept past the side road several miles before the worsening pain warned him. He cruised back and forth before he finally located the curving ramp that led across the cloverleaf ten miles east of Lawrence.

From this a ruined asphalt road turned east, and the pain in Harry's arm had dropped to an ache. The road ended in an impenetrable thicket. Harry stopped just before he crashed into it. He sat immobile on the seat, thinking.

He hadn't considered what he was going to do when he found Marna; he had merely taken off in hot pursuit, driven half by the painful bracelet upon his wrist, half by his emotional involvement with the young girl.

Somehow—he could scarcely trace back the involutions of chance to its source—he had been trapped into leading this pitiful expedition from the Medical Center to the governor's mansion. Moment by moment it had threatened his life—and not, unless all his hopes were false, just a few years but eternity. Was he going to throw it away here on a quixotic attempt to rescue a girl from the midst of a pack of cruel young wolves?

But what would he do with the thing on his wrist? What of the governor? And what of Marna?

"Ralph?" someone asked out of the darkness, and the decision was taken out of his hands.

"Yes," he muttered. "Where is everybody?"

"Usual place—under the bank."

Harry moved toward the voice, limping. "Can't see a thing."

"Here's a light."

The trees lighted up, and a black form loomed in front of Harry. Harry blinked once, squinted, and hit the squire with the edge of his palm on the fourth cervical vertebra. As the man dropped, Harry picked the everlight out of the air, and caught the body. He eased the limp form into the grass and felt the neck. It was broken all right, but the squire was still breathing. He straightened the head, so that there would be no pressure on nerve tissue, and looked up.

Light glimmered and flickered somewhere ahead. There was no movement, no sound; apparently no one had heard him. He flicked the light on, saw the path, and started through the young forest.

The campfire was built under a clay overhang so that it

could not be seen from above. Roasting over it was a whole young deer being slowly turned on a spit by one of the squires. Harry found time to recognize the empty ache in his midriff for what it was: hunger.

The rest of the squires sat in a semicircle around the fire. On the far side was Marna, seated, her hands bound behind her. Her head was raised; her eyes searched the darkness around the fire. What was she looking for? Of course. For him. She knew by the bracelet on her wrist that he was near.

He wished that he could signal her in some way, but there was no way. He studied the squires: one was an albino, a second a macrocephalic, a third a spastic. The others might have had physical impairments that Harry could not see. All except one, who seemed older than the rest and leaned against the edge of the clay bank. He was blind, but inserted surgically into his eye sockets were electrically operated binoculars. He carried a power pack on his back with leads to the binoculars and to an antenna in his coat.

Harry edged cautiously around the forest edge beyond the firelight toward where Marna was sitting.

"First the feast," the albino gloated, "then the fun."

The one who was turning the spit said, "I think we should have the fun first—then we'll be good and hungry."

They argued back and forth, good-naturedly for a moment and then as others chimed in, with more heat. Finally the albino turned to the one with the binoculars. "What do you say, Eyes?"

In a deep voice, Eyes said, "Sell the girl. Young parts are worth top prices."

"Ah," said the albino slyly, "but you can't see what a pretty little thing she is, Eyes. To you she's only a pattern of white dots against a gray cathode-ray tube. To us she's white and pink and black and——"

"One of these days," Eyes said in a calm voice, "you'll go too far."

"Not with her, I won't."

A stick broke under Harry's foot. Everyone stopped talking and listened. Harry eased his pistol out of its holster.

"Is that you, Ralph?" the albino said.

"Yes," Harry said, limping out into the edge of the firelight, keeping his head in the darkness, his pistol concealed in a fold of pants at his side.

"Can you imagine," the albino said, "the girl says she's the governor's daughter?"

"I am," Marna said clearly. "He will have you cut to pieces slowly for what you are going to do."

"But I'm the governor, dearie," said the albino in a falsetto, "and I don't give a——"

Eyes said sharply, "That's not Ralph. His leg's all right."

Harry cursed his luck. The binoculars were equipped to pick up X-ray reflections as well as radar. "Run!" he shouted in the silence that followed.

His first shot was for Eyes. The man was turning, and it struck his power pack. He began screaming and clawing at the binoculars that served him for eyes. But Harry wasn't watching. He was releasing the entire magazine into the clay bank above the fire. Already loosened by the heat from the fire, the bank collapsed, smothering the fire and burying several of the squires sitting close to it.

Harry dived to the side. Several bullets went through the space he had just vacated.

He scrambled for the forest and started running. He kept slamming into trees, but he picked himself up and ran again. Somewhere he lost his everlight. Behind, the pursuit thinned and died away.

He ran into something soft and warm that yielded before him. It fell to the ground. He tripped over it and toppled, his fist drawn back.

"Harry!" Marna said.

His fist turned into a hand that went around her, pulled her tight. "Marna!" he gasped. "I didn't know. I didn't think I could do it. I thought you were——"

Their bracelets clinked together. Marna, who had been soft

beneath him, suddenly stiffened and pushed him away. "Let's not get slobbery about it," she said angrily. "I know why you did it. Besides, they'll hear us."

Harry drew a quick, outraged breath and then let it sigh out. What was the use? She'd never believe him. Why should she? He wasn't sure himself why he had done it. Now that it was over and he had time to realize the risks he had taken, he began to shiver. He sat there in the dark forest, his eyes closed, and tried to control his shaking.

Marna put her hand out hesitantly, touched his arm, started to say something, stopped, and the moment was past.

"B-b-brat-t-t!" he chattered. "N-n-nasty, un—ungrateful, b-b-brat!" and then the shakes were gone.

She started to move. "Sit still!" he whispered. "We've got to wait until they give up the search."

At least he had eliminated the greatest danger: Eyes with his radar, X-ray vision that was just as good by night as by day.

They sat in the darkness and waited, listening to the forest noises. An hour passed. Harry was going to say that perhaps it was safe to move when he heard something rustling nearby. Animal or enemy? Marna, who had not touched him again or spoken, clutched his upper arm with a panic-strengthened hand. Harry doubled his fist and drew back his arm.

"Dr. Elliott?" Christopher whispered. "Marna?"

Relief surged over Harry like a warm, enervating current. "You wonderful little imp! How'd you find us?"

"Grampa helped me. He has a sense for that. I have a little, but he's better. Come." Harry felt a small hand fit itself into his. Christopher began to lead them through the darkness. At first Harry was distrustful and then, as the boy kept them out of bushes and trees, he moved more confidently. The hand became something he could depend on. He knew how Pearce felt and how bereft he must be now.

Christopher led them a long way before they reached another clearing. A bed of coals glowed dimly beneath a sheltering bower of green leaves. Pearce sat near the fire slowly turning a spit fashioned from a green branch. It rested on two forked sticks. On the spit two skinned rabbits were golden brown and sizzling.

Pearce's sightless face turned up as they entered the clearing. "Welcome back," he said.

Harry felt a warmth inside him that was like coming home.

Marna fell to her knees in front of the fire, raising her hands to it to warm them. Rope dangled from them, frayed in the center where she had methodically picked it apart while she had waited by another fire. She must have been cold, Harry thought, and I let her shiver through the forest while I was warm in my jacket.

But there was nothing to say.

When Christopher removed the rabbits from the spit, they almost fell apart. He wrapped four legs in damp green leaves and tucked them away in a cool hollow between two tree roots. "That's for breakfast," he said.

The four of them fell to work on the remainder. Even without salt, it was the most delicious meal Harry had ever eaten. When it was finished, he licked his fingers, sighed, and leaned back on a pile of old leaves. He felt more contented than he could remember. He was a little thirsty because he had refused to drink from the brook that ran through the woods close to their improvised camp, but he could stand that. A man couldn't surrender all his principles. It would be ironic to die of typhoid so close to his chance at immortality.

That the governor would confer immortality upon him—or at least put him into a position where he could earn it—he did not doubt. After all, he had saved the governor's daughter.

Marna was a pretty little thing. It was too bad she was still a child. An alliance with the governor's family would not hurt his chances. Perhaps in a few years—— He put the notion away from him. Marna hated him.

Christopher shoveled dirt over the fire with a large piece of bark. Harry sighed again and stretched luxuriously. Sleeping would be good tonight.

Marna had washed at the brook. Her face was clean and

shining. "Will you sleep here beside me?" Harry asked her, touching the dry leaves. He held up his bracelet apologetically. "This thing keeps me awake when you're very far away."

She nodded coldly and sat down beside him—but far enough away so that they did not touch.

Harry said, "I can't understand why we've run across so many teratisms. I can't remember ever seeing one in my practice at the Medical Center."

"You were in the clinics?" Pearce asked. And without waiting for an answer he went on, "Increasingly, the practice of medicine becomes the treatment of monsters. In the city they would die; in the suburbs they are preserved to perpetuate themselves. Let me look at your arm."

Harry started. Pearce had said it so naturally that for a moment he had forgotten that the old man couldn't see. The old man's gentle fingers untied the bandage and carefully pulled the matted grass away. "You won't need this any more."

Harry put his hand wonderingly to the wound. It had not hurt for hours. Now it was only a scar. "Perhaps you really were a doctor. Why did you give up practice?"

Pearce whispered, "I grew tired of being a technician. Medicine had become so desperately complicated that the relationship between doctor and patient was not much different from that between mechanic and patient."

Harry objected, "A doctor has to preserve his distance. If he keeps caring, he won't survive. He must become calloused to suffering, inured to sorrow, or he couldn't continue in a calling so intimately associated with them."

"No one ever said," Pearce whispered, "that it was an easy thing to be a doctor. If he stops caring, he loses not only his patient but his own humanity. But the complication of medicine had another effect. It restricted treatment to those who could afford it. Fewer and fewer people grew healthier and healthier. Weren't the rest human, too?"

Harry frowned. "Certainly. But it was the wealthy contributors and the foundations that made it all possible. They had to be treated first so that medical research could continue."

Pearce whispered, "And so society was warped all out of shape, to the god of medicine everything was sacrificed—all so that a few people could live a few years longer. Who paid the bill?

"And the odd outcome was that those who received care grew less healthy, as a class, than those who had to survive without it. Premies were saved to reproduce their weaknesses. Faults that would have proved fatal in childhood were repaired so that the patient reached maturity. Non-survival traits were passed on. Physiological inadequates multiplied, requiring greater care——"

Harry sat upright. "What kind of medical ethics are those? Medicine can't count the cost or weigh the value. Its business is to treat the sick."

"Those who can afford it. If medicine doesn't evaluate then someone else will: power or money or groups. One day I walked out on all that. I went among the citizens, where the future was, where I could help without discrimination. They took me in; they fed me when I was hungry, laughed with me when I was happy, cried with me when I was sad. They cared, and I helped them as I could."

"How?" Harry asked. "Without a diagnostic machine, without drugs or antibiotics."

"The human mind," Pearce whispered, "is still the best diagnostic machine. And the best antibiotic. I touched them. I helped them to cure themselves. So I became a healer instead of a technician. Our bodies want to heal themselves, you know, but our minds give counter-orders and death-instructions."

"Witch doctor!" Harry said scornfully.

"Yes. Always there have been witch doctors. Healers. Only in my day have the healer and the doctor become two persons. In every other era the people with the healing touch were the doctors. They existed; they exist. Countless cures are testimony. Only today do we call it superstition. And yet we know that some doctors, no wiser nor more expert than others, have a far greater recovery rate. Some nurses—not always the most beautiful ones—inspire in their patients a desire to get well.

"It takes you two hours to do a thorough examination; I can do it in two seconds. It may take you months or years to complete a treatment; I've never taken longer than five minutes."

"But where's your control?" Harry demanded. "How can you prove you've helped them? If you can't trace cause and effect, if no one else can duplicate your treatment, it isn't science. It can't be taught."

"When a healer is successful, he knows," Pearce whispered. "So does his patient. As for teaching—how do you teach a child to talk?"

Harry shrugged impatiently. Pearce had an answer for everything. There are people like that, so secure in their mania that they can never be convinced that the rest of the world is sane. Man had to depend on science—not superstition, not faith healers, not miracle workers. Or else he was back in the Dark Ages.

He lay back in the bed of leaves, feeling Marna's presence close to him. He wanted to reach out and touch her but he didn't.

Else there would be no law, no security. And no immortality.

The bracelet awoke him. It tingled. Then it began to hurt. Harry put out his hand. The bed of leaves beside him was warm, but Marna was gone.

"Marna!" he whispered. He raised himself on one elbow. In the starlight that filtered through the trees above, he could just make out that the clearing was empty of everyone but himself. The spots where Pearce and the boy had been sleeping were empty. "Where is everybody?" he said, louder.

He cursed under his breath. They had picked their time and escaped. But why, then, had Christopher found them in the forest and brought them here? And what did Marna hope to gain? Make it to the mansion alone?

He started up. Something crunched in the leaves. Harry froze in that position. A moment later he was blinded by a brilliant light.

"Don't move!" said a high-pitched voice. "I will have to shoot you. And if you try to dodge, the Snooper will follow." The voice was cool and cultured. The hand that held the gun, Harry thought, would be as cool and accurate as the voice.

"I'm not moving," Harry said. "Who are you?"

The voice ignored him. "There were four of you. Where are the other three?"

"They heard you coming. They're hanging back, waiting to rush you."

"You're lying," the voice was contemptuously.

"Listen to me!" Harry said urgently. "You don't sound like a citizen. I'm a doctor. Ask me a question about medicine, anything at all. I'm on an urgent mission. I'm taking a message to the governor."

"What is the message?"

Harry swallowed hard. "The shipment was hijacked. There won't be another ready for a week."

"What shipment?"

"I don't know. If you're a squire, you've got to help me."

"Sit down." Harry sat down. "I have a message for you. Your message won't be delivered."

"But——" Harry started up.

From somewhere behind the light came a small explosion—little more than a sharply expelled breath. Something stung Harry in the chest. He looked down. A tiny dart clung there between the edges of his jacket. He tried to reach for it and couldn't. His arm wouldn't move. His head wouldn't move either. He toppled over onto his side, not feeling the impact. Only his eyes, his ears, and his lungs seemed unaffected. He lay there, paralyzed, his mind racing.

"Yes," the voice said calmly, "I am a ghoul. Some of my

friends are headhunters, but I hunt bodies and bring them in alive. The sport is greater. So is the profit. Heads are worth only twenty dollars; bodies are worth more than a hundred. Some with young organs like yours are worth much more.

"Go, Snooper. Find the others."

The light went away. Something crackled in the brush and was gone. Slowly Harry made out a black shape that seemed to be sitting on the ground about ten feet away.

"You wonder what will happen to you," the ghoul said. "As soon as I find your companions, I will paralyze them, too, and summon my stretchers. They will carry you to my helicopter. Then, since you came from Kansas City, I will take you to Topeka."

A last hope died in Harry.

"That works best, I've found," the high-pitched voice continued. "Avoids complications. The Topeka hospital I do business with will buy your bodies, no questions asked. You are permanently paralyzed, so you will never feel any pain, although you will not lose consciousness. That way the organs never deteriorate. If you're a doctor, as you said, you know what I mean. You may know the technical name for the poison in the dart; all I know is that it is like the poison of the digger wasp. By use of intravenous feeding, these eminently portable organ banks have been kept alive for years until their time comes."

The voice went on, but Harry didn't listen. He was thinking that he would go mad. They often did. He had seen them lying on slabs in the organ bank, and their eyes had been quite mad. Then he had told himself that the madness was why they had been put there, but now he knew the truth. He would soon be one of them.

Perhaps he would strangle before he reached the hospital, before they got the tube down his throat and the artificial respirator on his chest and the needles into his arms. They strangled sometimes, even under care.

He would not go mad, though. He was too sane. He might last for months.

* * *

He heard something crackle in the brush. Light flashed across his eyes. Something moved. Bodies thrashed. Someone grunted. Someone else yelled. Something went *pouf!* Then the sounds stopped except for someone panting.

"Harry!" Marna said anxiously. "Harry! Are you all right?"

The light came back as the squat Snooper snuffled into the little clearing again. Pearce moved painfully through the light. Beyond him were Christopher and Marna. On the ground near them was a twisted creature. Harry couldn't figure out what it was and then he realized it was a dwarf, a gnome, a man with thin little legs and a twisted back and a large, lumpy head. Black hair grew sparsely on top of the head, and the eyes looked out redly, hating the world.

"Harry!" Marna said again, a wail this time.

He didn't answer. He couldn't. It was a momentary flash of pleasure, not being able to answer, and then it was buried in a flood of self-pity.

Marna picked up the dart gun and threw it deep into the brush. "What a filthy weapon!"

Reason returned to Harry. They had not escaped after all. Just as he had told the ghoul, they had only faded away in order to rescue him if they could. But they had returned too late.

The paralysis was permanent; there was no antidote. Perhaps they would kill him. How could he make them understand that he wanted to be killed?

He blinked his eyes rapidly.

Marna had moved to him. She cradled his head in her lap. Her hand moved restlessly, smoothing his hair.

Carefully, Pearce removed the dart from his chest and shoved it deep into the ground. "Be calm," he said. "Don't give up. There is no such thing as permanent paralysis. If you will try you can move your little finger." He held up Harry's hand, patted it.

Harry tried to move his finger, but it was useless. What was the matter with the old quack? Why didn't he kill him and get it over with? Pearce kept talking, but Harry didn't listen. What was the use of hoping? It would only make his torment worse.

"A transfusion might help," Marna said.

"Yes," Pearce agreed. "Are you willing?"

"You know what I am?"

"Of course. Christopher, search the ghoul. He will have tubing and needles on him for emergency treatment of his victims." Pearce spoke to Marna again. "There will be some commingling. The poison will enter your body."

Marna's voice was bitter. "You couldn't hurt me with cyanide."

There were movements and preparations. Harry couldn't concentrate on them. Things blurred. Time passed like a glacier.

As the first gray light of morning came on tiptoes through the trees, Harry felt life moving painfully in his little finger. It was worse than anything he had ever experienced, a hundred times worse than the pain from the bracelet. The pain spread to his other fingers, to his feet, up to his legs and arms toward his trunk. Harry wanted to plead with Pearce to restore the paralysis, but by the time his throat relaxed, the pain was almost gone.

When he could sit up, he looked around for Marna. She was leaning back against a tree trunk, her eyes closed, looking paler than ever. "Marna!" Her eyes opened wearily; an expression of joy flashed across them as they focused on him, and then they clouded.

"I'm all right," she said.

Harry scratched his left elbow where the needle had been. "I don't understand—you and Pearce—you brought me back from that—but——"

"Don't try to understand," she said. "Just accept it."

"It's impossible," he muttered. "What are you?"

"The governor's daughter."

"What else?"

"A Cartwright," she said bitterly.

His mind recoiled. One of the immortals! He was not

surprised that her blood had counteracted the poison. Cartwright blood was specific against any foreign substance. "How old are you?"

"Seventeen," she said. She looked down at her slim figure. "We mature late, we Cartwrights. That's why Weaver sent me to the Medical Center, to see if I was fertile. A fertile Cartwright can waste no breeding time."

There was no doubt: she hated her father.

"He will have you bred," Harry repeated stupidly.

"He will try to do it himself," she said without emotion. "He is not very fertile; that is why there are only three of us. My grandmother, my mother and me. Then we have some control over conception. Particularly after maturity. We don't want his children, even though they might make him less dependent on us. I'm afraid—" her voice broke—"I'm afraid I'm not mature enough."

"Why didn't you tell me before?" Harry demanded.

"And have you treat me like a Cartwright?" Her eyes glowed with anger. "A Cartwright isn't a person, you know. A Cartwright is a walking blood-bank, a living fountain of youth, something to be possessed, used, guarded, but never allowed to live. Besides"—her head dropped—"you don't believe me. About Weaver."

"But he's the governor!" Harry exclaimed. He saw her face and turned away. How could he explain? You had a job and you had a duty. You couldn't go back on those. And then there were the bracelets. Only the governor had the key. They couldn't survive long linked together like that. They would be separated again, by chance or by force, and he would die.

He got to his feet. The forest reeled for a moment and then settled back. "I owe you thanks again," he said to Pearce.

"You fought hard to preserve your beliefs," Pearce whispered, "but there was a core of sanity that fought with me, that said it was better to be a whole man with crippled beliefs than a crippled man with whole beliefs."

Harry stared soberly at the old man. He was either a real healer who could not explain how he worked his miracles or the world was a far crazier place than Harry had ever imagined. "If we start moving now," he said, "we should be in sight of the mansion by noon."

As he passed the dwarf, he looked down, stopped, and looked back at Marna and Pearce. Then he stopped, picked up the misshapen little boy, and walked toward the road.

The helicopter was beside the turnpike. "It would be only a few minutes if we flew," he muttered.

Close behind him Marna said, "We aren't expected. We would be shot down before we got within five miles."

Harry strapped the dwarf into the helicopter seat. The ghoul stared at him out of hate-filled eyes. Harry started the motor, pressed the button on the autopilot marked "Return," and stepped back. The helicopter lifted, straightened and headed southeast.

Christopher and Pearce were waiting on the pavement when Harry turned. Christopher grinned suddenly and held out a rabbit leg. "Here's breakfast."

They marched down the turnpike toward Lawrence.

The governor's mansion was built on the top of an L-shaped hill that stood tall between two river valleys. Once it had been the site of a great university, but taxes for supporting such institutions had been diverted into more vital channels. Private contributions had dwindled as the demands of medical research and medical care had intensified. Soon there was no interest in educational fripperies, and the university died.

The governor had built his mansion there some seventy-five years ago when Topeka became unbearable. Long before that it had become a lifetime office—and the governor would live forever.

The state of Kansas was a barony—a description that would have meant nothing to Harry, whose knowledge of history was limited to the history of medicine. The governor was a baron, and the mansion was his keep. His vassals were the surburban squires; they were paid with immortality or its promise. Once one of them had received an injection, he had two choices: remain loyal to the governor and live forever, barring accidental death, or die within thirty days.

The governor had not received a shipment for four weeks. The squires were getting desperate.

The mansion was a fortress. Its outer walls were five-foot-thick pre-stressed concrete faced with five-inch armor plate. A moat surrounded the walls; it was stocked with piranha.

An inner wall rose above the outside one. The paved, unencumbered area between the two could be flooded with napalm. Inside the wall were hidden guided missile nests.

The mansion rose, ziggurat fashion, in terraced steps. On each rooftop was a hydroponic farm. At the summit of the buildings was a glass penthouse; the noon sun turned it into silver. On a mast towering above, a radar dish rotated.

Like an iceberg, most of the mansion was beneath the surface. It dived through limestone and granite almost a mile deep. The building was almost a living creature; automatic mechanisms controlled it, brought in air, heated and cooled it, fed it, watered it, watched for enemies and killed them if they got too close. . . .

It could be run by a single hand. At the moment it was.

There was no entrance to the place. Harry stood in front of the walls and waved his jacket. "Ahoy, the mansion! A message for the governor from the Medical Center. Ahoy, the mansion!"

"Down!" Christopher shouted.

An angry bee buzzed past Harry's ear and then a whole flight of them. Harry fell to the ground and rolled. In a little while the bees stopped.

"Are you hurt?" Marna asked quickly.

Harry lifted his face out of the dust. "Poor shots," he said grimly. "Where did they come from?"

"One of the villas," Christopher said, pointing at the scattered dwellings at the foot of the hill.

"The bounty wouldn't even keep them in ammunition," Harry said.

In a giant, godlike voice, the mansion said, "Who comes with a message for me?"

Harry shouted from his prone position, "Dr. Harry Elliott. I have with me the governor's daughter, Marna, and a leech. We're under fire from one of the villas."

The mansion was silent. Slowly then a section of the inside wall swung open. Something flashed into the sunlight, spurting flame from its tail. It darted downward. A moment later a villa lifted into the air and fell back, a mass of rubble.

Over the outer wall came a crane arm. From it dangled a large metal car. When it reached the ground a door opened.

"Come into my presence," the mansion said.

The car was dusty. So was the penthouse where they were deposited. The vast swimming pool was dry; the cabanas were rotten; the flowers and bushes and palm trees were dead.

In the mirror-covered central column, a door gaped at them like a dark mouth. "Enter," said the door.

The elevator descended deep into the ground. Harry's stomach surged uneasily; he thought the car would never stop, but eventually the doors opened. Beyond was a spacious living room. It was decorated in shades of brown. One entire wall was a vision screen.

Marna ran out of the car. "Mother!" she shouted. "Grandmother!" She raced through the apartment. Harry followed her more slowly.

There were six bedrooms opening off a long hall. At the end of it was a nursery. On the other side of the living room were a dining room and a kitchen. Every room had a wall-wide vision screen. Every room was empty.

"Mother?" Marna said.

The dining room screen flickered. Across the giant screen flowed the giant image of a creature who lolled on pneumatic cushions. It was a thing incredibly fat, a sea of flesh rippling and surging. Although it was naked, its sex was a mystery. Its breasts were great pillows of fat, but there was a sprinkling of hair between them. Its face, moon though it was, was small on the fantastic body; in it eyes were stuck like raisins.

It drew sustenance out of a tube; then, as it saw them, it pushed the tube away with one balloonlike hand. It giggled. The giggle was godlike.

"Hello, Marna," it said in the mansion's voice. "Looking for somebody? Your mother and your grandmother thwarted me, you know. Sterile creatures! I connected them directly to the blood bank; now there will be no delay about blood."

"You'll kill them!" Marna gasped.

"Cartwrights? Silly girl! Besides, this is our bridal night, and we would not want them around, would we, Marna?"

Marna shrank back into the living room, but the creature looked at her from the screen, too. It turned its raisin eyes toward Harry. "You are the doctor with the message. Tell me."

Harry frowned. "You—are Governor Weaver?"

"In the flesh, boy." The creature chuckled. It made waves of fat surge across his body and back again.

Harry took a deep breath. "The shipment was hijacked. It will be a week before another shipment is ready."

Weaver frowned and reached a stubby finger toward something beyond the camera's range. "There!" He looked back at Harry and smiled the smile of an idiot. "I just blew up Dean Mock's office. He was inside it at the time. It's justice, though. He's been sneaking shots of elixir for twenty years."

"Elixir? But——!" The information about Mock was too unreal to be meaningful; Harry didn't believe it. It was the mention of elixir that shocked him.

Weaver's mouth made an "O" of sympathy. "I've shocked you. They tell you the elixir has not been synthesized. It was. Some one hundred years ago by a doctor named Russell Pearce. You were planning on synthesizing it, perhaps, and thereby winning yourself immortality as a reward. No—I'm not telepathic. Fifty out of every one hundred doctors dream that dream. I'll tell you, Doctor. I am the electorate. I decide who shall be immortal, and it pleases me to be arbitrary. Gods are always arbitrary. That is what makes them gods. I could give you immortality. I will; I will. Serve me well, Doctor, and when you begin to age, I will make you young again. I could make you dean of the Med Center. Would you like that?''

Weaver frowned again. ''But no—you would sneak elixir like Mock, and you would not send me the shipment when I need it for my squires.'' He scratched between his breasts. ''What will I do?'' he wailed. ''The loyal ones are dying off. I can't give them their shots, and then their children are ambushing their parents. Whitey crept up on his father the other day; sold him to a junk collector. Old hands keep young hands away from the fire. But the old ones are dying off, and the young ones don't need the elixir, not yet. They will, though. They'll come to me on their knees, begging, and I'll laugh at them and let them die. That's what gods do, you know.''

Weaver scratched his wrist. ''You're still shocked about the elixir. You think we should make gallons of it, keep everybody young forever. Now think about it! We know that's absurd, eh? There wouldn't be enough of anything to go around. And what would be the value of immortality if everybody lived forever?'' His voice changed suddenly, became businesslike. ''Who hijacked the shipment? Was it this man?''

A picture flashed on the lower quarter of the screen.

''Yes,'' Harry said. His brain was spinning. Illumination and immortality, all in one breath. It was coming too fast. He didn't have time to react.

Weaver rubbed his doughy mouth. ''Cartwright! How can he do it?'' There was a note of godlike fear in the voice. ''To risk—forever. He's mad—that's it, the man is mad. He wants to die.'' The great mass of flesh shivered; the body rippled. ''Let him try me. I'll give him death.''

Cartwright, Harry thought. Weaver must mean Marshall Cartwright, the original Immortal. But why would Cartwright attack the convoy, risk—eternity? Because, perhaps, he had learned that eternity was worthless without courage, without honor, without love. By hijacking the elixir shipment he had dealt Weaver a deadly blow.

Weaver looked at Harry again and scratched his neck. "How did you get here, you four?"

"We walked," Harry said tightly.

"Walked? Fantastic!"

"Ask a motel manager just this side of Kansas City or a pack of wolves that almost got away with Marna or a ghoul that paralyzed me. They'll tell you we walked."

Weaver scratched his mountainous belly. "Those wolfpacks. They can be a nuisance. They're useful, though. They keep the countryside tidy. But if you were paralyzed, why is it you are here instead of waiting to be put to use on some organ bank slab?"

"The leech gave me a transfusion from Marna." Too late Harry saw Marna motioning for him to be silent.

Weaver's face clouded. "You've stolen my blood. Now I can't bleed her for a month. I will have to punish you. Not now but later when I have thought of something fitting the crime."

"A month is too soon," Harry said. "No wonder the girl is pale if you bleed her every month. You'll kill her."

"But she's a Cartwright," Weaver said in astonishment, "and I need the blood."

Harry's lips tightened. He held up the bracelet on his wrist. "The key, sir?"

"Tell me," Weaver said, scratching under one breast, "is Marna fertile?"

"No, sir." Harry looked levelly into the eyes of the Governor of Kansas. "The key?"

"Oh, dear," Weaver said. "I seem to have misplaced it. You'll have to wear the bracelets yet a bit. Well, Marna. We will see how it goes tonight, eh, fertile or no? Find something suitable for a bridal night, will you? And let us not mar the occasion with weeping and moaning and screams of pain. Come reverently and filled with a great joy, as Mary came unto God."

"If I have a child," Marna said, her face white, "it will have to be a virgin birth."

345

The sea of flesh surged with anger. "Perhaps there will be screams tonight. Yes. Leech! You—the obscenely old person with the boy. You are a healer."

"So I have been called," Pearce whispered.

"They say you work miracles. Well, I have a miracle for you to work." Weaver scratched the back of one swollen hand. "I itch. Doctors have found nothing wrong with me, and they have died. It drives me mad."

"I cure by touch," Pearce said. "Every person cures himself; I only help."

"No man touches me," Weaver said. "You will cure me by tonight. I will not hear of anything else. Otherwise I will be angry with you and the boy. Yes, I will be very angry with the boy if you do not succeed."

"Tonight," Pearce said, "I will work a miracle for you."

Weaver smiled and reached out for a feeding tube. His dark eyes glittered like black marbles in a huge dish of custard. "Tonight, then!" The image vanished from the screen.

"A grub," Harry whispered. "A giant white grub in the heart of a rose. Eating away at it, blind, selfish, and destructive."

"I think of him," Pearce said, "as a fetus who refuses to be born. Safe in the womb, he destroys the mother, not realizing that he is thereby destroying himself." He turned slightly toward Christopher. "There is an eye?"

Christopher looked at the screen. "Every one."

"Bugs."

"All over."

Pearce said, "We will have to take the chance that he will not audit the recordings or that he can be distracted long enough to do what must be done."

Harry looked at Marna and then at Pearce and Christopher. "What can we do?"

"You're willing?" Marna said. "To give up immortality? To risk everything?"

Harry grimaced. "What would I be losing? A world like this?"

"What is the situation?" Pearce whispered. "Where is Weaver?"

Marna shrugged helplessly. "I don't know. My mother and grandmother never knew. He sends the elevator. There are no stairs, no other exits. And the elevators are controlled from a console beside his bed. There are thousands of switches. They also control the rest of the building, the lights, water, air, heat, and food supplies. He can release toxic or anesthetic gases or flaming gasoline. He can set off charges not only here but in Topeka and Kansas City or send rockets to attack other areas. There's no way to reach him."

"You will reach him," Pearce whispered.

Marna's eyes lighted up. "If there were some weapon I could take! But there's an inspection in the elevator—magnetic and fluoroscopic detectors."

"Even if you could smuggle in a knife, say," Harry said, frowning, "it would be almost impossible to hit a vital organ. And even though he isn't able to move his body, his arms must be fantastically strong."

"There is, perhaps, one way," Pearce said. "If we can find a piece of paper, Christopher will write it out for you."

The bride waited near the elevator doors, dressed in white satin and old lace. The lace was pulled up over the head for a veil. In front of the living room screen, in a brown velour grand rapids overstuffed chair, sat Pearce. At his feet, leaning against his bony knee, was Christopher.

The screen flickered, and Weaver was there, grinning his divine-idiot's grin. "You're impatient, Marna. It pleases me to see you so eager to rush into the arms of your bridegroom. The wedding carriage arrives."

The doors of the elevator sighed open. The bride stepped into the car. As the doors began to close, Pearce got to his feet, pushing Christopher gently to one side, and said, "You seek immortality, Weaver, and you think you have found it. But what you have is only a living death. I am going to show you the only real immortality."

The car dropped. It plummeted to the tune of the wedding march from Lohengrin. Detectors probed at the bride and found only cloth. The elevator began to slow. After it came to a full stop, the doors remained closed for a moment, and then, squeaking, they opened.

The stench of decay flowed into the car. For a moment the bride recoiled, and then she stepped forward out of the car. The room had once been a marvelous mechanism: a stainless steel womb. Not much bigger than the giant pneumatic mattress that occupied the center, the room was completely automatic. Temperature regulators kept it at blood heat. Food came directly from the processing rooms through the tubes without human aid. Daily sprays of water swept dirt and refuse to collectors around the edge of the room that disposed of it. An overhead spray washed the creature who occupied the mattress. Around the edges of the mattress like a great, circular organ with ten thousand keys was a complex control console. Directly over the mattress, on the ceiling, was a view screen.

Some years before, apparently, a water pipe had broken through some shift in the earth, a small leak that made the rock swell, or a hard freeze. The cleansing sprays no longer worked, and the occupant of the room was afraid to have intruders trace the trouble or he no longer cared.

The floor was littered with decaying food, with cans and wrappers, with waste matter. As the bride stepped into the room cockroaches rose in a cloud and scattered. Mice scampered into hiding places.

The bride pulled the long white satin skirt up above her hips. She unwound a thin, nylon cord from her waist. There was a loop fastened into the end. She took it out until it hung free.

Then she looked to see what Weaver was doing. He was watching the overhead screen with almost hypnotic concentration. Pearce was talking. "Aging is not a physical disease; it is mental. The mind grows tired and lets the body die. Only

348

half the Cartwrights' immunity to death lies in their blood; the other half is their unflagging will to live.

"You are one hundred and fifty-three years old. I tended your father, who died before you were born. I gave him, unwittingly, a transfusion of Marshall Cartwright's golden blood."

Weaver whispered, "But that would make you——" His voice was thin and high; it was not godlike at all. It was ridiculous coming from that vast mass of flesh.

"Almost two hundred years old," Pearce said. His voice was stronger, richer, deeper, no longer a whisper. "Without ever a transfusion of Cartwright blood, ever an injection of the *elixir vitae*. The effective mind can achieve conscious control of the autonomic nervous system, of the very cells that make up the blood stream and the body."

The bride craned her neck to see the screen on the ceiling. Pearce looked odd. He was taller. His legs were straight and muscular. His shoulders were broader. As the bride watched, muscle and fat built up beneath his skin, firming it, smoothing out wrinkles. His facial bones receded beneath young flesh and skin. Silky white hair thickened and grew darker.

"You wonder why I stayed old," Pearce said, and his voice was resonant and powerful. "It is something one does not use for oneself. It comes through giving, not taking."

His sunken eyelids puffed, paled, opened. And Pearce looked out at Weaver, tall, strong, and straight—no more than thirty, surely. There was power latent in that face—power leashed, gentled, under control. But Weaver recoiled from it.

Then, onto the screen, walked Marna.

Weaver's eyes bulged. His head swiveled toward the bride. Harry tossed off the veil and swung the looped cord lightly between two fingers. The importance of his next move was terrifying. The first throw had to be accurate, because he might never have a chance for another. His surgeon's fingers were deft, but he had never thrown a lariat. Christopher had described how he should do it, but there had been no chance to practice.

And if he were dragged within reach of those doughy arms! A hug would smother him.

And in that startled moment, Weaver's head lifted with surprise and his hand stabbed toward the console. Harry flipped the cord. The loop dropped over Weaver's head and tightened around his neck.

Quickly Harry wrapped the cord several times around his hand and pulled it tight. Weaver jerked against it, tightening it further. The thin cord disappeared into the neck's soft flesh. Weaver's stubby fingers clawed at it, tearing the skin, as his body thrashed on the mattress.

He had, Harry thought, an immortal at the end of his fishing line—a great white whale struggling to free itself so that it could live forever, smacking the pneumatic waves with fierce lunges and savage tugs. For him it became dreamlike and unreal.

Weaver, by some titanic effort, had turned over. He had his hands around the cord now. He rose onto soft, flowing knees and pulled at the cord, dragging Harry forward toward the mattress. Weaver's eyes were beginning to bulge out of his pudding-face.

Harry dug his heels into the floor. Weaver came up, like the whale leaping its vast bulk incredibly out of the water, and stood, shapeless and mostrous, his face purpling. Then, deep inside, a heart gave up, and the body sagged. It flowed like a melting wax image back to the mattress on which it had spent almost three-quarters of a century.

Harry dazedly unwrapped the cord from his hand. It had cut deep into the skin; blood welled out. He didn't feel anything as he dropped the cord. He shut his eyes and shivered. After a period of time he never remembered, he heard someone calling him. "Harry!" Marna cried. "Are you all right? Harry, please!"

He took a deep breath. "Yes. Yes, I'm all right."

"Go to the console," said the young man who had been

Pearce. "You'll have to find the right controls, but they should be marked. We've got to release Marna's mother and grandmother. And then we've got to get out of here ourselves. Marshall Cartwright is outside, and I think he's getting impatient."

How did Pearce know? Harry thought dazedly. But he knew the answer. Pearce's powers did not stop with healing. Allied to that, perhaps stemming from that, were other perceptions of people and locations, and things, sometimes of thoughts themselves. Christopher, too. He had picked it up.

Harry nodded, but he did not move. It would take a strong man to go out into a world where immortality was a fact rather than a dream. He would have to live with it and its terrifying problems. They would be greater than anything he had imagined.

He moved forward to begin the search.

DAW

Don't Miss These Exciting DAW Anthologies